XEELEE: VENGEANCE

XEELEE: VENGEANCE

STEPHEN BAXTER

This edition first published in Great Britain in 2018 by Gollancz

First published in Great Britain in 2017 by Gollancz
an imprint of the Orion Publishing Group Ltd
Carmelite House, 50 Victoria Embankment
London EC4Y 0DZ

An Hachette UK Company

3 5 7 9 10 8 6 4 2

A CIP catalogue record for this book is
available from the British Library.

ISBN 978 1 473 21719 5

Typeset by Input Data Services Ltd, Somerset

Printed and bound by CPI Group (UK) Ltd, Croydon CR0 4YY

MIX
Paper from
responsible sources
FSC® C104740

www.stephen-baxter.com
www.gollancz.co.uk

ONE

The wormholes are gateways to other times, other places.
They should be beautiful, like all great engineering.

Ambassador Flood, AD 4820

ONE

1

Timelike infinity

Even after the Xeelee had finally won their war against humanity, the stars continued to age, too rapidly. The Xeelee completed their great Projects and fled the cosmos.

Time unravelled. Dying galaxies collided like clapping hands. But even now the story was not yet done. The universe itself prepared for another convulsion, greater than any it had suffered before.

And then—

'Who are you?'
'My name is Michael Poole.'

2

AD **3646**

Beyond the flitter's viewing window, Jupiter loomed.

The light out here was eerie, Michael Poole thought. Or at least he was reminded of that whenever he had visitors from Earth. The light of the Sun, five times as far away as from the home world, was diminished, yet it was far brighter than any star or planet: a strange in-between light, unfamiliar, and the shadows it cast were sharp and rectilinear. The face of Jupiter itself, huge in the sky, was misty, elusive, an ocean of banded clouds.

Today, before that face, there drifted a wormhole portal, a spindly tetrahedral framework of electric blue. Automated monitor probes swarmed. And in the portal's faces, glimmering gold, another world could be glimpsed.

It looked perfect. It wasn't.

Something strange had been detected coming from that wormhole portal. Gravity waves: anomalous bursts of energy. Poole didn't understand this; nobody understood. And because of that anomaly the wormhole, beautiful as it was, was in danger of being shut down.

The wormhole was Poole's creation. His whole career depended on the success of the current trials. Indeed, he felt as if he were on trial himself. He was twenty-five years old.

There were four people in this flitter, including Poole: two corporeal, and two Virtuals, images projected over from Michael Poole's own ship, the *Hermit Crab*, whose elegant bulk was at rest alongside the flitter. Even though they were in zero gravity the flight deck of the *Crab Junior* felt crowded. The skinsuits they all wore, with helmets at their sides, didn't help.

Harry Poole, Michael's father, was one of the Virtuals. He raised a glass of single malt, as unreal as he was, and tapped the arm of the woman beside him. Shamiso Emry, the UN Oversight Senior Coordinator, soberly dressed, hair silver grey, was the second Virtual, hence her sensation of Harry's contact; Michael thought she stiffened against the touch.

Harry said, 'More whisky, Co-ordinator?'

'I've barely touched my glass – thank you, Mr Poole.'

'Harry, please. Beautiful spectacle, isn't it? Look, I know we're here on business—'

'We're here because of a suspected flaw in your prototype wormhole—'

'But when I bring people out here, I always encourage them to take a moment, and just look.'

Harry was fifty-six years old; AS-preserved, he looked younger than Poole himself. And with his wide grin, blond-white hair and blue eyes he was a contrast to his son, who was shorter, more heavy-set, darker – broad nose, brown eyes, black hair – more like the rest of his family. But then Harry hadn't been born a Poole. Harry, though, always had more presence than his son, Virtual or not. And so it was now, during this official inspection.

Harry grinned. 'What a sight!'

While Harry and Shamiso Emry sat on Virtual images of comfortable couches, projected from the *Crab*, Michael Poole and Nicola Emry – Shamiso's daughter, the fourth occupant of the cabin – sat in bulky, confining pilot couches, side by side.

Now Nicola looked around. 'What sight, pray? Jupiter, that big ball of gas? Or the ramshackle thing you Pooles built that's getting in the way?'

Poole was irritated by that jab. And it had galled him that Nicola had insisted on taking the left-hand seat, the pilot's seat, in *his* flitter. 'That "ramshackle thing" is an example of the highest technology in the Solar System right now.'

'So you say.'

'Yes. So I say. And look – can you see those flashes of blue, through the gold?'

Nicola squinted that way. She was shaven-headed, her features sharp. 'Earth, right? I see clouds, hints of continents – that grey-green splash is the big north European forest, I think. But I thought I saw multiple images. It was . . . kaleidoscopic.'

'Good observation,' he said grudgingly. 'Most people miss that.'

Poole found Nicola difficult to fathom, and intimidating. He knew that the only skill Nicola Emry claimed for herself was as a pilot – hence her monopoly of the left-hand seat – and her eyes, evidently without augmentation, seemed sharp enough. She looked maybe thirty years old. AntiSenescence treatments always turned true ages

3

into the subject of a guessing game, but such was her immaturity, in Poole's eyes, that he would have been surprised if she was much older – and besides, the mother, who seemed to have allowed herself to age naturally, was only about sixty herself.

'Look,' he said, 'this is just a prototype, the portal's a couple of hundred metres across. One day the finished articles will allow ships much bigger than the *Hermit Crab* over there to travel between Earth and Jupiter. Five astronomical units – that is, five times Earth's distance from the Sun, around eight hundred million kilometres – spanned in minutes. Effectively faster than light.'

Nicola raised an eyebrow. 'Gosh.'

He pressed on doggedly. 'As for what you can see through the portal – the wormhole is a short cut. It's as if we've folded spacetime and pinched together the locations of Jupiter and the Earth. But the transit itself isn't instantaneous; you still have to travel through the wormhole throat, a finite distance. That's because of instability problems. Make the throat too short and you find that the exotic-matter structures of the mouths interact . . . Well. Light from Earth can pass through the wormhole – that's why, sitting here, we can glimpse the planet – but the wormhole throat is long enough, you see, that there is more than one path for that light to travel. Hence the multiple images. Yes, some people call it kaleidoscopic.'

Now Nicola did laugh out loud, but with a kind of delight.

Shamiso Emry ducked her head. 'Well, I can't see it.'

Harry said solicitously, 'That's probably an artefact of the Virtual projection. We are in a different location from the youngsters.'

Curiously, Shamiso looked out now at the *Crab*, floating alongside the flitter.

The *Hermit Crab* was Poole's own design, based on GUTdrive technology long ago patented by earlier generations of Pooles. A spine, a kilometre and a half long and crusted with fuel tanks and antenna clusters, was fixed at one end to a block of ice taken from the crust of Europa, Jupiter's moon, pocked and blackened where it had been mined for reaction mass, and at the other to the gleaming hemisphere of a lifedome, a splash of Earth colours in the Jovian night. Somewhere in there were the originals of Harry and Shamiso. And so Shamiso was looking back at herself, Poole thought.

Shamiso said, 'Tell me again why we need to be in two ships?'

'Safety, Co-ordinator,' Harry said promptly. 'Backup options. Jupiter space is a pretty lethal radiation environment. Even as far out as

Ganymede you would pick up a lifetime dose of radiation in a couple of years; less, if unprotected. We always send out ships in pairs, or larger flotillas. All this was mandated by some earlier Oversight committee – oh, generations ago.'

Nicola grinned at Poole, and whispered, '*Oversight*. Isn't that a fine word? You engineers paid for this huge technology demonstration yourselves, didn't you? And now here we are, deciding whether to shut you down or not.'

Poole found her irritatingly intriguing. 'You talk big, but here *you* are running around after your mother.'

'Oh, I'm just a cab driver, I know that. Call it nepotism if you like. My mother gave me a choice: this or prison, or a dose of memory-editing.' She winked at him. 'I do have a habit of breaking the rules, you see. I'm not a scion of mankind like you and your illustrious forebears, Michael Poole. I'll tell you this, though. By Lethe, I'm a *good* cab driver.'

'Perhaps we could get on with it,' Shamiso snapped. Her face, square, strong, seemed not unfriendly, but her expression was stony. 'We're here, after all, because of anomalies you've yet to explain away. You spoke of instabilities in the wormhole structure. Could that be the cause—'

Before Poole could respond, Harry said quickly, 'I'm confident that's not the problem, Co-ordinator. Look – a functioning wormhole *exploits* inherent instabilities. We design them in, manipulate them. We understand this stuff.' He waved a hand at the gleaming blue tetrahedron. 'Left to itself, a wormhole would collapse quickly. So you have to thread the throat and portals with exotic matter—'

'That's the blue frame,' Nicola said.

'Yes. It's called "exotic" because it's a manifestation of negative energy.'

'Which is a kind of antigravity.'

She seemed to be understanding more than Poole had expected.

Harry grinned. 'You've got it. And that's essential to keep the wormhole mouths open – though the process has to be actively managed. You see, these are known, indeed useful instabilities, Co-ordinator.'

Nicola was looking out, the blue light casting highlights on the planes of her face. 'I know exotic matter is a quantum-gravity phenomenon, essentially. So those blue rods must scale accordingly. Line density with dimensions governed by lightspeed and the gravitational constant would be . . .' She conjured up a Virtual workstation in the air, worked it quickly. 'My, my. Says here that a loop of the stuff a metre across should mass as much as Jupiter.'

Poole was grudgingly impressed. 'That's the kind of estimate they came up with when the idea of traversable wormholes was first floated back in the nineteenth century. Or was it the twentieth? What you see out there is the result of a millennium and a half of engineering development since then. The portal itself is two hundred metres across, but its mass is no more than that of a kilometre-wide asteroid—'

'And he's longing to give you all the details you already read about,' Harry said, with a kind of mock fondness in his voice. 'How we pluck natural wormholes from the quantum foam . . . How we use Io flux-tube energy to extract exotic matter from the Hub, a manufacturing facility based around the quantum gravity field of a mountain-mass black hole suspended deep in the clouds of Jupiter itself . . .'

Nicola said, 'There's nowhere near enough energy density in the flux tube to enable you to build *this*.'

Again Poole was reluctantly impressed. 'True. But we use the tube as a siphon, a trigger for a nonlinear cascade which extracts mass-energy, via coupled magnetic fields, from Jupiter itself.' He smiled. 'You should see it. When we inject energy into the portal structure, it grows exponentially, doubling in size, and doubling again—'

'Spare me the sales pitch.'

Harry said hastily, 'Of course the most important detail of all this is the cost. Which will be, crucially – when we're up and running, and if you look at our business case which applies net-present-value discounting – astronomically *less* than the cost of running GUTships, like the *Crab* over there.

'It's not just the efficiency. It's the scale that will be transformative. One day our wormholes will link all the major bodies of the System, from Mercury to the Oort Cloud. And you'll be able to travel in a flitter like this, all the way to Earth, in a matter of minutes. Whereas now it takes six *days* in a ship like the *Hermit Crab*. And, crucially, with the new system, for the first time we will be able to transport *very* large masses between the worlds cheaply. For such grand purposes as, some day, taking nitrogen from a source like Titan to supply the great arcologies on Mars. Or even carrying food grown in Titan's organic-chemistry seas to feed Earth.

'All this will have an impact you can barely imagine. But we Pooles have been here before. Everybody thinks the story of the Pooles started with Michael Poole Bazalget.'

Nicola grinned. 'Even I heard of him. The Arctic guy.'

'Yes – in the twenty-first century, back in the Bottleneck – the Poole who stabilised methane deposits around the Arctic Circle, thus saving the world from a particularly savage dose of greenhouse-gas warming. One of the pioneering acts of the Stewardship generations . . . Long before *him*, though, Poole ancestors were involved in the great railway boom of the nineteenth century. The first great modernisation of transport, which opened up industrial development in Britain, and then Europe, America, Asia – and the global economy exploded. Now our wormholes, laid down by *this* generation of Pooles, are going to do the same thing on an interplanetary scale.'

Shamiso said dryly, 'That would be heart-warming if I hadn't read it all in your brochures. But it doesn't help us with the problem I was sent out here to resolve, does it? Shall we get to the point?' She waved a hand and brought up a Virtual display of her own, an orrery-like model of the Solar System, a plane centred on a gleaming, jewel-like Sun.

Nicola was peering through the forward viewing port, those sharp pilot's eyes intent. 'Mother . . .'

'Hush, Nicola. We monitor gravity waves routinely. They have been our main astronomical tool since – well, my grasp of history isn't as obsessive as yours. And, recently, we saw *this*.'

Another gesture, and fine, cherry-red lines shot out from the position of Jupiter, a pink ball in the Virtual model – streaks of energy crossing the Solar System. Most of these bolts were in the plane of the System, though they seemed to be laid down at random, not targeting a planet or any other obvious body. But some of them went spearing out of that plane, off into the emptiness of interstellar space.

Every time Poole saw this image sequence, he felt sick deep in his stomach. It really did look like a weaponised energy beam, he'd thought from the first time he'd seen it: thunderbolts spearing out of the wormhole portal. No wonder the Oversight committee had submitted its order for an inspection of the project. But the fundamental problem was that still nobody knew *what* this was.

Shamiso said, 'I should emphasise these energy tracks are harmless. Spectacular – an unprecedented gravitational-energy phenomenon within the Solar System – but harmless in terms of the perturbation of ships, habitats, still less moons and planets. But naturally the citizenry is concerned. Even more so when the source of these energy bolts was identified.'

Nicola was still staring out of the window. 'I think there's something out there.'

Harry spread his hands. 'Co-ordinator, I can assure you – look, there's nothing intrinsic to the wormhole, its morphology and dynamics, that can have anything to do with these pulses.'

'Yet they exist. Yet they are coming *from* your wormhole, evidently, even if they aren't caused by it. If I were to recommend shutting down the project—'

Nicola turned now, and faced them all. 'I think it's too late for that. By the waters of Lethe – *look*, Mother!'

At last her forcefulness broke through Shamiso's concentration. She looked through the view window. And Poole saw her mouth sag, almost comically.

Finally he turned around himself, swivelling in his chair, and looked out at the wormhole portal.

To see something coming through.

3

Even Harry seemed to forget the politics, his corporate role. He, or his Virtual avatar, drifted to the window, gaping in fascination at the thing, black and huge, that was emerging from the shining blue portal.

Poole himself saw a moulded black carapace, symmetrical with spiky protuberances, and sharp, curved edges between moulded planes. All of it pushing steadily out of the wormhole. Around this mass the portal face's golden glow shimmered, flickered, broke up. And behind it Poole made out flashes of light of another quality: purplish, lurid.

Harry checked the flitter's console. 'Are we recording all this?'

Poole called up a Virtual slave of the control desk of the *Hermit Crab*'s instrument suite, much more extensive than *Junior*'s. 'All of it, multispectral.'

'I'll call up Oversight backup imaging too,' Shamiso said.

'Those purple flashes look like particle cascades to me.'

'It's brushing the walls of the wormhole throat,' Harry said. 'Whatever *it* is. It's only just squeezing through. At that size it must be withstanding ferocious tidal stresses. And its surface doesn't look like any hull material we use. Not metal, not ceramic, not carbon composite. More like a kind of chitin. It looks . . . insectile, doesn't it? A huge beetle.'

'Maybe.' Now Poole could see a body behind that misshapen head, slowly emerging into the pale Jovian sunlight – what looked almost like shoulders, extending to some kind of wing.

'We're seeing more of those gravitational pulses,' Shamiso said now, glancing at a monitor. 'Spreading at lightspeed across the System. A storm of them. Evidently the signals we received before were a precursor of *this* event.'

Harry muttered bitterly, 'Well, that should keep your swarms of scrutineers happy for a while.'

Nicola laughed. 'You know, Harry, *this* is something – different. Alien, obviously. It's got nothing to do with us. Humanity, I mean.

Or with your wretched wormhole, even if that is how it's getting here. And all you can think of is that it's breaking your pretty toy.'

Harry glared.

Poole couldn't take his eyes off the portal. The steadily emerging anomaly – that head, attached to what looked increasingly like a slim body fitted with flaring wings . . . he felt a deep, instinctive revulsion. *'This shouldn't be here.* It doesn't belong.'

'And it's not alone,' Nicola said.

'What?'

She pointed away from the portal itself, to a shining dot, star-like, swimming against the face of Jupiter with its drapery of clouds.

Poole hastily checked his monitors. 'There's a swarm of those things – silvered spheres, each maybe ten metres across, squeezing out of the wormhole around the insectile mass. They're returning blank reflections from the sensors. Perfectly spherical, perfectly smooth, any irregularities beyond the reach of our instruments. And – look at this display – I think there's something else, a *third* class of anomaly, massive, but hard to resolve.'

Harry moved forward through the air. 'Just when you thought the day couldn't get any stranger.'

'I have it.' Nicola pointed. *'There.* Look, against Jupiter's face . . . A kind of shadow. Is that your third kind?'

'Show me,' Poole snapped.

Her eyes, augmented or not, really were much sharper than Poole's, and she had to manipulate recorded imagery to show him what she meant.

Translucent discs, passing over Jupiter's pale colours.

Nicola said, 'I thought at first they were some kind of reflection, or a lighting effect from your wormhole, like the multiple Earth reflections. But I made sure the *Crab*'s full sensor suite took a look at them. Look at the gravity readings.'

The 'phantoms' were actually regions of spacetime warped by dense concentrations of mass, Poole saw – just granules, but very dense indeed. They were visible through a kind of gravitational lensing, the distortion of light coming from behind the objects by their gravity fields.

'That's incredible,' he said. 'I'm seeing a kernel of matter compressed beyond nuclear densities. Like a knot of quarks. And then, within *that*, something denser yet, hotter. Those are the temperatures and densities we achieve in our GUT-energy pods.' He glanced at Shamiso, checking her understanding. 'GUT – Grand Unified Theory. We compress matter and energy to such densities that we emulate the first moments of the universe, and the forces of physics recombine. It takes us an accelerator wrapped around Copernicus Crater on the Moon to do this. So how can these – knots of the stuff – just be floating there?'

Harry leaned forward to see. 'Those silver raindrops of yours are sticking close to the main mass. The beetle. The phantoms are moving out more widely. Filling space. Almost as if they're searching for something.'

Shamiso said quickly, '"Searching"? I'd hesitate to use such words yet. Because they ascribe agency, you see. As we haven't encountered minds equivalent to ours anywhere beyond Earth, an assumption of intelligence ought to be a last resort. Of course some hypothesise intelligence in Grantt's Lattices on Mars, but—'

Nicola said impatiently, 'I don't think this is the time for an academic debate about bugs on Mars, Mother.'

Harry leaned forward, ignoring the pixelated sparkle where his Virtual self brushed a chair. 'Look, I think it's nearly all the way out of the portal now. The big mass.'

The two ships were so close to the portal that Poole's view of the anomaly was almost face on. He quickly manipulated the sensors' data streams until he had produced a composite three-dimensional image of the object as a whole that he could rotate, expand, explore. That central fuselage, the mass that had emerged first, was like a fist in a black glove, clenched tight. And from it, he could see now, two wings swept back, one to either side of the main body, almost paddle-shaped, but flat and sharp-edged – in fact, he saw, flat and sharp to within the resolution limits of the *Crab*'s equipment. And both black as night.

'Not like a beetle,' Harry said, wondering. 'Like a sycamore seed.'

Symmetrical, with smooth, sweeping lines, the surfaces seamless: if this was engineering, it was fine work. Yet it was not beautiful, as Poole had thought of his wormhole portal. Not ugly either. It did not fit into that category – or any human category. 'You do not belong,' he murmured.

Nicola looked at him, not unsympathetically. 'Whether it belongs or not, it's *here*.'

'But it only *just* got though,' Harry said. 'It couldn't have got through a wormhole much narrower. It scraped the sides, of the throat, the portal.'

Shamiso said, 'Got through from *where*? The other end of your wormhole is in Earth orbit – correct? Could this sycamore seed and its entourage have come through from Earth, then? Surely some alarm would have been raised ... Ah, but we're restricted by lightspeed; any warnings might still be on their way to us.'

Poole was doubtful. 'If it's come through from the Earth end we'd know about it. There are instruments in the portals, test data sent through the wormhole itself.'

'Oh, it's obvious this thing didn't come from Earth,' Nicola said impatiently. 'You're thinking too literally – you at least, Mother, if not these two brooding geniuses. One of the reasons the Pooles built this prototype was to understand wormholes themselves better. Correct? It says so in your prospectus. Mother, you think a wormhole is some kind of simple high-speed transit system? There's nothing simple about it. A wormhole is a flaw, a link between two events that shouldn't be linked at all. Events that can be anywhere in spacetime – in space, on the other side of the Andromeda Galaxy, or somewhere else in time, *anywhen*, in past and future. Even in other universes, some think.'

Harry scowled. 'What are you saying?'

'I'm saying that you hoped to build an interplanetary superhighway. In fact you opened a kind of crack in space that could lead anywhere. And that could let in anything. Didn't you even *think* of this, when you were doodling Earth–to-Jupiter subway systems on your softscreens? I'm getting you into focus, Michael Poole. You're the worst sort of visionary meddler. Like a weapons manufacturer. You can see the glorious technology, and you persuade people to give you the money to build it. But you don't see the consequences, do you ...?'

These ideas swirled in a fog of dread in Poole's mind. *A crack that could let in anything.* 'She's right,' he said. 'There's a *reason* that thing, the sycamore seed, is as big as it is – a reason it's shown up today, of all days.'

Harry still didn't get it. 'Why?'

'Because this is the first time we've built a wormhole big enough. You said it yourself; it only just squeezed through. This – thing – has been waiting. Out there somewhere. And as soon as we opened the door far enough—'

Shamiso looked at him in growing horror. 'In it barged—'

Her image broke up in a burst of cubical pixels.

The flitter lurched. Poole was thrown forward.

Suddenly the flitter was hurtling backwards. He saw that the portal had shrunk in his vision, as had the sycamore seed ship.

Nicola was at her controls, sweeping stylised icons through the air with sharp, decisive, very physical gestures. This was her style; it was possible to control a modern craft with the mind, without any bodily movement at all. Right now Poole found he approved.

As he hastily strapped into his couch Poole glanced over his shoulder. Harry and Shamiso's Virtuals, reformed, were both back in their projected seats, and both looked shocked. Poole snapped, 'Put on your helmets and close them up. Make sure the Co-ordinator does it right, Harry.'

His father nodded, silent for once, and complied.

Poole turned on Nicola. 'What did you do?'

'Moved us away.'

'Lethe, this is *my* ship.'

'So's the *Hermit Crab*. Look at it.'

She brought up a display showing the *Crab*'s status. The display was littered with red alarm flags. Poole had designed the display himself; he read it in an instant. 'Something is destabilising the *Crab*'s GUTdrive.'

'Yes. And you know what that something is.'

'The phantoms?'

'The third type of entities. Squirmy, ghostly things made of GUT-stuff themselves. I think that's what they were searching for – more sources of GUT energy. Feeding, maybe? Or refuelling. Well, they found one. The *Crab*'s drive pod.'

'And you reacted,' he said grudgingly. 'Faster than I did. You got us away. We should be OK in this tub; it only has a fusion drive. The *Crab*, though – Harry?'

'Here, son. I heard all that.'

'You need to get the *Crab* back to Ganymede. Use the attitude thrusters, not the main drive.'

'I'm way ahead of you.' Harry's Virtual was already throwing invisible switches. 'I'll broadcast warnings, to keep GUTships clear until we know what we're dealing with. I'll take care of your ship, son. And Co-ordinator Emry. What about you?'

Poole thought quickly. 'I'm going to Io. Miriam and Bill are there.

The flux-tube teams. Stuck down a deep hole in the middle of the magnetosphere's most intense region. And their radiation shields are powered by—'

'GUTengines. So they're in immediate danger. Take care.'

Nicola Emry watched Poole coldly. 'OK, since you ask, I'll come with you. Do you want me to send a message to Earth, the inner System?'

'Why?'

'Because that's where the sycamore seed ship is heading.'

When he looked out of the window, for the first time since Nicola's impulsive manoeuvre, he saw that the huge black object had gone.

4

Poole frantically tried to establish a decent link to Inachus Base, at Babbar Patera on Io. At first all he could get was a scratchy head-and-shoulders Virtual image of Melia, senior artificial mind at the base, and even that was prone to breaking up into a fluttering cloud of pixels. And the time delay between her responses, of a second or so, was heart-breaking. It was the kind of delay suffered between Earth and its Moon, and an indication of how far Poole still had to travel to get back from the wormhole site to Io. Such was the scale of the Jovian system.

But Melia, as she had been designed to be, was calm. 'I'm doing my best to restore contact with Bill Dzik and Miriam Berg. As soon as I have them I'll patch them through—'

'If the uplink can handle it.'

'Be assured we're on the case, Michael.' She smiled, sketchily. 'We follow your adventures with interest. As soon as it was clear that there was some kind of anomaly at the portal site, I called a general alert. Retrospectively endorsed by Bill and Miriam.'

'You made the right call. Though you know you didn't need that authorisation.'

'Better safe than sorry,' Melia said primly. 'Every second of down time costs money. The shareholders—'

'Are more unstable than Io's volcanoes, I know.' For Poole Industries the wormhole operation had always been out at the edge of the envelope of financial plausibility. And for an investor you couldn't get much more of a confidence-sapping glitch, Poole thought with gnawing anxiety, than some kind of alien artefact pushing its way out of your prototype wormhole. But for now there were more immediate priorities. 'How's the evacuation going?'

'In hand,' Melia assured him. 'We're lifting everybody up from the Hub, inside Jupiter. And every craft we can get hold of that can run independently of a GUTdrive, including your own flitter, will be enlisted to— I have Miriam Berg. Please hold.' The Virtual collapsed.

Nicola, piloting the flitter, glanced over at him. 'You guys run a big operation out here, but your comms link is worse than I had in my bedroom aged five.'

Poole looked at her with some contempt. 'So? This is the frontier. There's no larger human operation between us and the stars. And Jupiter is about as hostile a place you can come to work.' He shook his head. 'One power plant failing you can cope with. We never envisaged a contingency that could take them all out.'

'Then you lack imagination. Who's Miriam Berg?'

'She and Bill Dzik are the senior managers on the ground at Io, in this phase of the project.'

'And Melia?'

'Senior artificial sentience.'

'Senior this, senior that. I expect you've got an organogram. People like you always have organograms.'

He just glared. 'What I have is a hundred people down on Io, flesh and blood, and several thousand other sentients of various capabilities. Out there, on the surface, unprotected, you'd pick up a lethal dose of radiation in three hours. And without the GUTengines – without the electromagnetic shielding—'

'Inachus for Michael Poole.' It was Miriam Berg. Her head-and-shoulders image showed her peering out of a pressure-suit helmet.

'Miriam. I'm coming in.'

'We're doing what we can, Michael. We don't dare shut down the main GUTengine generators, but they're glitching all over the place.'

'Are you down in the lava-tube shelters yourself?'

She glared at him. 'No, I'm not, and nor is Bill, and nor would you be right now. We've got a crash schedule of evacuations set up and operating, with the usual priorities going out first – the young, our one pregnant woman, the injured. AS users last. I can pass it up for your approval—'

'I don't need to see that.'

Nicola put in, 'Finding somewhere to house a hundred refugees will be the next challenge. I know that even Daraville, on Ganymede, doesn't have the capacity. I've put out a general call for help. And I have a couple of ideas.'

'Thanks. That's actually helpful.'

She arched an eyebrow, quizzically. 'Nice to be appreciated. So, AntiSenescence users are at the back of the line? What is this, some kind of discrimination against the elderly?'

'Are you a user?'

'Of AS? Not my style, Poole.'

Despite the circumstances he had to laugh. 'You're serious, aren't you? Look – among the capabilities you acquire from AS treatment is a limited ability to repair cellular, even genetic injury. Meant to counter the effects of ageing, but it will work just as well on radiation damage. The studies show that an AS user with compromised protection might last a full hour on Io longer than a non-user. So it wouldn't save your life—'

'But it's enough to get you kicked out of the first lifeboats.'

'That's the idea.'

Miriam was frowning. 'Who are you talking to?'

'My cab driver.'

'Hmm. Listen, Michael. If you get the chance, and the comms capacity, follow the news. That intruder of yours, the big one—'

'The sycamore seed. On its way into the inner System?'

'Yes, and moving fast, about one per cent of lightspeed. *How* it's moving is another question. We're seeing no radiation, no evidence of exhaust. Whatever it is, it ain't a rocket. We are detecting some kind of gravity waves emanated by the thing, but—'

'Is it making for Earth?'

'Earth is on the far side of the Sun. It will actually come closer to Mars. The final destination's still unclear – some projections show the Sun itself, some Mercury.'

Nicola frowned. 'I can see why it might head for the Sun; that's where the System's mass-energy is. But Mercury? What in Lethe could it want there? And what about the other junk that came through the wormhole?'

Miriam glanced down. 'The silvered spheres you called raindrops followed the sycamore seed into the inner System – all of them, as far as anyone knows. But the phantoms have stuck around in Jovian space, unfortunately for us. Obviously they're tracking any GUTengine they can find. But some of them are diving into the Io flux torus.'

'They're hungry,' Nicola said. 'Looking for energy, for the high-density sort they need. Which they won't find in the flux torus.'

Miriam shrugged. 'Your cab driver may be right. But all we have is guesswork right now.'

'Noted,' Poole said. 'So let's stop guessing. I'll join the evac effort as soon as we can get there. I'll get off the line and let you progress your—'

'No, you won't get off this Lethe-spawned line.'

Miriam's head imploded in a cloud of pixels, to be replaced by the snarling visage of a man, apparently much older, his face deep-space pale, his white hair a tangle tied up at the back of his head. In his background, Poole glimpsed green leaves, like trees.

Nicola laughed. 'Now *that* is the look I want when I get AS-preserved.'

The man glared. 'Which one of you is the Poole?'

Poole leaned forward. 'I'm Michael Poole. Who in Lethe are you, and how did you crash my private comms links?'

'I'll crash a lot more than that before we're done, you foetus. *You* called *me*.'

'Strictly speaking, it was me,' said Nicola. She tapped Poole's shoulder and pointed to an alert from the onboard intelligence. The caller was identified: Highsmith Marsden, calling from Gallia Three. 'I told you I was looking for places to put your people.'

'I've heard of him,' Poole murmured. 'And the Gallias. Though I don't know much more than is scrolling before me . . . Highsmith Marsden. Over two hundred years old. A scientist, no present academic affiliation, specialises in bioinformatics, quantum nonlinearity, experiments in superluminal communications. Oh, now I know why I remember him. He consulted with Jack Grantt on the Mars Lattices. And Gallia Three's a cycler. Earth–Jupiter. A hollowed-out comet nucleus—'

'I know the idea. In the days before high-speed technologies like the GUTdrive, right? Elliptical orbit, dipping to Earth at perihelion, Jupiter at aphelion. You'd just climb on board and *live* in the thing as it carried you out to the gas giants – how long was the trip?'

'Over two years,' Marsden snarled. 'But the system has worked like clockwork for centuries. Which is more than can be said for your steam rockets today, isn't it, flyboy? Let alone your wormholes. Lethe, man, what have you done to us? Rapid transport system my eye. You ought to paint your wretched wormholes red so we know to avoid them.'

Poole said, 'Professor Marsden, you can see we have a situation—'

'Oh, I'm well aware of your situation. And I have my own priorities. You can consult the academic press to find out what I'm doing here. This is a space habitat already over a thousand years old, which shelters a biosphere of similar antiquity, and all of it relying on nothing more than comet ice and sunlight. Studying such an object is exactly the sort of project one *should* be pursuing, given the benefit of AS longevity, wouldn't you think? Not that those fools at Oxford who cut my funding decades ago would have agreed. And I would have thought, Michael Poole, that today of all days, when it appears that some sort of alien entity has erupted into the Solar System thanks to your infantile tinkering, you ought to applaud a transport mode that is all but powerless, invisible, silent.'

Poole made to answer.

Nicola waved him silent. 'Shut up, Michael. This old fossil is thinking more clearly than anybody else I've heard today. Professor, you're right. Gallia Three is about as safe a refuge as we could have found. Which is why I thought of calling on you. And – shut *up*, Michael – how big is the habitat? This report says it was designed to hold five hundred, at peak capacity . . . Where are you just now?'

'I'm near aphelion. Obviously, or I wouldn't be wasting my time trying to communicate with the likes of you.'

'Near Jovian orbit, then,' Poole said. 'And given the time delays, he's no more than light-seconds away.'

Nicola said, 'So we found a place to take your precious workers from Io, and their bot buddies. Your first lucky break of the day.'

'Not that lucky. There were three Gallias; the idea was that there would be one at Jupiter three times in every twelve-year Jovian orbit. So it's not that unlikely that—'

'Shut up. Thank you for responding, Professor. Michael. Contact the *Crab*. Speak to my mother. She's a UN Oversight Co-ordinator, remember; she has a lot of leverage. Tell her this old fart will open his door to your refugees.'

Poole, feeling dazed, resolved never to make an enemy of Nicola Emry. He turned back to the monitor. 'Professor Marsden – since we've got you on the line – what do *you* make of it?'

Marsden frowned. 'Of what?'

'The intruders. You've obviously been following events. We've been calling them the sycamore seed, the raindrops, the phantoms.'

He sniffed. 'Labels are irrelevant.'

'Of course they are. What do you think?'

'That they're dangerous. Almost bound to be hostile. And your irresponsibility in allowing them into the System—'

'Why dangerous? What's your logic?'

'It is that these are forms of life – and I do think they show the characteristics of life rather than technology; one of your "phantoms" even appears to have budded, to have reproduced already – these forms are quite inimical to our carbon-chemistry forms. Surely this is obvious.

'The "phantoms" – you must have identified this for yourself – are essentially knots of quagma, centred on a GUT-density core. *Quagma*: the stuff of the very early universe, created less than a millionth of a second after the first singularity – just after the GUT era itself and the age of cosmic inflation . . . The universe was filled with a kind of ultra-hot liquid, a soup of particles like neutrinos and photons, and electrons – and photinos, dark matter particles – and quarks; it was too hot yet for the quarks to combine in nucleons, protons and neutrons. A quark soup, a quagma. And yet there was life – oh, the theoretical modelling and relic anomalies prove it. Beasts of quagma, who fought and lived and died in their mayfly generations, and who fed, probably, on remnant islands of GUT matter, super-hot, super-energetic. Just a second after the singularity and it was all over. Most of the quark soup had congealed into nucleons, and the whole universe was no more exotic than the heart of a star. *But*—'

'But some of these quark creatures may have survived.'

'Indeed.' Marsden was almost whispering, eyes wide, voice hoarse, grey hair haloing his head; to Poole he was like a vision of some pre-Discovery-era prophet. 'To these quagma phantoms our universe would be a vast, cold, empty place, its days of glory long gone. But in pockets, here and there—'

Nicola nodded. 'There would still be delicious knots of left-over high-density energy, on which they feed. Such as the engine cores of Michael's GUTships.'

'Exactly. Life – but not our kind of life. *They do not belong here*,' he said with sudden, almost savage vigour. 'They do not belong *now*. As soon as they arrived, they started to spread destruction and chaos and misery. And *you* brought them here, you Pooles, with your hubristic meddling.'

Nicola grinned. 'I think we've got the first draft of your gravestone inscription, Michael.'

Poole's face burned. 'We have people in danger. I'm going down to Io. *Crab Junior* out.' He cut the line, peremptorily took control of the little craft, and threw it across space.

5

After a fusion-powered limp through Jovian space, the *Crab Junior* had to make a slow, cautious final approach to Io, such was the volume of traffic around the little moon. With the big GUTships abandoned for now, there were only small craft available for the evacuation, flitters and yachts and other special-purpose vessels, all of them fusion-propelled – and each capable of lifting only a handful of refugees.

But the slow descent gave the *Junior*'s crew a chance for a good look at Io, and Poole was grimly gratified to see Nicola Emry's cynical eyes widen with wonder.

Io, innermost major moon of Jupiter, mangled by tidal squeezing and battered by the giant planet's magnetosphere – and no larger than Earth's Moon – had more active volcanoes than all of Earth's landmasses. The great calderas were pits in the surface, black as night and stained with orange fire. There were lakes of lava too, of liquid sulphur dioxide, banded red and orange at their cooler perimeters. Meanwhile curtains of crimson lava reached hundreds of metres above the surface, gas plumes towered, and persistent, eerie aurorae haunted the poles.

It was the colours that got you, Poole always thought. Violent colours you would never have expected on such a minor body, vivid against a background of wan five-astronomical-units sunlight, and the pale glow of Jupiter, huge in the sky. Red and orange and black, and a lurid green.

And, only hours before, there had been a droplet of Earth blue too, the dome over Inachus Base.

The Poole Industries company town at Babbar Patera had been built on a kind of platform, standing on vast foundations pile-driven into the unreliable surface, with active stabilisation to cope with rock tides that amounted to fifty metres every forty-two-hour Io 'day'. But once the GUTengine-powered magnetic shields had gone, the dome had quickly collapsed, exposing buildings, bunkers, equipment stacks

– and humans in their hardened suits, scurrying for shelter. Away from that centre, the roadways and monorails and mass-driver slingshots, infrastructure constructed to extract Io's mineral treasures, were deserted and exposed, looking from above like the ribbing of an autumn leaf about to be thrown on the fire.

But that fire, the awesome energies focused on Io, was the reason the Pooles had come here. Io was so close to its parent that it orbited well within Jupiter's radiation-filled magnetosphere, twenty thousand times as strong as Earth's. Indeed, the moon's volcanic plumes injected electrons and oxygen and sulphur ions into the magnetosphere, so that Io orbited inside a wheel-shaped, highly energetic flow of charged particles: the 'Io torus'. More tubes of magnetic force connected Io's field to the poles of Jupiter itself: flux tubes, along which currents measured in millions of amperes routinely flowed. As a result, Io-Jupiter was like a single vast engine, Poole always thought, with linkages of electromagnetism and particle streams and tides, and spanning three million kilometres.

And it was this engine which industrialists had tapped for a thousand years or more, all the way back to the days when Poole Industries, Con-Am and others had first dug into the tortured crust for exotic sulphur compounds and other treasures. Those pioneers had simply draped superconducting tethers across the landscape to allow the shifting magnetosphere to drive useful currents. Now this world-engine was trying to kill the humans and machines that had dared to come here.

It was all his fault, came the nagging from a corner of Poole's mind. His ambition, or at any rate his family's, that had brought so many into a position of such peril. His lack of care, his headlong rush to complete the latest project, his hubris that had opened up the wormhole gate to the eerie, out-of-time peril that had caused all this. Nicola was right, and Marsden. All he could do now was try to put it right.

As soon as he could, he joined the evacuation operation, and went to work.

The operation was slow, a trickle. The collapse of the surface facilities saw to that, as airlocks and power plants failed, making transfers dangerous and slow.

As the long hours of the emergency went by, in between their own descents and take-offs – in a flitter that started to smell of the fear and exhaustion of the refugees who had passed through it – Poole and Nicola Emry took it in turns to grab some rest. Nicola slept a lot better than Poole did. But then, he suspected, she was not troubled by a conscience, and probably never would be.

It was after one of his non-sleeps that Nicola woke him, cautiously, to tell him that she had some news. 'From Mars.'

Poole felt groggy, baffled. It was already two days since the worm-hole invasion. He was strapped into a sleeping bag at the rear of the flitter cabin. He saw that they were on their way back down to Io once more, for another refugee pickup. He grabbed his flask of water from a bracket, drained it, and let it drift off in the microgravity. 'Mars? What has Mars got to do with it?'

'It's the sycamore seed, and its accompanying flock of raindrops. It still seems to be making for the Sun, or Mercury. But Mars happens to be close to that track.'

'I remember.'

'There's no indication that it's going to call in. But conversely the Martians have been calling it. Take a look . . .'

She set up a Virtual that played out on the floor beside his pallet. He saw a small figure, doll-like – a male – standing in what looked like a huge, glass-roofed hall. The man was looking out of the image, talk-ing to the universe. Poole saw a crowd of people behind him, behind a rope barrier, patrolled by Federal Police in their pale blue uniforms.

She pointed. '*That* is the Cydonia dome. And the show-off in the foreground—'

'I know him. Jack Grantt. He led the team that claims to have dis-covered intelligence on Mars. Vast bacterial networks—'

'Vast guesswork, more like. My mother has been to his funding pitches.'

'He's an old family friend. He was "Uncle Jack" when I was a kid. My father sent me for a season's study with his team, on Mars. Harry wanted us, Poole Industries, to develop an open mind about encountering exotic life. After all, we've been leading the way into many of the more unusual environments, like Io, that humans have yet explored. If anybody's likely to contact new life, it's us.'

Nicola pulled a face. 'People like you always *know* each other, don't you? Well, now Grantt thinks there's life, and maybe mind, coming at us through your wormhole. So he's been trying to signal to it.'

That amused Poole. 'Signal to it? How? Flashing lights, radio beams? With big triangles dug into Hellas Planitia?'

'Oh, there's more comedy value in it than that. He's

sending a broadcast – of himself, standing there spouting – via gravity waves.'

'Gravity waves? How? Oh – Phobos. He would have got the co-operation of the local representatives of Poole Industries . . .' In advance of the day when exotic matter might need to be manufactured in the Martian system for local wormhole-network links, the Pooles had established a trial black hole facility on Mars's moon, a cut-down version of the Jovian Hub. And it was by manipulating that black hole, Poole quickly confirmed, that Jack Grantt had attempted to catch the attention of the sycamore seed. 'Harry will have made sure the company got the appropriate credit. But as for the sycamore seed—'

'It just sailed by,' Nicola said with mock sadness. 'Grantt did succeed in signalling to his own species, I suppose – after all here he is, on all the news feeds – which will probably do his next funding application no harm. Of course the sycamore seed and its entourage are a sensation, across the inner worlds. Everybody's watching the various feeds. But there's controversy – well, you can see that.'

'You mean that crowd in the background? What is it, a demonstration?'

'Some commentators are calling it a riot.'

That word, redolent of the global disorders of the Bottleneck age, took Poole aback. 'A riot? Seriously?'

'Feelings are running high, Michael. Look, there's already been damage from this – alien incursion. People have *seen* the drifting GUTships, the chaos on Io. Not every Martian thinks it's a good idea to draw the attention of this ambiguous visitor to their world with gravity-wave look-at-me signals. Certainly Grantt has got no kind of public endorsement to do what he's doing. Who is he to speak for Mars? Let alone mankind.

'And counter to that there are others who think it's mankind's cosmic duty to welcome this visitor.' She sighed. 'Half of humanity seems to wants to adopt this visitor, the other half to blow it up. It's barely arrived, yet already it's disrupting our society. Makes you think, doesn't it? And—' She pressed a finger to her ear. Then, without hesitating, she hurled herself towards the pilot's couch.

Poole, confused, struggled out of his sleeping bag. 'What's wrong?'

'Inachus is breaking up. I mean, the stabilising platform under the base. The evac is nearly done, but three survivors are still to be picked up. My mother – she's the in situ UN coordinator of the operation – has banned making any more rescue attempts.'

'So what are you doing?'

'Making a rescue attempt. Wash your face and get up here.'

Even from high above Io, on their closing trajectory, Poole could see the problem. The raft on which Inachus had been built was itself tipping now, as if wrecked by the stormy sea of rock beneath it. The base facilities were slipping from the raft's surface, like crockery from a tilted tray, and lava from below lapped up and over the lower rim of the platform, which was beginning to dissolve into that ferociously hot pool.

Nicola, piloting the *Crab Junior*, hovered above the tilting surface.

'You looking for somewhere safe to land?'

'No. I'm looking for people. That's where I'll land, safe or not – *there*.'

A human figure had dashed out onto the open deck of the platform, in a brilliant green armoured suit, waving vigorously.

Nicola immediately brought the *Junior* down, a crash dive.

'Just her,' Poole said. 'She must have seen us.'

'Her?'

'That's Miriam. Miriam Berg. I bought her that suit. Three survivors, your mother said. Where are the others?'

A building collapsed, shuddering apart into panels and struts that hailed down across the tipped deck in low-gravity slow motion. The fleeing figure, already unsteady on her feet, had to scramble out of the way of the debris.

'*Lethe*. I'll be in the airlock.'

The *Crab* touched down, and was at rest for bare seconds before Poole, having sealed up his own suit, opened the small airlock, hauled Miriam aboard, and helped her brace for take-off.

As the flitter soared up and away from the collapsing base, they helped each other out of their suits. Miriam went to clean herself up. Poole heard her throwing up.

Then they made their way to the flight deck. Poole led Miriam to the co-pilot couch, beside Nicola. The command couches were the most comfortable seating in the ship; Miriam, seeming groggy, didn't object.

A few years younger than Poole, Miriam had brown eyes and hazel hair prematurely streaked with grey, cut low-gravity neat. Now she looked older, gaunt, exhausted. Poole insisted she let the ship's medical suite treat her for any radiation damage within the hour. But she refused food and water. For now she just wanted coffee, and to sit.

Eventually she said simply, 'Thanks.'

Nicola shrugged. Evidently she didn't appreciate gratitude.

'You need to go back to the wormhole, by the way.'

Without questioning, Nicola laid in the course.

Poole sat in a fold-out passenger chair. 'We were told there were three survivors.'

Miriam sucked coffee through a zero-gravity lid. 'I'm the only one who made it. Bill Dzik and Melia . . . We were the last, we three. Most of Melia's memory store had been uploaded; we had the rest of her in a core processor – a last-resort backup, a thing like a suitcase. The platform had already started to tilt. Melia wanted us to leave her behind, so we could escape on the scooters.' She glanced at Nicola. 'Low-gravity terrain-hopping vehicles—'

'I can guess.'

'Bill refused to dump her. So she charged the casing, and *shocked* him so he'd have to drop her. And while he was trying to get hold of her again, the platform tipped, and we had air tanks and other heavy-duty gear smashing through the partitions and raining down on us—'

'Bill Dzik,' Nicola said. 'Never met the man, but a name to remember. The first human to die because of all this, the incursion through the wormhole. And Melia, the first artificial sentient.'

Miriam nodded. 'Much of her memory can be reconstructed. But *she* has gone, yes. So we failed.'

'You did your best,' Nicola said calmly, surprising Poole. 'You came close to getting everybody out of there. What more could you do?'

'Not screw up.'

'Everybody screws up. Life's not perfect.'

'Well, it should be.' Miriam had finished her coffee. Poole handed her his own carton. She started to drain it, like the first.

'So,' Poole said. 'Why do we need to go back to the wormhole?'

Nicola said, 'I can tell you that. More chatter on the comms feeds. There's a new development. Something else coming through. You need to be there.'

'Us?'

'Not us. *You*.'

6

The wormhole portal, when they got to it, was surrounded by a cloud of ships, a rough sphere. Many of these were GUTships of the classic design, each a gaunt pole topped and tailed by lifedome and lump of comet ice. Because of the threat of the quagma phantoms, the ships were immobilised save for their secondary attitude-control thrusters. But Poole knew that some of the ships, including flitters belonging to the UN's Federal Police, might be armed.

There was some contact from these ships as *Crab Junior* arrived, including a hail from Harry Poole and Shamiso Emry in the *Hermit Crab*, returned from Ganymede, somewhere in the crowd. *Junior* was allowed to pass through the cordon, and then to approach the wormhole portal at the centre of the cloud, the spiky tetrahedron, its sky-blue structure as innocent-looking as it had been before the sycamore seed entity had pushed its way through. Approach until they were closer than any other ship, Poole realised uneasily.

And, finally, they confronted the new thing that had come through.

It was another enigmatic, anonymous form: a sphere, silvered, maybe a couple of metres across. It had a kind of belt around its circumference, like a lanyard to which a bright green pendant was fixed.

Miriam and Nicola, at the controls, studied this object with the flitter's sensors.

Poole just stared. 'It looks like a cousin of those raindrops that came through with the sycamore seed.'

'Don't think so,' Nicola said. 'Actually more massive. That thing weighs a tonne. Not quite as dense as water . . .'

'It's nearly featureless,' Miriam said, checking monitors of her own. 'But you can see it's rotating. Look at that lanyard around its equator. A lanyard with a pendant attached . . .'

Wordlessly Nicola brought up an image of the 'pendant'. It was a tetrahedron – small, only a few centimetres across, a green frame enclosing an empty space. 'Curious,' Nicola said dryly. 'Wherever this thing came from, how could it know that *this* end of the wormhole ended in a tetrahedron?'

'And curiouser yet,' Miriam said, 'according to the analysis by the UN observers, that green isn't any old green. That's chlorophyll green – Earth green.'

Poole was feeling uneasy, increasingly so. The lingering sense of *wrongness* that he'd felt since the first emergence of the sycamore seed from the wormhole was now deepening drastically, spiralling down within him like an Anthropocene-era drill sucking the last dregs of oil from a well. 'Maybe it's a universal,' he said. 'Chlorophyll, I mean. Maybe under any sunlike star, with a carbon-based biosphere, the laws of chemistry dictate—'

Nicola laughed. 'Your biologist buddy Jack Grantt wouldn't buy that. There are many ways to eat sunlight. And even if so, do you imagine that tetrahedral form is a universal too? *You* designed the portal. Why did you choose that configuration, anyhow? Why not a cube or—'

'Because it looked – well, right. Aesthetically. I wanted my wormholes to be beautiful. We sat up all night sketching.'

'So, an arbitrary choice?' Nicola looked back at him. Given the news she was about to reveal to him, he would later reflect, she didn't seem excited, or impressed. She said simply, 'There's something else. Your sycamore seed may not have spoken to us, but this spinning sphere *is*. Since it emerged. Across the electromagnetic spectrum, in neutrino pulses, even in gravity waves . . . A lot of trouble for a few words. Even if they are in Standard.'

'Standard?'

'She's right,' Miriam said, watching monitors of her own.

'Just tell me,' Poole said hoarsely.

'Here's a live broadcast, with a rough translation.' Miriam touched an icon.

The voice was flat, artificial, tinny. The intonation was odd, almost quaint, as if spoken by a non-Standard speaker, or as if this was some recording from the deep past. Poole found he needed the comms system's simultaneous best-guess translation to make sense of it.

'. . . Ambassador to the Heat Sink. I am here for Michael Poole. I am a Silver Ghost. That is, or will be, your name for us. Our kinds waged war for millennia. And yet I bear the Sigil of Free Humanity, as you can see. I have visited the tetrahedral cathedrals of the

Wignerian faith of which you, Michael Poole, are a prophet. And at the centre of the Galaxy, on a world dedicated to the billions of dead of the Exultants' war, there is a statue of you, Michael Poole. Two kilometres high. I have seen that statue for myself. I will be with you at Timelike Infinity, Michael Poole, where this burden will pass. I am known to my own kind as the Ambassador to the Heat Sink. I am here for Michael Poole. I am a Silver Ghost. That is, or will be . . .'

The flitter shuddered, as if a mass had detached itself from the hull of the small craft.

Then, through the window, Poole, disbelieving, saw a missile sail across space, silent, barely visible. It was a depth probe, he recognised, designed to hit a rocky asteroid or comet core at high velocity, to sample its deep interior. He knew it wasn't intended as a weapon. But it would *work* as a weapon. It was streaking across the gap towards the drifting, spinning 'Ghost'.

And it had come from the *Crab Junior*.

He glared at Nicola. 'Why in Lethe did you do that?'

'I didn't.' She was checking her displays. 'There was an override . . . *Harry*. Your father fired the missile.'

'What? This is *my* ship. He doesn't *have* an override.'

Miriam glared at him. 'Are you sure? More to the point, why would he do this?'

Nicola shrugged. 'To secure the safety of mankind. Or some such. That's what the public feeds are being told. Or possibly it's because this Ghost thing named *you*, not him? You two need to talk about your rivalry issues, it's not healthy.'

Still the 'Silver Ghost' spoke. 'I bear the Sigil of Free Humanity—'

And Poole saw the projectile, at a comparatively low speed, penetrate the Ghost's hide.

'—the tetrahedral cathedrals—'

The Ghost simply burst open.

That shimmering skin ripped, shredded, and a mess of biology came tumbling out: red blood, quickly freezing; masses like organs, muscles; even a kind of rangy, long-limbed body, with recognisable torso and limbs, foetus-like, coiled up. And what looked like a vegetable mass, or perhaps something fungal, that had evidently packed the shell.

Out of the dispersing mess that pendant came sailing, the green tetrahedron, still attached to a snapped lanyard.

Nicola broke the silence. 'I guess that souvenir is yours. You want me to go out and get it for you?'

'Do it,' he snarled. 'Sooner that than leave it for Harry. Then let's go to Gallia.'

TWO

'But the future is irrelevant.'
'It is?'
'Yes! If we can't get through the present.'

Tom and Michael Poole Bazalget, AD 2047

TWO

7

Nicola guided the flitter in towards Gallia Three, working her way through a crowd of other refugee-laden craft: more flitters, larger fusion-drive scows – slow freighters designed to carry cargoes of ore and ice – even a couple of gaunt GUTships, nudged this way by their manoeuvring and attitude control systems. One of these ships had brought Harry here, Poole knew. Not for the first time in his life, his father had overtaken him.

And Gallia Three was gradually revealed.

Gallia was a squashed ball of dirty comet ice about a third of a kilometre across – an oblate spheroid, like Jupiter itself, shorter from pole to pole than it was fat at the equator. The whole turned rapidly on that short axis; Poole, instinctively counting, estimated it completed a rotation in about half a minute. The outer crust was a dirty crimson-black, thanks no doubt to a layer of complex hydrocarbon molecules in the ice created by hundreds of years of Jovian radiation and inner-System sunlight. But as the spheroid turned, Poole glimpsed flashes of Earth green shining from windows, breaks in the black, there and gone. It was an oddly nostalgic view – at least, Poole supposed, if you had grown up on Earth.

This nucleus was only the heart of a wider mechanism. A lacy, dodecahedral frame was pinned to the habitat at its rotation poles. And to the frame was attached, by glimmering guide cables, an immense mirror, more than five times the diameter of the habitat itself. Reflected sunlight splashed on receptor panels at the habitat's poles. Poole saw repair bots crawling over the mirror, like beetles on glass, sending slow ripples washing across the gleaming surface.

Nicola was looking stuff up. 'They use that mirror-sail, not just for catching sunlight for their fields and forests, but actually as a sail, for position and momentum control. They tweak their orbit; they don't come too close to Jupiter, for instance. And across an orbital path that spans four astronomical units there's time to do all the tweaking they need. What an antiquated, ramshackle—'

'I'll tell you what's ramshackle, child, and that's your imagination.' Highsmith Marsden's Virtual head flared into existence once more above the flitter's comms console. 'Old we might be, crusty we might be, but right now we're the only safe haven for you and your wretched bands of miners and digger bots, aren't we? Now, if you want to come any closer you're going to have to shut down your fusion drive – you can manoeuvre with any chemical-propellant thrusters you have – and you can shut down your comms too. Passive sensors only; no pinging of my hull. We're running silent here, and if you keep wandering around lit up like an Earth Day display you can go dive into Jupiter itself for all I care. Is that clear enough?'

Poole tried to reply. 'Professor Marsden—'

'Oh, and by the way, that alien artefact you picked up—'

'The amulet,' Nicola said.

'Amulet?' Marsden mused. 'I haven't heard it called that before. An old word: an object that brings its wearer power or protection. Maybe that's appropriate. Don't even *think* of bringing it into my habitat.'

The link was broken; the talking head disappeared in a cloud of pixels.

Nicola sighed. 'I want to be like him when I grow up.'

'Paranoid old relic.'

'But he has a point. Let's do as he asks.'

The dock was situated at one non-rotating pole of the habitat, and Poole had to admire the skill with which Nicola guided the *Junior*, unpowered save for a few puffs of chemical-propellant exhaust, through a forest of structural beams, antennae and sensor gear. The mechanisms of dock and airlocks were scuffed and much patched. Poole wondered how much of the fabric of this ancient habitat was original.

Once they were through the lock they faced a brightly lit inner space, a squashed sphere with a belt of Earth-green landscape plastering the equatorial region. Sunlight shone up into the hab through radiation-proofed windows set in the artificial ground. The air was threaded with ropes and struts along which people and machines briskly swam, hauling equipment and cargo boxes. Harry Poole was already coming up to meet them at the axial lock, pulling his way along a cable. Poole could see Marsden himself bustling up, a good way behind, his shock of white hair unmistakable.

There was a tube of cloud along the axis, slowly churning. The landscape knotted up around the far pole, pale with mist.

Nicola was staring around with a reasonable facsimile of wonder, despite apparent efforts to maintain a veneer of scepticism. 'I wonder if it rains in here.'

'I doubt it.' Poole tried to remember what he knew of the Gallias. 'Not big enough. Sprinklers, though.'

Harry reached them, breathing a little heavily after the effort of dragging himself through the air; AS-youthful or not, Poole thought wryly, he had never been one for physical exercise. He shook his son's hand. 'Michael. Lethe, I'm glad you made it. How are you feeling?'

'I'm feeling I can't remember the last time you shook my hand, Harry. The last time you bothered to show up physically.'

Nicola seemed entirely unoffended to be ignored. She merely grinned, cynically. 'Ah, but you've never been so famous before, Michael. That thing, the mercury-drop alien that came through the wormhole – it named *you*, not him. Which is why you shot the Ghost out of the sky, right, Harry?'

Harry glared at her. He never looked older, Poole thought, than when he was angry. 'You still here?'

Poole still felt stunned by the memory. 'Why *did* you destroy it, Harry? Firing a missile from *my* ship.'

'Because it seemed a good idea at the time. Highsmith Marsden agrees, actually. We'd already let strangers into our Solar System. Enough's enough. We didn't need any more.'

'You'd make such a decision, on behalf of all mankind?'

'Sure. If I'm the one on the spot. Everybody was watching, by the way. The whole incident. The news feeds, the comment channels – they're calling it the Wormhole Ghost. It's a frenzy. They are talking about you too, Michael.'

'Oh, good.'

'And there's endless speculation about what this incursion means for mankind.'

Poole asked dryly, 'And what it means for the family?'

Nicola grinned again. 'Now who's the cynic?'

'It's a heck of a wave,' Harry said. 'And it's a wave we have to ride, son.'

'A wave that's likely to come crashing down on all your pretty heads!'

This was Highsmith Marsden, climbing up at last, with that glowering, evidently habitually angry face now red with exertion. He had a barrel chest, not a trace of fat about the belly, and muscles that bulged under a pale blue coverall. His arms and legs looked equally powerful, an odd symmetry. This was a body adapted for hard work in low gravity, Poole realised: the physique of a deep-space farmer. And, despite his obvious physical age, whether AS-preserved or not, Marsdsen seemed a lot fitter than Harry.

He was still talking.

'Worst case, following this incursion, is some kind of existential threat to mankind. A threat posed by agents of nature unknown, origin unknown.' He looked Michael Poole up and down. 'And since, unlikely as it seems now that I'm actually in your underwhelming physical presence, *you* were actually named by that spinning wormhole alien, you yourself, Michael Poole, may be a source of that threat, or a focus, whatever you say or do. Let's get on with it. Follow me.' He turned and scrambled along another rope that led away from this axis, and back down towards the habitat's curving hull.

The rest prepared to follow, more clumsily.

Marsden called over his shoulder, 'I've been speaking to your colleague, by the way. Miriam Berg. Sensible young person.'

Miriam had gone ahead to this place in a fast one-person skimmer, to help with the arrangements for settling the refugee population from the Io facilities.

Poole said, 'I'm glad one of us impressed you. So what do you think we should do?'

'Obviously, work out how to establish a stable human breeding population in a stealthed space habitat.'

Nicola raised her eyebrows. 'On any other day that would be an odd thing to say. Now, which way up am I supposed to be when I climb this rope . . .?'

8

It turned out not to be a foolish question.

At first, following Marsden's example, Poole pulled himself head first 'up' the rope, and so towards the curving landscape 'above' his head. But as they moved away from the spin axis it soon felt as if they were falling upwards, a disconcerting sensation. Poole hastily swivelled around, so he was drifting down feet first, slow as a snowflake, guided by touches on the rope.

The descent got easier yet about forty metres down from the hub, where the ropes met a kind of grand, sweeping staircase, one of several set out radially around the axis point. When Poole tried standing, it felt as if the gravity was about lunar strength – a healthy fraction of Earth's. As Poole had spent more than a year on the Moon, supervising an upgrade of the Copernicus GUT energy accelerator, this felt familiar. Once he'd got his balance he bounded confidently down the steps after Marsden, Nicola and Harry. And by the time he'd caught them up, the gravity was feeling stronger yet.

'So,' he said, as they walked on. 'A breeding population? You have the room in here?'

Marsden glanced at him. 'Well, we should. Current population one hundred, capacity for five hundred. You understand the theory of the station. Years-long unpowered cruises from Earth to Jupiter. The Gallias were remote descendants of the Aldrin cyclers that once connected Earth to Mars: an economical way to achieve interplanetary travel. And the Gallias necessitated, by design, long-term self-sufficiency.' He gestured at the landscape that was now unfolding before them. 'Hence all this.'

Looking straight ahead, Poole saw a green swathe of parkland broken by small lakes, with clusters of cabins built of what looked like bamboo. It was a convincingly Earthlike vista. But the green landscape rose up on either side, so that it was as if they were walking down a mountain pass into a tremendous valley – a valley with walls that rose like great waves to close over their heads, behind that axial tube of fluffy cloud. Those windows in the ground cast sunlight *up* through the moist air to splash on the habitat's far wall; the shadows were peculiar.

'Nice place for a vacation,' Nicola said. 'But it wouldn't be a vacation to live here, would it?' She glanced pointedly at Marsden's own muscular body. 'I'm no historian, but didn't the age of farming end – Lethe, I don't know, by the thirtieth century?'

'More like the twenty-seventh,' Poole said.

'You would know,' she murmured. 'I expect your ancestors took out the patent on the first food machines, right?'

From behind them Harry called breathlessly, 'You're more right than wrong. You can thank Michael Poole Bazalget for that, and those Arctic methane deposits he stabilised. A while later, once suitable methanotropic bugs had been bred, we were able to turn what might have been greenhouse gases into food. And then—'

'We don't *farm* here,' Marsden said with some disgust. 'What do you think we are, barbarians? We do have food machines. But as far as possible we do live off the land, so to speak. That old solar sail provides enough power for living purposes. A few metres of comet ice in the shell, strengthened against the spin stress, is enough for radiation shielding – even when we approach Jupiter. All for free, you'll note; all we need is a little input of repair mass every century or so. People living off the sunlight and the resources of space . . . It's as close to the dreams of the ancient Bernal as we're ever likely to see.'

Harry frowned. 'Bernal? Was he on our payroll?'

Marsden just snorted. Poole suspected Harry was mocking him.

'Yes, we're cranks,' Marsden said. 'Yes, most people see this as an eccentric way to live. But now our time has come, hasn't it? We'll be safe in here, living quietly and silently, while your star-hot GUTships are hunted down by the thing you call the sycamore seed, and the quagma-phantom infestation, and whatever in Lethe else seeks to come through those wormholes of yours. You'll see. Even your group leader, Dr Berg, agrees with me – and agrees about what must be done.'

Poole was surprised by that last remark. But as it turned out, when Poole finally met Miriam inside one of those bamboo huts somewhere near the equator of the craft, Marsden was right.

Here at the equator, the region of maximum spin gravity, the load was up to about seventy-five per cent of Earth's. Poole, who had been in zero gravity for some days, felt it in his bones. Harry, too, was evidently glad to slump down on one of the couches that littered the dirt floor.

Dirt floor, yes: Poole found himself inside a kind of tepee, constructed of long bamboo shoots interwoven with reeds. Marsden had dumped them in here and gone in search of Miriam.

Poole knew that bamboo cane was a popular choice of construction material in closed-loop habitats like this, fast-growing, sturdy and straight – and it served as a neat reservoir of carbon to act as a buffer for the ecological cycles. A doorway faced one of the window light-pools, so a glow like late afternoon sunlight was cast into the hut, and a gentle breeze washed in, feeling pleasantly cool to Poole, who had been brought up in Britain's temperate climate. Good, unobtrusive environment control, he thought. This tepee was actually pretty big compared to the others around it. Poole had learned that it was generally used as a kind of town hall. But today the floor was crowded with rows of sleeping bags and heaps of blankets – many of them Poole Industries issue – and with small piles of spare clothing, first aid packs, a water bottle or two. Evidently this place was already serving as a dormitory for some of the incoming evacuees from Io.

They didn't have to wait long before Miriam Berg showed up, carrying a tray. She handed out clay mugs of what tasted to Poole like coffee, but probably wasn't.

Then she got down to business.

'Well, here we are. Most everybody in this habitat is out working on fixing up the life support to cope with the new arrivals: almost a hundred of us, in addition to the hundred residents already here. Double the numbers. They have made us refugees very welcome, by the way. Though you can see that even housing is an issue.' She smiled. 'We're quite a mixed crowd, Michael. I don't know how many you met before. Aside from the Io crew there are ice-moon miners, and Oversight biologists who were there to make sure those miners didn't disturb the native bugs in the roof oceans, and ore miners from Valhalla on Callisto, and admin staff from Daraville – even a few stranded tourists, unlucky for them. Here we are all mixed up together.

'But what's to become of us is way out of our hands. The discussions have gone up through Shamiso Emry's Oversight committee and other bodies to the World Senate, and they have already decided to evacuate the Jovian system altogether until the emergency is over.'

Nicola sniffed. 'If it ever is.'

'So we're to be taken back to Earth. The trouble is, because of these quagma phantoms of yours, Michael, the GUTships are unreliable for the foreseeable future, and nobody knows if fusion drives, for instance, are going to stay safe. So we can't be moved on; we're stuck here.'

Poole said, 'Highsmith Marsden has already suggested keeping you here longer. Or some of you. Enough to maintain a breeding population, he says.'

Miriam looked at him over her coffee. 'He's gone further, actually. He wants to nudge Gallia out of its transit orbit back to the inner System and relocate it to the Trojans, out here in Jupiter's orbit. So we'd stay there permanently. Stealthed, you see. As long as we do it before your visitors notice . . . I think I agree with him.'

Nicola had followed the exchange between them with interest. 'Speaking of breeding populations. You two, Berg and Poole. You're together, right? Or were. Or you *will be*. I can tell. Trust me, I'm good with people.'

Miriam looked as if she wanted to punch her.

Harry just laughed.

'It's not a big deal,' Poole said quickly. 'We were partners in our teens. After that – well, we got counselled out of doing anything hasty.'

'Counselled? Ah. So you're AS-platonic . . .'

Poole remembered the therapy sessions when he had begun his own AS treatment, vividly and with some embarrassment. With AS treatment you could look forward to whole extra lifetimes – and, as the mayfly centuries ticked by and people refused to die, that was slowly changing everything about human society, from political power structures to the economics of inheritance to interpersonal relationships.

'Marry young,' Harry himself had advised his son at the time, 'and you'll divorce what feels like younger.'

'How would you know? You aren't so old yourself, not yet. You and my mother "married young". And she *died* young. If you hadn't come together when you did—'

'Save it,' Harry had said evenly. 'Save *her*. Miriam. Save her until you're both ready, and sure. But be aware that it will almost certainly end someday anyhow. Live long enough and you outlive anything, even your own younger self . . .'

Poole had always felt uncomfortable with such advice. Could you really plan a relationship – could you timetable love? Looking at Miriam now, competent, strong, but somehow defensive – they had both changed so much, even before this intrusion of alien mystery into their lives – he wondered if they had already missed some elusive chance.

'"AS-platonic." I don't like being labelled,' Miriam said now, coldly, to Nicola.

'I'm right, though, aren't I? One reason why I never had AS treatment myself.'

Miriam stared at her. 'Seriously? Your mother must have offered to pay for it. Why would you turn it down? I mean, the medical benefits alone—'

Nicola shrugged. 'Has AS made you happy?'

'Well—'

Poole was relieved when Highsmith Marsden came bustling in. 'I could hear you gossiping from across the habitat. What are you, children?'

Nicola grinned. 'So to business.'

Harry stood. 'Professor Marsden, I—'

Marsden ignored him. 'Shall we get to the point? Which is to assure the survival of mankind in the face of alien threat.'

Harry blew out his cheeks, and sat down again. 'You think big, don't you?'

Poole frowned. 'We don't know if there is a threat, let alone an intentional one.'

Marsden said heavily, 'So claims the man whose own GUTship is already a drifting hulk. And whose closest friend was the first human to die. William Dzik, yes? I follow the news too. *I* say we need to act fast, while we have the chance.'

'Hence this idea of a breeding population?'

'A couple of hundred should be enough. I took a quick look over your crews' genetic records—'

Harry scowled. 'How in Lethe did you get those?'

Marsden ignored him again. 'Purely by chance we have a good sample of genetic diversity on board right now. The present two hundred will do the job, with a little planned breeding.'

Nicola grinned, evidently enjoying this hugely. '"Planned breeding"?'

'In an emergency it's essential to act quickly. It's rather like the efforts to save endangered species during the late days of the Anthropocene. To have even just one reserve population, one viable breeding set, tucked away here in Gallia, which can run as silently as we like

41

– externally we're just a ball of comet rock with a derelict-looking sail and a slightly odd heat signature . . .'

'He convinced me,' Miriam said. 'Maybe that surprises you, Michael. Might strike you as paranoid, even. But whatever we're dealing with here is very strange, and totally unanticipated. I mean, it *named* you, Michael. Or that mercury-drop Ghost thing did. You of all people should have an open mind about what comes next.

'And after all, we are bottled up in the Solar System. All of humanity. A determined enough attack, from an advanced enough technology . . . I think the Professor's right. We have to plan for the worst case.'

Poole frowned. 'Which is?'

Marsden glared at him. '"Which is?" "Which is?" What kind of a question is that? Have you no vision at all, man? And they built you a statue at the centre of the Galaxy, did they? What does it have you doing, looking for your own arse by supernova light?'

Harry barked laughter.

Nicola seemed to marvel. 'I *love* this guy.'

Marsden growled, '*Extinction*. That's the worst case. Do you kiddies need to look that word up? As Miriam implied, right now a sufficiently determined adversary could destroy us all – all extant humans. Then it's not just our own potential deaths we are dealing with, but the deaths – or rather the non-existence – of our children and grandchildren, and off into the future. And the loss of whatever humanity might have gone on to achieve.'

Nicola said dryly, 'Such as statues at the centre of the Galaxy.'

'Shut up,' Poole said.

Miriam said, 'It might not happen. But, then, it might. And until – I don't know, Lethe, until that sycamore seed thing speaks to us and tells it what it intends to do, we can't even assess the probabilities. Hence, yes, I agree with the Professor.'

Harry snorted. 'You agree with a totally paranoid analysis. Fine, Miriam, Professor. You hide away here while the rest of us go experience the wonder of the age. An extraterrestrial visitor to the Solar System . . .! We'll have to figure out if you're still on company time, Miriam.'

That made Nicola laugh. 'Harry, I don't like you. But I do admire your black heart.'

'Professor, that doesn't mean I'm not grateful to you for taking in my staff *in extremis* the way you have—'

'Oh, I'm sanguine about that,' Marsden said breezily. 'But what I won't allow is any alien technology aboard this station. You must deal with that yourselves.'

Poole felt his face grow cool, as if the blood had drained from his skin. 'You mean the amulet.'

'I think it's time you went to face that mystery – don't you? But not in *my* habitat . . .'

'I agree,' Poole said.

Nicola looked at him. 'Where, then?'

'It's Poole family business. Evidently – it did name me. So I'm going home. I'll take that Lethe-spawned amulet with me, see if anybody there can help figure it out. You don't know us, Nicola. We're a family of conspiracy theories and secrets, most of which nobody's trusted *me* enough to know about, yet. Well, here's another spooky mystery. Then I'll decide what to do next.'

9

Poole's GUTship, *Hermit Crab*, was hastily refurbished at a base on Himalia.

This small moon followed a moderately eccentric path ten times the width of the orbit of Ganymede. The facilities were modest, even compared to the sparsely inhabited communities elsewhere in the Jovian system: just a handful of airtight shacks buried in loose, impact-shattered ice. But this irregular lump of rock had in fact been humanity's first cautious footfall in the Jovian system, one of the Recovery-age space projects back in the twenty-fifth century. And now, it was believed, Himalia ought to be safely beyond the reach of the swarming quagma phantoms, which seemed to have stuck mostly to the inner regions of the Jovian magnetosphere and the big human settlements there, no doubt in search of the high-energy-density sustenance they craved.

These days the small maintenance facility on Himalia was owned and operated by Poole Industries, though much of its work was under licence to various UN agencies and fulfilled by subcontractors. So the battered *Hermit Crab*, towed out here by fusion-powered tugs, was bumped to the head of a line of similarly afflicted hulks, and its GUTengine core, infected by quagma phantoms, dumped and replaced. The work was done in a couple of days.

Poole fretted over this; he always felt guilty when his position in the family company earned him what felt like privileges.

Nicola, who spent the wait mostly in a low-gravity sauna, just laughed at him. 'You're a Poole. You're supposed to have had your conscience extracted at birth. Just like we ejected that polluted drive system. Whoosh! Gone.'

'I didn't ask for any of this. I'd much rather be building my wormholes. And staying at the back of the line.'

'Well, tough luck. Isn't that what your father would say?'

'Maybe. What's more to the point is what my mother will say.'

Nicola stared at him. Then, with an evident and uncharacteristic effort at tact, she said, 'I thought your mother died.'

'It's complicated. Let's get out of here.'

It took six days for the *Hermit Crab* to drive herself across the Solar System from Jupiter to Earth, the GUTdrive burning all the way to deliver a solid one gravity's thrust: three days' acceleration to the turnaround, and then three more days of deceleration. Her peak speed was a little less than one per cent the speed of light, and throughout the journey she would be visible as a brilliant shifting star across the inner System.

There you had the paradox of GUT technology, Poole thought. The drive was, if anything, overpowered for interplanetary travel; a GUTship was capable of interstellar missions, journeys tens of thousands of times longer than this intraSystem hop – and, though a GUTdrive could never exceed lightspeed, it could get so close to that limit that time dilation would compress the subjective duration of such journeys into easily survivable periods. But within the Solar System, a GUTship was enormously expensive in terms of reaction mass, all for a cargo capacity of no more than a few hundred tonnes. Which was where Poole's own wormhole network was supposed to come in. Once built, it would enable the transfer of high-volume cargoes much more rapidly, and the economy of the Solar System would be transformed – although in fact it was the technology itself that attracted Poole's interest, not long-term theoretical implications he might never live to see.

If, he thought gloomily, the project wasn't abandoned altogether after this string of catastrophes attached to a mere prototype. The immediate future seemed galling. Young he might be but he'd already had to fight hard, alongside his father, to get this far – especially on an Earth which had just endured an age of recovery and cautious rebuilding, beginning with Michael Poole Bazalget's Bottleneck-era Stewardship movements. And now all this alien strangeness had thrown his plans into chaos.

He probably spent too much of the journey back to Earth telling a bored Nicola Emry all of this.

Not that she had any hesitation in telling him what she thought about it. 'You're a gloomy old fossil in a young man's body.'

It seemed a very long time before the *Crab* reached Earth.

10

At last the *Crab* docked at the Geostationary Node of the Sahel space elevator, in orbit over Africa. Here they had to wait for a tether-climber ride to the ground.

Poole and Nicola made their way to the Caravanserai, one of the Node's larger public chambers. A sphere of engineered carbon and radiation-proofed glass, full of cafeterias and reception desks for hotels and other facilities – and filled with light from the Sun above and the shining Earth below – this noisy, crowded volume was a place for passengers arriving from Earth or sky to acclimatise, to meet up, or just to come and be a tourist. Suspended as the Node was in geosynchronous orbit, circling the Earth in precisely twenty-four hours, there was only microgravity to be experienced; rather like Gallia, the internal space was spanned by a spider web of guide lines, and children and adults hauled their way along the lines with expressions of alarm or squeals of delight, depending, Poole supposed, on temperament and experience.

Nicola burned her way through the Node's facilities.

After a couple of hours she emerged from a pricy souvenir store laden with bags. 'Look at this junk! I got you this.' She held out a manikin, a muscle-bound man in a silver suit. 'The Mariner from Mars. Little boys like you always wanted to be the Mariner, right? And look at these.' A pair of earrings, with green tetrahedral frames for pendants. 'And this!' A Michael Poole facemask. 'Merchandising already. Your father must be smiling – as long as he secured the copyrights . . .'

After that, Poole stayed in hiding.

He found a quiet lounge, with a view outside. Seen through wide windows in the floor, a handful of spacecraft floated like toys in the sharp, startlingly bright Earth-orbit sunlight: one of them was the *Hermit Crab*, its hull stained crimson and black by Io flux-tube muck and radiation damage. And below, elevator tethers stretched down like gossamer to an Earth the apparent size of a large dish held at arm's length: a dish full of Africa.

He stayed here long enough to watch as the eastern coast headed into evening, the shadows of thin clouds stretching long. The terminus station of the tethers was lost in equatorial rainforests. Poole had seen images of how Africa had been in the days before the Recovery centuries – how, from space, you could actually have made out national borders in the straight-line edges between landscapes of different textures, here quasi-natural, here agricultural, here a desolation of war. All of it was gone now, the borders themselves washed away like the nations that had fought over them. But the renewed green was studded here and there with diamond needles: Towers, kilometres-high structures that could house as many as a million people in a single self-contained urban space, while making a minimal impact on the rest of the planet. A million living like colonists from space, it struck Poole now, on humanity's native planet. Well, sooner that than the sprawl of the Anthropocene age.

But even the great Towers were details in that continental green.

As the reduction of population from its Anthropocene peak had cut in seriously, Poole knew, humanity's target, at first an unconscious groping and finally a consciously realised, purposeful programme, had been to restore the Earth to something like its state at the end of the last great glaciation, thirteen or fourteen thousand years ago: long before the Neolithic and the farming revolution, even before Old Stone Age hunter-gatherers with their sharp blades and lethal hunting skills had so quickly overrun the planet. It had begun with very cautious programmes of carbon-dioxide drawdown – leading eventually to a Poole re-engineering of Antarctica. It had culminated in the rewilding of much of the planet. Poole wondered if any of the beasts restored to that huge, primordial landscape, the elephants and rhinos and the great apes, ever looked up at the peculiarly stationary star directly overhead, placed there by the same clever relatives who had brought them back from extinction.

Eventually Nicola found him.

Drifting in the air alongside Poole, she accepted a gratis flask of coffee from a passing bot. 'Bored,' she said.

'You can't stay still for a heartbeat, can you?'

'How many heartbeats are we supposed to hang around here for?'

'Harry said he'd meet us.' Harry, with Shamiso, similarly had headed back to Earth at the first opportunity, on an uninfected GUTship. 'He's overdue.'

Nicola laughed. 'Poor you. Did Daddy promise to turn up for your little-league baseball games, and never came?'

'We played cricket,' Poole said. 'Not baseball. I grew up in Britain.'

'I needed to know that. Well, he ain't here, is he? So now what? I guess we'd better jump the line for the next car down to the ground.'

'That won't be necessary.' An elderly woman approached them, smiling at Poole. 'Events are moving rather too rapidly for that. Welcome home, young Michael.'

She was shorter than either Poole or Nicola, stocky if not stout, and was dressed in a gown, colourful and tied at the waist, a little like a kimono, Poole thought. Her grey hair was pinned sharply back into a bun. Her face, broad, pleasant, was a mix, the skin olive, the eyes bright blue: a blend of the regional characteristics of mankind which, like the nation-states, had dissolved into history. She might have been fifty years old; it was impossible to determine age in an era of AS technology – and, Poole knew, it was particularly futile in the case of this individual. Poole hadn't seen her approach. Suddenly she was just *there*. But Gea was always discreet about such things; her manifestations were never jarring. Always well mannered, he thought.

'Gea.' He smiled and nodded; she nodded back – any more physical gesture being inappropriate in the circumstances. 'Did my father send you?'

'No,' she said wryly. 'But I spoke to him. He had every intention of meeting you—'

'Don't make excuses for him. It's kind of you to come meet us. Gea, this is Nicola Emry.'

'Ah. The daughter of Shamiso? A good friend and colleague on the UN Senate. She speaks well of you.' Gea bowed again.

Nicola bowed back, politely enough, but she laughed. 'Somehow I doubt that. And what – apologies, *who* – are you? Some friend of the family?'

'You could say that.' Gea waved her hand through the thin line of a guide rope; her flesh broke up into pixels. 'Ouch. Consistency protocols; the bane of my life. If I may use that word.'

'You're a Virtual.'

Gea smiled. 'I prefer "differently conscious". And rather elderly, though I have enjoyed more upgrades, over the years, than even Michael's beloved *Hermit Crab*. In fact the first Poole I, or one of my ancestral intelligences, ever encountered was called George, and *he* was the uncle of a man you may have heard of: Michael Poole Bazalget.'

Nicola's eyes widened. 'The polar-stabilisation guy? That was back in, what, the twenty-second century?'

'Twenty-first.'

'Wow.'

Poole said, 'Gea has been an influential figure in world affairs since – well, since Bazalget's day. She was once one of the most powerful artificial sentients in the world, working at the heart of the great conservation and recovery programmes. All the stuff that's now in the history books. In fact "Gea" stood for . . .'

Gea smiled. 'Global Ecosystems Analyser. The name was the unfortunate result of a long-ago brainstorm at the University of Oklahoma. But I'm used to it.'

'Gosh. I feel like I should ask for a picture with you.'

Gea laughed, a delicate sound. 'I like her, Michael. A lack of deference. She's probably good for you. Why are you travelling together, though?'

Poole frowned. 'I'm not actually sure.'

'Accident,' Nicola said. 'I was piloting my mother out at Jupiter, and now I'm piloting *him*. It's turning into a fun ride. Though not if we're going to be stuck in some space-elevator car for days.'

Poole said, 'You said you had some news about that, Gea.'

'Indeed. Urgent news, in fact. No need to wait for the elevator. Come this way.'

She led them out of the lounge and towards an airlock access gate.

Nicola asked quickly, 'You've got us a shuttle?'

'We – the Senate subcommittee handling this situation – believe that the environmental impact of an in-atmosphere flight is justified, in this case.'

'Thank the gods for that. Can I fly it?'

'Don't push your luck,' Poole murmured. 'Gea, you said something about new events—'

'It has arrived at Mercury. The entity you call the sycamore seed. Slowed there and stopped. Landed, possibly. It is not yet clear what it is doing there. There has been no communication, no response to our own attempts to contact it . . . But meanwhile, as for you, Michael, the news of your encounter with the silver-spheroid creature—'

'We know.' Nicola gleefully showed off her tetrahedron earrings. 'It's all over the place.'

'It has caused quite a stir. A stir with *you* at the epicentre, Michael.'

Gea sighed. 'Well, you're a Poole. This kind of strangeness is part of the package, it seems. And after all it's not the first time a Poole has come into contact with an irruption from – somewhere else.' She eyed him. 'I'm talking about Michael Poole Bazalget. In fact if not for that contact long ago it seems likely you Pooles would never have achieved the power and wealth you have.'

This was new to Poole. 'What about Bazalget? What contact?'

But she would say only, 'That's family business. Ask your mother about the Kuiper Anomaly.'

That meant nothing to Poole, but it wouldn't be the first time he'd been drawn, more or less reluctantly, into the deep family history. 'I'm on my way to see her. I'm shipping her the amulet, the artefact brought by the Wormhole Ghost. If anybody can make sense of it . . .'

'I'm afraid you're going to have to postpone that visit,' Gea said gently. 'More news. You've been summoned, Michael. Along with your father.'

'Summoned? Who by? The government?'

'Indeed. Specifically by a subcommittee of the World Senate, which has, considerately enough, agreed to convene in one of the Poole properties – the Goonhilly Mound, in Britain.'

'The Senate.' Poole clenched a fist. 'You know, I didn't want any of this.'

'But you have got it anyhow, so don't sulk,' Gea said, admonishing.

Nicola laughed out loud.

'Now, let's find that shuttle. A Poole Industries ship, of course, built for the lunar run . . . Do you have any baggage?'

Even with Gea's help, the journey down wasn't that quick, and, Poole observed with amusement, Nicola was soon chafing with impatience.

It was morning by the time the shuttle had dropped them at the sprawling Terminus station at the base of the space elevator, in what was still known, for administrative purposes, as northern Nigeria. Nicola had clearly expected to be flown all the way to their final destination, but such was the caution taken over environmental impacts now that the few allowed flights to space took off and landed close to the elevators themselves.

From there you took a monorail.

As the three of them waited to board a small compartment in a northbound train, Poole saw Nicola peering up at the sky: the multiple elevator tethers ascending into the blue, the sparks of orbital habitats and factories visible even in the daylight – a more lurid glow, sliding over the sky, that was probably a profac collector, a sub-orbital craft scooping up wispy nitrogen from the top of the atmosphere for export to the growing arcologies on Mars.

'You're not used to any of this,' Poole observed with some surprise. 'I thought you were born on Earth.'

'Grew up mostly on the Moon. And I was out of *there* as soon as I could steal a rock-rat shuttle and head out to the asteroids.'

'Then as a pilot you must have been self-taught?'

She grinned. 'I would never have been *taught* a lot of the stuff I do.'

After all the time they'd spent together, Nicola remained an enigma to Poole. 'You turn down AS treatments. You commit crimes you're dumb enough to get caught at.'

She laughed. 'Wouldn't call it crime. Just – playing. A bit of fraud and stuff, to get back at a few enemies of the family. A few enemies *in* the family.'

Gea sat with them as they settled in their compartment, an unreal flask of water set before her on a table as an integral part of her Virtual presence. Now Gea said gently, 'I think Michael's trying to work out why you're so self-destructive.'

Nicola shrugged. 'Look – I may have crashed out of my education, but I'm not dumb. I see the world as it is, that's all. It's full of artificial minds like *you*, who will always be smarter than I am, and a government that is run by a global class of old folk who are never going to die off and get out of the way. Like *you*, probably, Poole. So what is there to do but play nihilistic games?'

The train moved away now, smooth and silent. The buildings of the elevator terminus washed past, to be replaced by a primitive green. And as the forest thickened, Poole thought he heard an extraordinary low rumble, a growl, almost geological.

Gea smiled at his reaction. 'A lion.'

Nicola didn't seem impressed. 'Anyhow, after all of that escaping, here I am crawling around on the ground. I mean, a train all the way to England?'

Gea smiled. 'It's pretty quick. And wait until we pass from Africa to Europe, following the crest of the Gibraltar dam. One of the greatest of the late-Bottleneck engineering projects: a flood defence for the whole Mediterranean basin—'

'Whenever I'm on Earth I feel like I have to tiptoe, in case I wake the old folk.'

'Well, maybe that's not a bad analogy. But we know how precious Earth is now, if we didn't before. Look at this journey, for instance. Who wants to rip everything up again, just to get from one place to another a little quicker?'

'Oh, into Lethe with it. Just wake me when we get there.' She tipped over, shoved a folded-up jacket under her cheek, leaned against the window and closed her eyes.

Poole just shrugged at Gea.

Gea laughed softly. 'You know, Michael, she's right. The world is a rather elderly place, these days. I remember when it was *full* of children. In the Bottleneck, the age of migration, children everywhere, and their parents barely any older. Of course we have had the beginnings of AS technology since Michael Poole Bazalget's time – and remember to ask your mother about that, Michael.'

Ancient family secrets again. He felt vaguely alarmed.

'But it's only been in recent centuries that the demographic has changed enough for the elderly to – well, to dominate the discourse. Still, we will always need the young, or the young in spirit. It's a necessary stabilisation. A trade-off between chaos and order. Just like you and Nicola. Is she really asleep, do you think?'

'Probably.'

Gea smiled. 'In that case she'll regret not seeing *that*.' She pointed out of the window and counted down silently, using her fingers. *Five. Four. Three—*

Before she reached 'one', Nicola sat up.

They were on a viaduct, crossing a valley through hilly country. A Tower gleamed, unearthly, its glass walls a faint chlorophyll green. And on a crest, silhouetted against the morning sunlight, the elephants were walking.

11

At Goonhilly, Harry himself met Poole and Nicola at the monorail station. There wasn't room for them all in the small car he had brought, so Gea, with a smile and a promise to meet later, winked politely out of existence.

They had a short ride now in the solar-power smart car, smooth and silent, through a largely empty landscape. This was the Lizard Peninsula, a south-west corner of the British Archipelago. Near the station itself the precarious ruins of houses overlooked a collapsed cliff, a grey sea. Long before they got to Goonhilly itself the familiar profile of the Mound was visible, a spindly, organic-looking tower, with a cluster of antique, carefully preserved radio antennae at its feet – as if the Mound were a skinny human, Poole thought, standing in a meadow of metallic flowers. Another memorial to the family's complicated past.

During the ride Harry's conversation was little more than a high-speed monologue. There were times, Poole realised, when he barely looked at his son and his companion at all, so wrapped up was he in his own agenda.

'It's good to have you here in person, Michael. Listen, there's still a lot of interest in you just now. Which is to say, leverage for us.' He grinned, his blond hair bright in the misty sunlight of a June day in England; Poole thought he looked remarkably young, for once. 'But all this is clutter. We have to focus on the real goal.'

Nicola wasn't about to put up with being excluded from the conversation. 'And what goal is that, Harry?'

He glared at her. 'The wormhole project, of course.'

'But you can't seriously consider continuing. Not now. The first time you opened up a wormhole, some kind of alien menace swarmed out, and your own son was proclaimed a messiah of the future. Wouldn't it be better to wait?'

'Look, we may or may not have aliens wandering around the Solar System. But the logic of the project, technological, demographic—'

'Commercial,' Poole put in dryly.

'None of it has gone away. If humanity is to have a future in space we *have* to do this.' Harry gestured, and Virtuals swam in the air, equations, graphs: little figurines to represent people in their thousands and millions, their futures evidently to be shaped by the Pooles' schemes. 'It's already more than a thousand years, after a lot of half-assed exploration and failed pioneering, since we finally established respectably sized colonies off Earth: a few hundred each on the Moon, Venus and Mars, and so on. And they started to grow. On Earth, before the Anthropocene crash, population growth was around two per cent per annum. In space it's been much slower than that, simply because of the lack of room to grow *into*. Think about it. If you want your colony to double in size, first you have to *build* a place for all those new folks to live. So the growth rate has been more like one per cent per annum.

'But the wormholes will change all that. We're predicting growth rates more like colonial-era America. I mean, somewhere well over two per cent. In two hundred years you could have a population of billions in space. All enabled by our wormholes.'

Nicola laughed. 'Are you serious? You've only built one trial wormhole so far—'

'Two, actually,' Poole said.

'There's another?'

'We have an installation orbiting Mercury. Another of our conceptual schemes. We're going to drop a wormhole mouth into the Sun.'

Nicola gaped. 'Why in Lethe would you do that?'

Poole grinned. 'Partly for science – to study what's in there – you could use the wormhole as a refrigeration channel to protect a deep-entry craft. We call the project the Sun Probe. But the main goal is energy extraction. Through a wormhole, you could just pump out solar heat to anywhere in the System. Like miniature, portable stars, hanging out there in the dark. Moor it to a Kuiper Object and you have a graving yard for starships.'

Almost reluctantly, Nicola admitted, 'OK. That's a neat idea.'

Harry snorted. 'We're playing for the future. Billions of people in space. You hesitate, you lose. Lethe, no, we're not going to *wait*.'

Nicola glanced at Michael. 'Your father's either a genius or insane.'

'He's a Poole. And we're about to arrive at another family folly . . .'

*

Gea was waiting to meet them at the foot of the Goonhilly Mound.

The Mound was generally considered a masterpiece of cautious mid-Recovery-era architecture. When it had been built – initially serving as the seat of a British regional parliament – the relic antenna park at its feet, an emblem of an earlier space age, was already six hundred years old. But to a modern eye the Mound itself was a much stranger sight than those more ancient structures. Poole knew that travellers from Africa, for example, always immediately likened the building to a huge termite mound. And that was no coincidence.

Tall, slim, its exterior was smoothed over with an oddly contoured texture, as if it had been moulded from wet clay – its substance was actually based on nanotubes of carbon, strong and light. Inside, once Gea had them waved through security, Nicola gaped at lofty chambers with sculpted roofs, and shining floors across which walked UN senators and their aides. All this was soaked in a gentle light – nothing more than sunlight, Poole knew, filtered through walls that were as translucent as fine porcelain, though tinged green by layered panels containing blue-green algae, busily photosynthesising, eating carbon, producing energy.

But Nicola was soon distracted by the people, as usual. Sober, slow-moving delegates in floor-length gowns, black with silver inlays and stylised hoods.

'They keep staring at you, Michael,' Nicola said. 'I guess they're going to know all about you and your wormhole buddies. But – there, see *that* guy? – he looked at you, then looked away.'

Harry grunted. 'They're a pack of snobs in here, is what they are. Always been the same – you can read it in our ancestors' diaries, Michael – the political and moneyed classes have always looked down on mere engineers. Even though we're the ones who built the world.'

Gea demurred. 'That's a very partial point of view, Harry. My reading of history is that there has always been a tension between those who would build things, and those who would seek to oversee on behalf of the public good. In fact, as you will see today, a new UN Oversight panel has already been established, if on a rather ad hoc basis, to monitor the unfolding situation following on from your wormhole dramas. You have to see it as a compliment that they chose to come hold a General Assembly meeting here, at this famous Poole family monument, instead of one of the more traditional meeting places, in New York or New Geneva. In politics, symbolism can be everything.'

Poole said, 'Yet here I am in person, and they aren't so much as looking at me.'

Harry shook his head. 'When they figure out what they want to do with you, believe me, they'll look at you.'

Nicola wrinkled her nose. 'Well, personally I just want to go figure out somewhere to eat. But there's a smell in here that's putting me off. And is there a breeze? Maybe the air conditioning is faulty.'

'There is no air conditioning,' Gea said. 'Not in the sense you mean. In this building the flows of air, moisture, energy are organic – natural.'

Poole murmured, 'Think termite mound.'

'Seriously?'

Gea said, 'The whole point of the design is that humanity should fit once more into the natural flows of energy and matter on the planet – and by the time the Mound was constructed the experience of successful colonies on worlds like Mars had taught us a lot about how to build in a resource-constrained environment.

'Hence, a building like a termite mound. There is no air conditioning – no traditional technology of that sort, no pumps and fans. Instead, convection drives air through the walls, which are porous – the whole building is like a tremendous lung. And the heat which drives that convection comes primarily from the fungus farms in the basement levels, where, incidentally, much of the food you'll eat here is produced. Already nearly a millennium old, functioning as well as when it was designed – and aspects of it have served as models for the architecture of Towers around the planet.' She smiled, calm. 'And I was here at the opening, by its designer, Lilian Poole. Quite a day.'

Harry grunted. 'Well, Lilian has her plaque in the Princess Elizabeth Land mausoleum like the rest of them. But she doesn't deserve it. Not in my eyes. Pooles are about changing the world. Not living like some mindless insect in a hive.'

Gea said enigmatically, 'A shame you can't ask Michael's distant uncle George about that.'

A distant chime sounded.

'The sessions are resuming,' Gea said.

'Good,' Harry said grimly. 'Time to go to work. *Politics . . .*'

12

After a rest stop at their quarters, Gea guided the visitors to a meeting room in the building's subterranean levels, where they were shepherded into a kind of viewing room, walled off by soundproof glass.

UN General Assembly representatives, in person or as Virtual avatars, had already gathered in a main chamber that appeared a traditional setup to Poole, with semicircular banks of benches. The session's speaker stood at a central podium, a woman dressed in silver-black robes and hood, as were the rest of the delegates. The discussion was ongoing, and voices murmured softly in Poole's ear with offers of translation options.

Gea listened to the conversation for a moment. She was, after all, an artificial sentient, Poole reflected; even as a few words from a single delegate trickled into Poole's own ear, Gea could be consulting volumes of transcripts, cross-references and ancillary evidence.

At length she said, 'They're discussing policing options. Every time we have a crisis the same issue comes up: to what extent we need to expand the core of trained police operatives in the Federal Service . . .'

Poole understood the principle of Federal Service – and knew also about the debates that had surrounded it, probably since the system had been inaugurated, when the last of the world's armies had been disbanded centuries before. It was the duty of all citizens under the UN – thus all human beings born anywhere in the Solar System – to donate some of their time to the Federal Service, from which huge pool were drawn volunteers for the police forces, various peacekeeping functions, and the ongoing curation of Earth itself. Some professions gained you exemption, such as expertise in medicine. And of course for the influential and rich there were always opt-outs. Poole himself had ignored that, but in his late teens had accepted Harry's assistance in getting a placement in disaster recovery and trauma medicine, skills he imagined would become useful in the course of his own career.

The most important single agency was the Federal Police, a global force unified under the UN – and thus the only officially sanctioned quasi-military force in existence. Now, Poole learned, trying to follow the debate, the questions before the Assembly included a motion that perhaps a fully trained, permanently staffed military force, or at least the core of one, ought to be instituted.

'Good,' Harry growled.

'Of course we ought to have an army,' Nicola said, for once agreeing with Harry.

Poole wondered vaguely where *she* had done her Federal Service. He said, 'There's no "of course" about it. Earth has seen nothing like a war since—'

Harry said, 'Nobody's talking of waging war, a human war. But we do appear to face a possible threat from this bunch of alien species. Wouldn't it be better to have a trained militia ready before we need it? Why, the big armed nation-states of the Anthropocene would have done a better job of facing down this threat than we have so far. The right mind-set, you see.'

Gea said, 'Seeing conflict where none yet exists? This is the language used about the issue by some of our more, ah, paranoid delegates.'

Nicola snorted. '*He* blew up the Wormhole Ghost, remember. How paranoid was that? Paranoid, or calculating, Harry?'

Harry ignored her, and faced Poole. 'This is politics, son. Like I told you, I'm here to argue that we can't let this sideshow about aliens deflect the wormhole programme. And if it would reassure these kooks to have a bunch of Federal cops put on body armour and call themselves a militia, let them have it, I say.'

Gea laughed, a tinkling sound – not quite authentic, Poole thought, but none the less charming for it. 'Typical of you, Harry, if I may say so – if not of the Pooles I have known. But you may have a point.' She moved forward, so she stood between Poole and Nicola as they looked down on the assembly. 'The outcome of the debate is uncertain. You know, the UN is the sole survivor of the pre-Anthropocene political institutions – but these days the United Nations Organisation is neither united, nor do nations any longer exist, and nor, indeed, is it terribly well organised. In a sense little survives of the organisation its founders established bar that enduring name. But it's still the best global governance system we've got.

'Now, this is a subcommittee of the General Assembly, which is an advisory and scrutinising branch. The World Senate, the executive, sits separately, and from their numbers are drawn the Presidents. There are still representatives from geographical regions, if not from nations.' She pointed to delegates. 'The Congress of Europe. Beringia and the Arctic Circumference Zone. The United Americas. Sundaland. The United Asian Republic . . . And over there is a representative of the Lunar Controller, and a party from Mars. Other bodies are represented: ourselves, for instance, the artificial community. In fact President Younger is the first non-artificial sentience to be elected to the post in three terms. And there are lobby groups like the Paradoxa Collegiate, who as you know have long argued for more radical solutions to the world's problems.'

'Yes. Rare supporters of Poole Industries,' Harry growled. 'Even if half of them are struldbrugs like the rest of this talking shop.'

Nicola frowned. '"Struldbrugs"?'

Poole knew the term but not the derivation. 'Undying – *old*, basically.'

Harry grunted. 'Centuries old, some of them. And so nothing ever gets done.'

'Too true, Harry,' came a new voice. 'Here we are in old England, looking for a hero. And maybe, sometimes, you need Beowulf, not the Venerable Bede.'

Poole turned, startled, with the rest. Then he smiled. 'Jack?'

The man who had joined them was short, stocky. He looked perhaps fifty, his black hair sprinkled grey, his skin space-pale. He was dressed in an apple green coverall that was quite a contrast, Poole thought, to the austere black-and-silver robes of the UN delegates. But then, this was no ceremonial gown but a practical piece of kit – Martian kit, Poole knew, the green designed to stand out against that planet's ochre background.

The new arrival grinned at the group, confident of his welcome.

Nicola spoke first. 'You're Jack Grantt. The Mars life guy. Who tried to speak to the sycamore seed alien.'

He nodded, amused. 'That pretty much sums up my biography. And you are?'

'Nicola Emry.'

'Ah. Any relation to—?'

'Shamiso? My mother.'

Gea asked, 'Is Senator Emry on your Oversight committee, Jack?'

'You should know; she's chairing it.'

Harry punched him on the arm, affectionately but hard. 'Well, you're in trouble, she's tougher than you, old man.' Grantt gave as good as he got, trading mock boxing moves.

Nicola raised her eyebrows.

Poole murmured to her, 'We're all buddies. Used to visit when we were kids, at Cydonia—'

'You told me. "Uncle Jack." Heart-warming.'

Grantt laughed. 'I *like* her. Look, I thought I'd come fetch you on my own initiative before I got ordered to. Michael, Harry, the general session will need to see you later, but right now you're both asked to testify before Nicola's mother's committee . . .'

With resigned expressions, at least from Nicola and Harry, they followed him out of the viewing gallery, back up a stair, and through more corridors, past more meeting rooms.

'Our sessions have been going on for six days already. I've been co-chairing just to keep myself awake. But I accept the need for the effort. For now all we can do is monitor the situation, but the more time we have to generate options ahead of the end game, the better.'

Gea murmured, '"End game." An ominous phrase.'

Grantt snorted. 'I'm a biologist, not a politician. I don't choose my words. Don't read anything into that. And, believe me, I'm one of the optimists in that room, comparatively.'

They reached another viewing gallery. Beyond the window was a smaller copy of the General Assembly room, but here, among the rows of senators in their silver-and-black robes, were other delegates and assistants, more plainly dressed. The atmosphere seemed generally less formal. The attendees consulted data slates and Virtual displays that sparked around them, even as one elderly-looking man, on his feet, made his contribution.

'If it's that dull,' Nicola said, 'why bother staying around? I'd be out of here.'

'I've considered it myself.' Grantt rubbed his back. 'My kids, you know, and my grandkids, all of them were born at Cydonia. They grew up in Martian gravity, and they're like gazelles. Me, I was born on good old Earth, yet after more than a couple of days back I'm half immobilised by the gravity.'

'But you stayed here because—'

'Because we're talking about how we humans should respond to an authentic first contact event. What more important conversation could you have?' He gestured at the window. 'It's not just senators you've got in there. I'm not the only scientist involved, of one discipline or another. Commercial interests like you Pooles, various philosophical schools . . . There are even delegates from religious groupings. And then you have the existential-threat lobby, small but growing, and vociferous, a group that thinks we should just destroy these visitors, while we can. *If* we can. Take no chances. Some of us might have hoped that we'd advanced beyond such attitudes in our moral development as a civilisation.'

Nicola grunted. 'They should ask Highsmith Marsden.'

'But then there's also a strong lobby that believes it's all a hoax, or maybe some kind of money-grabbing scam. And *they* want you Pooles arraigned. Harry, you know I'd enjoy seeing you arrested just on general principles, but that ain't going to happen.

'But even if you concede it is all real, then *what* is it? Is it actually life we're dealing with, let alone mind? There are some lifelike behaviours, particularly of those "quagma phantoms" as you called them – an unscientific label that prejudges the issue, of course – but your "sycamore seed" with its entourage of silvered bodies has done nothing but spiral in relentlessly towards the innermost System since it emerged. It shows about as much sentience as a short-period comet, some are saying.'

Nicola said, 'What about the Wormhole Ghost? The creature who did actually speak to us, who mentioned Michael here by name—'

'Agreed. That's pretty convincing evidence . . . of *something*. The trouble is, nobody knows of what. I mean, if your Ghost is authentic – and if it came wandering through a wormhole from, well, somewhere else – how could it *possibly* know the identity of an individual human?' He pulled a face. 'In a way it adds to the confusion, and just weakens the general case. I guess it doesn't help that we had more or less accepted that we were alone in the universe, in terms of intelligence at least. With myself an honourable exception, as you know.'

Nicola asked now, 'So what do *you* think, "Uncle Jack"?'

He shrugged. 'I'm Mister Life on Mars, as you reminded me. The guy with the wacky hypothesis that the bacterial communities we've been studying on Mars are actually part of a global, possibly sentient network. And we're having trouble classifying *that*, let alone communicating with it – we can't even prove intelligence *doesn't* exist on Mars. Even though we've been walking around on the planet for over a thousand years. I suppose I'm just arguing for an open mind when it comes to this new phenomenon.'

Harry nodded. 'Fair enough. So what now?'

'Well, you need to clear your diary for a few days. The General Assembly wants to speak to you all about the whole background to the wormhole project, the incidents that led up to the alien emergence, how you responded . . . Looks like they're ready for you. I'll take you in.'

As the others moved off, talking quietly, Nicola grabbed Poole's arm, holding him back. 'Let's get out of here. Don't argue. Just walk.'

His heart beat faster as he followed. 'What? But—'

'Look, don't give me a lecture about responsibility. Do you *want* to spend days being grilled by a bunch of empty suits who know even less than we do? At least by coming here we're halfway to where the action is.'

'Which is where?'

'Mercury. The Sun. Where in Lethe do you think? Where the alien invaders have gone. You need to be *there*, Michael.'

'But we can't—'

'You said there were Poole facilities at Mercury. Building some other kind of experimental wormhole.'

'The Sun Probe, yes.'

'Fine. So you've an excuse to go out there.'

'I said I'd see my mother. That's why we came to Earth. I sent her the Wormhole Ghost amulet.'

'Well, then, give her time to think that over. For sure you didn't come all this way for *this*.'

He had to grin. 'I don't know whether you're good for me or bad.'

'But it's fun finding out, isn't it?' Now she took his hand, and said more seriously, 'Listen. All this hot air – it's futile, and missing the point. That Wormhole Ghost *spoke your name*. This is, somehow, all about you. And you have to face up to that.'

He took a breath and glanced around. Harry and Jack Grantt were a few paces ahead – and if Gea was aware of what they were planning she showed no signs of it.

He squeezed Nicola's hand. 'Follow me.'

13

The Poole Industries orbital base at Mercury was called Larunda. Poole and Nicola debarked from the *Hermit Crab* in the flitter, and crossed space to the habitat.

From this carefully selected location, the lowering Sun was hidden by the shadowed bulk of the planet itself, a perfect and permanent eclipse, with the face of Mercury itself in total shadow. Beyond the planet, the Sun's outer atmosphere was a gaudy sprawl across the sky. Whatever it was that had come through the Jupiter wormhole had gone down to Mercury, to the surface, and had done something there. Poole longed to go down and see for himself.

In this exotic setting, the Larunda base was an old-fashioned design, a spindly wheel a couple of kilometres across, rotating at a leisurely single revolution per minute for spin gravity. A hub with docking facilities was circled by concentric torus-shaped living areas, giving spin gravity of various strengths depending how far you climbed down from the centre. The wheel itself was surrounded by a cloud of solar sails and mirrors which almost shyly sailed out of Mercury's shadow and into direct sunlight.

In an arena of such huge energies the station had an oddly delicate look, Poole thought.

Inside, Mitch Gibson was waiting for them.

Gibson was Poole Industries' operations manager here; bluff, efficient, single-minded, and, at forty, with a bulk that he was failing to shed despite his beginning a long lifetime's course of AS treatment. 'Welcome to Larunda!'

Nicola wrinkled her nose. 'As Poole architecture goes, at least it doesn't stink so bad as that Mound in England.'

Gibson grinned, good-natured. 'Hey, it's just a work shack but we're proud of it. Look, I know you want to get down to business, but first I need to give you the novices' tour, so you'll know where to run in case of emergency. Company rules – well, you're the boss, Michael. *Your* rules. So let's get that done. Let me show you the way. Here we are at the hub. Our solar-storm shelter, among other functions . . .'

So they clambered down ladders through white-walled access tubes, moving away from the hub, and Poole soon felt a faint tug of spin gravity. The shaft walls were decorated with portraits, smiling faces, generations of previous staff members who had been rotated through the station.

'You understand we're at a Lagrangian point here,' Gibson said. 'L2. Equilibrium, the gravity of Mercury and the Sun balanced, holding us in place – though we have to apply a little thrust to control our position, a delta-V of a few metres per second per year. This is a uniquely hazardous environment, but we have got some breaks – such as the eclipsing of the Sun by Mercury. It's just a lucky chance that in the Sun–Mercury system L2 happens to lie just here, where the planet's cone of shadow reaches out, which reduces our need for shielding . . .'

Nicola was staring at him as if he was some exotic animal. 'Is this guy always like this?'

Poole grinned. 'Pretty much.'

Gibson himself smiled back. 'Sorry. But you can understand we don't get too many visitors here.'

They did pass a few people, laden with data slates or food, clad in company coveralls that had all been customised to some degree. They nodded to Poole as they passed. He knew them all pretty well; the station had a permanent staff of less than twenty. They stared curiously at Nicola, though. Poole knew the feeling; confinement made any novelty fascinating. They got glares back in response.

They reached the exits to the first habitable torus, where the hatches were marked with a smiling-face Man on the Moon, and there was a faint whiff of antiseptic. Poole knew that at this level the spin gravity was up to lunar, one-sixth of Earth, and the torus contained the base's surgery and rest areas. Low gravity was easy on conditions such as traumas, burns.

'If you overdo the sun tan, this is where you get the emollient cream,' Gibson said.

'Ha,' said Nicola, deadpan. 'Who was Larunda?'

Gibson seemed flummoxed. 'You know, I never got asked that before. Help me out here, Michael.'

'Consort of Mercury. Roman myth.'

Nicola said, 'We might be outgrowing religion if those pompous windbags in the World Senate are right about the moral development of mankind. But if not for all that junk from the past, what would we *call* stuff?'

As if in response to that, the second torus exit bore a strip-cartoon-god Mercury, complete with winged boots. Gibson stopped here. Poole climbed off the ladder gingerly; the gravity was substantial but light.

'OK,' Gibson said. 'Here we're at one-third G, which is Mercury's gravity – twice the Moon's. The outer ring down below, at Earth gravity, is mostly uncrewed. We use it for science observation posts, and for acclimatisation for anybody who needs to go back to Earth. This middle level is where we do most of our living, so we get used to surface conditions. You've got the accommodation areas, the games rooms, most of the work areas. The bar. Oh, and the restaurant. How could I forget that?'

'They have a dedicated chef,' Poole said to Nicola. 'Fully trained.'

'Actually she's the only full-time specialist,' Mitch said. 'The chef. We're a small staff here; we cross-train, keeps us busy. But we leave the chef alone.'

Poole said, 'Bases like these, with small staff numbers, long duration tours – Harry calls them the orphans of the Poole empire. We have a duty to keep our people comfortable. Indeed, healthy and sane. Good food is a prerequisite.'

Mitch Gibson faced them. 'Last page of the lecture. Look, I know you're itching to get down to the surface. To see – well, to see what you came all this way for. But this is pioneer country. The rule is, twenty-four hours at least at this one-third-G torus, so you adapt, and then and only then—'

'Fine,' Nicola said. 'You want to show me to my room? If it's got a shower and a food bar you can leave me be, and get back to explaining stuff to each other.'

'You know me so well,' Poole said.

'That's the trouble,' she said. 'I do.'

Mitch Gibson pointed along a corridor whose carpeted floor and unadorned walls curved upwards, distinctly. 'Fourth door down. But you just might want to see the view first . . .' He tapped one wall, and a section of panelling slid out of sight, revealing a dark rectangle.

Nicola walked to the window, and Poole, following, looked over her shoulder.

The background was only blackness, no stars; evidently this was a slice of the shadowed face of Mercury. But in the foreground was a sculpture of light, of electric-blue struts.

It was a wormhole portal.

'*That's* the Sun Probe,' said Poole.

Nicola shrugged. 'Look what you made.' She walked away to her room.

Gibson murmured, 'Why in Lethe did you bring that person?'

'It's more that she brought me,' Poole admitted. 'Everything's changed, Mitch. So what about the aliens? In transit we've been out of touch for a couple of days.'

Gibson said seriously, 'Michael, it's all been happening. I've sent some scrambled reports back to the corporate HQ on Earth, but the *Crab* wasn't seen as secure—'

'You did the right thing. Just tell me.'

'The sycamore seed. I'll show you what it did here, at Mercury. But then *it went into the Sun*. No deceleration, no deorbit—' He mimed a plunge, with a swoop of his hand.

Poole felt bewildered, then shrugged. 'OK. That's what I came to see, I guess.'

'You want to go find your room?'

Poole glanced at a chronometer on the wall. 'Shall we try the bar? Just so I can get used to the gravity, of course.'

Gibson grinned. 'You'll get pestered there. We don't get a lot of visitors, I told you. Especially not the boss. And a boss who's going to have a two-kilometre-high statue at—'

'Skip it.'

'I have a bottle of single malt in my own room.'

'Just one?'

'Just one you're going to know about.'

'OK.' They walked down the carpeted corridor, their footsteps silent. 'And you can fill me in on the Sun Probe project. Two weeks behind schedule, so I read on the way in. I suppose you'll use the excuse of an alien invasion to explain *that* away . . .'

14

The flitter was called *Lar III*, named like the rest of the station's shuttles after the Lares, mythical children of Mercury and Larunda. The little ship was piloted to the planet's surface by Mitch Gibson, somewhat roughly, with squirts of the main drive and bumps and bangs of the attitude control system. Nicola glowered in silent disapproval at his clumsy handling.

But she made no comment about the slowness of the descent, or the caution with which Gibson guided the flitter through invisible gravitational complexities.

Poole had never landed on Mercury before. He peered down curiously at a ground pocked with craters, around many of which distinct black splashes could be seen: a relic of a primordial ocean of liquid rock, he'd learned, magma topped by a thin crust of complex carbon compounds. During its formation Mercury had been extensively battered by planetesimals, fragments of more would-be planets, and the scars were still visible. Indeed, it was believed that one mighty collision with another young world had stripped off much of the rocky mantle of a once-larger Mercury, leaving the iron core exposed, and bequeathing the planet an unusually high density and a relatively strong gravity. But the overall mass concentration had been left uneven by that rough moulding; the irregular gravity field was a hazard for pilots.

They flew across a ragged terminator into night.

An inky darkness, marked here and there by beacons and navigation aids. In a way, the glow of the lights gave a better picture of the sparseness of the human works down there than the blasting daylight. Much of the material which had been used to construct the Sun Probe wormhole had been mined from Mercury. But even so the presence of mankind was a mere scrape. It was twelve centuries since the first tentative landings on Mercury – a hasty scuttle to the shadows of the polar craters, and back home with a handful of samples – but even now there was no permanent human station on the planet's surface.

Lar III emerged once more into sunlight, a ferocious, sudden dawn. Then the flitter dropped towards a plain, shadowed by crater walls, scarred by sinuous ridges. Poole made out more signs of humanity: a temporary camp dwarfed in the immensity, a golden rectangle that was a landing pad target, a cluster of domes, what looked like earthworks, banks and ditches dug out of the lunar-like ground. Artificial lights broke the shadows, but they were pale gleams compared to the excluded sunlight.

Mitch pointed ahead. 'And *that's* what we're here to see.'

Poole leaned forward. A dark rectangle had been cut into the ancient surface, sharp-edged, huge, like a giant mineshaft, surrounded by marker lights and vehicle tracks. Evidently artificial, but created by no human hand.

Waiting silently for them.

Mitch Gibson brought the flitter down without any fuss, not far from the edge of the rectangular shaft. 'Welcome to Caloris Planitia.'

The three of them suited up, and Gibson evacuated the cabin's air. They climbed down a short ladder to the surface.

Morning on Mercury: the Sun was just below the broken horizon, and only a few rays of its light touched the dusty plain. It was a dawn that would only slowly unfold, Poole knew: Mercury's tidally locked 'day' and 'year' combined to give a cycle of sunrises and sunsets that lasted, at any point on the surface, a heroic one hundred and seventy-six Earth days.

Once out of the flitter Nicola moved cautiously; she tried jumping, running, bending. Her suit was silvered, and reflected dazzling highlights whenever the low sunlight caught her. 'Yes, gravity's about like Mars. Running is easier than walking . . . Glad I spent that day in the habitat's one-third G.'

'Orientation,' Gibson said. He pointed towards the Sun. 'That way, it gets hot enough to melt lead. And thataway,' he jerked his thumb back towards the shadows of night, 'cold enough to freeze nitrogen. If there were any. You're wearing twilight suits.'

'Twilight?' Poole asked.

'That's what we call 'em. Designed for when the Sun is low, like it is now. If we ever have to operate in full daylight we have suits like tanks, with parasols and big radiator fins. If you were to stay out in *these* suits in full daylight—'

Nicola snapped, 'Before the sunlight broiled me, you'd bore me to death talking about it. Shall we get on with it? So, Caloris Planitia – I think I heard of that.'

'You should have,' Poole said. 'It was famous even before our sycamore seed came calling.'

'Follow me.' Gibson walked off, towards the sunlight, heading for a shadow in the ground, like the lip of a canyon: the edge of that big feature they'd seen during the descent.

Poole followed, more clumsily.

'In some ways this is typical Mercury terrain,' Gibson said. 'Basaltic rock pulverised by ancient impacts and ground to dust by more recent infalls. No air to protect it . . . Like the Moon you have craters everywhere, and old areas of congealed lava. But we have a few attractions you won't see on the Moon.'

He pointed to a ridge, perhaps a kilometre away. It looked like a huge worm-cast, Poole thought, sinuous, worn, meandering.

'They call those features *rupes*. Ridges and folds, kilometres long some of 'em, caused when the planet cooled, and *shrank*.' He clenched a gloved fist.

'Like the skin of a dried-out apple,' Nicola said.

'Exactly that. But even for Mercury *this* place is kind of unusual. Caloris is a big, circular plain. We're close to the centre here. And there are oddities. Radial cracks in the ground, I mean these are *major* canyons, lined up like wheel spokes. Old volcanic vents. Rim mountains kilometres high, but so far away they're over the horizon . . .

'You know what Caloris is, right? One vast impact crater. Fifteen hundred kilometres wide. Bear in mind that's about a third of the planet's diameter: just one crater. Even beyond the walls there are splashes of debris, rings of heaped-up ejecta, going out hundreds of kilometres. One of the biggest impact craters in the Solar System – and there's a feature almost as striking at the antipode, where the shock waves from the impact washed around the planet and collided, crumpling everything up. Mercury's biggest whack aside from the mantle-stripper itself.'

Nicola smiled. 'You're proud of this big hole in the ground, aren't you?'

'Shouldn't we be?'

Poole, not for the first time in this encounter with the alien, felt a deep, growing dread. 'So this is the site of one of the largest natural disasters in the history of the Solar System. Why do I get the feeling that it's not a coincidence that we've been drawn here?'

'Come take a look,' Gibson said softly. 'You know me, Michael. I'm no showman. Lousy at sales conferences, and pitches to the UN Oversight people, and so on. I don't mean to spring this on you like a conjurer's reveal. It's just that you don't get a sense of it, even from a low-flying flitter. You have to be down here to understand . . .'

He stopped a respectful few metres back from that apparent cliff edge, a sharp break in the ground, like the edge of some canyon. They joined him.

Gibson said, 'Basic safety stuff.' He wore a light pack; from this he drew self-fixing pitons and cable, strong carbon-fibre, on spools. The pitons, once triggered, lodged themselves in the ground, burrowing down through the dust, trailing cable, until they hit bedrock. Gibson quickly fixed the cable ends to loops in his own suit, and the others'. 'So we can't fall, come what may. Now – go ahead and look.'

Gingerly, dragging his cable, Poole made his way past Gibson to the edge of the 'cliff'. It was dead straight, stretching from left to right – or rather north to south, he thought, taking his bearings from the Sun. 'This edge is razor-sharp. It looks more like a quarry than any natural feature. An open-air mine. But—'

But when he looked, cautiously, over the edge, he saw no bottom to this 'quarry', nothing but shadow. And, looking ahead, he saw a sharp horizon, far away. But he was looking *down* on that distant edge, tilting his head.

He had a sudden, terrifying sense of falling. 'Lethe.' He stumbled backwards, clumsy in his suit.

'Hey.' Nicola was first to grab him, to steady him. 'Take it easy.'

Gibson was here now. 'I'm sorry. Should I have warned you?'

'Well, you showed us from above, but from down here – it's like the ground has been sliced off. What is this, Mitch?'

'A shaft,' Gibson said. 'Cut in the ground. Walls smooth to within the tolerance we can measure, and coated with some kind of – material – that we can't make any sense of. And the depth, well, we can't measure that either. Far beyond any depth where such a shaft ought to collapse in on itself.'

'And how wide? From space, the scale fooled me.'

'A hundred kilometres on a side, Michael. Near enough. And it's regular – a perfect square. When you look at it from space it doesn't look so odd, just a big hole in the ground. But down here – Michael, Mercury's horizon is only three kilometres away. The far side of this shaft is so far away that you're looking *down* to see it, by a degree or two, below the local horizontal. This is a well so big it cuts through the planet's curvature.'

'Enough. I get it. Show me how this thing was made.'

Mitch Gibson nodded. 'Time for a Virtual show. We got good records of the event, from orbit, even from down here. Don't be alarmed. Nothing is real . . .'

He clapped his hands.

The lip in the ground vanished. Suddenly the land was whole again, with a regular, if lumpy, horizon.

And a black sycamore seed hovered above the Mercury ground.

Nicola glared up defiantly. 'Our buddy from Jupiter.'

'This is what we saw,' said Mitch Gibson.

'We watched it coming, of course. Updates from Spaceguard, long before it got here. And it brought with it a swarm of the objects you called raindrops, the silvery spheroid forms. We lost track of those. And we did a lot of screening, but we didn't detect any of your quagma phantoms. Even so we kept our GUTships away from the area. '

Poole glanced at him. 'Larunda itself runs on GUT plant.'

'Yes. We actually made a partial evacuation, and ran down the power levels. Turned out not to be necessary . . . I think we expected the sycamore seed to make for the Sun Probe, our wormhole. Maybe it had come from one wormhole in search of another, we thought. No, it came straight here. Just about the geometric centre of the Caloris basin. Hovered in position for around an Earth day. And then it did *this*.' He clapped his hands again.

The sycamore seed began to rise, smooth, silent, without creating so much as a flurry in the dust. No exhaust, Poole realised, as a GUTship's thruster would have kicked up – as observed before, it seemed not to use any kind of reaction drive, a rocket, at all. And as the craft rose into the sunlight it remained perfectly black, featureless.

He remarked, 'I haven't seen it in such strong sunlight before. Where the light hits its hull – the casing, whatever – no reflection.'

Gibson nodded. 'The light conditions were different, of course, from this simulation. But that's an authentic detail. No reflection; perfect absorption as far as we could tell.' He took their arms. 'You might want to stand back from the edge. We can't be harmed, of course, but the visuals coming up are impressive.'

Nicola, like Poole, allowed herself to be drawn back. 'The visuals of what?'

'The geologists say that this basin, Caloris, was created in the early days of the Solar System. Mercury itself was barely formed, when – wham! The impactor struck. We guessed it was just another planetesimal, a planetary-formation fragment, or maybe even a comet, around a hundred kilometres across. There were plenty of objects that size roaming around the young System . . . Well, we got the mass right, but that was all.'

The ground shook now, visibly. Poole looked down to see dust rising up around his feet, only to fall back quickly in the absence of any air to suspend it. And where the rocky ground was exposed, near the cliff edge, a swarm of cracks ran across the surface. Poole's stomach clenched, and he felt profoundly uncomfortable, even though – or perhaps *because* – the visual effects, of this apparent tremor, did not translate into actual motion under his feet.

But he was missing the main action.

'Look,' Nicola murmured. 'Michael. *Look.*'

He lifted his head.

The ground ahead seemed to be exploding – literally, as if implanted bombs were going up, smashing the bedrock to rubble and dust and hurling it high into space. Tilting back his head, Poole saw a kind of fountain of the debris, rising straight up, some of it even slamming into the base of the sycamore seed itself, which still climbed steadily.

All this in an eerie, airless silence.

'We watched from Larunda. From up there it looked as if somebody had pricked Mercury with a pin, and its innards were just gushing out, a fountain . . .' Gibson was shouting now, as if unconsciously trying to make himself heard above the non-existent noise. 'Most of the debris was hurled upwards with such violence that it reached escape velocity, and just dispersed in space. And then—'

A shadow washed across Poole, blocking out the Sun. Even as the rock and grit and gravel continued to fountain out, something else was rising from the ground now, vast, vertical. A smooth wall of what looked like milky-white glass.

'It's like a building,' Nicola murmured. 'A huge building. Just rising up out of the ground, like it's on some giant elevator platform.'

Gibson nodded. 'Exactly that. But bigger than any building we ever constructed before the arcologies on Mars. It's a cube, in fact, a hundred kilometres on a side – and as massive as if it is one vast block of water ice. Gravimeters told us that. Walled with the same stuff as the shaft it left behind – well, we think so; it gives us the same kind of reflectance signature. Nicola, Michael, behold the Caloris impactor.'

'Lethe,' Poole said. '*This* is what slammed into Mercury five billion years ago. And all that time it's been down there. Waiting to be – summoned.' And he looked up, at the sycamore seed that still rose smoothly up above the great slab, as if evoking this vast structure into existence. 'It must have known this thing was here. The sycamore seed. It must have *expected* to find this.'

'Keep watching.'

Now the whole of the object had emerged from the pit, Poole saw; he glimpsed the Mercury plain under the sharp lower edge. The tremendous cube was suspended in space, invisibly supported, it seemed, by the rising sycamore seed.

'The two objects – the sycamore seed, this big cube – spent another day, roughly, in Mercury orbit. And then they made for the Sun. Everybody watched them go. The whole crew on Larunda, I mean. Under strict instructions not to talk to anyone from outside the station, until ordered.

'The scientists will tell you that all we can say for certain is that the two objects flew in a kind of formation. You ask me, I think the sycamore seed *towed* the Cache.'

'Cache?'

'We had to call it something . . . And once they got there—'

'Turn it off,' Nicola said now, tightly. 'Enough. Consider me overwhelmed. Let's get back to the flitter. *Turn it off!*'

15

The three of them huddled in the flitter cabin, windows opaqued, coffee mugs in their hands. Mitch Gibson had produced silver survival blankets that they draped over their shoulders.

Survival blankets, in the middle of a morning on Mercury. They had created a little human nest, Poole thought. Aside from the gravity, they could have been anywhere. They had made no contact with the rest of mankind since getting back to the flitter, save for Mitch making a routine status report back to Larunda. It was as if they had needed to escape, for a while.

'So,' Gibson said at length, 'there you have it. The sycamore seed came to Mercury, and snake-charmed that structure out of the ground.'

'Where are they now?' Nicola asked. 'You said they headed for the Sun.'

Gibson tapped his data slates. 'The Cache seems to have landed *on* the Sun . . . I know that makes no sense. It's sitting on the photosphere anyhow, on the visible surface. Latest update is it's still there. Growing.'

Poole couldn't take that in. *'Growing?* Never mind.'

Nicola asked, 'And the sycamore seed?'

'I told Michael. It dived *into* the Sun.'

Poole shook his head. 'Some kind of suicide dive?'

Nicola snorted. 'I hardly think so. We just don't understand, is the truth. The what, the why, or the how of it.'

Gibson looked at them uncertainly. 'We still have some puzzles left here. At Mercury, I mean. As I said, most of the debris thrown up when the Cache emerged was lost in space, but we sent a couple of probes flying through the cloud before it dispersed. We found biological traces in there. Complex molecules – carbohydrates, but not like the amino-acid suite Earth life uses—'

Poole felt bombarded again. 'Whoa, Mitch, that's one mystery too many. Biological? How could that be?'

Nicola was less fazed, and seemed to be thinking more clearly. 'What if the impactor – the Cache – was brought here in some kind of ship? Or dragged, as the sycamore seed seems to have dragged it back out again. And if the ship made landfall itself, or couldn't get away – maybe there was some kind of survival.'

'Life? How?' Poole snapped. 'This is Mercury. Hot enough to melt lead, remember? And this was billions of years ago.'

'Yes,' Gibson said cautiously, 'but actually there is water here. As you know, Michael. Ice, at the poles, in shadowed craters. And where there's water of any kind – we learned this from Mars – life can follow, or survive anyhow. Even if the raw sunlight is lethal, you can burrow into the ground, where there's shelter, and thermal energy is available from volcanism, minerals. And in the shattered ground over the impactor there might have been room to grow and spread – spaces between the boulders and the dust grains. So it's possible.

'We may never know. If there *was* something surviving in the extraction zone, at the centre of the crater – after all this time – unless it spread away from the crater, which is possible, it's lost now, blasted to space with the rock and the rubble.'

One mystery too many. Poole shrank inside himself, staring into his coffee cup, his mind churning with more or less wild speculation.

'This has changed everything for us,' Mitch was saying. 'Mercury's not a place you're ever going to love. But it has resources. You can transfer lunar mining techniques, which we've perfected over centuries, straight here to work the upper regolith. Then you have that lovely iron-rich core, only a few hundred kilometres deep. And free energy from the Sun – six times the power density per unit area as at Earth. Mercury could become the workshop of the Solar System.' He sighed. 'Or it could have. Now we have this sycamore seed and its progeny rampaging around the inner System, and I guess everything is on hold. Maybe I ought to fix us some food.' He folded up his blanket and went to the galley area at the rear of the little craft.

Nicola shuffled over to Poole. 'Tell me why you're so quiet.'

'I've a lot to be quiet about.'

'Such as?'

He glared at her. 'Think about it. The sycamore seed came along and dragged this – Cache, whatever – out of the Mercury rock. A Cache that was implanted there *five billion years ago*. Since when it's been sitting, waiting until it's needed. How in Lethe did the sycamore seed *know* the Cache was there? And what caused the Cache to be put there in the first place, all that time ago, when the Solar System was forming? Is it just coincidence, that it's there when it's needed?'

Nicola thought that over. 'The principle of mediocrity.'

'The what?'

'See, I'm not so vacuous as you think. Mediocrity. A guiding philosophical principle of science. The idea is that we shouldn't expect to find ourselves in a special place, or a special time. We're a typical sample of the universe. Which kind of feels right, doesn't it? More than the alternative anyhow, the idea that we're special, which sounds – well, grandiose. Then again I'm not a Poole, I don't do grandiose. But, you see, if our Solar System is typical, then maybe *every* young planetary system gets an early visitor, and some inner planet gets whacked with one of these Caches—'

'Just in case it's ever needed.' He looked at her. 'So we're dealing with some kind of agency that had the power to emplace these Caches in *every* system, across the Galaxy . . .'

'Anyhow, all that is irrelevant.'

He had to smile. 'Maybe this is why I'm travelling with you, Nicola. For comments like that. A Galaxy-wide superpower meddling in the formation of every stellar system, irrelevant? Compared to what?'

'Compared to what the sycamore seed is going to do next, and how we deal with it. So it's dived into the Sun. Why? What's it looking for? What's it going to do when it finds it?'

'I don't know.' A knot of defiance formed, deep in Poole's heart. 'But that's *our* Sun.'

'That's the spirit. Not only that, it's *your* fight. Don't look at me like that – the Wormhole Ghost went to a lot of trouble to tell you so. Now we have to figure out what to do next.' She grinned. 'Of course, I have an idea.'

Poole knew about her ideas. His heart thumped faster.

Mitch Gibson called over, 'You two want salt in your mashed potato?'

'No,' Nicola said boldly. 'But I do want your wormhole.'

Mitch glanced at her, back at his potatoes, over at her again. A classic double-take, Poole thought. 'You want *what*?'

'The Sun Probe. Think it would take a pilot's couch? Mitch, you're burning those potatoes.'

'Oh, Lethe—'

16

It took Mitch Gibson's Mercury-shadow hermits less than a week to rig up a crewed capsule inside the existing infrastructure of the Sun Probe. Poole wasn't particularly surprised; the engineering of human survival was a much less novel technological feat than that of delivering a functioning scientific probe to the inner layers of the Sun in the first place. Once they'd grasped the mission, in fact, the Larunda team had enjoyed the challenge.

'But by the time we're done with you two,' Gibson said with a certain relish, 'you won't know where your own bodies end and the probe begins.'

Poole knew he wasn't kidding.

The basics of the design were drawn up in hasty sketches during a single coffee-fuelled night shift. An adapted flitter would sit inside a wormhole portal. A compact GUTdrive would propel the craft through the Sun's interior. The negative-energy fields which propped open the wormhole portal would help shield the flitter from the dense plasma of the solar environment, while the wormhole itself would keep the little craft cool by the simple means of refrigeration: by pumping out solar heat through the wormhole's higher-dimensional throat and dumping it into space in Mercury's orbit, where the other end of the wormhole drifted amid a cloud of construction shacks and observation posts.

The new crewed compartment, built into the existing 'Solar Module', was to be a sphere, for structural strength. Though the sketchy mission plan was minimally ambitious, Gibson had insisted that the capsule be over-engineered: made capable of surviving all the way down to the edge of the Sun's fusing core itself, where the temperature was measured in millions of degrees, and gamma and X-ray photons hammered through a high-density gas of electrons and protons.

Nicola Emry was, predictably, more interested in their new craft's propulsion system. This would not be just a simple descent, but a powered exploration. A GUTdrive would still function inside the carcass of a star, as the Pooles' venerable Grand Unified Theory technologies relied on a realm of physics – the unification of electromagnetic and nuclear forces – even more energetic than the hydrogen-fusion processes that powered the Sun.

Nicola had whooped as she took the modified probe, a neat sphere, for its first test flight above the plains of Mercury.

The one aspect of the Sun's environment from which their sturdy craft would not be able to shield them was the star's gravity, which would be as much as twenty-seven times Earth's at the surface. Even Jupiter's gravity, at the upper cloud layers, was only some two and a half times Earth's; people had ventured there and returned safely, but the Sun's challenge was ten times harder. Poole Industries had experimented with exotic-physics inertial screens, but they were inadequate for this challenge. And so more old-fashioned methods had to be used.

It took the whole of the last day before the descent to prepare the travellers for this. With the help of two young, kindly, medically trained techs, Poole, with Nicola at his side, was immersed in a thick, gel-like, oxygen-rich fluid, which would fill Poole's lungs, his stomach, the cavities in his body. Even the fluid in the spaces in his skull, around his brain, was reinforced; even the fluid in his eyes. And, too, a network of nanotech robots crawled through his body, strengthening his muscular and skeletal structures, bracing cartilage and muscle and bone. Despite anaesthetics, he thought he could *feel* much of this.

Nicola, typically, blustered through it. When they endured the final lung-filling injection of support fluid, an experience that felt like nothing so much as drowning, Poole watched a monitor showing Nicola's face, behind a thick glass plate. She opened her mouth, dragged in the fluid, coughed once, and then glared out, grinning. 'So what's next?'

For all the bluffing they were both relieved, Poole thought, when the preliminaries were done, and the moment of launch arrived.

Mitch Gibson crawled into the pod to shake their gloved hands.

But their very last human contact – before the pod was sealed and the air replaced with a clear suspension fluid – was with the two young techs who had taken them through the medical stages. Again their hands were shaken.

'The naming of names,' said the male tech.

Poole asked, 'Names?'

'We need call signs. Commander Gibson suggests *Anaxagoras* for the control station at Larunda. And *Cecilia Payne* for your descent module.'

'Anaxagoras,' said the female tech. 'A pre-Socratic philosopher who was the first to speculate that the Sun might have a physical nature, as opposed to divine. He imagined the Sun was a ball of hot iron mere thousands of kilometres above the Earth.' She laughed. 'He was misled by a lack of understanding of the curvature of the Earth. Still, not a bad guess. And Cecilia Payne was a late-Discovery-era solar physicist who made rather better guesses.'

Poole nodded brusquely. 'Good names. *Anaxagoras* and *Payne* it is.'

'I hope you will remember us. We have worked so closely together. Physical contact brings a bond, does it not?' She shook Poole's hand. 'My name is Asher Fennell.'

'And mine,' said the other, 'is Harris Kemp.'

'We will remember,' Nicola said, gravely enough.

Poole suspected they were both relieved when the cabin was finally sealed, and the suspension fluid cautiously pumped in. 'Nicola, I appreciate you not laughing at them.'

'It took an effort, believe me. Those earnest kids.'

'Who will never forget this moment, whether we live or die.'

Nicola just shrugged.

Now Gibson called. '*Anaxagoras* here. Larunda control. *Payne, Anaxagoras*—'

'*Anaxagoras, Payne.* We have you loud and clear,' Poole replied. Even if that wasn't quite true; the suspension fluids had left his hearing slightly muffled, his vision blue-tinged.

'Then if you're ready for the final pre-launch preparations—'

Nicola snapped, 'Enough chatter already. So long, Mitch.' Her finger stabbed down on a glowing slate.

And the *Cecilia Payne*, dragging an electric-blue wormhole frame, lurched into free space. Within minutes they had fallen out of the shadow of Mercury, and faced the raw Sun.

17

First they had to travel from Mercury's orbit to the surface of the Sun: not an inconsiderable distance in itself, nearly sixty million kilometres, forty per cent of Earth's distance from the star. And, given the stress on their systems, human and mechanical, the sooner that distance was spanned the better.

So, following the prepared flight plan, Nicola ramped up the GUT-drive to an acceleration of twenty gravities – less than they would suffer at the Sun itself, but a good test of the interlocking systems that should shelter them from that ferocious pull. At that rate it would be five hours to turnaround, then an equally ferocious five hours of deceleration, before they hit the edge of the Sun's outer atmosphere . . . The edge, at least, as the Larunda crew defined it for practical purposes. Poole knew that to the physicists the star's extended atmosphere reached theoretically to interstellar space, where the solar wind brushed against the wider galactic breezes.

Once the thrust was engaged and she was satisfied the craft was performing as expected, Nicola turned to Poole – moving very cautiously – and winked at him through her faceplate and a blue wash of suspension fluid. 'Wake me if there's an alarm.' She closed her eyes.

After a few minutes her breathing was deep and regular.

Mitch Gibson spoke in Poole's ear. '*Payne*, *Anaxagoras*. How's it going, buddy?'

'I'm glad of the company. That woman could sleep through the end of the world.' Although, he thought, maybe that wasn't something he should joke about just now.

'We rate you at just shy of twenty G. Any problems?'

'Not that I can detect. Breathing is no more uncomfortable than before. Vision seems normal. As the acceleration ramped up I had a few pressure points.'

'We saw them. Your neck, the bottom of your spine—'

'The smart systems compensated before I could report.'

'Unless you want anything, I'll shut up. Follow your pilot's example and try to sleep. You'll face a long day when you wake up.'

'I don't suppose you stowed away any single malt on this tub.'

Gibson laughed. 'Sure. The state you're in you'd have to inject it straight into your brain pan. Sleep tight, my friend.'

Perhaps he did sleep. So strange, so unreal was the situation, this cocooning in a technological womb while the Sun's disc slowly grew before him, it was difficult to know if he was asleep or awake.

In the end it took the soft chime of an alarm to alert him that the descent phase was over. That was shortly before the GUTdrive faded, and the acceleration softened to zero.

Nicola woke, stirred, went to rub her eyes, and found her gloved fists thumping against her faceplate. She looked at her hands, listened to the whirr of the exoskeletal multipliers that enabled her to close her fingers, and laughed at herself. 'Are we there yet?'

'I guess so—'

'I can tell the drive shut down, evidently on cue.' She checked a monitor. 'And it left us with the right residual velocity. We're free-falling, more or less, at the best part of four hundred thousand kilometres an hour . . .'

The drive had cut out with the craft still about two solar radii above the photosphere, the visible surface: about one and a half million kilometres high. But already they were descending through a hugely energetic environment. This was the corona, the Sun's outer atmosphere, a realm of super-hot, super-thin gases. And this was the fastest they would travel, Poole knew, until – and if – they emerged safely from the heart of the Sun.

'Four hours to the photosphere.'

Poole glanced at her. 'You haven't looked outside once since you woke up, have you?' He tapped a button.

The craft's hull turned Virtual-transparent. It was as if the two of them, in their couches, with instrument and control banks before them, were suspended in light, with, just behind them, the spectacular frame of the wormhole portal they'd dragged all this way.

And, dead ahead now, walling off half the universe, was the Sun. A disc that spanned the sky. As seen in hydrogen light it was coloured a vivid orange-brown that crawled with detail. This was the photosphere, the Sun's visible surface. The texture was grainy, almost as if pixelated – or, Poole thought more brutally, it was like some vast wound infested by a billion squirming insects. But each of those 'grains' was typically the size of Great Britain, or larger. Here and there he saw sunspots, huge dark scars; those close to the horizon were foreshortened, and seemed depressed below the general horizon, like craters.

This lightscape was not tranquil, but turbulent: lashed by huge energies. He saw spicules, fountains of wispy, glowing gas, bursting out of the granulated surface, as well as still more elaborate features: prominences, great glowing arches. These were much more easily seen out towards the horizon of the Sun than head on. The prominences were manifestations of the Sun's powerful magnetic field, generated deep in its interior – at a zone into which, Poole realised queasily, if all went well, he was scheduled to descend in this frail craft. It was a disturbing thought that such immense limbs of energy might be reaching out towards him even now, all but invisible as seen from dead ahead.

Mitch Gibson's voice, calm, reassuring, whispered in his ear. '*Payne, Anaxagoras.*'

'We're here, Mitch.'

'Hope you're enjoying the light show. You'll be aware that we checked the solar weather predictions before we set the date for your mission. We didn't want to lower you down in the middle of a storm.'

Nicola laughed. '*This* is calm?'

'Comparatively. Take a look up to, umm, your top right.'

Poole had to lean forward to see, muscle multipliers whirring. There, beyond the edge of the Sun, Poole saw a kind of effigy against the black sky, apparently a rough circle, distorted, glowing. He had no way of judging its size. 'Got it.'

'That's a coronal mass ejection, or the relic of one . . .'

The Sun's magnetic field, distorted by differential rotations in the star's layers, could become entangled. And, erupting through the surface, every so often these tangles could, in the physicists' term, *simplify*: the fields lost that knotted-up complexity all at once, and in the process dumped a load of energy. Tremendous explosions pushed gouts of matter from the surface, amid a hail of high-energy radiation. And in a 'coronal mass ejection' a great knot of the magnetic field itself could be expelled, carrying a mountain's mass of plasma with it, hurled out at a million kilometres per hour. That was what Poole was watching now. Earth's fragile but recovering technological civilisation had been hardened against such storms for centuries, but solar weather remained a hazard for all of spacegoing mankind.

But not today, Poole murmured. Not today. They were descending, as Mitch had observed, into comparative calm.

Their sphere steadily falling, dragging the electric-blue portal with it – Poole imagined the invisible tunnel of the wormhole stretching behind them – it took the full four hours for them to pass through the corona, and a denser, brighter layer called the chromosphere that was only as thick as the Earth's diameter – a mere detail in this huge landscape – and finally to approach the photosphere itself.

The surface of light.

Mitch Gibson took them through final checks before entry. *'Payne, Anaxagoras.* How's the neutrino scanner?'

Nicola checked it over. 'Nominal . . .'

Poole turned his head, cautiously but with interest, to see the relevant display: a first close-up scan of the interior of the Sun.

He knew that as hydrogen fused to helium in the Sun's core, a flood of gamma ray photons was released, packets of energy that had to batter their way through the Sun's inner layers, absorbed and re-emitted over and over, and out to the surface. Such was the density in that crowded deep that this process was a stop-start random walk, and it could take hundreds of thousands of years for the energy carried from the core by a single photon to reach the surface, and then sail unimpeded through space, to illuminate a target like planet Earth. To neutrinos, though, another product of the fusion processes – ghostly particles to which even the densest matter was far more transparent than air was to sunlight on Earth – the journey out of the Sun took mere seconds after their creation in the core. And so the neutrinos offered a way to look within.

Once, as Poole, a fan of archaic technology, had learned, to detect even a fraction of these neutrinos had taken huge, ungainly, mass-heavy 'telescopes': vast tanks of fluid stuck down mine shafts on Earth, for instance. Now the neutrino scanners whose results Nicola consulted were smaller than Poole's fist.

And the data they delivered was interpreted in the consoles as a ghostly image, as if the Sun was rendered transparent as glass, save for a star-like object contained in its very heart – the core itself, a fusion engine larger than Jupiter. Away from the core only the faintest of details could be seen, for now. But Poole knew that it was hoped that as the descent progressed this suite of instruments would be sufficient for them to detect the Sun's recent visitors.

'OK,' Nicola called. 'Coming up on the photosphere. Hold on to your lunch . . .'

Under Nicola's command, the angle of their fall abruptly flattened out. Poole felt a deep, savage surge of deceleration, and the Sun tilted, turning from a wall of light ahead into a kind of landscape beneath him. As he sat in his couch a tremendous weight dragged on his bones; he found it suddenly an effort to take a breath. But the manoeuvre was over, and now the craft settled into a low, rapid glide over the solar surface. With the hull still set to Virtual transparent, Poole could see how he and Nicola were underlit by a complex carpet of light.

He dared not turn his head. But a monitor showed him Nicola's grinning face – a lopsided grin, distorted by the gravity. She said, 'Welcome to the Sun.'

'*Payne, Anaxagoras*,' Mitch called. 'We've got good telemetry. The ship's systems, your own medical signatures, everything shows nominal.'

'How reassuring,' Nicola said.

'And enjoy the view. We're getting great imagery up here.'

Now it was as if they flew over some immense cauldron, its surface dominated by huge, slow-swelling bubbles, hundreds of kilometres across, each traversed in minutes. These 'granules', some of them organised into vaster clusters, were the termite-like infestation Poole had seen from afar. Close to the surface they seemed less lifelike, more mechanical. That analogy of a cauldron was apt; what he was seeing were the upper reaches of huge convective fountains that stretched deep into the Sun's interior. Further ahead he could see sunspots, distinctly foreshortened now, with wisps and arches of glowing gas reaching up into space. The sunspots were scars that showed where the Sun's magnetic field disrupted the deep convection flows, creating cooler patches.

'*Payne, Anaxagoras*. OK, guys, you're coming up on your first target. Should be over your horizon in five, four—'

'Mitch,' Nicola said, cutting him off. 'I already *see* it . . .'

And, looking ahead, so did Poole. A huge form pushing out of the glowing photosphere. Like a wall, smooth-faced, sharp-edged, pale.

A building, on the Sun.

'The Cache,' he breathed.

'That's the one,' Mitch Gibson reported. 'Glad we could bring you down close enough for a visual. You may see that it's half-immersed in the photosphere – as if floating there. But neutrino and other scans show it has the same proportions as when it emerged from Mercury. A precise cube.'

'Same proportions, maybe,' Nicola murmured. 'But look how far away we are from the Lethe-spawned thing, Poole. How big was the Caloris impactor? A hundred kilometres across? Whereas *that*—'

'*Payne*, it's now more like a *thousand* kilometres across. I did say it started growing as soon as it came out of Caloris.'

Nicola somehow laughed. 'Yes, but you didn't say *this* much. It's like the box Ceres came in.'

'Mitch, is it still growing?'

'No – well, not that we can see. Michael, we think that the material of which that big hull is made is some kind of light-energy receptor. A perfect solar cell. And it turns the energy it captures, with perfect efficiency, to mass. The bigger it gets, obviously, the more light it can intercept, and the faster it can grow—'

'Exponential growth,' Nicola said.

'That's the idea. Of course the rate at which it grows depends on the input energy flux. It was already growing, we think, as it approached the Sun, behind the sycamore seed; now it's bathing in light. Our observations of the early stages are patchy. But we think it had a doubling time, in terms of surface area, of a couple of hours.'

Nicola thought that through with characteristic quickness. 'OK. So it grew to its current size in, what, twelve, fifteen hours?'

'Something like that. Then it stopped.'

'Do we know why?'

'Internal complexity,' Poole guessed. 'First it inflated the shell to the required size. Now it's growing inside, not out. Some kind of infrastructure filling it out.'

'And the result will be what?'

Poole shrugged. 'Whatever those who planted it in Mercury, five billion years ago, intended for it.'

'We've no way of telling,' Gibson said. 'The sycamore seed seemed to monitor it for a while, having, apparently, guided it here from Mercury. Then, as you know, the seed just dived into the Sun. We do have partial observations that indicate that some of the objects you called raindrops – the silvery spheroids – may have *entered* the Cache, once it was settled. But that's disputed. As for now, not even neutrino scans can penetrate that material. Which is why, incidentally, we hope that the sycamore seed will show up in your own scans, at least as a shadow against the core-neutrino glow. We are sending probes past the Cache, and seeing how they're deflected by its gravity. Hoping to pick out some internal detail that way.'

Poole looked at the shining box. 'I'm itching to look inside that thing. Find out what in Lethe they're doing in there.'

'That's for the future,' Nicola said firmly. 'We have a job to do. Let's get on with it.'

Poole didn't see her move a muscle.

But the *Payne* tipped up and plunged straight into the surface of the Sun.

18

The so-called convection zone – the outer layer of the Sun's deep, stratified structure – was indeed a cauldron, a great spherical pot of boiling material wrapped around the Sun. A cauldron more than a hundred thousand kilometres deep.

Poole knew he was falling into a tremendous heat engine, whose principles would have been recognised by Discovery-era thinkers – indeed the basic physics of the Sun, and of all stars, had been worked out in that age of engines of steam and internal combustion. The Sun's material here was a gas, ionised, but not so hot that atomic structures broke down. So, just like Earth's air, it was a gas that was capable of absorbing and retransmitting the heat energy of the photons singing up from the Sun's core. And this gas boiled, exactly like a pan of water heated from below, with the heat energy transported by convection: the rising of hotter fluid, the falling of cooler.

And so they descended through great fountains, themselves hundreds or thousands of kilometres across, their structure and their cycling flows dimly visible in the neutrino images. Towers taller than worlds, all around them. The temperature slowly clicked up, from a few thousand degrees at the surface, then into the tens of thousands, and then hundreds of thousands. The density quickly increased too, up to that of breathable air – the photosphere, for all its drama and spectacle, was very rarefied – and then beyond.

The *Payne*'s speed had been drastically reduced; it would take more than eight hours to pass through this hot density.

'After all that drama at the surface,' Poole reported, 'this is kind of calm. I feel sleepy. Nicola *is* asleep, I think.'

'*Payne*, *Anaxagoras*.' Mitch Gibson's voice was carried now on modulated neutrino streams sent from Larunda, though there was a backup, a less trusted link passing through the wormhole itself. 'Sleepy is good. After all, you're inside a star, dangling at the end of an experimental wormhole technology that is the only thing that is keeping you from flashing to carbonised ash. But it's working. We can see a healthy fountain of hot gases erupting out of the external portal. The data shows your GUTdrive is functioning perfectly too, and a bleed-off of electromagnetic energy from the drive is deflecting the solar plasma safely away from your hull. Calm is *good*. Look, take it easy. Accept the process. You're just a bit of grit in a big pan of boiling water, falling with the currents . . .'

The pod lurched sideways, with a shove hard enough for Poole to feel, despite the dominant twenty-seven G that kept him pinned to his couch. He didn't try to fight the restraints that kept his head rigidly still. But he glanced at the monitor fixed on Nicola's face.

She was awake, wide-eyed, grinning. Piloting.

'What in Lethe are you doing?'

'Avoiding *that*. Take a look.'

And in the monitors, he saw now, a huge form was rising from the depths below. It was like a shining worm, he thought, or a sea snake: silvery it was, in the false-colour neutrino imaging. But this worm had no head or tail: a loop of string, then, rising from some deeper tangle.

'A flux rope,' he guessed.

'*Payne, Anaxagoras*. That's exactly it.' Gibson sounded excited. 'Another magnetic phenomenon. A kind of self-reinforcing structure where the field lines gather into a tube, that holds in matter like a hosepipe – but the contained matter is lower density than the average, and so the tube just floats up, up through this zone to the photosphere, and the surface. Buoyancy: simple physics, here in the heart of a star.

'Michael, Nicola did the right thing to get you out of the way. Even if she didn't need to jerk you around quite so hard.'

'How did you know?' Poole asked Nicola. 'I didn't notice any proximity alarm. And I thought you were asleep.'

She just grinned again. 'That's why I'm here. *Anaxagoras*, how about a tweak to the mission plan? What if we follow this flux rope all the way down to the tangle it came from? Maybe that will guide us away from any others.'

Gibson hesitated. 'Maybe. The modelling is uncertain.'

'I'll take that as a yes. Do you heroes ever make a decision without your bots' permission?' With subtle motions, Nicola worked her controls, and the apparently transparent craft glided alongside the great curving pillar of light. 'Be more fun to do some steering, anyhow. Let me know when your modelling catches up.'

Poole snorted. 'Once a pilot, always a pilot. Maybe you ought to give me a chance to play too.'

'Get some sleep first. You get crusty when you're tired, Michael.'

Well, he didn't sleep any more. And nor did she give him the controls, not through the rest of that phase of the descent.

All the way to the tachocline.

Even Nicola instinctively slowed the craft as the next interface approached.

Eight hours in, they were now more than a hundred thousand kilometres below the Sun's surface. That was about a quarter the distance from the Earth to the Moon, Poole reflected uneasily. In fact the whole Earth–Moon system could have been contained within the body of the Sun.

The neutrino imaging showed a kind of carpet beneath them now, a flat-infinite plain in which ropelike structures were embedded, lying roughly parallel. But even as Poole watched he saw those structures move, writhe, as if trying to escape that apparently infinite floor: huge forms, motivated by huge energies. If the granulated surface had seemed infested with life, at least from a distance, and the great bland convection cells by contrast had felt mechanical, a vast engine, here again he had a sense of a kind of quasi-life. He wondered what Jack Grantt would make of such observations.

'*Payne, Anaxagoras*. OK. You know where you are. This is the outer boundary of the radiation zone. No more atomic matter further in, just the debris of broken atoms: electrons and protons and neutrons and a hell of a lot of scattered radiation. The temperature is already around a million degrees – but the pressure's not so bad, like a shallow ocean.'

'More flux tubes,' Poole said. 'That's what we're seeing down there. Correct . . .?'

He knew the theory. If the convection zone was about steam-engine-era heat flows, the next part of the inner Sun, deeper yet, below this boundary, the tachocline, was like a simple electromagnetic motor.

The Sun's magnetic field was created and shaped by rotation. The core and the radiation zone, everything below this layer, rotated with a period of about twenty-five days, like a giant, solid planet. But the layers above the tachocline, the convection zone and photosphere, rotated more slowly, taking around twenty-seven days at the equator, and differentially at other latitudes. With uniform rotation the Sun's magnetic field would naturally have been like Earth's, with a north and south pole, and flux lines tamely following lines of longitude, north-south. But the fast-spinning central core screwed up that neat pattern. The magnetic field was everywhere dragged along by the local spin: twenty-five days below the tachocline, twenty-seven days above. So, here at the tachocline, in this zone of shear, the flux lines were pulled west to east, stretched like elastic, wrapping around the tachocline, this spherical surface. Just as Poole saw below him now.

And every so often one of these great flux tubes, stretched too far, would break away from the tangle, rise up through the convection zone, and ultimately burst out through the photosphere. Thus all of the Sun's weather – the solar flares, the mass ejections that plagued technological Earth, even the aurorae of the polar regions – was rooted in this tremendous hidden engine.

Mitch Gibson said, 'I got experienced physicists up here salivating over the images you are returning. Some of them are complaining that we didn't timetable in more observations. If only they could see a flux tube actually break away . . .'

Nicola just ignored that. 'Continuing with the flight plan.'

'*Payne, Anaxagoras.* Concur.'

Now, with great delicacy, Nicola manoeuvred their improvised craft through the tangle of flux ropes. It was a loose array, Poole saw as they descended, but it was three-dimensional and mobile, and he had to applaud, if silently, Nicola's skill as she guided the vessel through this puzzle – and *out*, down through that complex roof, and into a featureless glow beneath.

Featureless save for that steady neutrino-shine coming out of the fusing core itself, far below.

'That was easy,' Nicola said. 'You made the simulators too hard, Gibson.'

'Take it up with my boss.'

'I did feel a sideways kick as we passed through that interface and entered the faster-rotating central region. Compensating. And reducing speed . . .'

Poole knew the drill. Each successive stage of the journey, deeper into ever more challenging environments, was being taken at lesser velocities. It was not anticipated that the *Payne* could survive an entry into the fusing core itself. But still it would take forty-eight more cautious hours before they reached the outer boundary of that zone.

Unless events intervened.

This radiation zone might be a physicist's dream, a realm of enormous congregations of mass and energy. But there was nothing to see but a smooth gas of electrons and protons, immersed in a bath of continually scattered X-ray photons. The complex structure of the convection zone was a memory now; here, nothing changed save for abstract readings of density and temperature and pressure, and the slowly brightening glow in the neutrino imagers of that central core, the star within a star that was the source of all the Sun's heat and radiation. It was, Poole thought, like falling down the slope of some mathematician's abstracted graph.

Time seemed to pass even more slowly.

He tried to eat – meaning, taking solid food as opposed to the nutrients that were continually pumped into his system. The psychologists on Larunda had advised it would be good for his morale. But, despite exoskeletal support, the effort made his jaw muscles ache, the heavy gravity fighting him all the way, and he gave up.

Nicola was silent for such long periods it was hard to tell if she slept or not. Even Mitch Gibson went off air for a time, taking his own biological downtime.

And with nobody speaking to him, Poole, lost in his own thoughts, in an environment of sensory deprivation, actually grew bored. He couldn't always tell if he was asleep or awake.

Until Nicola murmured, 'Michael. We found something.'

19

Poole took one look out of the faux-transparent hull.

Then he looked away. He studied his control panels, trying to get his bearings.

He must have slept, after all. They had been passing through the radiation zone for nearly two days – only another few hours before they were due to reach the boundary of the core, and would have to turn back. They were just a third of the solar radius out from the centre now, with nearly five hundred thousand kilometres of starstuff over their heads. The view outside was empty, with only that still-brighter core glow from beneath showing in the neutrino monitors.

Empty, save for the fish that were swimming past the windows.

'Fish?' Nicola asked.

Poole hadn't realised he had spoken out loud. He looked again.

Fish, yes, they were like flatfish, or rays: roughly circular forms, thicker at the middle, thinner at the edges – lenticular – pale, greyish, translucent, almost transparent in the imagers' rendering. But big, each maybe fifty metres across. Individuals were difficult to make out, such was the size and density of the flock.

Swimming past his window. In the heart of the Sun.

'Not a *flock*,' he said, almost to himself. 'A school? A school of fish. Yes. But, fish inside the Sun?'

'*Payne, Anaxagoras*. Stay calm down there.'

'Easy for you to say,' Nicola snapped.

'They're all around you. As soon as you were spotted by outliers, this flock—'

'School, Mitch,' Poole said. 'School.'

'Whatever. They rose up in a big cloud, from deeper in the core. We can't make out individuals well from up here – we can't even see the lower edge of the cloud, the school. But now we know what to look for, we can tell they're there. All around the core, Michael. A shell of them. Incredible. A feature nobody saw before.'

'Not a *feature*,' Nicola said scornfully. 'What kind of word is that? I don't know if Michael's "school" is right. But *they're alive*, Gibson. Alive, inside the Sun. And they are swimming around in this high-energy gloop of protons and electrons like it was thin air.'

'To them, it is,' Gibson said. 'We can tell what those things are made of—'

'Dark matter,' Poole said, guessing wildly. 'Correct?'

'You got it,' Gibson said, sounding surprised. 'That's what our tame physicists are saying. Dark matter only interacts with our kind of matter – baryonic matter – through gravity. On the large scale, dark matter is the stuff that gives the universe its structure, of galaxies and clusters of galaxies, and superclusters of clusters , , , And now, on the small scale, here it is gathered in the heart of a star. Nuclear, electromagnetic forces don't mean a thing to dark matter. So these objects are swimming through this super-hot electron-proton plasma as if it didn't exist. In fact our imagers can only see them by their very occasional interactions of the particles they're composed of with normal matter, and some very subtle gravitational lensing, a deflection of the neutrino streams . . .'

Nicola glanced over. 'That's surprisingly acute for you, Poole.'

'Well, what else could pass through this stuff like it was mist?'

'I can't believe nobody knew this was here before. Somebody must have guessed.'

Gibson hesitated, evidently consulting. '*Payne, Anaxagoras.* Quite right, Nicola. There were speculations, at least. A dark matter, umm, *cloud*, was the best explanation of certain anomalies about the heat distribution in the centre of the Sun. First detected millennia ago, actually. More recently we've detected peculiar flows of helium from the outer layers into the core. You understand that the Sun is around a quarter helium by mass anyhow, and that excess helium is "ash" created by the core fusion processes. So it's as if somebody was shovelling ash onto a burning fire . . . It was one of the goals of the original Sun Probe project to check all this out. Nobody expected *this*, though.'

'Life, you mean?'

'Well, let's not jump to conclusions—'

Nicola seemed uncharacteristically thoughtful. 'Maybe we shouldn't be surprised. Isn't that what they used to say about the old planetary explorers? *Everywhere the humans went, they found life* . . . But what do these dark matter fish eat? Maybe they consume Sun-core fusion energy – no, it can't be that; they don't interact with electromagnetic fields, do they? Maybe it's something to do with the gravity.

Maybe the hearts of stars are breeding grounds for them, wherever the gravity wells are deep enough for them to gather, and they feed off gravitational waves, and shovel helium into the cores for fun . . . Uncle Jack would love this, Michael.'

Poole said now, 'One question. Did these – fish – come here with the Cache?'

'*Payne, Anaxagoras.* We don't believe so. My guys are rechecking our old records. We weren't specifically looking for dark matter entities, but the scans should have shown up any such change. Best guess is that these fish of yours have been here a long time, Michael.'

Nicola said softly, 'But *that* hasn't.' She pointed.

It hovered beyond the window. Suddenly there.

Black wings sweeping behind a blocky body, and its blunt head-like prow squarely facing the *Payne.* Where the dark matter fish were pale, translucent, this was solid, black in the neutrino imaging. And where the fish looked blurred, soft-edged, this was hard, sharp.

The sycamore seed.

'Wow,' Nicola said. 'Suddenly this scow seems fragile.'

'We didn't see it coming,' Gibson admitted. 'We're tracing it back – it must have moved through the solar medium at a murderous pace.'

'No creeping around like us, then.'

'No, Nicola. As far as we can tell it seems to have been inspecting these flocks of dark matter fish. Orbiting the Sun's core with them . . . Then, suddenly, it came for you. Your craft is trying to talk to it, by the way.'

'What?'

'One of the mission objectives has been to attempt to contact the intruder, if you ever got close enough. So you have the systems to fulfil that.'

Nicola laughed. 'Are we counting out the primes one neutrino pulse at a time?'

'You're not entirely wrong.'

Poole couldn't take his eyes off that blunt, powerful form. He struggled against the ferocious gravity, scarcely lessened even though they were so deep in the Sun's substance; he longed to stand, to face this thing on his feet, but he could not. 'Who are you? Why are you here? Are you studying these fish creatures? What in Lethe do you want?'

Nicola said, 'Actually I think I know what it wants, right now anyhow. Look at this, Michael Poole.'

A Virtual reconstruction congealed in the air before him. Poole saw a small spacecraft embedded inside an electric-blue tetrahedral frame, facing another artefact, much larger: black as night despite the torrent of light around it, a compact body with swept-back wings.

'That's us,' Nicola said, pointing. 'Us and the sycamore seed. Or, to be precise, here's *us*.'

The spacecraft shape dissolved, a glimpse of a complex interior, burning away. Two figures were left, seated on nothing, floating in the glowing air. Facing the sycamore seed.

'Us. Me on the left, you on the right. Bye, Nicola.'

The left-hand figure dissolved in a spray of pixels.

Leaving the sycamore seed, and that right-hand figure. Facing each other, head on.

'Lethe, Michael. It couldn't be clearer. I've set up some precision measurement routines . . . Somehow the sycamore seed knew you were in here. And it has come to rest right in front of you. *Right* in front. You're on its axis of symmetry. Michael, the sycamore seed isn't just here for these dark matter fish. It's here for you.'

With an angry gesture, he dismissed the Virtual.

Outside, still the sycamore seed lingered. Then, abruptly, without warning, it did a kind of back-flip, and shot away, out of sight.

For a long interval there was silence.

Poole said, 'We've seen what we came for. Get us out of here.'

For once Nicola didn't answer back. With tentative high-gravity gestures she worked her controls.

The school of dark matter fish followed the *Payne* for a while, as it rose back up into the glowing sky from which it had descended. Then they turned away, returning to their own endless circling of the core of the Sun.

It had taken over two days for the *Cecilia Payne* to descend into the heart of the Sun. It took another two days to return, to climb back through the photosphere, and once back at Larunda it took longer still for Nicola and Poole to be extricated from their unique craft.

In the weeks that followed, the data they had gathered were scrutinised with fascination, fear, and academic rigour. Debate was intense as to whether Nicola was right that the dark matter entities could be called 'alive'. But they appeared to show co-operative behaviour, in their flocking: they reacted to each other's presence, at least. There was much debate too as to what energy source they used: what did they eat? – as Nicola had first asked. And there was some speculation as to what might eat *them*. Could there be a whole dark matter food chain, embedded deep in the heart of the Sun?

Was there even intelligence to be found there?

And what impact might this inner canker have on the Sun's own internal processes? Ancient studies were dug out, old hypotheses dusted off, suggestions that a dark matter cloud in the heart of the Sun might diffuse the core's intense heat, or that additional layering of helium ash might suppress the rate of fusion reactions – perhaps it might even, ultimately, destabilise the Sun in some way.

Maybe the dark matter fish weren't even natives of the Sun. The Sun was just another star, after all; perhaps they inhabited many stars, and had migrated here . . .

Arguments raged.

Meanwhile, as far as anybody knew, the sycamore seed continued to lurk at the heart of the Sun.

After a month, though, the great artefact called the Cache – surely it *was* an artefact – detached itself from what appeared to have been a fuelling station on the surface of the Sun, rose up, and began a long, slow spiral out away from the star and out among the orbits of the planets. It would take months to span the tens of millions of kilometres between the inner planets – years to return to Jupiter, if it went that far.

It seemed a new phase was beginning.

A few weeks after the Cache's detachment, Nicola left too, on a routine supply ship. She didn't tell Poole where she was going, or what her plans were. Evidently she'd just got bored with going over old data.

Poole stayed on Larunda.

He continued to follow the study of the dark matter fish, and the Cache. And he helped out with the station's routine duties – everything except the cooking. He kept himself to himself at first, but gradually opened up in the company of the station's staff, Mitch Gibson and Fennell and Kemp and the rest. They were his kind of people, after all, as well as being Poole Industries staff. Slowly, he recovered from the physical side of his descent into the Sun.

And maybe, he thought, he was healing in other ways too. At least here he could stay out of sight of a lingering public fascination in him and his apparent central role.

Then, a full year after his Sun-dive, his mother summoned him home. 'You can't hide away for ever, Michael.' And her projected image opened one hand, to reveal the green amulet on her palm.

THREE

The girl from the future told me that the sky is full of dying worlds.

Michael Poole Bazalget, AD 2048

20

En route to Earth Poole sent a note to Nicola, asking her to join him, more in hope than expectation. He wasn't even sure he wanted her to respond. Not even sure why he felt he needed the support of such a disruptive individual.

Anyhow, she came.

They met at the space elevator Node over Singapore. After descending, they took the intercontinental monorail to the Red Centre of Australia, and then to Tasmania.

Nicola did more sleeping than complaining.

And from there to Antarctica, in the middle of the southern winter.

For the last leg, having obtained UN dispensations through Gea, Poole piloted a small, low-powered, scrupulously clean flitter himself: south across the Southern Ocean until his lights showed the gleam of crumpled ice – the continental glaciers, as opposed to the smoother sea ice – and then west across what was still called, on some maps, the Australian Antarctic Territory. When they got far enough south the sky was pitch dark, save for the faint glow of aurorae – an echo of the energies of the now-distant Sun – and the sparks of a few polar-orbit comsats and habitats and power stations, and the splayed purple glow of a refrigeration laser, dumping waste heat into the sky as it had since its construction in the Recovery era centuries before. Poole flew with spotlights illuminating the icescape below, to give Nicola something to look at.

Meanwhile Poole monitored what was going on out in the Solar System.

Teams of observers were tracking the slow, spiralling trajectory of the Cache, outward from the Sun from which it had detached more than a year ago. This trajectory had already taken the Cache back past the orbit of Mercury, and then to Venus. And then it had sailed closer to Earth than the planet's own Moon, to be greeted by a flock of human vessels, all resolutely ignored. Now, it seemed, the Cache was preparing for a similarly close fly-by of Mars.

Meanwhile the sycamore seed object was still lost in the heart of the Sun, visible only to neutrino scans and occasional deep-penetrator probes: still sitting deep in the radiation zone, evidently doing no more than observing.

After a year, Poole believed, things had calmed down a little in the wider universe, as well as in his own head. The first sensation at the arrival of alien objects in the Solar System had faded quickly. It had helped that the objects had adopted this apparently orderly behaviour, predictable on a timescale of years. Harry, Poole's father, had laughed cynically about this. 'You got to love the human race – shallow as a puddle. An alien craft the size of a small moon is sailing around the Solar System, and another one is sitting *in the Sun*, and after a few months nobody gives a damn. But at least it lets the serious folk get on with some work . . .'

Work that went on without much public scrutiny, as human ambitions accreted around the alien objects – not least Harry's own schemes, Poole was sure, though Harry rarely shared any of this with his son.

But the news flow was there if you wanted to tap into it. Regarding the Cache, a steady stream of imagery and other data was being returned by the Spaceguard observatories, and by the small fleet of specialist probes, government and private, that with the passing months had gathered to trail the enigmatic object as it made its painstaking way through the inner System.

And, if you paid attention, every so often there was something genuinely new.

'Dimples,' Poole murmured.

Nicola frowned, distracted by Antarctica. As they flew, overlays on Virtual displays showed landscapes hidden under the ice beneath the prow: lost twenty-fifth-century townships built on exotic, archaic geographies that had, in the end, been only briefly ice-free. Nicola gazed at these with morbid interest, and without comment.

Now she turned to Poole. 'Dimples?'

He pointed to a Virtual image, a gleaming cube. 'On the face of the Cache. Something new. Circular patches, a little darker than the rest. There's different radar reflectivity when the walls are pinged.'

'Impact craters? There's a lot of junk in the inner System, Earth-crossing asteroids and such. And that thing is a big target.'

Poole shrugged. 'Not as simple as that. We've even observed a couple of impacts on the Cache. Mostly the debris just splashes away, or you might get residual rubble clinging to the centre of one of those big square faces. The thing has a non-negligible gravity field of its own. But there's never any sign of damage, no cratering.'

Nicola looked away, apparently losing interest. 'Something else, then.'

Poole felt vaguely irritated. 'Not everything the Cache does has to be mysterious, you know. I keep thinking that this phase of its operation, at least, would have been familiar to the old space pioneers.'

Nicola snorted. 'You mean, to people like Michael Poole Bazalget? To a Poole, history is about whichever of your ancestors was perturbing the world at the time.'

'Earlier than him. Well, I think so. Back in the twentieth century, when they sent the first uncrewed probes out to the planets. The machines themselves were dumb, and for propulsion they only had chemical rockets and gravitational slingshots. So all they could manage was flybys, of Mars and Venus, the outer planets. But it was good enough for a first quick scout to see what was out there, to direct the more ambitious programmes to come. Maybe this is doing the same thing – the Cache, I mean. It's already taken a good look at what we're doing on Mercury, Venus, Earth, Moon. Now it's on the way to Mars . . .'

'I heard the Martians are planning some kind of response just as they sent a signal last time the sycamore seed sailed past. This time they're talking about sending a crew out to meet the Cache when it gets there. A mission. Your honorary Uncle Jack is involved again. Well, he is an exobiologist. "Welcome to Mars. Give me a urine sample."' She laughed, and looked down at the fleeing ice of Antarctica. 'And meanwhile, here we are. It's like Europa down there. Lethe, what a planet this is. Deserts like Mars, those huge salt-water oceans, and *this*, all jammed together on one world. It's amazing anything ever evolved here in the first place . . . This ice, though. Is there subsurface life, like the ice moons?'

'It's complicated.' Poole glanced at her. 'You really don't know your history, do you? Yes, there used to be subsurface life, in deep, icebound lakes, and at the surface, in sunlit droplets of liquid water under a frozen crust. But it was all endangered when the ice was melted after the Anthropocene. Lost, except for what we could save. And then, when the land was refrozen, we put the life back.'

'We? We Pooles, right?'

'We contributed,' he said dryly. 'Take a look at the South Pole.' He tapped a softscreen. Up came an old image of an ice field in spring-time, a low Sun, a clutter of buildings half-buried in fresh snow – and a spire, crystalline, too tall to fit into the frame, set precisely at the pole itself.

'Wow,' she said ironically. 'I give up. What is it?'

'That's a monument to how Gabriel Poole saved the world, when it was his turn.'

Nicola laughed. 'I *knew* it . . .'

It had been in the twenty-fourth century that a kind of minimum point in the post-Anthropocene evolution of Earth's climate had been reached. At that time most of Antarctica's ice sheet had been desta-bilised and lost – the coastal flooding around the world reached its peak – and the concentrations of greenhouse gases in the air reached their highest level. The geosphere, too, was finally responding to the great climatic changes: the solid Earth itself. The ice lost from Green-land, Iceland and Antarctica destabilised long-dormant volcanoes; there were landslides, tsunamis. Human civilisation was an adaptive complex system, a mesh of tightly coupled networks and feedback loops of food and water, raw materials and manufactured goods, energy, money, information, people . . . At that time there were fears that under an unprecedented strain this complex system could col-lapse. And if it did, it would stay collapsed.

It was a turning point.

'People finally decided something had to be done. The first space elevators were built, for instance. And geoengineering was suddenly fashionable . . . As for Antarctica, Gabriel's plan was simple. Even if it took a few centuries of arguments, demonstrations and trial runs to get it approved.'

Ice-free Antarctica had been slowly turning green, colonised by hardy lichen, mosses, a few early tufts of grass. It would have been a long process. The various biotas would have had to adapt to Antarc-tica's low light levels and odd seasons: months of darkness every year, then months of continual daylight. But life had adapted here before, as the fossils proved.

'Once there were forests of huge broad-leaved trees down there. Given millions of years, something like that would have evolved again. But in the end the continent was only ice-free for a few centuries before—'

'Gabriel Poole got in the way.'

Gabriel had proposed to freeze back out all the water ice Antarctica had lost, thus reducing sea levels and recovering at least some of the lost shoreline territory on all the continents.

'Oh, and in the process Gabriel was going to draw down some of the excess greenhouse-gas carbon dioxide too. It's all down there now, in the new ice, stored in stabilised layers – an artificial clathrate, almost, like the methane-bearing permafrost layers Michael Poole Bazalget had stabilised in the north centuries before. The time was right. By the twenty-seventh century the issues had been debated and worked over – and there were already terraforming efforts proposed on Mars. Why, Venus's atmosphere was already being frozen out.'

'By another branch of the family?'

He ignored that.

Nicola did seem interested. 'Big stuff, then. I like big stuff. So how was this achieved? Sun shields, like at Venus?'

'The UN oversight agencies wanted more control than that. A gradual solution. Nobody wanted to do it too quickly, if it was to be done at all, to risk destabilising the climate *again*. It was all pretty controversial.'

'But Gabriel got his big refrigerator?'

'Pretty much. He built huge pumps that lifted sea water to the centre of the continent, to the top of the old ice dome, and froze it all out, metre by metre. It took five centuries for the drawdown to be complete – the sea-level drop was contained at about a centimetre per year, and the carbon dioxide drawdown at about a gigatonne per year. So the power required was relatively trivial, year by year, a fraction of the planet's annual output in the Anthropocene days. Now the programme has settled down to long-term stabilisation; you need less refrigerating power because so much of the sunlight is deflected by the ice itself. The power generation nowadays comes from a GUT facility: more compact, cleaner. Even though there was a lot of controversy about applying interplanetary-engine technology to the Earth itself.'

'But it worked.'

'It worked.'

Nicola said sourly, 'And all they gave Gabriel was that poky tower? If they really are going to build a statue to *you* at the heart of the Galaxy some day . . .'

But then she shut up. The flitter was suddenly flying over a green landscape, vivid in the spotlights, a crumpled plain walled by diverging ice cliffs and scoured deep by ravines and rivers. The contrast with the blankness of the ice was startling.

105

Poole grinned at her reaction. 'Gabriel and his successors needed a base on the continent to run the freeze-out programme. So he kept *this* ice-free – and this is where my mother lives now. Welcome to Princess Elizabeth Land. Listen, my father's going to be down there too.'

'Harry? I thought your mother—'

'She's the host. And she's the one with something to say, apparently. But Harry has muscled in, not for the first time in my life. It's complicated.'

'You are Pooles. It's always complicated.'

'Just don't provoke him.' Poole punched a comms console. 'Strap in, we're on our way down.'

21

When they arrived, Harry Poole, clutching a drink, was pacing the floor of Muriel's reception room.

He didn't seem pleased to see Nicola Emry walk in at the side of his son. 'You. Why in Lethe do you need to be here? This is a Poole estate. Family business.'

Poole said mildly, 'Everything that's happened since the sycamore seed came through the wormhole affects all humanity. Maybe it's a good idea to have one perspective from outside the bloodline, don't you think?'

'Perspective? From her? She's nothing but a trickster, Michael, and she'll lead you astray one way or another.'

'Anyhow, why are *you* here?' Poole knew his father. When he was around his son, especially in person, it was usually because Harry wanted something; conversely he generally wasn't around if he didn't. Now, something about his sheer intensity made Poole nervous.

But Harry grinned easily. 'We'll get to that. Anyhow I brought backup of my own. I'm not about to be outnumbered . . . Ah, here comes Muriel.'

Poole seemed to see the scene through Nicola's cynical eyes. This reception room was huge, a hall with an ice-like, translucent floor over which cushions, chairs, tables were scattered, as well as a few softscreen stands. Any humanity was overwhelmed by the sheer scale. The main feature was an arching picture window facing north – of course north, when looking out from the south pole. Under the glare of artificial lights, a garden was visible, a carpet of green studded with tree clumps that stretched to an ocean shore, on which could be glimpsed sea ice. Poole had no idea what technology was used to keep the huge estate free of Gabriel Poole's restored ice, even in the Antarctic winter; whatever it was, it was subtle and unobtrusive.

And now, across the light-filled floor, his mother walked. 'Outnumbered? Backup? Do you have to use such confrontational terms, Harry?'

Muriel wore loose, pale green shirt and trousers, and her reflection was flawlessly rendered in the floor's smart surface. Even the shoes she wore clicked softly as she took each step. Where Harry was tall, blond, thin to the point of gaunt, Muriel was shorter, darker, with Mediterranean features, grey-streaked hair tied back – and pale grey eyes, a feature associated with the Pooles for centuries. Muriel was the one with the Poole ancestry, in fact, Harry the outsider who had married in and had taken his wife's surname – as had been the habit with the Poole clan for generations. Michael had got his brown eyes from his father, and had been told they were the 'wrong' colour more than once in his life. Ironically Harry hadn't even kept his own brown eye-colour when he had got himself AS-rebuilt, opting for a more spectacular blue.

Watching her approach, Poole was uneasy, his feelings as complex as ever when he was around his family.

Meanwhile Muriel had a companion at her side. Short, serene-looking in a floor-length robe, it was Gea, the ancient artificial intelligence, adviser to various UN government arms and a member of the Oversight committee responsible for monitoring the sycamore-seed incident – and thus, Poole realised, an ally of Harry's just at the moment, if you needed to use such terms.

Harry was grinning. 'You're working it out, Michael. Yes, right now Gea's with me.'

Gea half-bowed, stiff but graceful. Poole realised she was trying to project a subtle aura of artificiality and age, a Virtual avatar politely reminding them of who she was, what she was. 'I echo Muriel. I have been a friend of the Pooles since the age of Michael Bazalget or even before. Or so I like to believe. I am an ally of all. And I hope that our meeting today will be characterised by sharing, not confrontation. This is family, after all.'

'Not my family,' Nicola said quickly. 'And not yours either, robot lady.'

'We must contribute as best we can.'

Now Poole's mother approached him, smiling. She looked tired, he thought, and perhaps a little older than when he'd last seen her. But, of course, everything about the Muriel he saw was deliberately projected. 'Come, sit.' She led them across the cool floor to a cluster of furniture. A small bot rolled out bearing a tray of drinks, snacks. 'We'll talk. Have dinner later. I'm promised that the aurora tonight will be spectacular. It should be visible just as we take dessert . . .' As they took their seats, Muriel kept smiling. 'Well, Nicola. Welcome to the inner circle. It's only courteous to make sure you know that I too am in fact a Virtual. Like Gea.'

'Yes, I—'

'And as to how I came to be this way – I don't imagine Michael or Harry has told you the full story.'

'How you died young?'

Poole winced.

Harry laughed. 'You don't mince your words, do you?'

Nicola was unperturbed. 'I'm guessing it was an accident. Your death. Some overwhelming trauma? AS treatment can fix most health issues, after all. And you Pooles would have had the best.'

'I'm afraid you're quite wrong. In fact, when I was young, my body rejected my preliminary AS treatment.'

Harry growled, 'It was worse than that. She had an adverse reaction . . . One in a million. The AS actually killed her.'

'At the various clinics I attended, my fellow patients, mortals all, shared a lot of black humour: somebody has to be sacrificed to balance out the actuarial statistics, and so on. And then there was Harry. We decided to try for a child despite my problems.'

Harry grunted. 'To sum it up, I gained a son. Michael. I lost my wife.'

Poole studied his father. 'I don't *think* he blamed me,' he said bluntly to Nicola. 'Some parents would.'

Harry smiled crookedly. 'You have to give me credit for that. I blamed the universe. And the Lethe-spawned, inadequate pharma industry that gave my wife an apparently life-extending drug that killed her before she was forty. Although of course the Pooles themselves owned most of the patents. That was the only reason I didn't sue. But I didn't care about the rest of the family, and I still don't. I just wanted you back.'

'And it looks like you got her,' Nicola said. 'Kind of. What was it, consciousness download through the corpus callosum?'

Harry shook his head. 'Muriel's decline happened too quickly.'

'And besides,' Muriel said, 'I didn't actually *want* that. To have my mind pumped out of the neural bridge between the two halves of my brain? I'd accepted my fate. But Harry . . .' She looked directly at Nicola. 'I'm an emulation, Nicola. Which Harry created from recordings of my life, my work, my journals – testimony from my friends and family.'

Including a very young Michael Poole, who had barely remembered his mother at all, but had been forced to talk about her to strangers for hours, in order to 'populate' this simulation. He kept his gaze fixed on the floor, but he was aware of Nicola watching him.

'Created,' Muriel added, 'without my prior consent.'

Nicola observed, 'This is an old argument.'

'But since then,' Harry said breezily, 'consent or not, you've had decades of life. Of consciousness, at least. Thanks to me. You even went back to your career.'

Muriel said to Nicola, 'I am a historian, of sorts.' She picked up a drink from the table before her, a glass of fruit juice; the integration of the Virtual with the real was seamless. 'Though I'm generally restricted to this environment. I'm interested in long-term trends, Nicola. The way the Anthropocene crisis and its long aftermath have reshaped humanity.' She smiled, looking oddly tired. 'Of course it's a paradox for *me* to be studying the effect of AS technologies on human societies. Yet the effect is undeniable. As the age profile of mankind has changed, so the way we think has evolved. We look beyond short-term fixes to long-term solutions. Our institutions have responded too. This was certainly a factor in the post-Anthropocene recovery. And, individually, we have changed. We are more *patient* . . . In studies on animals, this is known as life history theory. Put starlings, for example, in a harsh and deprived environment and they will fight for scraps of food, they will neglect their own physical state. Give them a more predictable and nourishing place to live—'

Harry snorted. 'Patience. Ha! Too much of that for my liking. You can't just sit there being patient until the dying Sun eats the Earth. Some of us have to be out there pushing.'

Muriel said, 'Whereas you didn't even have the patience to ask if I wanted to live again, did you?'

Poole glared at them both. 'This argument has been going on as long as I can remember. But the truth is, you're only here today because of me. Right?'

Harry looked at Muriel. 'So we get to the point. You want to start, or shall I?'

Muriel, calmer, sipped her drink.

Harry got up, paced around, spread his hands. 'OK. Look, Michael, I think we all saw why you hid away at Mercury, for a year. You needed time to adjust to it all. The strangeness, the disruption. Anybody would. Maybe we all needed some time. I'm having trouble myself getting used to the idea of aliens in our midst.

'But you know that it's not just your family who are taking notice of you now, son. You have been watched ever since the Wormhole Ghost showed up. Surely you must have expected that. Even during your jaunt into the Sun. You found out a lot during your Sun-dive, the two of you, and for that I applaud you. But the key moment, as all humanity witnessed, probably, was when the alien faced you. *You*, Michael. Just as Nicola here recognised at the time, to her credit.'

'Thanks,' she said dryly.

'And everybody saw it, boy. That's my point. You can't hide from it. Somehow you're central to all this, Michael. You always have been.'

'You must understand our concerns, Michael,' Gea said now. 'We are after all suffering an alien incursion into the Solar System – an incursion that's been going on for a year now, though no harm has yet been done, or only trivially—'

'Trivially?' Nicola snapped. '*That* is a bot's perception. People have died. From the beginning.'

Gea acknowledged that with a nod, but continued. 'And we must make best use of *all* the evidence available to us. Muriel . . .'

Muriel nodded. 'But this is also the culmination of centuries of family history. Millennia, even.'

Poole felt queasily alarmed. Enmeshed in unwelcome family history. 'What does *that* mean?'

'I have studied the relic the Ghost brought,' Muriel said. 'As you requested when you sent it here, Michael. Your amulet. A term of magic, though there's nothing magical about it . . .'

Nicola was interested. 'What, then? Have you discovered what it's made of, for instance?'

Muriel shook her head. 'We do know it's not of human manufacture. That's something, if only a negative data point. Modern human manufacture anyhow. Some are suggesting that it's made of the same substance as the alien artefact, the Cache. Which some call "hull plate", the shell that grows in the sunlight. There are aspects of the reflectance spectra . . . But since we don't know what *that* is either, it's not a very useful comparison.'

Nicola was growing predictably impatient. 'Then what do you know?'

Muriel smiled now. 'Did you ever try looking at it? Or rather, through it?'

Poole thought back. Perhaps he hadn't. Maybe that had seemed too obvious. 'Tell me what you found.'

'We – aren't sure. A deflection of the light. Some have suggested there are images stored in there; if so, no deconvolution routines we've tried so far have worked. It's as if there were a very strong gravitational field working inside the amulet. Or as if the amulet itself was made of exotic matter, holding open a spacetime warp, like one of your wormhole portals—'

'That's ridiculous,' Harry said. 'Our portals each have the mass of a small asteroid. To think you could compress such a thing down to the size of a toy you can hold in your hand—'

Nicola laughed at him. 'I thought you Pooles had big imaginations.'

Muriel said calmly, 'Whatever it is, it is certainly very advanced.'

Poole said, 'This thing *is* from the future, then. Just as the Wormhole Ghost claimed about itself.'

Muriel nodded. 'It seems so. Or a possible future. Which is why, tangentially, I have brought you here.'

He began to feel still more profoundly uncomfortable. 'What does that mean?'

'You see, we have more evidence, Michael,' Muriel said, almost sadly. 'From a different source. About the future, or futures. Prophecies of a kind which have been held in the Poole family archives for generations. Prophecies you now need to know about. *And which are made available only to the bloodline* – to which you belong, and of which I, even as this Virtual memory, count as part, and Gea, as a longstanding ally of the family—'

'Aha,' Nicola said quickly, her gaze flashing between them. 'I'm working it out. But *you* aren't bloodline, are you, Harry? So you've had to come here, to this simulacrum of your dead wife, to get access?' Harry made to speak, but Nicola kept talking. 'In fact – oh, I get it now – *is that the real reason you brought Muriel back*? So that this unreal copy of your dead wife could be your key to the spooky family archives?' She shook her head, as if admiring. 'My, my. You do think ahead, don't you?'

Harry glowered at Nicola. 'You little runt. Why are you still here? *You* aren't bloodline, for sure.'

'She goes, I go,' Poole said bluntly.

Nicola laughed at them all.

Muriel looked disgusted. 'Oh, Harry, drop the histrionics. And, you, Nicola, stop provoking him.'

112

Poole said, 'And enough of the screwed-up relationships. Mother, just tell me what you know.' He frowned, digging for memories. 'The Kuiper Anomaly, for instance. Does this go back as far as that?'

Muriel looked faintly shocked. 'Who told you about that?'

He was careful not to glance at Gea. 'Just tell me.'

And so she did.

22

She spoke softly and steadily, her account supplemented with details supplied by Gea, who had actually witnessed some of the distant-in-time, resonant events Muriel described.

She spoke of George Poole in the early twenty-first century, who had lost his sister to some kind of metahuman cult in Rome . . . and whose lifetime had seen the arrival of a spaceprobe, of evidently very advanced manufacture, in the outer Solar System. The Kuiper Anomaly, as it had been known, had orbited slowly in the Kuiper Belt, out beyond the orbit of Neptune, before disappearing just as discreetly.

And she spoke of George's nephew Michael Poole Bazalget, the visionary engineer who had averted the danger of a massive release of greenhouse gases from the Arctic permafrost . . . and who claimed to have suffered visitations of his own.

Gea, consulting her inner archive, repeated words from Bazalget's personal account: '"The girl from the future told me that the sky is full of dying worlds . . ."'

Muriel said, 'In the twenty-first century, we – at least, Bazalget – *were visited from the future*, Michael. There seems no doubt.

'All we have is fragmentary. It seems the Kuiper Anomaly somehow – mediated – the journey of the traveller from the future. Bazalget claimed he received specific advice from her, but of course his visitor had her own agenda, which we don't fully understand. But he got from her enough to inspire his development of the clathrate-stabilisation programme. And enough to kick-start modern AntiSenescence research. It's said that the starting point for *that*, by the way, was a study of advanced features in the girl's genome . . .'

'Either of which,' Harry said, the envy obvious in his voice, 'would alone have been enough to found a commercial dynasty of a kind the world never saw before.'

'Our knowledge is partial,' Muriel said. 'Sketchy. Even contradictory. And what the Wormhole Ghost added only fleshes it out a little more.'

'Just tell me,' Poole said, his voice gruff.

She took a deep breath. 'Well. To begin with, we think mankind is destined to survive this age, to prosper, to become more powerful – to go out among the stars. There are hints of races we will trade with, or be conquered by—'

'Or conquer,' Harry said brutally.

'The *Silver Ghosts*. Well, you met one of them. And the *Qax*.' *Chh-aa-kss*. 'We know virtually nothing of these beings but their names. But from various hints we have worked out a little of the history of the future . . .'

The Qax had conquered humanity.

Whereas the Ghosts had warred with mankind, but had been defeated. And, ultimately, driven to near extinction. But at least some of the Ghosts, including the Wormhole Ghost, had apparently evolved a cult of worship of their conquerors – with Michael Poole himself remembered, a human become mythic. Quite a measure of their defeat, Poole thought.

'Now, the Wormhole Ghost's language was interesting in itself,' Gea said quietly. 'It spoke an approximation of our own Standard. Which as you may know is a product of the Bottleneck, the age of the great migrations, with a core of old English supplemented by dialects and pidgins – Eurafrican, Eastasian, Panamerican – and a later consolidation with Han Chinese, which—'

Nicola frowned. 'I'm picking my way through all of that. You're saying that the Wormhole Ghost's attempt to speak Standard *itself* contained evidence of the epoch it came from. The drift from our own speech.'

Gea smiled. 'Exactly. The linguistic drift adds authenticity to its account.'

Poole sat back, blowing out his cheeks. 'You mean, its account of *me*.'

Muriel leaned forward. 'Michael, the future is still largely a blank – and who knows how current events, even our own foreknowledge, may be perturbing it? But we do have two dates. One is from your Ghost visitor. The linguistic drift indicates that it came from a future beyond twenty thousand years ahead, give or take. When, as the Ghost told us, humans will win a war at the centre of the Galaxy.'

Nicola grinned. '"A war at the centre of the Galaxy." *Lethe*. Every time I hear about that I'm glad I bothered to come.'

'The second date,' Poole said heavily.

'Much further out. Perhaps half a million years hence. This is the era that Bazalget's girl from the future came from, we think. When humanity reaches some kind of peak of power and influence – and, maybe, wisdom. The dominant class of that era called themselves – *will* call themselves – Transcendents. They seem to have had some knowledge of the even deeper future. A future they planned for. And they wanted, somehow, to reach to the past – to the Pooles . . . It's all fragmentary. Shards, hints, seen through a glass darkly. *But still you will be remembered, Michael.* Listen to this . . .'

Gea recited the transcript.

Even after the Xeelee had finally won their war against humanity, the stars continued to age, too rapidly. The Xeelee completed their great Projects and fled the cosmos.

Time unravelled. Dying galaxies collided like clapping hands. But even now the story was not yet done. The universe itself prepared for another convulsion, greater than any it had suffered before.

And then—

'Who are you?'

'My name is Michael Poole.'

They sat in silence, absorbing these words.

Nicola spoke at last. 'Who are these Xeelee?' *Ch-ee-lee.*

Gea said gently, 'As best we understand it, these are the creatures – the race – who humanity will defeat in the Core of the Galaxy. But in the end—'

'They win,' Poole said gruffly. 'And the story ends. The cosmos dies. And there *I* am.'

'Yes.' Muriel made to grasp his hands; she flinched when her flesh crumbled against his. She always seemed to forget her own Virtual nature, Poole thought, and had to learn a painful lesson over and over. 'You will be brought back somehow. Preserved. Or at least remembered, yet again.'

'Why?' Poole demanded. 'Why would that happen?'

Gea looked at him steadily. She quoted, '"The story was not yet done." Evidently you are – will be – part of that ongoing story. The cosmic story. You, or some vestige of you, preserved somehow to the very end – perhaps ultimately by these Transcendents, who evidently had the power to reach into the past. And they believed you would have some role to play, in that distant end time.'

'And that name. Mankind's ultimate enemy. It has to be the name of the sycamore seed, the thing that has come out of the wormhole, the thing that seems to be so interested in me. Or whoever built it. And the reason it's come here—'

Muriel said gently, regretfully, 'You know why. You can put the pieces together.'

'Like the girl from the future. Like the Wormhole Ghost, maybe. It came from future to past. And it came to change its own past – our future. It came to change *my* past.'

Michael Poole spoke the name, for the first time.

'*Xeelee.*'

That was when the arguments started.

Poole closed his eyes and clenched his fists. 'I don't want any of this.'

'You don't have to accept it,' Nicola said.

'You,' Harry said. 'Shut up. This isn't your business. Not your family.'

'And Michael isn't *yours* either. His future is his own. He doesn't have to accept these spooky hints and scraps. And he doesn't have to follow whatever agendas you lot build out of them.'

Poole, eyes still clamped firmly shut, heard Gea say, more gently, 'But we don't know if that is true. Perhaps the future is ordained . . . I was there, remember, with Michael Poole Bazalget, when he had his own encounter with the future. I and others have striven to keep this strange knowledge secret – private, even within the Poole family circle. We must be sure—'

'Nicola's right.' Poole stood up. 'You all want to manipulate me – everything about me. You, Mother – even you, Gea – all this murky stuff from the past. And *you*, Harry.'

Harry glared at him. 'Well, can't I? Haven't I the right?'

Poole looked around at them all, uncomfortably aware that they were all staring at him with a kind of awe. Even his ambitious father – even Gea, a sentience sixteen hundred years old – even his mother.

All but Nicola Emry.

'Nicola. Let's walk.'

He stalked over to the room's vast window.

Stared out.

Counted flecks of sea ice on an ocean rim, illuminated by flood-lights. Tried to drown out thought.

After a couple of minutes Nicola joined him, bringing a drink. 'Single malt. Your mother tells me it's your favourite.'

'Not now.'

'Take it.' She waited until he obeyed. 'Is it always like this? Your family.'

'Lethe, yes. This is one of the good days. So what do you think is going to happen now?'

Nicola seemed to think it over. 'Look, I'm new to your family dynamics. But you just *know* they're not going to work together.'

'You got that right.'

'Your mother spoke about studying long-term trends. I think *she's* going to look at this visitor as a gift from the cosmos. She's going to want to make contact. Exchange diplomatic envoys. Enter into a pan-galactic civilisation of harmony and peace. You know the kind of thing. And she will want to use *you*, and this odd connection you have with the Xeelee, to achieve that. Whereas your father, and Gea – well, there you have the government. And I know from my own mother that Oversight agencies are always cautious. It's their job. *They* will want to be sure this Xeelee does no harm, at least.'

'They'll destroy it.'

'If they have to. If they *can*. There are going to be splits. Factions battling over differences of opinion.'

'My father will want more than that. To be the new Michael Bazalget, getting rich on gifts from the future – that will be his dream. He would destroy the Xeelee *and* steal its technology, if he could.'

'But again, he's going to need you to achieve that, Michael. If he's going to franchise the alien.' She laughed, unexpectedly. 'I'm sorry. It's hard to take it all seriously. I guess I'm a shallow person.'

'No. Keep laughing. I might stay sane that way. So I know what my parents want, what the government wants – but none of them is seeing the whole picture. They're all stuck inside their own prejudices and ambitions.'

'Right. And the question is, what do *you* want?'

He just looked at her.

'Remember what I said, Michael. I can understand you being crushed by all this. But you're free to act, no matter what's written about you, in the past or the future. *This is the present*, and you control it.'

'Yes. Yes, you're right. So we look for another option.' He chewed a nail. 'There's Miriam, in Gallia Three. With Highsmith Marsden. A mad genius, surrounded by hundreds of our own super-smart people from our Jupiter projects. And nobody knows they're there, because of Marsden's paranoia.'

'And hopefully not the Xeelee.'

'Right. That's one channel to explore. I'll get what I can from the archive through my mother, and whatever data the various agencies have been collecting on the Xeelee since it got here. Plus whatever else my mother can dig out of that Lethe-spawned amulet. Let's give it all to Marsden and see if he can come up with options.'

'Fine. In the meantime, what about us? Before they lock you up in some vault and start studying *you*—'

'I need to get out of here and *do* something. To act, not talk about acting.' He looked at her. 'Jack Grantt, on Mars. You said he's assembling a mission to the Cache.'

'So I did.' Nicola grinned. 'You think he needs a pilot?'

23

In the months that followed, the Cache was cautiously and discreetly tracked as it continued to follow that lazy spiral outward, a twisting groove cut through the plane of the ecliptic, the plane of the planets' orbits. Its motion was obviously under motive power, but the nature of that power remained a mystery.

Eventually, though, it became clear that the Cache was adjusting its trajectory.

Mars, fourth planet out, had always seemed the next obvious target, once it had passed Earth. But now the Cache was slowing, and it did indeed appear to be preparing to settle in near-Martian space – perhaps at one of the Lagrange points, most people guessed, stations of stability in the combined gravitational fields of Mars and Sun.

As Nicola had told Poole, Jack Grantt had long been leading a campaign in the Martian science institutes to mount a mission from Mars to the Cache as it passed. If it was going to wait around near Mars, at such a location, that opportunity was only more welcoming.

And as Nicola had suggested, she had campaigned for Grantt to make room for Poole and herself on the jaunt. Not that Grantt had taken much persuading. It was clear enough to him, as to everybody else who was following the story, that Michael Poole was somehow central to the whole mystery. Who else would you want in your crew?

But, slow as it was moving, the Cache wouldn't reach Martian space for the best part of another year. And that, Poole told Miriam, had determined for him where he was going to wait out that year. 'At least I'll get to see Mons Olympus again. *And* I can get out of sight of my screwed-up family . . .'

24

You couldn't just land on Mars.

Nicola complained loudly as she brought the *Hermit Crab* into a dry dock, one of an extensive cluster surrounding Mars's moon Phobos. 'You have to *park*? What is this, New York?'

Poole grinned. 'Well, Mars is Mars.' He glanced out of the *Crab*'s lifedome, beyond the dusty limb of Phobos, at the surface of the planet. Below it was evening, and domes and arcologies shone blue and green against the Martian red. 'Ten million people down there now. It's taken us fifteen hundred years to get this far – but that's about as many humans as were alive on Earth when they invented agriculture, and everything took off. Maybe that's an omen for the future.'

'Let's hope your Xeelee pal agrees,' Nicola said. 'And if you're done quoting tourist brochures at me you can help me with the docking protocols . . .'

Then, even from Phobos, you couldn't just hop in a flitter and land where you liked. They had to take a scheduled shuttle to Nerio, the Martian space elevator, named for a mythological consort of the war god.

Nerio's anchor Node was permanently positioned over the Tharsis uplands, and specifically over Olympus Mons, one of the great shield volcanoes and the tallest of all. Olympus was inconveniently offset from the equator, the ideal location for an elevator – but Poole knew that the mountain was so high its summit poked out of most of the air, and the elevator cable thus avoided the hazard of dust storms. And with this location the elevator cable also avoided the two moons, Phobos and Deimos, which both orbited the planet *below* the altitude of the space anchor.

From Nerio, anyhow, they had a great view of Mars. But their descent down the tether from space took days.

The beginning was bad enough. The tether climber, fitted out like a small mobile hotel, was cramped and homely and crowded, at least compared to its more expansive counterparts on the Earth cables. Then on the third day somebody recognised Poole, and tried to pump him about wormholes, about the alien intruders that had been all over the news, about a job. After that Poole hid away in his cabin.

Nicola spent a lot of time in the bars.

She emerged only when the descent drew to a close. Poole suspected the heavy use of antitoxin medications. And she studiously avoided the company of a couple of the male passengers, and one female. Poole didn't ask.

From the summit of Olympus they took a short ride aboard a bus, a pressure-cabin blister on big balloon tyres, down the volcano's shallow slope. Then, joining other traffic, they followed a road of what looked like toughened glass, burned into the desert, to Kahra, political capital of the quasi-independent UN region that was Mars.

Kahra had been one of the earliest off-Earth settlements established in the brief late-Bottleneck wave of resumed spaceflight. The proximity to Tharsis was no accident. Kahra's founders had had the foresight to recognise that the space elevator must come here some day, and so here was where they would build their town. More than a thousand years later traces of that first settlement effort were still preserved: small prefabricated domes within a sprawling, glassed-over heritage area, at the heart of a city of towers of Martian glass.

Jack Grantt himself was unavailable, out on an intensive field expedition in the Vastitas Borealis, the great dry ocean bed that dominated much of Mars's northern hemisphere. Nicola and Poole had time on their hands. And Kahra, for all its historic significance, was a small town by Earth standards, and didn't have much of a nightlife.

So, by the second week, Nicola had them booked on what was optimistically billed as a 'safari': a guided tour of the Valles Marineris.

Most of what Poole knew about Marineris came out of comic books. In the backstory of his favourite childhood superhero, the Mariner from Mars, the Valles had been created when the alien ship carrying the Mariner had skidded across the hemisphere. But Marineris itself, a system of valleys that ran east of Tharsis and Kahra, was a great flaw comparable in length to the radius of the planet. Though it was essentially geological rifting that had shaped this great feature, water and ice had once flowed here, and it was the promise of the terraforming lobby that someday the cold rivers would flow once more.

The tour itself was a mixed pleasure. Six people were shared out over three rovers which crawled along the canyon, the planned duration being twenty days. In the beginning they passed through spectacular country, a maze of canyons called the Labyrinth of Night. Further down, though, the canyon system was so vast that it was draped over the curvature of the planet itself; you could see either one wall or the other, and sometimes neither. It was a classic complaint of sightseers on Mars that many of its great features were simply too vast to be seen from the ground.

In the end the stops turned out to be more fun. Their walks in skin-suits outside the rovers were called EVAs, a very old acronym that referred back to the days when the only humans on Mars were astronauts from Earth. Poole enjoyed the sense of freedom the EVAs gave him. He would walk away from the rest as far as the safety rules let him, and run, jump and swing his arms. Night walks were spectacular too (as long as you avoided the dust storms), with the brilliance of Jupiter and of the twin planets Earth and Moon dominating the sky. It made up for the shrunken Sun of the daytime, Poole thought.

He said to Nicola, 'I've travelled the Solar System from the heart of the Sun to Jupiter and beyond. But I've spent almost all my time in space cooped up in a box, breathing in somebody else's recycled farts.'

'Mostly mine, recently.'

'If you want room to run around and swing your arms you're always going to need a planet.'

'True. And let's hope we still have planets available to do that when this is all over.'

At the Marineris terminus station, Nicola, on impulse, decided she'd like to go on to visit Hellas Planitia. Out here in tourist country the best way to get there was to fly, by airship.

From the eastern end of Marineris to the western flank of that great crater was a mere thousand kilometres or so. Nicola complained most of the way, however. In Mars's tenuous atmosphere the ship's lift bag, full of heated carbon dioxide air, had to be enormous to heft a decent load, and it overwhelmed the small gondola slung at its belly. 'I feel like I'm swimming under a whale. Can't see the sky at all. And they ought to ban *any* flying vessel that can't do a barrel-roll . . .'

Hellas contained the lowest point on Mars – where stood a human colony called Lockyerville – and, it was claimed, some of the modern planet's highest architectural achievements. Even as the airship crossed immense ranges of rim mountains, Poole could make out the glimmer of a glass roof, kilometres high, a blister pushing in from the crater's rim. This was the Hellas arcology.

The spectacle inside the arcology, once they had landed and debarked, was astonishing too. Unsuited, with Nicola at his side, Poole walked forward over a floor of roughened glass broken by lawns and flower beds, while ahead of him slim towers supported a gleaming roof, three kilometres high. Poole was becoming used by now to Mars's great natural features being too large to comprehend from the ground. So was the Hellas arcology, the difference being that this was human-built – and not more than a tenth finished.

Feeling overwhelmed, he concentrated on the nearest tower. Perhaps half a kilometre broad at the base, glittering with glass, it narrowed as it rose, its four sides converging – it was like the ancient Eiffel Tower, perhaps, he thought, blown up to a vast height and coated with glass. Looking up, he saw another such monster standing tall perhaps a couple of kilometres further away, and another, to the right of that – and still another to the left, and more in the mistier air beyond. He could see that some of the lower levels of the towers were inhabited: internal lights glittered, and he glimpsed people moving to and fro. All across Mars stood such buildings, cousins of the great Towers that now served as home for much of Earth's population, hardened for the environment of Mars.

But for these huge structures habitation was only a secondary purpose. Set out in a neat hexagonal array, the towers supported that roof of tremendous panes of Martian glass, kilometres above the ground. For now the scheme covered only about a tenth of Hellas's vast circle, but Poole knew that the ultimate goal was to bring the whole of the planitia under one vast ceiling. And the Martians planned ultimately to go much further: to spread this single structure right around the lower-latitude regions of the planet, sheets of glass crossing mountain ranges on ledges and platforms. The vision was as much about economics as engineering; with such a structure the Martians could make much of their planet habitable for humans at only a fraction the cost, in terms of the imported atmosphere needed, of full terraforming.

'You're standing on the flowers,' Nicola said.

He looked down at her, dazed by scale. 'What flowers?'

She pointed at his feet.

They had been walking on a lawn of green grass, and he had indeed strayed into a bed of flowers – pretty and yellow, he thought they were celandines. He stepped back hastily. Now, when he glanced around, he realised there was more vegetation: trees, larches, firs, pines, even what looked like young redwoods. A high-latitude biota on Earth, he recognised, and so preadapted to cold Mars with its weak sunlight. He knew that in the very early days of colonisation biota from Australia had adapted comparatively well to Mars: life from a similarly depleted landscape, an ancient arid continent from whose soil most of the nutrients and minerals had long since washed away. He imagined there would be surviving samples in terraria, somewhere under this vast roof.

Meanwhile, celandines.

Unexpectedly, Nicola laughed. 'Flowers,' she said. 'Growing in the open, on Mars. Kind of.'

On impulse, he took hold of her hand. Generally they didn't do physical stuff. 'Come on,' he said. 'Let's go to a party.' And he dragged her away.

As it happened, a party wasn't hard to find. This was the Martian southern hemisphere, and it was autumn at Hellas: time for the return of the polar migrants.

It turned out that thousands of settlers, living in great mobile habitats, spent each southern summer at the fringe of the south pole, where water ice was exposed at the surface. Here they focused the low sunlight to melt the ice, and planted their crops under collapsible plastic greenhouses – all the while, Poole learned, taking care not to harm the fragile native life that huddled in liquid-water droplets just under the ice's sunlit surface.

But in the Martian winter it got so cold that at the pole the very atmosphere froze out, and there was nine months of total darkness. And so, every Martian year (twice as long as an Earth year), the migrants packed up and rolled a few thousand kilometres north to Hellas, to see out the season.

This had been going on for centuries.

It had taken a lot less time than that for the return of the wanderers to become the excuse for a bout of partying that, Poole decided after the first couple of days, strove to emulate the scale of Hellas itself.

It was a relief, for Poole at least, when Jack Grantt called on the third day, and said he was ready to discuss their jaunt to the Cache.

25

There was no easy way to get by scheduled transport from Hellas to Cydonia, in the northern hemisphere, where Grantt had his base. So Poole used family money to hire another airship, big enough for a dozen passengers, inside which the two of them rattled around for the three days' journey.

From the air the giant Cydonia dome, largest on Mars, was a splash of Earth green-blue in the red desert – but it would have been dwarfed by Hellas. 'If the arcology ever gets finished they're going to lose the tourist market here,' he said glumly as they descended.

'You say that,' Nicola replied, at the controls. 'Look over *there*.'

To the north-east, Poole saw, checking a smart map, was a plain called Acidalia Planitia, one of Mars's classic desert locations – and the place where, so he claimed, Jack Grantt had discovered a unique form of native life. Craters and dunes and sandy waste, like much of Mars.

But right now it looked like a small war was going on.

Through a magnifying window Poole made out camps of stout-looking domes, walls and fortifications, and pressurised vehicles and warriors in mechanised suits tearing at each other across the dunes. Aeroplanes shot through the thin air, wispy Martian craft that looked like they were made of bamboo and paper. All of this was obscured by billowing dust.

'Looks like fun,' Poole said doubtfully.

Nicola snorted. 'None of it is real. Or hardly any of it.' She pointed to a softscreen display which showed local energy usage. The Cydonia dome glowed bright in false colours; on the 'battlefield' there were only a few scattered lights. The 'war' was Virtual, a brilliant sham.

They descended on a private airfield a few kilometres out from the dome, alongside a cluster of more basic, older buildings, made of Martian brick and grounded-spaceship hull sections, which Poole surmised was Grantt's biology lab. Jack Grantt himself came out to greet them: 'Welcome to Cydonia!' Grantt, a burly Earthborn, looked clumsy and a little impatient in Mars's slow-motion gravity, as if he'd never properly adapted. And his skinsuit was extensively patched: a much-loved relic of a lifetime of fieldwork, Poole guessed.

Nicola asked about the war next door.

'Of course it's not real. Virtual tourists . . .'

He led them indoors to show them. The living area was cluttered, the walls covered by softscreens, the tables and chairs heaped with grimy clothes or bits of equipment – though big windows offered glimpses of a sealed-off lab area that looked sterilised and pristine.

Grantt swept a surface clear of junk, found a particular screen, and poked around until he got an aerial image. 'We run drones to keep an eye on things.' He showed them a diorama of the battle they'd glimpsed from the airship. 'I guess that's what you saw. *This* is the reality.' He tapped an icon, and most of the battle scene evaporated – the vehicles, the warriors, even most of the thrown-up dust. Only a handful of scattered figures were left behind, running or crawling in the dirt. 'Gaming, see? Mars has a lot of desert, and sadly there are only so many earthworms who want to spend their money on exploring rock and dust and sunsets. They go shopping in the arcologies, and gawp at the Age-of-Heroes space probes, but as for the landscape . . . Well, some bright spark saw its potential as an empty canvas. So we mount fantasy games and historical re-enactments.

'You can see we get a few players who want to come out in person, although that limits the experience: in a skinsuit we can't yet simulate Earth gravity. But most are projections, from Cydonia, or Kahra, or Hellas – even from orbit, though the time lag gets tricky.

'So there you have it: humans battling space aliens on Mars, most of them entirely unaware that under their feet, a few hundred metres down, you've got the real thing. Alien life. Actually I'm happy for this crap to be going on, so long as the visitors stick to the rules. If those grockles did any real damage, Lethe, I'd be on Earth slapping samples of my Lattice down on the desks of the UN Oversight committees so hard—'

'Lattice?' Nicola asked. 'Oh. Mars life.'

'I mean, you wouldn't believe the proposals I've had to fend off, particularly hydrological, for aquifer mining, and running canals from the polar cap—'

'And now,' Poole said quickly, sensing Grantt, always a garrulous man, was these days spending too much time alone, 'you've made a proposal of your own. For a mission to the Cache.'

'Yes! Look, you're in good time. I'm just waiting for final confirmation that the Cache is indeed heading for the Lagrange point – L5, to be precise. I've had a lot of support from the government, actually – I mean the Martian regional council – they're always keen to back projects that add prestige to the planet.'

'You mean,' Nicola said, and Poole knew her well enough now to see she was being mischievous, 'projects like your investigation of the Lattice.'

'Yes! You want to go see? Don't take off your skinsuits . . .'

After that he couldn't be stopped. He sealed up his own suit and led them back out into the desert, ignoring the space-opera battle flaring in the distance.

Still, it was a wonderful story he had to tell.

It had begun with life, not unlike terrestrial life – probably it was related, connected by migrant bugs spread between the worlds by meteorite impacts – life which had flourished in the briny seas of young Mars.

Not unlike Earth life, but differing in crucial details, specifically in its biochemistry.

On Earth as on Mars, primitive life had once used variants of the giant molecule RNA both to transmit its genetic information and to build the structural components of living things. That starting point was thought to be commonplace, Grantt said; a warm soup of RNA was a product of relatively simple chemistry, and likely to show up on any world stocked with carbon, nitrogen, hydrogen, oxygen. On Earth that primitive system had evolved, eventually, to use proteins as the building blocks, and DNA for genetic transfer, with RNA only peripherally involved. Mars life – under pressure almost immediately from a collapsing climate, as the planet, too small, too remote from the Sun, began to freeze over – had been forced to adapt more quickly, and instead had evolved a highly efficient variant of the primal RNA system.

'Then, physically, as Mars cooled and dried and the surface became uninhabitable, life followed the water as it receded to the aquifers underground, or froze at the polar caps. Oh, some traces of it live as life on Earth does – clinging to salt deposits, or scraps of liquid water under the ice crust, and *that* is what the Age-of-Heroes explorers concentrated on looking for. And they found it: like vast stromatolites, bug colonies the size of small nations, just under the surface dust. But to focus on that alone – treating Mars as if it was another Antarctica, a marginal environment on Earth, while missing the bigger picture entirely – talk about a category error!

'Look – on Mars there are huge seasonal transports of mass and energy, as all the dust in the world gets blown around every year, and, more significantly, the very air snows out at the winter pole. Well, life follows the energy flows, on Mars as on Earth – the great snows, even the tides in the deep aquifers – life, microbial life, on a grand scale, powered by planetary cycles. And *organised* on a planetary scale too.'

'Which,' Poole prompted, 'is where your Lattice comes in.'

'Exactly.' He led them to a kind of terrarium, a deep ditch under a porous dome. He clambered clumsily down into the ditch, cleared away maybe half a metre of loose dirt with his gloved hands, and showed them what looked like cables, embedded in the ground, worm-pale, heavily interconnected.

'I brought this sample up for test purposes. And for funding reviews. Go down a hundred metres or more, anywhere on the planet away from the poles, and you'll find *this*. A network, a kind of natural planetary network, that I call the Lattice. Biological, of course, self-repairing, unimaginably ancient – and connected through the wider microbial ecology to the planetary energy flows.

'*This* is life on Mars. Maybe even intelligence; it's complex enough. Or so I argue. But I'm horribly under-funded. I can't yet be sure.

'Look, all the way up to World Senate level we have a commitment to preserve all the life we encounter, in all its forms, wherever we go. But, naturally, familiar forms attract the most attention, and the money. I mean, if there were silicon-based kangaroos bounding around out there I could open a theme park. The Lattice is too . . . strange.

'It doesn't fit any of our earthly categories of life. It's most like a biofilm, perhaps, but not. And its actions are widespread, but they're subtle – even as it participates in the great cycles of air and dust and water, it manipulates its environment on microscales, trapping vented gases here, releasing water there. I'm pretty sure there's a global communication network working down here, and not restricted to chemical signals either. It may even be electromagnetic, borne through strata of iron-bearing minerals. Of which, as you can tell from the global rust, there are a lot on Mars.

'But it's all too strange for people to perceive, to accept.' He looked restless, agitated. 'You see, if I had *one other* example of extraterrestrial life in such straitened circumstances, surviving and co-operating on a global scale to deliver a sustainable environment, it would help my case regarding the Lattice. A lot.

'And it's possible we already lost another example of this kind of life strategy, in the Solar System. *Venus*. Life kicked off there when the Solar System was young, but Venus got too hot, rather than cold like Mars. A remnant biosphere survived, bugs floating in the acid clouds fifty kilometres up, where the conditions were temperate, almost Earth-like. And they participated in more planetary cycles. They somehow created storm systems, for instance, that threw up mineral-rich dust from the ground. Or so it's thought. Then, back in the twenty-seventh century, along came one of your ancestors, Michael.'

Poole frowned. 'I know there's a statue of Jocelyn Lang Poole—'

'On Maat Mons, yes. A highland. Except it's not strictly a statue . . . You should go see it some time. Jocelyn promoted the great atmospheric freeze-out, built a sunshield to achieve it. A kind of clumsy terraforming. Well, her "Sunset Day" in 2657 turned Venus into a huge carbon mine, but—'

'But it killed off your acid-eating bugs,' Poole said.

'And the planetary cycles were destroyed before they were properly understood.'

Nicola asked, 'And you really think it's smart? Your Lattice? Like a planetary mind?'

Grantt winked at her. 'A single great neural network? Each day like a single thought, a cycle of summer and winter like a heartbeat? Communicating with other living worlds, maybe, with radio waves – even gravity waves? Every non-scientist I bring here asks that. Every scientist I bring is sceptical. I have to keep an open mind; I'm a scientist myself. I hope someday to prove it. Or even disprove it.'

If you have time, Poole thought sadly. *Because now, strangeness is on the way.*

A comms patch on Grantt's suit lit up. A message from Kahra. They had confirmation: permission to fly to the Cache.

They got drunk. They slept it off.

Then they got down to planning the mission.

FOUR

'Look at it this way. I still cut my lawn. Now, my evolutionary divergence from the grass is, what, half a billion years deep, more? And yet we communicate . . . It asks me if I want it to grow over five centimetres, or start colonising the verges. It tells me this by actually doing it, you see. I say no, with my mower and my strimmer. So we communicate – not in symbols, but with the primal elements of all life forms, space to grow, food, life, death.'

'And you think it might be that way with intelligent aliens?'

'If there is no possibility of symbolic communication, maybe. But if they have the capability to reach us then they will be the ones with the lawnmower.'

George Poole and Michael Poole Bazalget, AD 2047

26

The ship Jack Grantt acquired to take his small exploration party to the Cache – himself, Michael Poole, Nicola Emry – was called the *Bellona*.

It was a Poole Industries design, a matchstick with GUTdrive and asteroid-ice reaction mass at the business end, a compact lifedome at the other. But *Bellona* was wholly owned by the Martian regional government, and had been heavily modified from the standard commercial configuration. Poole promised himself a look around when he got the chance.

Still, it was a GUTship, with the usual performance capabilities – and that dictated the mission profile.

The Cache had finally settled into place at Mars's L5 Lagrange point, a location in Mars's orbit that trailed the planet itself by sixty degrees, so that Sun, Mars and Cache were the corners of a neat equilateral triangle. Unlike the position of Larunda at Mercury's L2 point, the Sun and Mars created a kind of minimum here in their combined gravitational field, so that an object sited here tended to stick around, as if resting at the bottom of a shallow well. Indeed the L5 point, like its twin ahead of Mars, L4, was already cluttered with natural debris that had gathered since the formation of the Solar System. Well, Poole thought, now that junk had been enhanced by something that was not natural, and certainly, it seemed, not mere debris.

Given the geometry, the distance from Mars to L5 was the same as Mars's orbital distance from the Sun – about half as much again as Earth's – a distance that any GUTship could travel, under full one-gravity thrust, in less than four days. Once they left Phobos, however, acting under strict orders from the Martian authorities, the *Bellona* proceeded cautiously, taking more than twice that long. The point was to avoid looking like a missile aimed at the Cache. In addition, as they approached, the ship bathed the Cache in friendly messages, using every medium anyone could think of from visible light through to neutrino beams and gravity-wave pulses.

Meanwhile, during this slow cruise. they were accompanied by a small armada: more Martian ships, a few UN vessels flown out from Earth, a swarm of uncrewed monitor probes, all operating under similar restrictions.

Nicola the pilot chafed at the pace of the operation, and Poole felt uncomfortable under the scrutiny of their escort. But at least the low thrust, only a little in excess of one-fifth gravity, didn't put any pressure on Grantt's Mars-adapted physiology.

And, while Grantt was distracted by preparing for what might turn out to be the scientific mission of his life, the slow pace gave Poole a chance to snoop around the Martian craft.

Poole scoured the lifedome, noting an unusual clutter of internal partitions. He descended along the ship's spine, which was the usual skeletal assemblage of struts, cabling and antennae. He even put on a radiation-hardened skinsuit to go take a look around the GUTdrive compartment. He found an emblem affixed to the GUTengine hull itself, a female warrior on a chariot dragged behind four snorting horses.

'That's Bellona,' Nicola told him when she and Poole compared notes. 'Sister of Mars, and a warrior herself.'

'Hmm. The ship's pretty much a standard design,' Poole said.

'With extras,' Nicola said pointedly.

'With extras. Such as a *lot* of compartmentalisation of the lifedome. You could shoot a lot of holes in that bubble and still have the crew survive decompression. I haven't noticed anything that *looks* like a dedicated weapon . . . However,' he said heavily, 'the GUTdrive thrust nozzles seem unusually manoeuvrable. I mean it's a standard-capability engine, even though we're throttled down to this walking pace. But if you can direct the exhaust out of those nozzles—'

'You have a flamethrower to take out any moths that fly too close.' She was whispering, though Poole had a feeling that anything they said aboard this ship could be heard by Grantt, if he paid attention, if not by other agencies. 'So here we are, approaching an alien visitor with polite caution, firing off friendly messages, in a covertly weaponised ship. Some would say it's a sensible precaution . . .'

'And some,' Poole said, 'like my mother, would say it's a provocation. When we ought to be showing a peaceful intent, at least.'

'Well, whatever the rights and wrongs of that, there's another mystery here. Look, you're the engineer. Do you think it's possible that this ship could have been designed and built with all these customisations *since* the Xeelee and its entourage showed up in the Solar System? Don't answer. I looked it up; Poole Industries keeps records too. In fact ships of this class have been coming out of the Phobos yards for years now.'

'How did you—? Never mind.'

'Now why, do you think, has the peace-loving Martian government been building warships, for years?'

Poole rubbed his nose. 'I don't follow politics much.'

She grunted. 'That's typical. Harry says the Martians are restless. I know there are factions agitating for independence. They want to be able to press ahead with their terraforming initiatives, for instance, without having to argue against what they see as Earth's lingering post-Bottleneck psychological problems about geoengineering. Mars, with ten million people already and growing fast, with its own ship-yards, and envious eyes looking out to Titan and other resources – it will be a long time before Earth is happy to let *that* fledgling leave the nest. And so here are the Martians quietly preparing for a day when negotiations with Earth might heat up a little.'

'A war for independence? Well – maybe that shows how seriously the Martians are taking the Xeelee issue, that they'd risk tipping their hand to Earth over this covert armament.'

'Maybe so. The Cache is in their back yard, their Lagrange point. Mars is the front line – for now.' She grinned. 'I know there are uto-pian types – like your mother, no offence – who like to think humanity has grown up, that we have put behind us war and religion and such. Yet the first time somebody pokes our own particular ant nest with a stick, we come swarming out, armed to the teeth. Gladdens your heart. *Bellona*, goddess of war.'

'Yes,' Poole said sourly. 'And like Harry says, you're Loki, the trickster.'

'Wrong mythology.'

'Whatever. Come on, let's get back to Grantt, we don't want him getting more suspicious of us than he already is . . .'

And while the days of the journey went by, as they explored and speculated and schemed, the Cache grew in their field of view, from a grain of light, like a single pixel blinking in a faulty screen, to a discernible solid form.

To an artefact.

27

They came down on the Cache from above the ecliptic, the plane of Mars's orbit.

The Cache itself was an enormous box, tipped towards them.

From a distance it looked featureless, Poole thought, pale grey-white, shining softly as if from some inner power source. But telescopic images proved that its surface in fact bore slight imperfections. There were splashes of debris from random collisions with natural objects, the dust and rocks and asteroid fragments with which the Solar System was littered: impacts which had left behind rubble, but seemed not to have harmed the Cache itself. And there were those *dimples*: some kind of intrinsic marking, it seemed, scar-like discolorations, roughly circular, perhaps a hundred metres wide, one on each of the six faces. A new feature since the Cache's emergence from the Sun.

All this was surrounded by a loose cloud of sparks in the night: ships and drones from Earth, Mars and elsewhere, some of which had accompanied this thing from the Sun. None approached close.

Soon the *Bellona* had passed through the horde of monitors, and drew closer than any other crewed vessel so far.

And as they approached, the Cache grew until it filled the frame of the lifedome viewing windows, and then further, until its edges were lost beyond the perimeter of Poole's field of view, and the upper surface opened out like a landscape.

When they had still been far out, Poole didn't seem to have found it difficult to accept all this. He was used to big artefacts in space, after all; he had grown up among them; he had built his own two-hundred-metres-wide tetrahedral wormhole portals in the Jovian system. But this giant spanned a thousand kilometres, larger than some moons, and now it was so close it was too big even to see properly. It presented a clash of categories – the huge scale of natural objects overlapping with the engineered precision of artifice – that disturbed him on some deep level.

Nicola said, 'We're being nagged for comments. Lots of public interest in you, Michael.'

'What in Lethe am I supposed to say?'

Grantt murmured, 'Just tell them what you see.'

'Well – it's kept the same shape. Ever since the Xeelee dug it up out of Mercury . . .' *The Xeelee*: they had shared that enigmatic family-archive name with Grantt days ago; Poole was confident any such lapses would be filtered out before his message was shared more widely. 'It's still a cube.'

'Precise to the limits of our measurements, yes.' Grantt checked a record. 'We can't see through that hull. Even neutrino probes don't work. But we do have some data on the internal mass distribution from the deflection of flyby probes. Although the overall mass hasn't increased significantly since it left the Sun, the internal structure has changed. You have an outer shell, very thin, of the sun-catcher material they're calling hull plate. Inside the box appears to be some kind of gas, with a big dense mass at the centre – an object the size of a respectable asteroid. And other objects moving around in there, in swarms. There's speculation that they are like the objects that tailed the Xeelee out of your wormhole, Michael, what you called raindrops. A lot more of them, though. Meanwhile, from a pilot's point of view, those are nice flat surfaces to land on.'

Poole was startled. 'Land on?'

Nicola looked electrified, as Poole might have predicted. But she recovered quickly. 'At last, we learn about the mission plan. So secretive, you Martians.'

Poole shot her a warning glance.

Grantt nodded. 'It's the logical next step. And the mission designers have prepared. We won't take the *Bellona* down, obviously. We have flitters. Hopefully the artefact's gravity will be enough to hold on to a landed ship, and we have adhesive pads that might work on that surface. The labs in Kahra produced prototypes.'

Nicola smiled. 'Or if the worst came to the worst, I guess we could use thrusters to hold us down. Just a gentle, continuous firing downwards.'

Grantt turned in his couch and faced her. 'Hold *us* down, Nicola. Me and Michael. Not you.'

'What are you talking about?'

'About mission rules. Set out by the Kahra government. Look, you lived on Mars for months; you *know* our culture is shaped by adaptation to a basically lethal environment. We take our safety rules seriously. And as commander of the mission and representative of the government that sponsored it—'

Nicola's expression was blade-hard. 'You're leaving me behind.'

Grantt continued calmly, 'Two land. One stays in the *Bellona*, at a safe distance, maintaining the integrity of the mother ship, ensuring comms links between the landing party and the monitoring fleet and Kahra, and providing abort options. Basic protocol. It's an essential part of team operations in a situation like this.'

Nicola, angry, disappointed, snapped back, 'To Lethe with the team. Why me? I'm younger than you, and smarter than *him*. And I'm more disposable.'

That forced a laugh from Grantt. 'I admire your honesty. But it was made plain to me before we launched that Michael and I would be the landing party. Michael because, well, he's Michael Poole.' He looked at Poole quizzically. 'I haven't been briefed on it all. Interplanetary politics, even family friendships, don't yet allow *that*. But all of mankind knows you're somehow central to all this, Michael.'

'I wish I wasn't,' Poole said.

'Liar,' Nicola muttered.

'And me because I represent Mars. They gave me flags to take down.'

She sounded disgusted. 'You're like some tin-pot Anthropocene hero.'

Grant grinned, almost shyly. 'Childhood dreams.'

Poole asked, 'And why didn't you share this plan with us before?'

'What, and jeopardise our carefully wrought team harmony? She'd have thrown me off the ship. Or you. Now, do we have a problem with this? Shall we abort? Because, incidentally, the same rules forbid me going down there alone, in case my crew mutinies.'

Poole touched Nicola's arm. 'Look, whatever the outcome today, I don't think this is the end of the drama. You'll get your chance.'

A moment of silence between the three of them, while the Cache loomed ever closer, a plain of light spreading further – and with some detail visible to the naked eye now, Poole saw: a pale lake of discoloration, a scattering of sparkling ice, or dirt.

Grudgingly Nicola said, 'You have a point. Let's do this.'

28

So Poole, for once, took the left-hand pilot's seat. Without further comment, for sake of disturbing the crew's uneasy truce, Grantt strapped in to his right.

The flitter was attached to brackets under the lifedome. Looking up through big blister windows Poole could see the lifedome's base, a flat surface studded with cabling, sensors, ducts. To his right the ship's spine, a complex pillar of engineering.

And below him a shining plain. It was no longer possible to think of the Cache as an artefact. It was as if he was suspended over some calm sea into which he was about to plunge. He looked away and got on with his work.

With the grudging co-operation of Nicola, stranded up in the lifedome, Poole ran through system checks. If the *Bellona* was a covert warship, Poole saw no signs of weaponisation about the flitter. In fact there seemed to have been additional safety features incorporated into the flitter's standard systems.

He remarked on this to Grantt. 'I know we mustn't look hostile, and I guess we don't want the thing accidentally blowing up, in these circumstances. But I'm afraid that if I sneeze the main drive will shut down.'

Grantt laughed. 'Then don't sneeze.' Going through his own check-list of backup checks, he sounded uneasy, even tense. Poole saw through the man's faceplate that he was sweating heavily.

Poole tongued a switch and spoke privately to Nicola. 'Jack's kind of on edge.'

'*I* wouldn't have been.'

'Too late for that. You think I should say something to calm him down?'

She laughed softly. 'Michael, you may have the Poole genius genes from your mother, but you've got your father's tact. Keep it zipped. Ready for launch, by the way. In five, four, three . . .'

*

The descent seemed agonisingly slow.

That near-featureless surface expanded below him, the distance to its milky uniformity continually fooling Poole's eye. But the instruments worked; whatever this Cache was made of, it was material, and returned echoes to sensors ranging from radar to neutrino pulses.

'One kilometre up,' Grantt called. 'Nine hundred metres. Eight. Is this helping?'

'Keeps me awake as the flitter flies itself down.'

'I suppose you're used to this. The cautious pace of big engineering projects in space, huge masses drifting in close proximity. Six hundred. But, don't you feel self-conscious? You get the sense that everybody who's awake in the System is following us. I guess you're used to that too.'

Poole shrugged. 'Not so much. I mean, not before the Xeelee incursion. Unless we do something spectacular – like the first time my father and I flew through a test wormhole – most of our scrutiny is from the specialist technical press, or from our investors, or the various Oversight boards.'

'But you're a Poole. You were a famous baby.'

Poole winced. 'My father shielded me from *that*, at least.'

'Coming down nice and easy. Four hundred.'

'You're right, though,' Poole said. 'A routine docking wouldn't be taken much faster. Of course this isn't a regular docking.'

'Three hundred. *Bellona*, you know, has anti-impact safeguards. Some kind of laser shield to destroy any interplanetary debris in its way. Two hundred. I wonder if the Cache has similar defences.'

'Well, there's already debris down there, on the surface. It doesn't seem to care about minor impacts. I don't know what would happen if we threw Ceres at it—'

'One hundred. Nice and easy.'

'But evidently smaller objects are no threat. And we're moving slower than any space rock. We've done all we can to appear harmless.' He touched a softscreen control. 'Slower still, now.'

Grantt shut up, at last.

The view expanded further, and the closer they got the more lost Poole felt. He found himself searching for detail, a scrap of that meteorite debris, anything, to give himself a visual anchor. But they'd deliberately picked out a clear area of the hull to approach, and now he was so close there was nothing to be seen, no detail. A descent into abstraction.

The landing was feather-light.

They just sat still, for five seconds, ten, allowing the systems to settle.

Then Poole glanced over at Grantt. 'OK. We rebounded slightly, from the give in the flitter's undercarriage. That surface is hard as basalt. Harder. And that one per cent gravity is holding us down, for now. Trying the adhesive clamps.' He touched a control.

The flitter shuddered softly.

Poole checked his instruments. 'Seems to be holding. The flitter's not going anywhere soon. Time for the footprints and flags, Jack.'

Grantt grinned. 'It's my home world we came from. You don't mind if I . . .'

Poole shrugged. 'Be my guest.'

They both crowded into the flitter's airlock. They closed up their suits, and, at Grantt's insistence, checked them over with a care Poole hadn't been subjected to since training school.

Then, at last, Poole slapped a control to open the hatch.

A milk-white plain.

The sun was low over a geometrically precise horizon, and the flitter's landing gear cast long shadows. The sky looked black to Poole's light-adapted eye, but he saw a bright spark that must be Mars, and others sliding across the dome of the sky: ships, points of fusion light or GUTdrive radiation glaring in the dark.

Trailing a safety umbilical attached to the flitter, and moving with care in the virtual absence of gravity, Grantt drifted down a couple of ladder rungs. And he set foot deliberately on the Cache's hull. 'A human footstep on an alien ship,' he said softly. 'Nothing like this has happened in our history. Let's hope this is the start of a peaceful and productive encounter.'

Nicola growled in Poole's ear. 'Should've been me.'

'Hush. He's talking to the Solar System. And his grandchildren.'

Grantt took one step, two, drifting up into the vacuum each time, falling back like a snowflake, trailing his umbilical. 'Nothing seems strange,' he reported. 'Or at least, unexpected. I can sense the gravity, just, a definite up-down sensation. The view is – stark. Testing my boots.' More adhesive grippers had been fixed to the soles of their boots; now Grantt tapped a control on his suit's right leg, and took more steps, one, two, out of the flitter's shadow and into the Sun's glare. 'Walking feels kind of sticky . . . OK, Michael, come on out.'

Poole slid out of the flitter's hatch easily, letting himself fall, checking his umbilical didn't snag. He took a few steps, joining Grantt. 'Sticky, yes. I trained with magnetic-grip boots once; it feels like that.'

Grantt opened a small compartment on the side of the flitter. He drew out two slim flagpoles that telescoped open, and two flags that he draped over fold-out bars. One flag was the ancient UN standard, pale blue, the laurel wreath cradling a schematic Earth, the other the defiant red of a canal-strewn Mars, symbol of ancient fantasies and future dreams.

Then, as they had hastily discussed in advance, Grantt and Poole stood side by side, checking they were in full view of the flitter's cameras. 'Here,' Grantt said softly, 'the children of two human worlds first set foot on a craft from beyond the stars. We came in peace for all mankind.' And, awkwardly, evidently self-consciously, he saluted the flags.

Poole, still more embarrassed, followed his lead.

Nicola chuckled in his ear. Poole ignored her.

With some relief, Grantt rubbed his gloved hands and turned to Poole. 'So that's over. Let's get on with it.'

The flitter's exterior cargo hold was packed with instruments: beacons, sensors both fixed and mobile. They quickly unloaded the gear.

As Grantt set up the science stuff around the flitter's landing site, Poole opened another hatch which, as Grantt had informed him on the way down, contained a surface vehicle. It was just a frame, a couple of bucket seats, a small GUTengine motor, and big balloon tyres fitted with the same kind of adhesive pads that had been applied to their boots and the ship's clamps. All this had evidently been adapted from lunar and Martian technology, centuries old and supremely robust. It was a trivial task for Poole to unfold the frame and set it up – indeed, the vehicle was smart enough to do most of it for itself.

Everything on the mission had backups, Poole realised, including, for the rover's passengers, a couple of jet packs. If they couldn't drive back to the flitter in this thing they could, cautiously, fly home . . . Or indeed the flitter, piloting autonomously or controlled by Nicola in the *Bellona*, could come and get them. And if all else failed, Nicola could fly down in the GUTship itself and make some kind of pick-up. Multiple abort options.

Grantt spoke as he worked, for the benefit of the watching overseers as much as Poole, or himself. 'We'll be leaving much of this gear in place when we depart. I doubt frankly that we'll learn much that we haven't already discovered from remote sensing, but in science you never know until you get in there and measure something . . .'

Poole was an engineer. A tinkerer. Half his mind, almost, was engaged in the pleasurable chore of checking out the surface rover. The other half, almost, listened to Grantt's distracting patter.

But that left a little of his mind to be distracted by the view.

Under low sunlight, he was standing on a plain, flat and all but featureless, that stretched far away. He was in vacuum, so there was no mist to give a sense of distance – and he knew that there was no curvature as on a planet, so no horizon. He was close to the centre of a vast square plate, a full thousand kilometres across – he was a flea on a vast packing case – and in theory he should be able to see all the way to the edges, even to the corners. Yet he could make out nothing of the edges. And the human clutter that they were spreading out around the flyer, bright in the sunlight, seemed a gross intrusion, out of place against this clean geometry . . .

Nothing but a plain, an abstraction, that cut the universe in two: above and below . . .

An infinity that drew his gaze . . .

A figure stood in front of him, a face dimly glimpsed behind a plate filtered for sunlight protection. 'You OK, buddy?'

For one second Poole didn't know who this was. 'Jack. Yes.'

'You weren't here for a moment.'

'I'm sorry. I— '

'Don't sweat it. We're talking through a direct link, OK? Nobody can hear, just us for now. It's the perspectives, right? It is kind of hypnotic.'

Poole was embarrassed. 'I'm supposed to be the space engineer.'

'This isn't anything you built, my friend. Or any human. No wonder it awes us. Maybe that engineer's imagination is more easily dazzled; you understand it better than I do. However, we have got work to do.' With one booted foot he kicked the tyre of the surface rover. 'This thing checked out?'

'Ready when you are.'

'You drive.'

Poole jumped into the left-hand seat and strapped in. He started the engine; he felt a hum, a subtle vibration.

'So, which way, Nicola?'

'You want to make straight for an edge?'

'Seems the simplest plan. Which edge? We're right at the centre of the face here, so equidistant—'

'The Sun's to your right, yes? Call that east. So head north. Neither into the Sun, nor away from it.'

Poole glanced at Grantt, who shrugged. 'North it is.'

Poole swept his hand over a softscreen control, and the rover surged forward.

29

For the first few minutes Poole gave the rover its head. He tried sharp turns and emergency stops, and ran the vehicle up to its advised limit, of a hundred kilometres an hour. The virtual absence of a downward gravity pull was confusing, but it was a little like driving on a low-gravity world like Earth's Moon, even Io. The ingenious adhesive wheels worked smoothly, so far as he could tell.

Just as the GUTship and indeed the flitter were both bright with messages of friendship for any Cache aliens, so, as they drove, was the rover, Grantt told him now.

Nicola had them stop after five kilometres. Here they adjusted their suits and bucket seats, checked over the rover, and took gravity readings. They even set up a manual plumb line on a three-legged stand. The downward direction of gravity here diverged from the vertical by half a degree: far too slight to notice, but easily measurable.

Nicola said, 'There's the proof that you really are driving around on a big box. The gravity field is complex, but the mass of the box itself is a fraction of that of the central object inside – whatever *that* is. And even that is extended. Still, to a first approximation gravity points to the centre of the box. And as you move away from the midpoint of a face, the gravity vector tilts away from the local vertical and back to that centre. From here on in it will be as if you are climbing an increasingly steep hill. But you'll barely notice the effort.'

Poole packed up the plumb line. 'So we move on. Next stop a hundred kilometres? If all goes well.'

'Actually,' Nicola said, 'take a slight diversion. A couple of degrees to your right. Something interesting for you to pick up on – a probe just spotted it. Don't worry, Jack; all this has been approved by your bosses in their nice safe domes on Mars.'

Grantt frowned as he strapped himself in. 'Another of those dimples?'

'Not that. Something that might have come out of one of those big holes, though . . .'

Poole and Grantt exchanged a glance. Without a word, Poole accelerated away.

It took an hour to reach the destination, eighty-eight kilometres from the flitter at the centre point. As they approached Poole saw a scatter of debris, what looked like pulverised rock dust – presumably the relic of the splash of a meteorite against the Cache's resilient hull plate. But, half-buried under the debris, there was something else. It looked like a scrap of silvered cloth.

They stopped a cautious distance away. Again they made a manual check of the local vertical: gravity was now ten degrees away from the floor's perpendicular. When Poole stood, he could feel it now, feel how the ground under his feet seemed to tip up before him.

Poole and Grantt approached the small debris field together. Cautiously, Poole knelt down, gazing at the skin. It looked like very fine reflective film.

'OK,' Nicola said. 'Good imaging. Let me tell you what the various boffins are making of this. Michael, remember the raindrops?'

'The silvered spheres that chased out of the wormhole after the sycamore seed – the Xeelee.'

'Yes. They went to Mercury with the Xeelee. Many of them seemed to have entered the Cache then, before it got to the Sun, and more of them have come and gone from inside there since then.'

'Hmm. Maybe via the dimples, the surface marks.'

'The only indication we have of any kind of entrance, yes. We don't know if these are the same critters as came from the wormhole or not, or if they are being created in there.'

'Or if they're breeding,' Grantt said softly. 'But then I'm a biologist. I would say that.'

Poole said, 'And what we're looking at now—'

'It seems that one of the raindrops got hit by a stray meteor fragment. Just dumb bad luck, caught as it crossed the surface. Its partners came out to collect the remains. But—'

'But it looks like they left a scrap of skin behind,' Grantt said. 'We know something about this stuff too, from remote studies. Same kind of material as the hull plate, same kind of self-growth capabilities in sunlight, same density, but finer. We've been calling it *membrane*.'

Poole frowned. 'I heard that hull plate is thinner than a soap bubble. Thinner than that?'

'A *lot* thinner. Think of a proton's width.'

Poole shook his head. 'I'm an engineer, not a physicist. What force could hold something like that together?'

Grantt just shrugged. 'Best guess is it's something like a Bose-Einstein condensate. That is, matter which displays quantum phenomena on a macro scale. The material equivalent of lased radiation. Although to get such behaviour you generally have to chill stuff down almost to absolute zero. Well, if we take a sample, we might find out.'

They moved forward together. Cautiously, with their gloved hands, they brushed away the meteor debris. The scrap of membrane exposed was small, no larger than a handkerchief, Poole thought.

Grantt took this in his hands, in the shade of his body. 'I don't feel anything,' he reported. 'No suit alarms ringing. I don't think I'm being harmed in any way.'

Nicola said, 'Get it stowed.'

'No. Wait.' Poole stared at the scrap. 'If this stuff has the same properties as the hull plate, if it can convert radiant energy into mass – if it grows in sunlight . . . The hull plate growth was pretty spectacular, remember. On the surface of the Sun, it doubled in area every couple of hours. Out here the Sun is more than two hundred million kilometres away. The radiant energy is a lot less. But this stuff is *much* finer than hull plate. So it might need much less sunlight to make it grow.'

'You're seriously suggesting I hold this stuff up in the light and see what happens?'

Poole grinned. 'We're here to explore. Try it.'

Nicola said, 'Listen, you've got my vote. But there's a yammering of protest in my ear. Michael, stand back – just in case.'

Poole went to stand on the far side of the rover.

When Grantt held up the scrap, the membrane grew, visibly, in his gloved hands, expanding, spilling out in the sunlight. It looked to Poole as if he was shaking it out, unfolding a sheet.

Later they estimated that, in Martian sunlight, a given area of membrane would double in size in just seconds. Light to mass, effortlessly. Poole the engineer thought this was utterly wonderful.

They packed up the membrane blanket in a light-sealed bag and drove on.

From then on they barrelled towards the edge in their rover, making a hundred kilometres in each hour, or a little more. Periodically they stopped to check their systems, to make local measurements.

At two hundred and fifty kilometres out from the flitter the ground felt as if it were tipped up at nearly thirty degrees. Looking ahead wasn't so bad, but looking back was like staring down a tremendous slope. The flitter, of course, was long since lost in the detail; save for the trail of their nanocarbon umbilicals the surface was unmarked.

There was intense debate now among those overseeing the mission, on the wisdom of going any further. But Grantt was robust. 'Well, aside from the fact that we have several ways to get off this box, and that our suits will keep us alive for twenty-four hours at least . . . Also, the slope looks worse than it is. Remember the gravity is only one per cent; we can barely feel it. Why, we could just lie on our backs and slide all the way back to the flitter. And finally – Lethe, having come all this way, I want to reach that edge. Michael?'

Poole grinned.

Nicola said, 'I am never going to forgive you for this, Poole.'

So they drove on. Fleas clambering over that packing-case, a minuscule expedition. Steeper and steeper the slope became, approaching one in one.

Almost six hours after they left the flitter landing site, they reached the edge.

They parked up the rover, clambered out, and walked, side by side, the last few metres. There was the edge, visible before them, a dead straight line against the stars. Another step and another, as if climbing a pitched roof.

And they reached the peak. Poole took one more stride so he comfortably straddled the edge itself, one foot to either side, and the gravity, such as it was, pulled him straight down. It really was like standing on the roof of some vast building, with the twin plains, as featureless as each other, sweeping away to either side.

He laughed softly, in wonder. 'Somebody *made* this.'

'They did indeed,' Grantt replied. 'And here we are.'

'O brave pioneers! If your heads swell any more you won't get your helmets off.'

Poole grinned. 'You got news for us, Nicola?'

'Yes. Another fresh observation. But it will mean another detour.'

'An observation of what?'

'Back down the face, about a hundred kilometres past the flitter. Remember those dimples where we guessed the hull might open up?'

'Yes?'

'The hull just opened up.'

Grantt and Poole stared at each other.

Poole said, 'And what's happening there?'

'Raindrops, coming in and out.'

Grantt asked, 'What are our options?'

'Well, you can scoot back to the flitter and run home to Mommy. I'd say that's the consensus recommendation.'

'Or?' Poole prompted.

'Or you can go back in the rover, drive down, take a look. Drop in a probe, maybe.'

Poole hardly dared breathe. 'Or, better yet, we just fly inside in the flitter.'

'Yes – just checking that out – the lesions are big enough. Although flying the flitter inside the Cache rules out all sorts of abort options. Mission rules and all . . .'

'Jack, what do you think?'

Grantt took his time to answer. 'Nicola, you think we could get trapped in there?'

'Well, the dimple took its own sweet time to open. And it's *big*. No reason to think it's going to snap closed. If you don't stray too far from the hole, I think you'd be safe enough. You've got the whole Solar System watching over you, after all.'

Now Grantt faced Poole. 'Michael?'

'We came to explore.'

'Yes. And this may be our only chance to get inside there. In fact, our only chance for first contact. As people have dreamed of for centuries. We have to do this.' Grantt looked around. 'But I'm going to come back out here another time, and climb a vertex. What a view *that* would be, the junction of three faces. Like a mountain summit, a thousand kilometres tall.'

'But not today.'

'Not today. Let's go get that flitter.'

30

They had to get to the Cache's hull breach before it closed again – ideally, Poole thought wryly, they needed to get in *and* out of the interior before the breach closed.

So they got back to the flitter as quickly as their rover would let them. Poole, driving aggressively, learned to ignore the pings and stern vocal warnings of the vehicle's onboard sentience.

If anything Grantt was even more impatient than Poole himself, and as they skidded down the shallow apparent slope, he cursed the reluctant rover imaginatively. That reaction wasn't necessarily a good one, Poole realised. Poole had every respect for the Martians and their record for survival on a lethal world, but suspected that Grantt, as he dug his cautious trenches in the Martian dirt in search of traces of his Lattice, had never faced a situation as novel, as full of unknowns as this – and potentially as fast-changing.

Whereas Michael Poole had built spacetime wormholes in the middle of the Io flux tube, and mined exotic matter from the clouds of Jupiter.

Nicola fed them updates. 'Your lesion is staying open, and stable at a hundred metres across. In fact the panels of armchair philosophers who are following your progress are wondering *why* it needs to be that big; it's a lot bigger than any raindrop we've seen. I'm figuring out ways for us to talk, if you do go inside. The hull plate won't pass our comms, not even a neutrino beam, but I can position a relay probe over the lesion.

'Oh, by the way, there are a couple more lesions – that's the emerging consensus term for them – opening up on other faces of the cube. Three in total. Nobody knows how or why; we have drone ships investigating. And why three, not one or six . . . And why *now*? Maybe you're just lucky. But it's as if you're being invited in, Michael. That spooky Poole charisma's working again.'

Poole didn't respond to that.

'You're nearly at the flitter. Any last-minute doubts about going inside Pandora's box?'

'More mythology, Nicola?'

'What's your choice, heroes?'

Grantt grinned. 'What do you think?'

At the flitter they boarded quickly, leaving their other gear, including the rover, scattered on the surface.

Within minutes, the flitter was poised over the lesion in the hull plate.

Poole set the flitter's hull to Virtual-transparent. Now, suddenly, he could see below his feet the Cache surface, a floor beneath the craft that divided the universe in two. The lesion was a breach right beneath him. A kind of soft pink light shone up through the breach – evidently elsewhere this interior light was blocked by the hull plate.

And Poole's sensors showed that the environment in there was *warm*; the underside of the flitter was bathed in infra-red radiation. The Cache's internal temperature was maintained at a balmy thirty degrees, like a tropical summer's day on Earth. Not what Poole had expected, but nothing the ship couldn't handle. What was odder still was that there was some kind of material in there: gases, a sparse atmosphere – moist, warm air of some kind – air that failed to rush out of the Cache despite the huge breach in the hull. Another mystery among many, Poole thought.

And, deep inside, Poole glimpsed some kind of mass, locked up within this tremendous box. A glimpse of landscape, almost, folded over, all the colours wrong . . .

Poole blipped his thrusters. The descent began.

The ship dropped easily down through that hole in the hull.

Poole saw the breached surface rising all around him, a layer evidently blade-thin – the thickness of a soap bubble, as he remembered the analogy. It was like a gentle elevator descent through the roof of some huge Martian arcology, perhaps. And the passage was smooth, without turbulence or juddering. If there was some kind of force field holding in the interior air, it didn't impede the flitter as it passed.

Soon, so the sensors informed them, they were bathed in warm, moist gas. And below, that big mass, clearly visible now, a ball of crimson and black some six hundred kilometres across, the irregular surface sculpted with toy landscapes, miniature mountain ranges, valleys. The gravity-field surveys had reported some immense object hidden inside the Cache. Well, here it was.

Sensors poked out of the flitter's hull, and Grantt, staring into his screens, devoured the data as they came in. 'I'm detecting compounds in that air: carbon monoxide, methane . . . A very carbon-rich mix. Traces of water. A decent air pressure too. *All* of this was presumably manufactured at the Sun, transmuted from solar hydrogen and helium – or even just created direct from the radiative energy, I suppose, like the hull material. Of course, as per orders, we're sending out a stream of messages of all kinds, from optical blinks to neutrino pulses. Hi, we're friends! No response yet . . .'

Poole, silent, looked outside.

With the thrusters turned off now, they were falling slowly, slowly, into warm air. Above, Poole could see a tremendous flat roof, a panel of pale light like diffuse sunlight, with that hundred-metre breach above, a window of darkness through which stars gleamed. When Poole looked from side to side, through air that was dense, misty, he saw ragged clouds floating, and sparks descending, like shining raindrops. Without windows, presumably the hull plate itself was the source of interior light for this – environment. And for the heat, perhaps.

Beyond the clouds he thought he saw more walls, the side faces of this cubical container, walls hundreds of kilometres away. Walls beyond the sky.

Grantt shook his head. 'So many marvels. The hull material, the membrane. The containment field over the lesion. Whatever transmutation technology was used to create all this in the first place. Technology so advanced it *looks* elementary, simple. Maybe miracles always do.'

Poole was distracted. An angel was floating down past his view window.

'Miracles . . .?'

It was a raindrop, as they had come to call them. An apparently perfect silvered sphere a few metres across.

It really was not unlike the Wormhole Ghost that had come out of another universe to speak to him, Poole realised, but he had a deep intuition that that was just a coincidence of form: spherical shapes were robust, if you were containing pressure or trying to keep it out, and a silvered surface helped with thermal control . . . There was none of the sense of mass, of clumsiness, about this creature, as he had observed about the Ghost in those brief moments of contact. This was something far more advanced – or evolved.

And now the raindrop began to do something the Ghost had not done.

The perfect sphere was perfect no more. Lines appeared on its surface, running from pole to pole as Poole looked at it, lines of longitude scratched onto a silver-gilt globe. Those lines widened, thickened – darkened, and each flashed briefly with cherry-red light. Then the spherical shell split open, along the bright lines, and its segments peeled away. The angel was opening its wings, Poole thought.

To reveal a cluster of diamonds.

Diamonds, yes: the thing exposed was made of a glassy material that glimmered in the pale light shining from the hull plate. Like its abandoned container, it was a rough sphere in overall form, but it was open, a network of struts and planes, studded with jewels that gleamed. And it spun, slowly.

As the flitter hung in the air, more of these objects joined this first visitor, shedding their silver carcasses as they went, until they were suspended all around, like chandeliers hanging from some invisible ceiling.

Grantt was staring. 'By Ares' balls! Apologies, an old Martian expression . . .'

'You're forgiven. They look alive . . . Sorry – you're the biologist.'

Grantt was smiling. 'Yes. But your intuition is good, Michael.' He seemed to have to force himself to turn away, to look down at his data screens, to tap instructions for fresh analyses. 'Our visitor out there is exactly what it looks like, a structure of carbon – of diamond, essentially, that's the basic substance, though I can see other forms in there: graphite, carbides, even some kind of monomolecular filament. And alive? It has a lot of the characteristics of life, at first glance. That structure is orderly, but it's fractal – lots of similar patterns on a variety of scales, from the molecular on up. It looks as if it has *grown*.'

Poole had spotted another crowd of these 'creatures', out of his left-hand window. The newcomers looked like smaller copies of the big beasts in the main window, maybe a dozen of them, swarming around each other, rolling, glittering, shining, moving so quickly they were hard even to count.

He pointed. 'And *they* look as if they are still growing.'

Grantt laughed out loud. 'They do look young, don't they? Immature. Not just because they are smaller. They're playful! And they seem more interested in each other than in us. That's kids for you. Believe me, I have children and grandchildren, I should know.'

'Life made of diamond, then.'

'More importantly, carbon. Michael, *you* are a creature of carbon compounds. It's just that the carbon molecules lying around on Earth when it came time to evolve your ancestors were obviously rather different than in the environment these fellows evidently came from.'

'Raindrops.'

'Hmm?'

'That's the nickname we gave these creatures when the first of them came through the Jupiter wormhole. Because of those silver carapaces; they looked like raindrops when you saw a crowd of them. That name doesn't seem appropriate any more.'

'No. Quite right.' Grantt searched for more data. 'Those outer carapaces, as you put it, appear designed to be discarded. As we put on pressure suits. *This* is their true form. Not only that, as you know, the carapaces are made of the light-growth stuff we've been calling membrane, which is something different. Not molecular carbon at all. Like the hull plate, it's more like some kind of condensed matter.'

'Manufactured, then? As we manufacture pressure suits?'

'Maybe. Maybe not. The condensed-matter tech doesn't fit with the rest . . .' More softscreen-tapping. 'We've got whole panels of observers following our every move, via Nicola's relay. I get the sense you don't like the scrutiny, but for me it's useful, an ongoing brainstorm by some of the smartest people in the Solar System – although some of them, such as on Earth, are too far away to respond quickly, thanks to lightspeed delay. Anyhow they roughly back up our conclusions – these entities seem more usefully described as living, than not.' Grantt grinned. 'This is science in action, Michael. Hypothesising on the fly. But for sure, the name you gave them is wrong.'

'Paragons,' Nicola called.

'What's that?'

'I'm listening in too. A consensus is emerging about a better name. "Paragons." The word can be a synonym for "diamonds". And those beautiful pictures you're sending – your father says he's already had queries about image rights.'

Poole had to laugh. 'That's Harry.'

'Well, maybe you Pooles deserve it,' Grantt said. 'You got us here, after all. Someday we'll dream up a biological nomenclature for these creatures, and whatever ecology they come from. But for now, Paragons it is.'

Nicola said evenly, 'We don't exactly have a timetable here. There's no sign yet of that lesion you entered through healing up, or its partners in the other faces. *But* . . .'

'Time may be short,' Grantt said. 'And we need to be data-gathering. Theorising comes later.' He glared out of the forward window, at the nearest, slowly turning Paragon, which continued to inspect them back. 'A rough axial symmetry. Which probably implies an origin in a strong-gravity environment, and an evolution for buoyancy – did they evolve in some kind of ocean?'

Poole said, 'You know, Jack, for a pioneering exobiologist you can be remarkably unobservant. About the big picture anyhow. You're looking for an ocean? How about *this* one?'

He tipped the flitter up on its nose. That didn't trouble Poole – the gravity in here was negligible anyhow. But Grantt gulped and grabbed hold of his harness.

And there before them, just as Poole had glimpsed before, was the Cache's inner world.

A rough sphere, like a captive asteroid, dominating the inner space. A hasty check of Grantt's data showed that it was six hundred kilometres in diameter, compared to the Cache's thousand. Yes, about the size of a big asteroid, like Vesta.

But this was a miniature world, of land and oceans, lakes that shone like mirrors as they reflected the soft light of the distant, planet-sized walls. On the land Poole thought he saw uplifted plains, even chains of stubby mountains cut through by winding river valleys. The object was Earthlike in some ways, then, but not in others; aside from the whole being so small, these landscapes were wrought in dark colours, sombre crimsons and greys and blacks.

But like Earth it was clearly inhabited. Clusters of lights shone on those dark plains, and along the river valleys. There were even what looked like roads, threads through the compact geography along which some of those gleaming shards seemed to travel.

'Like Earth,' Poole murmured. 'But – not.'

'More puzzles! There's a pretty dense layer of air wrapped around that miniature world. I say *air* – the same stuff as we're swimming in, the mix of carbon monoxide and methane and other carbon compounds. But the pressure is a lot higher – more than a bar actually, more than Earth's atmosphere.'

Poole nodded. 'OK. So what keeps that layer of air sticking to the planetoid?'

'Not gravity.' Grantt consulted his data streams. 'At a guess, the same kind of barrier that's sealing up the lesions in the box itself. Something that's permeable to massive objects, impermeable to gases: a smart force field. And it wraps up the whole world. Maybe this is an emulation of the environment of a much larger world. Like our own arcologies, boxes with Earthlike conditions inside.' He grinned. 'My friends in Hellas would love this. An arcology the size of Vesta. The data's pouring in . . . Our first interpretations can only be impressionistic. Those gleaming light clumps are Paragons, I think, grouped together, maybe even joined physically somehow – they look as if they could interconnect, interlock. Maybe they can form composite organisms. Even group minds.'

Nicola murmured, 'Are our imaginations running away with us, gentlemen?'

'Sorry. But, meanwhile, the heat profile is remarkable. The surface is at the same temperature as the bath of gas within which this little world swims. You know, this environment reminds me of something. Planets floating in a warm sky. I'm sure there's an analogue in cosmological theory, papers I've seen somewhere . . .'

'Those Paragons,' Poole said, peering ahead. 'There's a group. Down on the planet, directly ahead of us. Look like they're working on something. Something big.'

Grantt smiled. '*Ahead* of us. I keep forgetting we're dangling nose-down over this thing, like some huge ornament.'

'Nicola, it's hard to see through this murky air. What are they doing down there? Digging a pit, maybe. Like a mine shaft?'

'A deep one,' Nicola said. 'That's what your radar echoes show. Yes, some kind of shaft; can't tell how deep. And it's a hundred metres across, give or take. Which is suspiciously similar in size to the big hole in the Cache you're sitting right underneath.'

A faint alarm sounded in Poole's head as he visualised that: a huge shaft underneath a breach in the hull. 'You have an interpretation?'

'Not yet. We're working on it. Me and a Solar System full of avid geniuses. Many of them have fixed on the detail about the carbon, Jack. Carbon-based life forms, OK. And you said the air around you is dominated by carbon products—'

'That's it,' Grantt said eagerly. 'I think. Carbon! The references I was trying to remember. And even the planetoid in front of us – I have a deep-scan report here somewhere . . .' He stroked a screen with one finger, scrolling through pages. 'Here it is. Michael, what would you guess that worldlet itself is made of?'

Poole shrugged. 'I'd guess the same stuff every small object in the Solar System is made of, from Vesta up to the Earth. A mix of water ice and rock.'

'By rock you mean silicate minerals? Well, you're wrong. According to this deep scan. That's a world, hosting carbon-based life, that is itself *made of carbon* – of graphite, carbides, what's presumably a diamond core. Very little in the way of silicate compounds, because there's very little silicon present. And even less iron, and other heavy elements. Those shallow seas are water, though, but so heavily carbonated they probably fizz . . .'

Poole shook his head. 'I'm no planetologist. Where would you find a world made of carbon?'

Grantt shook his head. 'Wrong question. I'm finally putting all this together, I think. Kind of slowly, but it is a novel situation.

'Michael, the question isn't so much *where* you'd find a carbon planet, but *when*.'

32

Jack Grantt spoke of the deep past of the universe.

Of ages still warmed by the afterglow of the Big Bang itself, the titanic spacetime explosion that had begun the cosmic story.

'It's ten million years after the singularity. Fifteen, maybe. The universe is expanding at lightspeed, but it's still small, and dense, all that mass and energy jammed in tight. There's light, lots and lots of radiant energy. And there are already stars, big bloated beasts that run through their lifecycles in a couple of million years, and then detonate, spewing their fusion products into a universe that is otherwise still composed of pretty much nothing but the hydrogen and helium that had come out of the Big Bang.'

'Those fusion products,' Nicola said. 'Aside from helium—'

'Mostly carbon, oxygen, nitrogen. Only traces of heavier elements so far, through to iron. It was the *later* generations of stars, that formed from the debris of the primordial giants, that pushed the fusion processes further, and produced silicon and iron in bulk. But in those early times there would have been *masses* of carbon, busily combining with oxygen and hydrogen to form molecules.'

'Carbon monoxide and methane,' Poole said.

'Yes. And you'd have carbon grains, even bits of diamond, coming together to make dust and rocks and planetesimals and—'

'Planets,' Nicola said.

'Correct. Carbon worlds – of which *this* is a shrunk-down scale model. Very rapidly formed. Water on the surface maybe, but only traces of iron in the interior – certainly no big hot iron cores, like Earth.

'You had more stars being formed, of course – but these odd worlds were kept warm from the beginning, even away from the stars. *Warmed by the glow of the sky.* By the afterglow of the Big Bang itself. Once, remember, the universe had been so hot that the very structure of spacetime had been broken down. Already it was cooling, on its way to the chilly three-degrees-absolute temperature we see today.

But *then*, a mere ten million years in, in between those two extremes, you had a sky that was still glowing with a comfortable heat: warm enough in itself to keep water liquid on a planet's surface.

'Today, in the Solar System, what we call the habitable zone is pretty much where Earth is: not so close to the Sun that the oceans boil away, not so far out that they freeze. Back then, the *whole universe* was a habitable zone, where you could potentially find liquid water on any planet, no matter how far from a star. The cosmos was probably never so welcoming to life again. So, carbon-rich worlds, crawling with carbon-based life, evolving fast in all that rich warm chemistry. Just as we see here. Incredible. But what are they *doing* here? Or, in fact – why are they here *now* . . .?'

'Michael.'

'I'm here, Nicola.'

'Reading something new.'

Poole felt his heart beat a little faster, a surge of adrenaline. Working around the Io flux tube you acquired certain instincts: any change was something to be wary of. 'Tell me.'

'That mine shaft before you.'

'Looking down its throat right now.'

'And the others. There's a build-up of energy . . . A *lot* of energy.'

Poole pictured it again. The great barrel before him. A hole in the Cache shell right behind him. His small, fragile ship in the way. And now, on the surface of the worldlet itself, right in front of him, he saw a flow of light sparks fleeing from the hole in the ground, clusters or multiples of the Paragons.

He kept his hand on the thruster control.

'This is why we've been able to get in here,' he said softly. 'Why those holes in the hull opened up. Nicola. That's not a mine shaft at all, is it?'

Light and smoke spewed from the pit in the ground.

'It's a cannon,' Nicola said softly.

Poole watched, amazed, as billowing smoke gushed out of the cannon mouth and into the air, rising until it was trapped under the Cache roof, soon turning the whole world into a kind of smoke globe.

Meanwhile, down in the pit, that central light was growing brighter. In that vast muzzle. And the flitter was still in the line of fire.

Poole yelled, 'Hang on!' He yanked at the thruster control. His body seemed to work independently of his conscious mind, his reflexes taking over. Lateral thrusters kicked in, throwing the flitter sideways, ignoring any obstacles in the crowded air, a motion savage and uneven.

Taken by surprise, Grantt was jolted hard, and he grunted, hanging on to his harness.

And a gleaming mass, glowing white-hot, smashed its way out of the muzzle. The projectile screamed past the flitter, just, and flew straight out through the hole in the Cache hull.

In the thin air there was enough of a wake to make the flitter buck and twist, and Poole wrestled for control.

Later Poole would learn that the projectile was one of three, shot out of the three apertures in the Cache, from three identical cannons. Each projectile appeared to be a mass of diamond, a rough sphere some forty metres across, massing about a hundred thousand tonnes and, once they settled on their final trajectories, travelling at two hundred and fifty kilometres a second. When they shot out of the Cache and into space, two of them were aimed roughly at the Earth–Moon system. The third was heading for Mars.

For now, Poole could only fight to keep control of the craft, to keep it from slamming into the Cache wall – to find a way out of this box in the sky, before it sealed itself up again.

More shock waves washed. The flitter bucked and rocked.

Jack Grantt was braced against his couch. He yelled, 'Some first contact!'

33

Once the flitter eased out of the lesion and rejoined the mother ship, the *Bellona* raced after the diamond missile from the Cache – the one that was heading to Mars. The *Bellona*'s GUTdrive was easily able to outrun the Probe's two hundred and fifty kilometres per second, at which rate the diamond mass would take about eleven days to reach Mars itself.

The Probe: that was what the Oversight groups and the official agencies were already calling it, and the term was spreading rapidly through the communities millions strong who were listening in, on Earth as well as Mars and elsewhere. But to an engineer that word implied a certain intention, Poole realised. If it *was* a probe, like his own Sun Probe, all it wanted, presumably, was information. Nothing more sinister than that about this Mars-bound mass, and its siblings heading for Earth and Moon.

This interpretation was based only on hope. What was real and certain was that the object's trajectory, without modification, would take it direct to an impact on Mars.

An impact, it soon emerged, square in the heart of Hellas Planitia.

Without waiting for orders, or consent, Nicola launched the *Bellona* on a parallel course.

Two days out from Mars, Poole spoke to his colleagues on Gallia Three. Not that there was much to confer about.

As far as anybody could tell, once the diamond lump was launched from the Cache, its trajectory was modified by no further propulsion system, either onboard or external. There was no flaring of exotic rocket exhausts from the Probe itself, no high-intensity laser beams pushing at the carbon lump as it sailed towards Martian space.

'Nothing that we or anybody else have been able to detect anyhow, Miriam,' Poole murmured into his comms system. 'The Probe just sails on through space, following a ballistic track, sending no messages, responding to no hails. Tracked by a growing crowd of ships, sightseers, science-institute craft, official government vessels. And Federal Police cruisers, the kind adapted for deep-space operations in the asteroid belt. The police are the only armed ships, as far as I know . . .'

A crowd that now included the *Bellona*. There were just two days left until the object's scheduled encounter with Mars. His words were being fired out from the position of the Probe to Jupiter orbit, to the Gallia Three habitat, on a tight neutrino beam, virtually undetectable.

'I know there's a forty-minutes lightspeed delay before you'll hear this, Miriam. Another forty minutes minimum before a reply. And, look, given the way Mars and Martian orbit are blanketed with ships and probes, with artificial eyes and ears, you mustn't reply unless you're sure it's safe . . .

'Maybe it's nothing more than what it looks like: a lump of diamond sailing through space, towards Mars. A cannonball. Although the one big modification we witnessed, since Jack and I were almost in the line of fire of that Lethe-spawned weapon inside the Cache, is that it's somehow got itself wrapped up in Xeelee hull plate – a rough ovoid of the stuff, that apparently assembled itself around the projectile. Maybe it grew in the sunlight from some kind of seed: a *Xeelee flower*, Jack calls this hypothetical object. Anyhow, it's a shell that's added virtually nothing to the mass of the thing but presumably has given it some kind of additional protection. Armour plating, Nicola says.

'But that kind of language – armour – is forbidden, it seems, by the UN Oversight group and the various think tanks they're consulting on Earth, and elsewhere. Even though, from the moment it emerged from the Cache, its projected track has been steady, its target unchanged – slap in the middle of the Hellas basin, the biggest bullseye target on the planet. But we can't say "target" either . . .

'I keep thinking of when I picked you up from Io. You know better than I do that the emergence of the Xeelee from the wormhole portal in the first place came associated with violence, with damage. But you could put that down to – well, to carelessness. Accidents. There has been no specific evidence of a destructive *intent*, let alone a warlike one. Not so far. Even the various crafts' refusal to answer any hails you can ascribe to cultural misunderstanding. *This*, though, a hundred thousand tonnes of diamond dropping out of the sky onto an inhabited world – and a couple of similar "Probes" heading for the Moon and Earth itself – I get the impression that still nobody *wants* to believe . . .

'Well, I guess the reaction to the entire incursion, for better or worse, is going to be shaped by whatever happens here at Mars.

'Jack Grantt wants to be down on the planet, when the impact comes – if it comes. Jack, of course, has family. And after all, his bugs in the rock, the Lattice, his dreaming planet-sized Martian mind, if it exists – I guess it's *their* world, not ours, and they're threatened just as much as the human colonists. We've sent him ahead in the flitter.

'Not colonists, Nicola reminds me now. Wrong word. There are human lineages down there more than a thousand years old. This is their world as much as anybody's. Fair enough.

'As for Nicola and me, we'll cross to the *Hermit Crab* at Phobos, and stay in orbit. Given my, ah, personal involvement, I don't want to be any kind of distraction. Anyhow, we'll watch the show from up here.

'And, you see, there are the other two Probes. If anything bad does happen here I have a feeling I may want to get back to Earth quickly.

'I increasingly think that Highsmith Marsden was right to hide you all away in Gallia.

'Please get back to me. But above all stay safe . . .'

Poole and Nicola were left in peace for twenty-four hours. Then, with just one day left until the Probe reached Mars, Poole was ordered to face an Oversight scrutiny committee.

In other words, he got a call from his parents.

34

Nicola cleared out of the lifedome for the duration of the conference.

She closed up her skinsuit and drifted down to the engine pod, buried deep in its cache of asteroid ice, to run, she said, some routine maintenance and upgrades. That was tactful, for her, but Poole had no doubt she would be listening in; he prayed she didn't disrupt what was always going to be an awkward session.

Awkward, even though Poole was the only person actually present.

They sat in a loose circle. Save for Poole, they were all Virtual people on Virtual couches: Harry, Muriel, and Gea. As usual, consistency protocols mandated that the illusion of reality should be maintained; in a freefall environment, they were strapped, if loosely, into their couches. Even the drinks at their sides were in sealed cups with adhesive bases: coffee for Harry, water for Muriel – what looked suspiciously like engine oil for Gea, and Poole, who knew that one of the sentience's first avatars had been a mock-up of a clanking toy robot belonging to his distant ancestor George Poole back in the twenty-first century, wondered if that was some kind of elaborate joke. If so he appreciated the touch, and he thought he detected the slightest of winks on that wise but almost immobile face when she saw he was looking.

And it was Gea who spoke first.

'So, is it down to business straight away? This is a family gathering of a sort – and here we have Michael, your son, so recently restored to you safe and sound. What, not even a hug? I'm sure Michael could create an avatar which—'

'We're Pooles,' Muriel said, sounding amused. 'We don't do hugs. Descending into pits of peril, yes. Not hugs.'

'Even if any of us were actually here,' Harry said. 'Aside from Michael.' He glanced away, as if at a clock visible in whatever environment he was calling from, as if he had more important matters to attend to. 'By the time we're done, and whatever conclusions we come to are posted back to our originals on Earth, more minutes will be lost from this final day, before – well, before the Cache Probe reaches

Mars, and whatever follows. Shall we get on with it?

'For the record: I am an authorised Virtual representation of Harry Poole. Citizen ident codes follow.' He closed his eyes, and Poole saw his lips move, reciting a string of digits. 'Harry Poole is not present in person, on this ship in Martian orbit. Nor are Muriel Poole, or the entity known as Gea. The purpose of the projection of this Virtual is to provide real-time responses to Michael Poole, here on the *Bellona*. And the purpose of the meeting itself is to share knowledge; any conclusions or recommendations will be fed back to our principals, along with a syncing of the experience itself, for ratification or rejection. Everybody agree?'

Muriel sighed, made a similar statement a little less pompously, as then did Gea.

Poole, restless, got out of his couch and drifted over to the galley area. 'Well, I'm here in person, authorised, ratified or otherwise. And I need another coffee. Lethe, a family gathering with everybody hundreds of millions of kilometres apart. Just like old times. As you said, Mother, we're Pooles. Once, you know, Gea, at a birthday party when I was a kid, they got one of the company staff to blow out my candles for me. Because Virtual parents have no puff.'

Gea laughed. 'You have my sympathy.'

Harry snorted. 'You're spending too much time with the Emry runt. She's feeding you lines.'

Poole just smiled. 'I think she'd be pleased you remember her, Harry. She seems to be the company I need right now. As opposed to absentee parents showing up like manifestations of unreliable gods.'

'Shall we get to the point?' Muriel asked. 'As you said, Harry, we're running out of time.'

'OK.' Harry regarded Poole. 'But really, this is one last go-round; Michael's been pretty thoroughly debriefed since his journey into the Cache. You came out of there with a slew of data and interpretation. If not for you, son, we'd be even more baffled than we are.'

Gea put in, 'Harry's right. The records you returned are unique, and invaluable. And Professor Grantt's preliminary analyses hold up too. Your Paragons do seem to be a carbon-based life form, adapted to life on a world suspended in a warm bath of radiation – the interior of the Cache is like a fragment of a globally habitable universe, as ours was when young. One interesting point is that the hull plate cloaks the Paragons wear, when they emerge from the shelter of the Cache – and which covers the Probes too – *don't* seem to be characteristic of

Paragon technology, such as it is. Grantt observed this at the time. The Paragons can build a space cannon; they could not make *that*. It is far more advanced, technologically.'

'The Xeelee, then,' Harry said. 'The material is Xeelee in origin.'

'Presumably. The speculation is that the Paragons are some form of client species of the Xeelee. Partners, under their protection. Recipients of gifts.'

Muriel frowned. 'But if the Paragons are relics of the early days of the universe – from ten, fifteen million years after the Big Bang? If the Xeelee have partnered them for that long . . .'

'Impressive continuity,' Harry said.

'Well, we know the Xeelee think on big scales, in time and space.' She quoted, *'The stars continued to age, too rapidly. The Xeelee completed their great Projects and fled the cosmos . . .'*

Poole suppressed a shudder.

Harry said, 'Yes, well, whatever happened thirteen billion years ago isn't so significant as what will happen in the next few hours when that Probe reaches Mars.'

Gea waved a hand, and images and records scrolled in the air. 'There is a great deal of public concern on Mars, as may be imagined. There have been demands to destroy the Probe, protests at inaction.'

Harry snorted. 'Protests? Riots, you mean. Such as outside federal buildings at Kahra.'

'Certainly the official position so far, such as it is, has been based on the premise that this is indeed a probe. That this is still a basically peaceful contact, benevolently intended. We cling to that assumption. Even though we've had no response to our own attempts to make contact.'

Muriel said, 'Still, we have to try. I and my colleagues have studied theoretical first-contact scenarios, and have long settled on the conclusion that intention is everything, in such a situation. If you *intend* to be peaceful, you must show it—'

'Ha!' Harry's laughter was a bark. 'You always were lost in the clouds, Muriel. Sometimes I wonder if you really are a Poole. Well, I admit you've been winning the argument. In as much as there's been no serious attempt to follow up the alternative hypothesis about this "Probe". That it is what it looks like, right now, as it rifles in at Mars. That it is in fact a weapon.'

'But what could we do?' Gea asked. 'We don't have warships, Harry. The police have some weapons, though it's been centuries since they were used in anger on any large scale. We have technology we could weaponise, of course. There have been hasty studies . . .'

Harry snorted. '"Hasty." You know as well as I do that the independence-minded factions on Mars have been playing around with weapons tech for decades. But none of these have been deployed against the Probe. Right?'

'This is not a warlike age, Harry,' Muriel said. 'These visitors to our Solar System, welcome or not, are *here*; they are evidently super-advanced, super-powerful. A war with such creatures could be disastrous – most likely for us, not them. This is what our theoretical studies show. We don't want to be the ones to start the war, if war isn't inevitable.'

Harry snorted. 'Tell that to the poor saps sitting under this thing at Hellas.'

Gea said evenly, 'Actually the Hellas region has already been evacuated. Mostly. Only those who insist on staying, for whatever reason, are still present, in the hypothetical impact zone.'

Harry frowned. 'Who in Lethe would want to stay?'

Muriel said, 'Optimists, frankly. Those who still don't believe there is harmful intent here, and have stayed around to show that faith.'

'Faith?' Harry sounded incredulous. 'A faith on which you would gamble your life?'

'It is still possible,' Muriel said. 'Even if the Xeelee came from a future of war – even if Michael is some kind of target – perhaps it comes here to create a peace.'

Harry snorted. 'Peace? Tell that to the survivors. Maybe it's time we started showing it just how insignificant we are. Oh, this is getting us nowhere. I guess we've done what we came for. Which was to see if any of us has anything new to say, before that Lethe-spawned probe falls. Evidently not. I've got work to do.' He drifted out of his chair.

Muriel, as if reluctantly, followed suit. She turned to Poole, forcing a smile. 'Goodbye, Michael. I'll speak to you on the other side of all this . . .'

Gea nodded gravely.

Harry glared at Poole, and shrugged.

Then the three of them popped out of existence, turning to transient clouds of pixels that glowed, faded, vanished. Suddenly Poole was alone; the lifedome was big and empty.

Almost plaintively he called, 'Nicola?'

'I'm still here. And we got a message, from Mars.'

'From who?'

'Jack Grantt . . . Actually it's a message to the human race.'

Poole listened. And he kept listening as the last hours wore away.

35

'This is Grantt, of the Cydonia Aboriginal Biology Institute, University of Kahra. Recording my uninformed observations for posterity, I suppose. The date and time . . . well, you'll have those from the recording stamp.

'My family are safe, come what may, on Phobos. Wife, children, grandchildren. I dedicate this record to them. I am far from home. Half a world away from Cydonia.

'I am in a flitter, strictly my Institute's flitter, over Hellas. I am somewhat cautiously circling over Lockyerville, at the heart of Hellas Planitia, and close to the predicted impact site of the object known as the Probe – though as it approaches, still maintaining its speed of fifty times Mars's escape velocity, that name seems increasingly inappropriate.

'On a sparsely populated world, Lockyerville is actually a relatively substantial community. And it is at the centre of a radial network of roads that connect it to satellite communities scattered across the Planitia. Lockyerville's significance is its unique location, of course. The geometric centre of Hellas, the deepest place on the planet, is not only a place of great scientific interest, it is also a unique tourist destination. Travellers like to return home, and point to images from telescopes good enough to pick out Hellas, and to be able to boast, *"That's* where I was, right there. You can see it from Earth."

'And it is presumably that geometric singularity that has drawn the attention, today, of our new visitors.'

'Later.

'Not long to go, to Probefall. I am trying to ensure I am at an altitude high enough, and far enough away, not to be caught by the impactor, if that is what it proves to be, or by the predicted side-effects of its fall. Not that any distance short of half the planet's circumference would suffice to reassure the flitter's on-board sentience, it seems; I have had to override its safety protocols.

'The spacebound observers are still recording no deflection in the path of the object. Not yet. Perhaps there is still time for it to turn away.

'I have a great sense of solitude, actually. Not an unusual feeling for a field scientist. And I know that in a sense I am alone. Almost all the population of Hellas, which numbered over a million in the flesh, has been evacuated. Even the big arcologies far to the west are emptied. Those glass roofs must have seemed very fragile today.

'Those who remain at ground zero are hoping, even now, for a peaceful outcome. A soft landing. Handshakes and an exchange of flags, I suppose. A brass band . . . As I said, I have moved my own family far away.

'*Ground zero*. That itself is a ghastly, antiquated, Anthropocene-war-era term. But that is the language in which it appears appropriate to discuss this event. A forty-metre-wide diamond, cloaked in hull plate, coming in at two hundred and fifty kilometres a second – friction with the thin air of Mars will barely slow it – will deliver kinetic energy equivalent to nuclear weapons of eight hundred megatons. A unit of measure that itself dates from the ages of war—

'Ah. I think I *see* it. A flash, high above. I am allowing the flitter's sentience, now, to move us away . . .

'Impact!'

'I must – it was so fast – I must record my impressions. And the sequence, much of it too fast to follow with the naked eye, as unscrambled by my instruments.

'I've seen meteors fall. Every Martian has. Small objects often reach the ground, on Mars; the thin air is a poor shield compared to Earth's. They flash, detonate, rupture; they are generally friable, fragile lumps of rock or ice, and suffer catastrophic damage themselves before reaching the ground.

'Not this time. Not this time. I think of the cohesion of the diamond core of it – I saw it myself, remember, in the Cache – and then there is the unknown protection yielded by its hull plate coat.

'It screamed through the air, coming down almost directly towards me. I saw the glowing plasma of the tortured atmosphere, and my instruments tell me that the object itself was unharmed. Intact, all the way to the ground.

'It came down – that flash—

'Where Lockyerville was, and that wretched city was right

underneath the impactor, I saw a point of unbearable brightness. I still have spots before my vision. On the ground, those close in must have died instantly, those further out blinded.

'Then a moment of what looked like an upward hail – molten, red-hot rock droplets, I imagine, washing back up the tunnel of vacuum left by the passage of the Probe. Molten rock, and perhaps superheated vapour. Mars's permafrost layer flashed to steam.

'Then, a pulse of heat crossed Lockyerville. It was a wave of compressed, superheated air, washing out from the impact site. I saw detonations among the domes and shelters of the town: anything, I suppose, that contained oxygen to feed fire exploded and flashed into fragments. The very surface of the glass roads melted.

'Then a tremendous ripple of energy washed out through the ground, at supersonic speeds, a circular shock wave travelling out through the landscape itself, tracking the air shock. I could *see* it. It overwhelmed the material strength of the rock itself, pulverised the upper ground, shattered bedrock. This wave travelled kilometres before stalling, with a great mound of overturned strata heaping up to form a circular rim. And I saw a kind of rebound too, a reflected wave that smashed back to the centre, the point of impact, to throw up a rough-edged mountain there. Thus, a new crater.

'All these events happened in mere seconds, you understand. The mechanism is well understood. At the point of impact, the tremendous kinetic energy of the Probe had hammered down on the bedrock beneath, compressing, vaporising it. That caused a tremendous sub-surface rebound: a secondary explosion.

'But even after this monstrous beginning, even as rock fragments begin to hail back down to the ground, a wave of destruction washes out from the epicentre through the atmosphere: a great circular storm already kilometres across, of wind and heat and red Martian dust, driven by the impact heat, an obliterating wave travelling at the speed of sound. It will be spectacular when *this* reaches the arcologies at the rim of Hellas.'

'Later.

'I am high, now, obeying the cautious flitter's safety mandates. So high I can see the curve of the world. I feel as if I am halfway to orbit.

'And I can see the impact region, clearly. A new crater at the centre of Hellas, perhaps six kilometres across. It is sharply defined. So new, so perfect in its symmetry, that it is almost beautiful. Innocent.

'Lockyerville is entirely gone, of course. Not even the graves remain. Beyond that, the landscape has been scraped clean of human traces across perhaps twenty kilometres. Nothing is left of those who lived here for generations, or any of their works.

'And the damage to the terrain of Mars itself, and the organisms I study, is extensive, across perhaps two hundred kilometres.

'Above me the sky is darkened by a plume of ejecta hurled up into the atmosphere. There will be cooling, across this small planet.

'What savagery! An impact that was felt in seismic echoes right around Mars. And deliberately aimed. Those who directed this thing *must* have understood that there were living creatures in the impact zone. I think now of the similar packets of destruction heading for the Moon, and Earth. I wonder what will come of this day.

'Yet, I reflect.

'I reflect that for all this barbarous destruction, Hellas is an impact crater ten times wider than this new blister of damage at its centre. Even the Xeelee hasn't matched *that* act of nature. Not yet, anyhow.

'I reflect that for all the harm it inflicted, perhaps this ugly weapon really was a probe, as much as a tool of destruction. Michael Poole tells me that some fine-grained observing instruments have seen what appear to be flecks of debris rising up from the impact, riding the thermal currents from the disaster site, even rising to the top of the thin air, reaching space. Chips of carbon, it is reported. Perhaps, somehow, this object is even now reporting back to its maker: about the planet it encountered, about the nature of those who inhabit it.

'And as a biologist I reflect that the great pulse of heat delivered by that impact must have melted the permafrost layer that lies deep beneath the Martian soil. A warmth that can linger for a thousand years. We know there are organisms on Mars adapted to take advantage of such "impact summers". If the Xeelee's intention was to inflict death, for whatever motive, it is somehow a comfort that on one scale at least it may, inadvertently, have given life.

'But it's a small comfort. I am a Martian. Now Martians have died, through the actions of the Xeelee – and there can be, now, no question about its intent. I look back at my own naïve reactions to my exploration of the Cache – which has turned out to be a weapons platform – with shame. How could I have been so foolish? Well, no more.

'All that for tomorrow. Now, I, like the rest of mankind, turn to the problem of how we are to deal with this proven destructive presence amid our worlds, the Xeelee.

'And how we are to deal with the objects heading for Earth and Moon.'

36

Six hours after the Hellas impact, Poole and Nicola pulled the *Hermit Crab* out of its dry dock in Martian orbit. At two gravities thrust, they raced to intercept the second and third Probes, which were still following their direct route from the Martian L5 point to Earth and Moon.

They overtook the Probes two days out from their presumed targets.

Poole settled the *Crab* into a trajectory parallel to the course of the Earth-bound Probe, less than ten kilometres from that milk-white hull plate shell. Just as with the Mars device, they found themselves once more in a crowd of craft, most of them uncrewed, some of which had been trailing the Probes ever since they had left the Cache at the Martian L5 point. Some of the ships splashed light on the Probe, but its seamless hull merely reflected a diffuse, featureless glow.

In the further distance, visible only telescopically, the Moon-bound Probe raced along its own path.

'It looks unreal,' Nicola said, munching a nutrient bar for breakfast, staring at the Earth Probe. 'Like a dragon's egg.'

'More old mythology?'

'Isn't that appropriate? We're facing the Xeelee as Beowulf faced Grendel's mother, armed only with an iron sword, and with about as much comprehension. Yet he fought her in the end, and won. Although eventually a dragon killed *him*.'

'Whereas when the Mariner from Mars took on the King of the Sand People, he *lost*, first time.'

Nicola smiled. 'Just goes to show, when you go to war you have to choose the right legend.'

'You think this is a war now?'

She glanced out at the Probe, bathed in light. 'Don't you? We should take on this Lethe-spawned thing. Hit it with all we've got. Us and this ragtag navy around us. I'm talking windows of opportunity, Michael. If we manage to destroy this thing, fine—'

'That seems doubtful. Have you seen the latest reports from Hellas?

Came in while you slept. There are indications that the Mars Probe *survived* after all. Mass surveys of the crash site have detected it, buried in the smashed bedrock. The damage to the planet was inflicted by the kinetic energy the Probe shed on impact, but *it* is still down there. That hull plate is tough stuff. Whatever we try we may not be able to destroy the Earth Probe—'

'At least shove it aside, then. And the sooner we try that the better. It's like asteroid deflection, Michael. Spaceguard. If your killer rock is far enough out, a slight deflection can cause it to miss its target by thousands of kilometres . . .'

'Any such attempts are vetoed for now.'

This was Harry's voice. His disembodied head sparkled into Virtual existence in the middle of the lifedome. Naturally, Poole noticed, the head was a significant fraction larger than life-size, the head of a heroic statue. That was Harry for you.

'Hmm. An immediate response to my remark,' Nicola commented. 'We're still light-minutes out from Earth. Are you another Virtual copy, Harry?'

'It seemed only polite, rather than keep you waiting for replies. Usual caveats apply; I am a top-quality authorised representation of Harry Poole. But don't take anything I say seriously until I've had time to sync back to my original, on Earth.'

Poole grinned. 'Harry, I never take you seriously anyhow.'

'Tell me about it. Just to reiterate, from what I overheard of your conversation: any hostile action against the Probes, either of them, is still forbidden. Even active sensors are ruled out. Not so much as a ping with a single neutrino. Even those floodlights are controversial. I do take your Spaceguard logic, Nicola; if all we can do is deflect these things, the sooner we try it the better. But—'

'But you're not going to try at all.'

Harry sighed. 'You kids understand so little. You *know* so little. There is no "you", to "try" or otherwise. It's not as simple as that.

'You're dealing with the democratically elected government of a more or less united planet – a planet in danger, and with its neighbour the Moon under similar threat, or a greater threat, actually, in pro-portion to the Moon's size and population – *and* with the background of the disaster that's already hit Mars, and the complication of the consequent relief effort we have had to mount there.

'Plus you have such difficulties as the AS lobby: the struldbrugs, always slow to come to a decision, slow to react. And the activists, groups like Paradoxa who, having cut their teeth on learning how to manage the long-term implications of climate adjustment, now think they're ready to deal with the alien. You want to know more about that, ask your mother, Michael.

'And then there's the public mood. Which is of growing anger, as you'd expect. Why hasn't somebody *done* something yet? Why was this allowed to happen? And so on. A lot of this is remote-link chatter, but I think we've all been surprised to see how people have been prepared to show up in a mass, like this was still the early Anthropocene. In person, I mean. I'm talking about mobs. The Federal Police had to contain a noisy demonstration outside the UN headquarters in New Geneva. Look – I'm trying to tell you that there's no simple entity to handle the situation, no clear decision-making process. It's more as if we're waiting for a strategy to emerge from a planet-wide conversation.'

Nicola said, 'And so everybody sits around gassing while this weapon falls from the sky. You know, we don't need a bunch of Virtuals and old folk in charge right now. We need Beowulf.'

Harry frowned. 'Who? . . . Looking it up. Oh. Iron Age-type warlord. Well, maybe, Nicola, or maybe not. We aren't that kind of society any more, where almost everybody died before they grew old, and the leaders were testosterone-pumped young men dreaming of nothing but glory in the afterlife for themselves, and wealth and power for their kids. The irony is, of course, that if we *had* stayed that way we probably wouldn't even be here, as targets for the Xeelee's diamond bombs.' The inflated head sighed hugely, its every motion magnified almost to comic effect.

'All this philosophising, even as the knock-out blow is heading for Earth–Moon.'

'I didn't say I agreed with it,' Harry said grimly. 'I'm just trying to show you the debate. *But . . .*'

Poole looked up now; he hadn't been paying full attention. 'I know your buts, Harry. But what?'

Harry's floating head turned to him, and grinned. '*Power is shifting*, Michael. At the highest echelons, under the pressure of this Xeelee incursion. Even though most people don't realise it, even those at the heart of government. Even though what they *think* is shifting is, not power, but blame.'

'Blame?' Poole asked. 'Who are they blaming?'

'Us. Me. The Oversight committee appointed to advise on the Xeelee incursion, all the way back to the irruption from the wormhole in the first place.'

'I hate to say it,' Nicola remarked, 'but that's unfair. Even to you.'

'Of course it is. Since when has fairness mattered in human affairs? Especially at the top. We overseers were just a bunch of industrialists and engineers and scientists and philosophers – not politicians, not soldiers, not security experts, not even police – drafted in to advise the UN agencies. We had pitiful resources, we had no executive power, we have generally been forbidden to act in any positive way for fear of upsetting the intruder. And now that Hellas has been diamond-bombed, they're saying it's all our fault. But, you see, at least it shows a subtle shift of attitude. It's a small step from "Why didn't you do something to stop that?" to "What are you going to do about the next time?"'

Nicola grinned back. 'And you see that shift, and you're ready to capitalise on it. Harry Poole, I withdraw my previous insults.'

'Why, thank you, Nicola. Please disregard various contemptuous sneers likewise.'

Poole, meanwhile, was feeling increasingly uncomfortable. 'What are you saying, Harry? That you and your buddies are mounting some kind of slow-motion coup?'

'Did I say that?'

Nicola looked at Poole. 'Michael, *somebody* needs to do *something*. I can understand the dismay that the first alien to show up in the Solar System is this ugly bomb-lobbing anomaly, instead of your Mariner from Mars in his crystal spaceship. But we can't just hide away in some fantasy of love and cosmic peace. We have to deal with this. We need somebody to *lead* us.'

'Maybe, but even if that's true – not my father. Not Harry Poole! Nicola, I've watched him pursue his own agenda ever since I was born.'

'A little father-son rivalry is understandable, Michael.' Harry sounded unperturbed. 'But you have to see—'

'No. I've seen enough.' Poole slapped his palm on an override control.

Harry's Virtual head seemed to expand, and then softly detonated in a cloud of fast-dissolving pixels.

'Well done,' Nicola said sourly. 'So because of your childhood issues you've cut us off from contact with the government. Very mature.'

Poole was frustrated, angry. 'You don't get it. Harry doesn't *care* about anybody else. All he cares about—'

'You told me. But at least he seems to be trying to do something about this situation we face. What are *you* doing?' She drifted closer to him, her scuffed jumpsuit loose, the remnant of her breakfast bar still in her hand. 'Come on, Poole. You're not facing up to this. You can rage about your father's character flaws all you like, and your mother's. Poor little Michael. But the truth is *you* are central to all this, somehow. It was your wormhole that let the Xeelee into the Solar System in the first place.'

He had to grin. 'You keep pushing me, don't you?'

'Somebody has to.'

'You already made me go into the Sun. And made me risk my life, and Grantt's, inside the Cache.'

'Only because he wouldn't let me come in with you.'

Poole gestured at the monitors, which showed a drifting cloud of ships around that central, egg-like anomaly. 'Now we're in the middle of all *this*. What am I supposed to do? We're not *allowed* to do anything.'

She snorted. 'Allowed by who? By a paralysed government? By a society that's become so old and clogged-up by its own past that it can't respond even to an existential threat? By a father, who, if you're right, is trying to use all this to grab power for himself? You're on the spot, Michael. What do you *feel*? Right now? Come on. Don't think about it. Tell me.'

He looked again at the cabin's softscreens, at the image of the Probe, at its projected orbit which arrowed almost straight, now, towards Earth – in fact to the Atlantic, according to the latest projections. He said slowly, 'I *feel* – outrage.'

'And what are you going to do about it?'

When he didn't reply, she left the lifedome in disgust.

37

Twenty-four hours out from Earth – over twenty million kilometres in distance, still fifty times further out from Earth than the Moon – the Probe's likely impact was narrowed down to a specific corner of the eastern Atlantic Ocean.

Poole and Nicola got ready for the encounter as best they could. They took doses of stimulants to help them keep awake, relaxed, alert. A full day before planetfall, at Nicola's recommendation, they donned skinsuits.

Around the Probe itself, though, little changed. Poole monitored the activities of the improvised accompanying fleet, the drones and crewed vessels, all backing off before the Probe's advance. Even now, hopeful, hapless efforts to contact the Probe continued. At one point, a huge Virtual of a human face was projected before the Probe, smiling wisely and mouthing words of peace and welcome.

'And I thank the gods who swim in the black waters of Lethe,' Poole said, heartfelt, 'that that face is *not* my father's.'

None of it got any response.

And on Earth, meanwhile, as that twenty-four-hour mark passed, the evacuations began in earnest.

Nicola said, '*Look* at this. You can see the refugees from space.'

She was looking at images of the North American Atlantic seaboard, the part of the continent most under threat. Under a clear sky, the Towers and other modern buildings shone like jewels against the green, and the old cities of the coast and the lowland plain were splashes of urban sprawl: Boston, New York, Philadelphia, Baltimore, Washington, saved during the age of flooding, preserved ever since, and now under threat once again. And all along the coast the western routes leading inland or to the higher ground were black with traffic, slow-moving as seen on this scale but a continuous, deliberate, dense flow. Monorail lines were continuous blurs of motion, in the air waves of craft could be seen working their way through unusually crowded skies, and here and there the spectacular fireworks of space-capable craft shot up from the ground.

Poole said, 'I guess you would see this all around the Atlantic coast. In South America, Europe, Africa . . .' He checked a news feed. 'The regional governments are already organising drops of food and other supplies into safe areas. Refugee camps.'

She snorted. 'Safe until what? Until the next time the Xeelee decides to take a pot-shot at the planet?'

Poole shrugged.

Now he found a feed about activities on the Moon. The lunar colonists were, by comparison, a handful, and for the Moon to be treated as a sideshow of Earth was, Poole knew, the satellite's perpetual fate. That was so even now. But that second Probe was on its way nevertheless, carrying just as much lethal kinetic energy as the one destined for Earth.

Poole discovered that the lunar Probe's impact area had been narrowed down with similar precision to the calculations about the Earth-bound weapon: to the region of the Mare Serenitatis, in fact, where, as it happened, the Pooles had been constructing a massive accelerator, part of a new GUTengine manufacturing facility.

Poole had spent a lot of time there, working with the lunar branch of mankind. Tall, spindly after generations of the lower gravity, their skulls big, their joints thick, they were stronger, wirier, faster-moving than they looked. And the miners and heavy engineers – who cracked the air they breathed out of the very rocks, and dug deep for iron and other minerals under the Moon's thick mantle, and sculpted swathes of that forbidding surface to build vast engineering systems like the Poole accelerator, all in hard vacuum – were the toughest of all. Now Poole, fraught with guilt, sent messages of support to the staff and their families at Serenitatis, people working for the company part-owned by the man who had, it seemed, brought this calamity down on the Solar System. He signed off only when he was satisfied that a complete and timely evacuation had been arranged.

Nicola watched over his shoulder. 'That will knock a few per cent off the share price.'

'Yeah, yeah. What's next?'

Next, at last, was action.

Eighteen hours out from Earth, some of the ships from the ragged accompanying fleet started to move, taking up a new, loose formation around the Probe.

Poole stood off and watched the formation gather, trying to guess the strategy. He'd heard no comms link chatter. As far as he could tell this operation hadn't been authorised by any central body, any government arm. Not even the Federal Police – though the cop ships in the travelling cordon hung back, for now. Local decision-making.

Then there was a flash, dazzling across several of the lifedome's screens. A storm of light around the Probe. Through filters and using telescopic views, Poole could see projectiles bouncing off that hull plate carcass, and its milky surface shone with intense reflected radiation.

A part of him exulted. Action, and obviously co-ordinated. Fifteen million kilometres out from Earth, and at last, for the first time since it had emerged from the Jupiter wormhole portal, the Xeelee's works were under fire from human craft.

'Well, that's the kind of message to the alien *I'm* talking about,' Nicola said, reading a scrolling analysis. 'Looks like they're using lethal-level projectile weapons, meant for the police as last-resort options. Surprised they've got hold of them. Also lasers, apparently comms weapons intensified to do some damage. *They* would slice open our lifedome like it was an eggshell.'

'But they're not doing the Probe any damage, are they?'

'Not a scratch.'

Poole rubbed his nose. 'Highsmith Marsden might say that all this is bound to fail. That if the Xeelee hull plate is indeed some kind of condensed matter, then you're not going to be able to harm it with conventional weapons. The way you can't crack an atomic nucleus with chemical explosives. The orders of magnitude of the forces, the energies involved, are just too different.'

'But you have to try.'

'Yes—'

Even more brilliant light blossomed on all their external-view softscreens, silent, wordless, dazzling even as transmitted through the screens.

Nicola hurried to a monitor. 'Phase two. I think that was a nuke. Thermonuclear explosion, a shaped charge – presumably meant for deep mining, on the Moon maybe. We've been hit by a pulse of hard radiation, heat energy.'

'We'll be safe enough in the *Crab*'s lifedome.'

'I know,' she said evenly. 'Message incoming . . .'

The monitors showed that in the vacuum of space the fireball from the nuclear detonation had dispersed almost immediately. And now Poole saw the smooth carcass of the Probe emerge from the glare, like some tremendous whale. Still laser light bathed the Probe; still projectiles spanged off that featureless surface. The alien seemed entirely unaffected.

'Maybe the nuke weakened the hull plate, at least.'

'Doubt it,' Nicola said. 'The Xeelee went swimming in the Sun, remember, the biggest fusion engine in the Solar System. It probably just soaked up the energy and grew a bit.'

'What about that message?'

'It's a warning, from one of the attacking ships. For us, and the rest of the congregation.' She looked at him. 'I was right about the nuke. It was sent by some bunch of lunar rock rats. Fighting harder than their terrestrial cousins, it seems.'

Poole shrugged. 'I know some of them. Not much appetite for ethical debates among those guys.'

'Well, now they're warning us all to stand off.'

'Stand off? After they just set off a thermonuclear weapon? What else—'

'I suggest you do as they say.'

'Yes. Grab hold.' A blip of thrust from the *Crab*'s drive pushed Poole back in his couch, and quickly put some distance between the GUTship and the Probe.

Before another flower of light and energy blossomed.

Nicola swore. If she was invoking more old gods, Poole had never heard of them. '*That* was matter-antimatter,' she said. 'Total conversion of mass to energy.'

Poole frowned. 'I wonder where they got that? Even Poole Industries uses antimatter sparingly, it's so expensive.'

She brought up more images. The hull plate whale swam on, utterly unperturbed. 'They wasted their money. Or possibly yours.'

Poole said, 'I'm copying all this up to Highsmith Marsden, on Gallia. All the imagery, the sensor data – anything we have. I guess every failure tells us something about the nature of what we're fighting.'

'But we didn't even deflect its course,' she said bitterly. 'Not by so much as a degree. I think the show's over. The lunar guys are sticking around, and some of the police ships. But the rest are dispersing. You can't blame them. They can't follow this thing all the way down into Earth's atmosphere . . . Lethe, I need a shower, I've been in this skinsuit too long. And I'm hungry. How does that make sense? I've just been a few kilometres from an antimatter bomb and I have a craving for synthesised breakfast bars.'

'Shows you're still human,' Poole said.

When she'd gone, he stayed at his station, glaring out at the Probe. Unwilling to take a break.

Formulating a plan, of a sort.

Wondering if he'd ever sleep again.

Six hours out from Earth. Less than twenty light-seconds, just a few million kilometres. Earth and Moon were clearly visible in Poole's sky, the disc of Earth less than a degree across.

Still the *Hermit Crab* trailed the Probe.

The alien artefact was entirely unperturbed by all that humanity had thrown at it so far. Only a handful of ships remained of the monitoring fleet, most of them uncrewed observer drones. A couple of police ships had stayed around, but, Poole understood, only because the lunar miners who had attacked the Probe were technically under arrest.

Messages from his father, among others, sat in the log, unread.

Poole had asked Nicola to check out the flitter. He said they should prepare it for helping with disaster relief efforts to come on Earth: fix up the hold to take passengers, for instance. Somewhat to his surprise she'd bought the lie, and had gone out to the *Crab Junior*.

So, right now, he was alone, in the lifedome. In his own ship, the *Crab*, positioned seventy kilometres from the Probe. Considering the one option he had left.

Time to act.

Poole tapped a comms link. 'Nicola? Where are you?'

'Here, Michael. In the flitter. System checks done. I just—'

'Good.' He tapped a pre-programmed control, a single stroke that set in motion a string of operations.

Nicola, predictably, detected the result immediately. 'Hey. Hey! What have you done, Poole?'

'Cast you adrift. Well, I say adrift – you're safe, in a flitter that could take you back to Mars if you felt like it. I just shoved you out of the way.'

'Out of the way? Of what?'

'Of *this*. Turning the ship . . . Reverse thrusters . . .'

In his control displays, and in his mind's eye, Poole saw it: the kilometre-long baton that was the *Hermit Crab*, turning in space, the lifedome pointing towards the Xeelee Probe, the GUTdrive compartment and its huge chunk of asteroid ice swinging away like some tremendous drawn-back fist.

Then the main GUTdrive opened up. An exhaust of superheated matter poured out at a velocity that was only one five-hundredth part below lightspeed itself. Poole was thrust back in his couch by a full gravity.

And the *Hermit Crab* hurled itself, lifedome first, at the Xeelee Probe.

Nicola called from the detached, left-behind flitter. 'Poole, what in Lethe are you doing?'

'What we maybe should have done from the beginning. I've given the *Crab* as much of a run-up as I could. The cops probably thought I was backing away.'

'Collision in less than two minutes. You'll kill yourself!'

'*That's* not the plan. Although, given all this is in some sense my fault, that would be fitting.'

'Don't talk like that.'

'You know,' he said through gritted teeth, pressed by the acceleration, 'my first job, working for my father, was as a GUTship designer. I designed this ship, the *Crab*. But further back, at college on Earth, we were put through some pretty intensive ethical and political courses. Legacy of the Recovery era, my mother always says. A civilisation capable of building ships fast enough to reach the planets wields energies such that, if it ever waged war, you're talking about suicide. Anyhow, ironically, during those courses about peace I realised that any GUTship is a potential lethal weapon. Time to put that theory to the test.'

Lights lit up across Poole's consoles and warning alarms chimed insistently as the ship itself became convinced of the reality of the upcoming collision. But as the seconds wound down, Poole's override commands were holding.

He pulled up his skinsuit hood, sealed it up, jammed on his helmet.

Nicola said, 'Looks as if we're being hailed by every ship in this raggedy fleet of ours. Especially by the police. Orders to explain what we're doing. Orders to stand down. A couple of more positive notes. "Give that Lethe-spawned thing one for me, Mike Poole." That's the lunar miners. Wouldn't have thought they'd be so polite.'

'Ignore them all. Whatever their orders, whoever has stayed with us this far wants to do this thing harm as much as we do. They'll make a lot of noise, but they won't stop me. Anyhow it's too late, almost . . .'

Everything about this operation was hasty, improvised. He'd only had a few hours, after all, to dream up the option, to simulate and game-play it a couple of times, to set it all up. And now, at this crucial moment, Poole wondered if it was just as well that he hadn't had more time to think about it.

'Your time's nearly up. If you want a countdown—'

'Do I sound as if I want a countdown? Just keep an eye on the automatics. If they do their job . . . around about . . .' He braced against his couch. '*Now*—'

Another jolt, a violent shove sideways, as secondary thrusters cut in.

And the whole lifedome, as Poole had intended, sheared off from the spine of the GUTship, taking Poole, the sole passenger, with it. Poole felt the severance almost as a physical pain, almost as if his own head had been ripped from his body . . . Or maybe that was just anthropomorphism, his too-close identification with his ship, which he was now beheading.

The separation in extremis of an intact lifedome was actually a safety feature which he'd designed in case of a sudden and disastrous failure of a GUTship's main drive, a last-resort option to save the large populations of the big, heavily inhabited generation starships of the future. But it was pretty much experimental. The detachment mode had certainly never been tested on a full-scale ship, in high-speed flight.

Now it had. Somewhat to his relief, it had worked.

And as the lifedome, unpowered and helpless, spun away, his screens gave him a grandstand view.

Of the decapitated remnant of the *Crab* driving itself like a spear into the hull of the Probe. Of the ship's spine crumpling and cracking as it encountered the hull plate, lengthy sections wheeling out of the collision. Then, seconds later, the main GUTdrive pod itself, still wrapped in its huge block of asteroid ice, hurtled towards the Probe.

Poole roared, 'Probe *this*—'

Just as Poole had set it, the engine overloaded on impact. A pulse of GUT energy, the energy that had once driven the expansion of the universe itself, was released right up against the hull plate surface of the Probe.

Another astounding explosion, that must briefly illuminate all the worlds of the inner Solar System.

The lifedome was hurled aside, like a grain of dust in a storm on Mars. Poole, shoved back in his couch by a force of many gravities, bared his teeth and yelled, wordless. The hull plate might be able to eat fusion heat and annihilating antimatter. Let it eat GUT energy . . .

But – it did.

His monitors showed the Probe sailing serenely out of another dispersing fireball.

The light faded.

Michael Poole breathed out.

The lifedome seemed to have held, but Poole was unwilling to put that to the test by opening his suit. The whole dome was spinning uncomfortably rapidly, though.

In his ear was a kind of slow clapping.

'What in Lethe is that?'

'It's meant to be applause. Ironic applause, but applause. Well played, engineer.'

'Did it work? Did I do any good?'

'If you mean, did you deflect the Probe—'

'I didn't expect to destroy it, but I thought that the sheer momentum of the ship itself and the reaction-mass ice ought to be enough to turn it aside.'

Silence.

'No deflection?'

'No deflection,' Nicola replied.

'Another data point for Highsmith.'

'You know, Poole, you were a meek and mild engineer when I met you. A real stickler for the rules.'

'Now look at me.'

'Right. Well, I take the credit for the improvement. Seriously, Michael, it was worth a try. If it had worked—'

'But it didn't. And we don't have anything left.'

'That we don't. And now—'

'Earth's in the way.'

'I suppose you want picking up.'

'The lifedome is spinning. The intercept might be tricky . . .'

'I could handle it in my sleep. Shut up and admire.'

*

After that, the final hours seemed to wear away quickly.

Then, safe in the *Crab Junior*, Poole and Nicola watched as the Xeelee Probe struck Earth.

39

The Probe came down at approximately latitude thirty degrees north, twenty degrees west. This was in the eastern Atlantic, not far west of the Canary Islands. Poole saw it from space: a brilliant spark of light that must have been the hull plate-clad diamond block hitting the sea floor, flash-vaporising ocean-bottom muck and rock as easily as its sibling had scattered Martian dry-ice snow. And he supposed that, even as the consequences of that impact unfolded, the Probe itself survived, embedded deep in the Earth, just as its sibling was now lodged somewhere inside the carcass of Mars.

But it was those consequences that Poole witnessed next.

A tremendous explosion. For a few moments Poole could see bare sea bed, as a great disc of ocean water was flashed to steam, exposing mud and rock smashed, melted and ruptured. Just as on Mars the layers of rock under the impact point had been compressed and then rebounded, catastrophically. A great pillar of glowing rock fragments and steam shot briefly into the sky, ejecta hurled up through the transient tube of vacuum cut through the air by the impactor.

But this was not dry Mars. Already the wound in Earth's grey sea was healing, cool ocean water closing over a well of tremendous heat. And then, as Poole watched, it was as if a great blister rose up on the surface of the sea, a shining silver dome.

Nicola said quietly, 'The energy pulse released was equivalent to a powerful earthquake. Or even a limited Anthropocene-era nuclear war.'

'It feels like I'm watching a slowed-down recording.'

'We're seeing it from space,' Nicola reminded him gently. 'It's hard to grasp the scale of things, from up here. If it looks slow, it's not; it's *big*, and very fast.' She skim-read reports. 'Seismometers across the planet are dancing . . . The impact may have set off some kind of undersea earthquake, or landslide. Which will in turn have added to the oceanic disturbances . . .'

As Poole watched, that great blister of overheated water was already collapsing in on itself. Around a turbulent centre, over which a spiral of cloud was gathering – among other things, Poole realised, the in-falling Probe had created an instant low-pressure weather system – a great ring wave was gathering, shining, flecked with white.

Receding rapidly from the centre.

Nicola tapped a couple of screens, calling up interpretations. 'Wow. *That* is some wave. Coming out of the collapse of that initial dome of water. More than a kilometre high, moving at more than a thousand kilometres an hour.'

'A tsunami?'

She pointed. 'You can see how the wave is diminishing as it spreads out. But it's going to pile up again when it reaches the coast. The flit-ter is handshaking with various global systems . . . Only about three dozen news outlets want to talk to us, so far. You want to go up to high orbit? You can imagine the sky is crowded today.'

'High orbit?' Poole felt distracted. 'For a better view of the mess we made? No.'

She nodded. 'Where, then?'

Poole turned helplessly back to the softscreen images. It looked as if a wave of cloud was racing ahead of the tsunami front now: wind and rain, he thought. 'Fifty kilometres up, over the Canary Islands. Tenerife.'

She nodded. 'Right. Where our tsunami will make its first landfall.'

'I wonder how many people have died already.'

'Let's go find out,' Nicola said. She swept her hands over the controls.

The flitter descended towards Earth, like a stone thrown into a blue bowl.

40

Tenerife, one of a scatter of islands on the breast of the Atlantic, looked from the air like a dusty jewel, green and grey, surrounded by the steel blue of the ocean. Its core was Teide, a volcanic summit, not quite dormant, a cratered mound of ash layers more than three kilometres high that looked very lunar. Teide was, Poole learned, looking it up, the third largest volcano on the planet. And a glittering modern city stood on terraces cut into the broad summit of the mountain, connected by monorail links to the coastal plain, shining threads against grey ash. The mountain city was called Achinet. The coastal plain was, this bright morning, a muddle of structure, of towns, roads, parkland, the detail too fine for Poole to resolve from the air. But that was where the wave would hit first.

And Poole, on impulse, decided to project a Virtual avatar down to the ground. To a spot on that coastal plain picked at random. He needed to see this.

Without consulting Nicola, he stabbed a softscreen tab.

He emerged from the transition crouched over, from his seated posture on the flitter. He stood up, staggering a little.

He found himself standing on dark sand, near some kind of coastal resort. He wasn't quite by the ocean itself. Between him and the water stood a line of small huts, some kind of bar, a row of palm-like trees. Beyond, the sea glistened in sunlit glimpses. Inland the ground sloped up to a heavily vegetated parkland, studded with shining glass buildings. Hotels? And beyond that rose the grey slope of the mountain, misted by distance, a smooth-walled cone that reminded him, from this angle, of the Tharsis volcanoes of Mars. Towers of glass stood on its slopes. There seemed to be nobody around. As on Mars, there had been plenty of warnings, and the evacuations had been comprehensive, if, probably, not quite complete; there were always some who refused to move.

He heard a rustling, cracking noise.

Clouds were fleeing across the sky, he saw, distracted. Heading for that mountain. And then birds, flying high, calling out. They were heading inland, like the clouds. He heard a kind of crackle, like a distant fire. And there was a breeze, that picked up bits of debris at his feet. Blowing inland, like the birds.

He turned back to the sea. And he saw those coastline trees falling, one by one. That was the splintering sound he had heard.

Then, beyond the trees, he made out what looked like a wall of steel, rising up. It was the wave itself, visibly advancing. A ridge of silver water piled up far higher than the huts before it.

Poole knew the basic physics. As the wave's leading edge slowed in the shallows the mass of water flowing in from the rear piled up into this looming wall. But to see it in action, only a few hundred metres from where he was standing, was visceral, astonishing, terrifying. For this wall of water was *moving*, advancing steadily on the land, almost like some tremendous piece of engineering. Moving with a terrible implacability.

The last of the trees were overwhelmed. And when the wave's foot reached the strip of coastal huts, it was as if they exploded, engulfed entirely, erased, with only smashed wood panels and scraps of broken plastic wheeling out. So loud was the roar of the water now that Poole could hear nothing of these small disasters.

Poole gave in to instinct. He turned and ran, heading inland, making for the higher ground.

But after a few paces he came across one other person on the beach, and he stumbled to a halt. A woman, dressed in sensible, sunlight-deflecting silvered coveralls. Unlike Poole she stood motionless, looking out to sea, at the approaching wave. He had no idea why she should be here. A first-contact optimist, perhaps.

He yelled back at her, 'Get away. Run! I can't help you . . .'

She looked at him. Silver-haired, smooth-faced, she was AS-ageless. He couldn't even tell if she was flesh, or a Virtual witness as he was. Either way there was nothing he could do for her.

The wave was nearly on them. Yet he hesitated. He couldn't just leave her.

He saw the water smash into the woman. Hunched over, she was snatched away like a leaf in a gale.

Just before the wave engulfed Poole himself. The suddenness of it was shocking. He was picked up, turned around, pulled and pushed. The very breath was driven out of him as if by a huge punch.

Then, immersed after the initial shock, in the deeper water behind the wave front, he was floating, almost as if he was back in zero gravity, surrounded by debris – bits of panelling, huge splinters from wrecked and uprooted trees – detritus so densely suspended in the water that he was in near darkness, save for glimmers of sunlight through the cloudy murk. He couldn't even tell where the surface was, whether he was upright or inverted.

Yet he had a great sense of speed. He imagined himself being dragged far inland.

His lungs began to ache, as he longed to take a breath the Virtual software wouldn't allow.

A tree, ahead of him, not yet uprooted, was rushing at him. A fixed point. Instinctively he made to grab for it; if he could just hold on until the wave passed—

He was impaled, straight through the heart.

He fell into blackness.

And into light.

He lifted his head. Pain shot through him, his arms, his chest, his throat. He was back on the flitter, loosely strapped to a couch.

Nicola was in the pilot's seat, checking softscreens, within which he glimpsed devastation.

He tried to speak, coughed, and that made his chest ache some more.

'Don't talk,' Nicola said.

'Where are we?'

'I said—'

'Just answer me.'

'At our station. Fifty kilometres above Tenerife.'

'How long was I out?'

'Thirty minutes. Hurt yourself enough, did you? You missed Casablanca.'

'Casablanca?'

'The wave got there half an hour after it hit Tenerife. You can get killed in a Virtual projection, you know, if you push the consistency violations too far. If that was what you were trying to do—'

'If I was suicidal, I'd pick a more efficient way. A Poole way. There have been precedents.' Grunting, he released himself from the couch and drifted forward. He ached all over, but at least there was no gravity to make things worse. 'Show me.'

'Tenerife? Since your jaunt, the first wave – the one that caught you – has receded. It smashed up a lot of the coastal infrastructure, shoved the debris kilometres inland, and now has scraped it all back out again. You can imagine the damage. And then the second wave came.'

'The second?'

'That's what a tsunami does, Michael. It – sloshes.'

She waved a hand. A screen showed a composite recording, a view from space, of the island as it had been before the wave. There was the grey central mountain with its crowded terraces, the cities on the strip of coast, and the ocean, in this image a grey, placid sheet of water.

'And then came the first wave,' Nicola said. She tapped at screens. 'Before and after.'

After the passage of the waves, the ocean around the island looked disturbed, foam-flecked, surging, in some places pushing into what had been dry land, in others withdrawing far from the coast. And that neatly inhabited coastal strip had become a blur of smashed buildings, washed-out roads, sheets of mud, broken trees, trapped lagoons of sea water: a band of raw grey-brown, right around the island.

Yet there was movement. Poole touched the screen, zooming in on detail. All along that coastal strip there were swarms of black dots that Poole at first thought must be rocks, or maybe stranded marine creatures. When magnified they turned out to be people, individuals or groups, struggling in the mud. They were coming together, evidently helping each other. And Poole saw aircraft of many makes and sizes, landing and ascending, like sea birds feeding off worms and crabs, he thought.

Nicola pointed out a beached ship, huge – perhaps a tanker, or a cruise liner, it must have been the length of the lost *Hermit Crab*. This great vessel lay tipped over on glistening sea-bottom mud. A stupendous disaster in itself that was just a detail, today.

'Oh,' Nicola said. 'And your mother wants to speak to you.'

'My mother?'

One screen blinked clear blue for a second, then filled with an image of the face of Muriel Poole. 'Michael.'

'Where are you? I mean—'

With only a brief time delay, she responded with a smile. 'Understandable question. I'm safe. I'm being projected from highly protected stores, including some off-planet. I'm going to be fine.'

'I'm thinking of coming down.'

Muriel nodded. 'In person? Might be a good idea.'

Nicola frowned. Without comment she touched controls; the flitter began to descend.

Muriel said, 'You may be safer on the ground. This isn't your fault, but there are plenty of hotheads who are looking for somebody to blame. Of course I can be anywhere. Come down to Tenerife itself. Ground zero. I'll meet you at Achinet. It's kind of appropriate, isn't it?'

41

So, once again, Michael Poole descended to Tenerife, this time incarnate.

They had to wait for landing clearance, delivered by some automated system: artificial sentience talking to artificial sentience. The sky was crowded with rescue craft, every one of which had a higher priority than Poole's flitter.

At last they were guided down to a landing pad, high on one of those mountain terraces around Achinet.

Poole and Nicola climbed out onto a hard, rough pavement. The Sun was high and brilliant; this was a late spring day. Poole's skinsuit had turned reflective to keep off the sunlight. They were close to the high-altitude centre of this summit city. Nearby, one great Tower stood gleaming, its clean lines rippling in heat haze. And in a noisy, almost chaotic sky, flying vehicles crowded, coming to and from the lowland fringe of the island.

Poole saw that, in the west, a heavy load of cloud was gathering. Advancing visibly, boiling. It wouldn't be sunny for long. Another gift of the Atlantic Probe.

Nicola pointed to a woman standing alone, just outside the fenced-off landing area. Poole thought he recognised the image of his mother, not tall, soberly dressed. Leaving a swarm of bots from the airfield's maintenance facility to tend to the flitter, Poole marched that way, with Nicola in his wake.

But as he walked Poole battled dizziness, a slight nausea, a rubbery feeling in his limbs. They had both been some days in zero gravity. When he felt the suit stiffen up to offer him exoskeletal support as he walked, he slapped a console on his chest to shut down its smart functions. The physical weakness only irritated Poole, making him feel self-indulgent given the calamity that was unrolling across the planet, even across this island.

If Nicola was similarly struggling, he didn't look back to see.

They reached his mother. Muriel stood alone before a security gate that led into a terminal building, where no doubt on a normal day customs and security processing would be performed. She wore a plain grey robe that swept to the ground. There was something slightly wrong with her representation today, Poole thought: perhaps the shadow was not quite sharp enough, the play of the strong sunlight on the material of her robe not quite convincing. If resources to support her projection were scarce, he could hardly complain.

'Michael.' She stepped forward, with a smile that looked forced.

Poole had no idea what to say.

'And Nicola Emry. You're proving a good friend to my son. I followed you as you tracked the Probe towards Earth. Well, of course I did – and so did much of mankind. Your assault on the Probe – I understand you had to try. But without you at his side, Nicola, I fear he might have killed himself in the process.'

Nicola looked away. She never took praise well, Poole reflected.

But he was irritated himself. 'Even if I had burned myself up – and even though it hadn't made a Lethe-drowned scrap of difference to the Probe – wouldn't it have been right?'

Nicola faced him. 'Only if you believe in some kind of atonement. Like Christ on the Cross, giving up His life to save mankind. Is that what you think you are? You know, I'm glad I'm looking up all these old religions. It's helping me make sense of *you*.'

'Nicola—'

'She has a point,' Muriel said. 'You always were a complicated little boy, Michael, even before you became some kind of avatar of the future. It was not arrogant of you to imagine you might succeed in deflecting the Probe. But if you had self-indulgently thrown your life away – yes, that *would* have been arrogant, unforgivably so. I'd have grieved, you know that. But I'd have been furious too.'

'So would a lot of people,' Nicola said. 'I mean, when this is all over, who else are they going to prosecute?'

That made him laugh, if bitterly. 'So,' he said, 'why did you call us down here, Mother? You said the location was appropriate.'

'So it is. Walk with me.'

They followed her through the port terminal building. The power was on in this bright, airy space; bots and automated vehicles passed to and fro. But there was nobody here, flesh or Virtual. And, Poole noticed, the big softscreens that coated the walls were blank, pale, featureless as Xeelee hull plate, he thought.

Once through the building, in brilliant sunlight once more, Poole was dazzled, and shaded his eyes. He found himself in a kind of square, backed by the terminal, and facing spectacular structures: what looked like a cathedral, a cluster of crystal blocks topped by a slim crucifix, and beyond that a taller Tower. Even the ground underfoot was exotic, a tough floor of what looked like compacted volcanic ash covered by a glassy skin. Almost like a Martian road surface, Poole thought. Overhead, monorails swept on slim trestles across the terraces, even cutting through the interiors of some of the grander buildings. And what looked like the cables of funicular railways ascended in neat straight lines up the side of the sculptured mountain.

There was no motion on the transport systems. Nobody in sight.

Muriel led them to a small café, one of several set out along one side of the square. They were all open; none had patrons as far as Poole could see. Muriel found shade, and pointed to chairs. 'Sit. You need a break, to reorient. Both of you.'

Nicola shrugged. 'If you're paying . . .' She sat, tugging open the neck of her skinsuit.

'I prescribe orange juice, fresh squeezed,' Muriel said, sitting opposite them. 'And still water, iced. I'll have an unreal equivalent. Are you hungry, either of you? No . . .?' She snapped her fingers, and a bot came rolling from the interior of the café and began to serve them efficiently.

'Beautiful city,' Nicola said, between gulps of juice. 'Never been here before.'

'I have,' Muriel said. 'The city's called Achinet, after the name the island was given by the Guanches, its pre-Discovery-era inhabitants. You saw the layout of the island from orbit: the populated coastal fringe around the core of the volcanic mountain? Santa Cruz de Tenerife was once a major city. But the island suffered badly in the Bottleneck sea-level rise. Two million people were displaced from their homes in the lowland. At times the island was abandoned entirely.

'But when the Recovery came, the island became a kind of administrative district for the rebuilding and reclamation of the coastlands of the whole south Atlantic region. The UN built this city, Achinet, as a symbol of a new way of doing things. Eventually, when we Pooles brought the sea levels back down, the lowland was reclaimed. Santa Cruz itself was rebuilt, a homage to the past. You see, these islands have been ground zero before, and have recovered before. Which was why I thought it was appropriate to meet here.'

'Nobody around, though,' Nicola observed.

'Well, we did have plenty of warning. Most people were evacuated from the endangered zones. There are always some who stay, for reasons of their own.'

Poole said, 'I think I met one of them, on the beach.'

'Even to the end, even after Mars, some people believed that the Probe would turn away. It became an article of faith, you see. And it would have been a beautiful gesture if the Probe had not, in fact, fallen as it did.'

'But it did fall,' Nicola said harshly.

A shadow crossed the Sun. Looking up, Poole saw curdled clouds rolling across the blue sky, coming from the west.

Muriel said, 'We're nearly a kilometre high here. Achinet itself is under no threat from the tsunami, but—'

The rain started, a sudden flood coming from the sky. Nicola and Muriel huddled under the table shade: Muriel the Virtual responding to another ancient reflex, Poole thought.

But Poole stayed where he was, in the rain. He raised his face. The impact of the heavy drops stung his skin, almost painfully. And when he let the water run into his mouth he tasted salt, and sea-bottom mud.

The rain cut off, as suddenly as it had started.

There was a soft whirr. Looking around he saw that a bot, comically, was approaching from the café, holding out towels for the customers.

Nicola grabbed a towel and threw it at Poole. 'What's this? More penance? Throwing yourself bodily at alien spaceships is one thing. Sitting in the rain is just showing off. Get dry, Poole.'

Muriel grinned. 'I always thought you were good for him, Nicola. Now – we can shelter in the Iglesia. It's no longer consecrated – is that the right word? But it's the most beautiful building in the new city, and I can't think of anywhere more appropriate to sit the rest of this out.'

Poole frowned. 'The rest of what?'

Nicola said, 'The rest of the aftermath. The tsunami didn't stop here. I told you. The wave rolled on. Casablanca was next. An hour later, Lisbon. And then—'

Poole stood up. 'We must help. Get back to the flitter.'

Muriel didn't move. '*No*, Michael. I understand how you're feeling. Well, I think I do. But there's nothing you *can* do. You don't have the skills; leave it to the experts. Frankly, you're exhausted. And

– everybody knows your face now. You might get yourself lynched.'

Poole slumped back down. 'I'm too exhausted to argue. The cathedral then?'

Nicola grinned. 'They used to call it sanctuary.'

As they hurried across the plaza, arms linked, ahead of the return of the rain, Poole thought he heard distant explosions. Thunder from the curdled air, perhaps, or the next giant wave, crashing on the island.

42

They crossed a shining, empty floor, under a vaulting roof supported by crystal pillars. The Iglesia de la Concepción, itself a millennium old, was extraordinarily beautiful, Poole thought.

'That ceiling seems to defy physics,' Nicola said. 'Reminds me of Mars . . . At least, Discovery-era Martian fantasies. Crystal towers by the shores of thousand-kilometre canals.'

'There was never a rainstorm like this on Mars,' Poole said sourly. 'Not for a billion years.'

'In here,' Muriel said.

She led them into an alcove, which Poole would learn was called a side-chapel, a calm area with sofas, a table. Enclosed, yet there was a fine view of the overall architecture.

A distant rumble of thunder, a clatter of rain on glass.

'If we wait, a bot will serve us,' Muriel said. 'Food and water. I scoped this out earlier. A place of refuge. We can ask for cots – there's even a shower, if you want it.' She made to touch Poole's hand, that habitual misplaced human instinct, and drew back. 'I knew you would need a place to—'

'Hide away?'

'To rest.'

'I need to know what's going on.' He glanced around for a soft-screen, saw none apparent. He swiped his hand at random across a tabletop, which lit up with menus and imagery.

So they spent the rest of that day, and into the night, eating, napping, talking desultorily.

And they followed the progress of the Atlantic disaster as it unfolded.

As Nicola had said, the Canaries, Tenerife, had only been the first target. Slowly, slowly, the tremendous ripples of the tsunami spread out from the Probe's strike point.

After three hours, the wave reached the southern coast of Britain. Muriel asked for reports from Goonhilly, the country's principal Poole

STEPHEN BAXTER

compound. At nearly a hundred metres' elevation and well inland the site was not affected by the tsunami surge, but the weather was soon battering the ancient Mound. The south coast of England would be hit hard, but London was comparatively secure.

After six hours, the wave reached the Atlantic coast of North America.

Reports started to come in from the old east coast cities, from Boston and New York through Miami, many others. Once, before the post-Anthropocene flooding, forty million people had lived within a few tens of kilometres of the east coast, and a mere ten metres or less above the pre-industrial sea level. Today the population was much smaller, and the surviving cities were jewels, preserved through millennia. Now, after all that history, such cities were being threatened again.

Listening to even the most factual reports on all this, Poole sensed a growing, global anger.

After another few hours a report came in from Harry, on Manhattan Island.

By now it was night at Achinet, and the pillars of La Concepción glowed with a soft, inner light. In New York it was still daylight. Harry was standing in what looked like a lane cut through a landscape of rubble.

'Look around, Michael, Muriel. Can you see? I'm standing on the ancient Via West 72, near the Hudson shore. And I'm really here, by the way.' He bent, picked up what looked like a lump of concrete, and tossed it aside. 'See? In the flesh. I wanted to come see for myself.' He pointed back over his shoulder at the river. 'You remember the old flood defences? Standing high out of the water, from the days when they beat back the sea level. Left intact as monuments. But they were never designed for this.

'When it was New York's turn, when the wave reached us . . .' He walked forward; the viewpoint tracked back to keep pace. He pointed. 'So the wave came over here, broke, smashed everything flat, and *then*, as it drained thataway, it dragged the debris back. Which did even more damage, as it scoured its way through the streets. Now, in places, the rubble is piled up five or six metres high. The labour of centuries turned to a heap of junk, just like that.

'You can see they barely started, not even to clear it, just to create a way through. Many of the food synth machines are down, and even the medical-supply fabrication stations. So there's a massive air effort

202

going on to maintain supplies of food and clean water. There are fears of dysentery and other diseases. Dysentery! In New York, in the thirty-seventh century . . .!'

The view jumped sharply. Now Harry, grimy, looking tired, was walking across green grass. In the distance was a wall of skyscrapers, some of them very ancient – and some of them bore the discolouring, still, of the most extreme post-Anthropocene flooding, ancient tide marks worn like badges of courage.

'He's in Central Park,' Muriel said. 'Look. There's the Paradoxa dome.'

This was a silvered sphere four hundred metres tall, containing tens of millions of tonnes of dry ice: carbon dioxide sequestered from the air.

'The water got in even here,' Harry said. 'Into the Park. Garbage, rubble everywhere. But – look up.'

The camera angle swivelled to show a sky crawling with points of light, even in the daylight: the habitats and factories of near-Earth space.

'The human sky. Full of industry and enterprise and life. And on the ground, rubble and floods and debris. Because of the Xeelee. Now look at me again.'

The viewpoint swivelled down, to show Harry's hard, dirt-smeared face.

'You know, even those who tried to explain away the Hellas impact as a "probe", as if it went in just a little too hard, won't be able to justify *this* as anything but wanton destruction. The labour of centuries, casually erased. And for what?

'I can tell you, this is going to change everything. Everything about how we handle this Lethe-spawned Xeelee situation. Everything about the way we run our affairs in the future – even beyond the Xeelee crisis.'

Watching, Muriel sighed. 'Much as it's hard to disagree with him, *that* prediction makes my heart sink. If I had a heart.'

'And, by the way, take a look at this.' Harry pointed to the sky again, a lower elevation this time.

The camera swivelled, zoomed, focused. The face of the Moon, almost full, was clearly visible in a clear, daylight sky. And there – Poole spotted the anomaly immediately – in the distorted left eye of the face of the Man in the Moon, in the grey patch that was the Sea of Serenity, a brilliant spark flared.

*

The next day, the real work of recovery and restoration began. Poole himself stayed around, working mostly anonymously within Poole Industries recovery projects. But not Nicola. Once again she chose to disappear from Poole's life.

The first days were the worst. Even after the bodies had been removed, and the initial trauma victims found and treated, whole populations were left without power, food and medical machines, without shelter from the rain in some cases. Even without clean water.

The blame game soon started.

As the days turned to weeks, if relief didn't come quickly, in places the reach of the UN government crumbled. There were police actions against local hoarders and warlords. Even minor wars.

A few months on, more exotic damage unfolded. The great heat of the impact, it turned out, had created a flood of nitrogen oxides in the air, which in turn had damaged the ozone layer. There was a slow plague of burnt skin, cataracts, skin cancers. The natural world suffered too, with savage wildfires tearing through the Saharan forests and other vulnerable landscapes. And against this background relief efforts had to be mounted on Mars and the Moon.

The healing was desperately slow. The anger gathered.

Six months after the Probe strikes on Earth and Moon, the Xeelee craft emerged at last from the Sun. It rendezvoused with the Cache, which had sailed in from the Martian L5 point to meet it. The strange flotilla began a new spiral path, outward from the Sun, through the Solar System. Something new, it seemed.

Six months after *that*, Harry Poole summoned his son.

FIVE

And Mars is *old*. The oldest landscapes on Earth would be among the youngest on Mars. But of course even the old can hide a few surprises.

Luru Parz, AD 24973

43

The emergency convocation of the UN's governing councils had been called by Harry himself, as a member of the Xeelee Oversight committee. It was to be held in Britain. And Harry made it clear that he expected his son to attend, in person.

'Look – I called this meeting, and that's about as much control of it as I have. But I'm using whatever leverage I can. I picked the location with that in mind. And you, son, have to be here, to remind these windbags and do-nothings of what is possible.'

'You mean what I did last year, when I went for the Earth Probe with the *Crab*? It didn't even work. I was a fly banging my head against a concrete block. I'm no hero.'

'Oh, yes, you are, for the duration. You ever heard of the kamikazes? Look it up. You have a story, son. And just by being here, you'll tell that story, even if you don't open your mouth . . .'

So, a full year after the Probe strike in the Atlantic, Poole found himself alone in an automated surface-to-surface flitter completing a UN-authorised flight towards the south-east coast of England.

This was Kent, and, as he descended, he saw the chalk cliffs, a line of white sunlit brilliance sandwiched between the grey waters of the English Channel and the countryside's sparsely forested green. Much of this part of the country had been allowed to revert to the wild; Poole's flitter spooked a herd of some kind of wild cattle, long-horned, that fled through a scraping of ruins.

Then, directly below him, not far from a disused surface road – a straight-line discoloration in the green – he saw a more open area, a couple of hundred metres across: exposed, chalky earth. Around this wound in the forest stood a few compact structures, and one more substantial building, low, glassy. Further out, a rough airfield hosted a huddle of craft not unlike his own. An unusual sight in these conservative times, and itself a marker of a global emergency.

Near that big glass building people walked, out in the sunlight.

Poole saw that some of them cast no shadow: Virtuals, then, and not the most expensive variety of projection, which came with shadows. But this was a time of frugal resource usage. So, cheap Virtuals.

Before he was brought in to land Poole called down to his father. 'Where am I, Harry? And what's with the ruins?'

'We're near the site of an old community called *Fokes Tone*. And, not by accident, near some archaeology. Take a look.'

Under Harry's direction Poole's aircraft banked over that cleared site, and, obediently, Poole looked again. Archaeology? Yes, that made sense; he could see that a layer of topsoil and vegetation had been stripped back, leaving that pale scar in the ground. There was some kind of threefold earthwork towards the middle of the dug-out area, centred on a lumpy mound on a central platform – he touched the smart window to have it magnify the view – no, not a mound, it looked like a statue, a seated figure, arms wrapped round its legs. Headless.

'A recent discovery,' Harry said. 'Found by orbital surveys. Routine stuff in the aftermath of the Probe tsunami, though this place wasn't directly affected by the waves. The scans picked out that buried statue. Its interpretation is controversial. *I* think it's relatively recent. A relic of the Anthropocene, that got lost in the chaos that followed.

'Michael, you know that in the early Anthropocene era the old British nation went to war with continental neighbours who had succumbed to a kind of technological dictatorship – Britain itself was more or less democratic at the time. Air power was still primitive, but it seems to have been a conflict in the air that was a turning point in that particular war. You can imagine the mythology: outnumbered British fighter planes turning back hordes of continental bombers. I think, for all its archaic look, that this is a monument to that key battle.'

'How can you tell? I don't see a sculpture of a plane down there.'

'No, but that trefoil earthwork is very like the propeller from one of those primitive planes. *You* know about that stuff.'

'Kites with fossil-fuel engines?'

'That was all they had. Yet they went up and fought even so.'

'And the statue?'

'A seated figure. The head lost. Too eroded for meaningful detail to be interpreted, and a lot of records were lost in the Bottleneck. But he, she, could be a pilot. A hero.'

'I don't feel like arguing, Harry. So, suppose you're right. Why are we here, rather than in some more comfortable UN location like New Geneva?'

'We Pooles are British, remember. Or were. History shows the British were as rapacious a bunch of imperialists and colonisers as anybody. But in that particular conflict, at that particular moment, they were alone and vastly outgunned. And they didn't surrender; they stood, and kept fighting until the enemy backed off.'

'Symbolism, Harry? Kind of obvious, isn't it?'

'I'm dealing with a lot of stubborn do-nothing people here, Michael. I told you, I'll use anything I can get to win the day. Now, you ready to come in?'

44

The next morning, the elderly artificial sentience Gea was the nominal chair of the opening session of the meeting of what was formally a subcommittee of the World Senate. Shamiso Emry was here; she nodded gravely to Poole.

Gea stood up and made brief introductory remarks.

Then Harry, evidently intent on dominating from the off, got to his feet, tabled a draft agenda, and without preamble began a brisk presentation.

The air at the centre of the room, over a big circular conference table, filled up with a Virtual image of that blunt yet beautiful sycamore seed shape, black as night, by now horribly familiar across the Solar System. One delegate moved back the pitcher of water on the tabletop before her, as if the ship might sideswipe it.

'So,' Harry said, 'after the strikes on Mars, Earth and Moon, the Xeelee came out of the Sun at last.'

The Xeelee: by now, everybody on the planet called it by a name that had once been restricted to the Poole family archives.

'And when it emerged from the photosphere, it found the Cache there waiting for it. The Cache itself, its work at Martian L5 evidently done, had made a rapid return to solar orbit.'

He snapped his fingers, and the display changed to a kind of orrery. There was the Sun, and the inner planets hanging like fruit. A path unwound from the Sun to run through the plane of the worlds.

'And then both craft sailed away from the Sun. Right now, both Xeelee and Cache, moving in formation, are following the same kind of trajectory as the Cache did on its last outing: that is, a spiral track through the plane of the ecliptic. Moving more slowly, if anything.

'Naturally we're tracking them both with a small flotilla of drones and crewed craft, just like before. Under orders, for now, not to try anything provocative, although we're still attempting to send messages.' He grunted, sceptically. 'Even now, trying to initiate a contact. And, just as before, we can't detect any trace of the motive power used

– no exhaust emissions, no waste heat, nothing. It will presumably take them months to get anywhere. At least that gives us time to plan.

'But this time, *unlike* before, already they're doing harm. Here's what else we've been observing.' He tapped the tabletop.

The Cache appeared in mid-air, a neat cube. Harry ran a short sequence showing the Cache opening up, displaying the kind of lesions that had allowed Grantt and Poole to enter the great artefact before. Now, though, there were more lesions, many more, through which Probes emerged. More diamond cannonballs, of a range of sizes.

Harry paused, stretching the silence.

Poole glanced around the room. He was met by uncomfortable stares, of curiosity, perhaps hostility. Formally he had no specific role to play and would not speak unless called, but evidently he was a familiar face. And in turn he knew most of the people here, by name and reputation if not personally. He could tell immediately that the key players were Harry himself, and Shamiso Emry, Nicola's mother, the leading voice of caution. Gea, meanwhile, was formally nothing more than the first speaker – but Poole knew not to underestimate a mind as supple and resilient as that of the ancient machine consciousness, whatever formal role she played.

And there was one group he didn't recognise: six, seven women and men in what looked like field camouflage from some antique war, blotchy grey and green. Some kind of allies of his father, Poole was willing to bet. They stared frankly at Poole, curious, not unfriendly.

Harry watched the faces of the delegates.

'The Cache is firing off more Probes,' he said. 'As you can see. And as I'm sure you know, this time, so far, the Probes – though I think we're justified in simply calling them weapons now – have been targeting lesser objects. Last time it was Earth, Mars, the Moon. Now it's minor bodies, and our own habitats – anywhere, it seems, where there are signs of human presence. To put it bluntly, anywhere inhabited that comes within range of Xeelee and Cache as they spin out from the Sun gets a Probe. And the results – again, I'm sure you're all familiar with much of this material . . .'

He hurried through a list of targets, all burned in Poole's memory. Larunda, the habitat at the Lagrange point of Mercury from where Poole had launched his own jaunt into the Sun. Venera, an Anthropocene-era monument of a station orbiting Venus, that had been used as a construction shack by an ancestral Poole for the great project that had ultimately frozen out Venus's deep atmosphere. Both stations smashed.

'The Probes are energetic enough to destroy utterly pretty much any object smaller than seventy kilometres diameter – inner-system asteroids, for instance. And of course any habitats they target are obliterated. A handful of lives have been lost; mostly we've been able to mount evacuations in time.' Harry looked around the room grimly. 'I think we already must regard the inner Solar System, from the orbit of Venus inward, as lost to the enemy . . . I have to say I hope the statue of Jocelyn Lang Poole on Venus is still standing. One bit of defiance.'

Gea smiled. 'From what I remember of Jocelyn, she'd find that quite appropriate, Harry.'

'Well, I object,' said Shamiso Emry, sounding almost weary, getting to her feet. 'Not only to the use of that pejorative – *enemy* – but also to the none-too-subtle undertone with which Delegate Poole has presented every element of his so-called factual summary.'

Harry, still standing, faced her across the table. 'And how would she have liked me to present all this, Speaker? To a musical accompaniment? These are the facts. The Xeelee and its associated artefacts have been destructive since the moment they arrived in the Solar System—'

'In *our* System, through *your* wormhole.'

'Hardly fair, Delegate Emry,' Gea said softly.

Emry pressed on. 'Of course I can't deny the destructive consequences of the Xeelee's actions. But we still know nothing of its ultimate intent. I mean, why would it *do* this? Why cross the stars, simply in order to smash everything we built? Or, put it another way – if it really is intent on destruction, why be so restrained? For example, we know that it is capable of diving deep into the Sun. Well, then, *why not destabilise the Sun itself*? Create some tremendous flare that would lick the faces of the planets clean?'

One of the camouflage-equipped men snickered. 'Don't give the Lethe-spawned thing ideas.'

Harry grinned. 'As you say, we don't know its motive. We don't know *why*. But, whatever in Lethe else this Xeelee is, it seems to me honest: brutally, transparently honest. It's doing what it came here to do. Those first Probes were destructive, but they tested us too. Through our response the Xeelee found out about where we live, how we live, what kind of a fight we could put up – how we die. Now it has started targeting the places we live, anywhere we have settled even in small numbers – in one instance it took out a handful of miners on a carbon-rich Apollo asteroid not much larger than this room.

'The strategy is clear. The Xeelee isn't out to destroy the Solar System. Not for now, anyhow. *It is out to destroy us. Humanity.*'

'Or maybe just your son,' somebody murmured.

Poole couldn't identify the speaker. He dropped his eyes, feeling as if everyone in the room, and the legions of remote observers watching this session, were looking, right now, at him.

Gea stood up. 'Perhaps we need to widen the discussion.'

Harry had stayed on his feet throughout, and he kept standing now. 'Good point, Speaker. In particular we need to look at the effect the Xeelee incursion is having on wider human affairs.'

And he launched into another bleak, impressive, depressing presentation.

Aside from its own recovery efforts following the Probe's Atlantic tsunami, Earth was now suffering a fall-out from the Xeelee assaults on the daughter colonies offworld. There had already been a significant number of evacuations to Earth from the Moon and Mars, from dwellers of domes and arcologies that suddenly seemed very vulnerable. Even if, as events had proved, Earth itself was hardly a haven.

Meanwhile, interplanetary trade and commerce were increasingly disrupted. Both Mars and the Moon depended on flows from Earth of foodstuffs, complex chemicals, and volatiles on a large scale: Earth-atmosphere nitrogen collected by the profac scoops, for example, to fill those airy arcologies on Mars. But Earth itself was dependent on imports from space: on solar power collected in orbit, on metals extracted from Mercury's crust, even on fusion-reactor helium isotopes mined from the atmospheres of the giant planets. The great triumph of the conservation lobbies in the Recovery era had been to establish a protective view of the Earth and its intricate cargo of life: a scraping of nitrogen could be taken to nourish a new Mars, but overall the Earth had to be seen as something to cherish, to protect. Earth was a park, a garden. But that meant a dependence on power generation, mining and other industries that had been moved off-planet. Now that dependence was being tested.

'Meanwhile,' Harry said, 'we're seeing a growing distrust in our world institutions. All of us here must be aware of that. A growing withdrawal of consent, from those we presume to govern but have been unable to protect.

'You don't have to witness a riot outside some UN office to see that. A study of news bias and conversational trends shows there is a growing regionalism, a fragmentation of the global society. Some Earth regions have refused to take Martian migrants, for instance. We haven't yet reverted to Anthropocene-era nationalism, but perhaps that's only because the old nations are so deeply buried in history. But there has been a revival of various old religious forms, even cultism.'

Poole thought of Nicola's mocking allusions to long-dead religions. In her irreverent way she had predicted some of this, he realised.

Harry went on grimly, 'There's even evidence that a handful of groups have started to worship the Xeelee. Worship: is that the right term? I'm no expert in these archaic modes of thinking. They *pray* to it, just as we assume our pre-technological ancestors once helplessly prayed to gods of thunder and volcanoes to spare their lives.'

And, Poole thought grimly, just as the Wormhole Ghost implied that one day a defeated alien species would have come to worship humans. Would have, if not for *this*.

So the discussion went on, dispiriting, even crushing, without relief. When Speaker Gea called a break, Poole doubted that anybody in the session was more grateful of it than he was.

Outside, it was raining softly.

Poole walked alone, coffee flask in hand. The air was warm and still, and Poole's costume, though no skinsuit, was weatherproof; the rain didn't bother him. Gentle English weather, as might have been experienced by Poole's ancestors all the way back to Michael Bazalget and George Poole, and even deeper in time. Back to the age of the subject of the archaic statue, maybe.

The rest of the delegates had stayed indoors. Huddled in the meeting room or in the surrounding hallways. Harry called this 'cluster space', room for the between-sessions informal conferencing that, he claimed, was the most significant element of such meetings. Poole left them to it.

On impulse, Poole walked to the centre of the trefoil earthwork – Harry's 'propeller', though Poole thought it was just as likely to be a sheepfold – and sat on the moist ground before that central statue, hands clasped around his knees, mirroring its casual pose. 'Were you a god, once? Or a hero?'

There was no reply.

Poole tapped his temple, and voices murmured in his ears.

He was linked into an ongoing feed from Gallia Three, his stealthed nest of colleagues out in near-Jovian space, all of forty light minutes away. No direct conversation was possible because of the time delay, but the two ends of the long comms link kept up an out of sync dialogue.

Right now Highsmith Marsden was discussing his analysis of Xeelee technology.

'. . . Each successive failure of our weaponry provides information of a sort. In that it provides a new lower bound on the capabilities of Xeelee technology.

'You see, the weapons launched against the Probe's hull – including nuclear-energy and antimatter detonations, and Poole's own ramming – not only failed to make a mark on the hull's surface, they did not deflect the Probe's motion. This was suspected by observers on the spot, but it has taken us a year to establish this securely from the data returned by the fleet of ships; its trajectory didn't vary by so much as a fraction of a degree. Never mind super-tough armour: what of the conservation of momentum? The Probe *should* have been pushed sideways, given its known mass, by a measurable angle – even if it that deflection might not have been enough to save the Earth.

'You may know that I – unlike the babbling children who now swarm through my habitat like spermatozoa in search of an egg – am uncomfortable with groundless speculation. Nevertheless I have been forced to hypothesise how this is possible. And I believe, and this idea needs to be tested, that the Xeelee have a drive that somehow *anchors* an object like a Probe to spacetime itself. All this is guesswork. But if, *if* it is so – or anything like this hypothesis holds – then the Probe, you see, will behave as if it has *infinite* inertia. Immovable. As if even the largest force cannot deflect it . . .'

Poole knew that Nicola Emry was out there at Gallia right now, with Miriam and Marsden and the rest – ostensibly finding out how Marsden's secretive studies of the Xeelee phenomena were advancing, presumably developing ideas for defence and weapons options, but also getting as far away from her mother as she could. Nicola would take any excuse for that, and thinking of his own family Poole couldn't blame her.

Miriam Berg murmured in his ear now, delivering a gloss on Marsden's peroration. 'Michael, Highsmith is concentrating on theoretical details about the Xeelee, and devising sensors to gather specialised kinds of data to test out his hypotheses. He keeps insisting there are a lot of clues in the gravity-wave data the Xeelee craft is giving off – he is confident it *is* a craft, by the way, a technological creation, or at least not simply biological. Gravity waves: ripples in spacetime . . . Highsmith thinks the Xeelee might even move by harnessing some aspect of spacetime itself. Well, it's his nature to pursue such questions. But I keep trying to draw him back to the fact that the exotic-drive vessel in question actually seems to be some kind of battleship that's approaching Earth and Mars once more, and what we *need* is some way of stopping it . . .'

Poole let her familiar voice wash through his head. As if they were still out there at the Io flux tube, working on the details of a mass-transport system that was supposed to have been the wonder of the age. It all seemed a long time ago.

He had a dread sense of inertia.

Just as Harry repeatedly complained, the leaders of humanity, even now, even in the ranks of this specially convened council, simply weren't taking responsibility, weren't making decisions fast enough. And Poole suspected that even Highsmith Marsden was unable to focus on the true problem of the Xeelee, its deadly threat, so distracted was even he by its alluring, unfathomable strangeness.

All the while the Xeelee approached, indifferent, following its own timetable.

'Wish I was out there with you, Miriam,' he said now. 'You know, the *Hermit Crab*, the first ship I built, was the nearest thing I ever had to a home, I guess. Which tells you a lot about my personal life. I always thought that when I was older I would take sabbaticals. Just go off alone, in the *Crab*. Out to the Oort Cloud to pursue some long-term science project – studying those quagma phantoms in the wild, maybe. Lethe, we have AS; we all have centuries before us; we have *time* for sabbaticals. Or we would have . . .'

A soft chime in his ear: the recall to the formal session. 'Later, Miriam.' Poole stood up with a sigh, set his clothing to dry off, gave an ironic salute to the seated god-pilot, and walked back to the conference hall.

When he got to the chamber the session had already resumed. The delegate on her feet was one of Harry's row of stern-looking camouflage-wearing warrior types, all of an indeterminate, AS-blurred age.

And she was speaking of weapons.

She ran through a diorama of the various assaults that had been made on the Earth-bound Probe, from tickles with a comms laser to Poole's own brutal, all-out ramming. Now Poole was the recipient of glances more of admiration, even envy, perhaps, than reproof.

'Those who took on the Atlantic Probe did everything that could have been done,' Harry's tame expert said. 'And showed more courage than any of us who weren't out there fighting alongside them had a right to expect. But it was futile, of course. Now, as the Xeelee itself approaches Earth or Mars—'

And Shamiso objected that the Xeelee's destination still wasn't yet proven.

The weapons advocate dismissed that. 'Well, I for one don't wish to risk *either* of our beautiful worlds. We have to prepare ourselves, ladies and gentlemen, for war. However, we live in an epoch of peace. We don't know *how* to make war – and of course it's just as well that we conditioned ourselves out of war-making before we moved into space and were handed technologies that could reshape worlds, or smash them. But our ancestors *did* make war. They got so good at it they came close to killing themselves off entirely a couple of times. And now, in this time of unprecedented existential peril—'

'Objection, Speaker.'

'Noted. Get on with it, please, without the purple prose.'

'Facing such a threat we have to reach back to the wisdom of our ancestors – their deadly wisdom. And ask ourselves, how would *they* have responded?'

'What's the point?' another delegate spoke up. 'We have already gone beyond our ancestors' toys, their fusion bombs. Our most dense source of energy is the Poole GUTengine, and we threw one of those at the Earth Probe and didn't leave a scratch.'

'Sure. But still, we have the resources of an interplanetary civilisation to deploy. There are tactics to try . . .'

With support from her colleagues, the presenter ran through a number of options. Such as battering the Xeelee with a swarm of kinetic-energy projectiles: dumb drones, massive, fast-moving – even relativistic, hurled at the Xeelee at close to the speed of light: 'Missiles intended as planet-smashers, in a darker age. Ultimate deterrents.' Or the Xeelee could be subjected to a sustained assault from a fleet of GUTships, bathing that sycamore seed hull in their hyper-energetic exhaust plumes.

'Sure, it survived the frontal attacks by the lunar miners, and

Michael Poole's supremely courageous ramming. And meanwhile we've tested that scrap of membrane material retrieved by Jack Grantt and Michael Poole from the surface of the Cache – tested it to the limits we're capable of. Haven't made a scratch. But perhaps even so there is some limit to the resilience of the Xeelee's armour, some limit to its capacity to soak up energy and momentum. And even if not, there are other ploys we could consider. We could even send in decoys . . .'

Poole noticed Harry murmuring a note to his own screen about that idea.

'Anything we can do to delay its progress. We won't know unless we try. And the minute the Xeelee shows any weakness—'

Shamiso stood, interrupting her. 'You people – I heard your names and affiliations, but who *are* you? And what makes you qualified to suggest strategies for planetary defence?'

Harry stood up, grinning; Poole could see he'd been waiting for the question. 'What these guys are is the nearest we have to experienced soldiers, leaving aside the Federal Police. Because these guys have been down there fighting: on Mars, in Acidalia, in Tharsis Province.'

And then Poole got it. 'War-gamers,' he said, wondering. 'You brought war-gamers into this UN session.'

Shamiso Emry goggled. 'Are you serious, Harry?'

'Never more so.' Shamiso was still on her feet, but so was Harry, thus breaking protocol, and he leaned forward, intimidating. 'Who else is there? Who in Lethe did *you* bring?' He glared around. 'What have any of *you* brought to the table? These guys know weapons, they know war – and if you think one of their Anthropocene-era nuclear-battlefield simulations is easy, go try it some day. They're the nearest thing to experts that we have, believe me . . . Thank you, Bella, I'll take it from here.'

He nodded to the war-gamer, who backed away and sat down.

Harry left his place and started to stalk around the table. More protocol broken. Nobody objected, not even Shamiso, who took her seat. Gea, the Speaker, stayed silent.

Poole sensed that the climax of the event was approaching: the moment Harry had been working up to since he called this meeting – and probably for months before that. He wondered if in fact Harry had set up all this with Gea's complicity from the beginning. He knew his father; Harry was nothing if not a cautious planner when it came to the key moments in his life, his career.

For this was the moment, Poole realised, that Harry was mounting his coup d'état.

'So,' Harry said, 'one lesson I have learned from my own studies of the past is that if you want to fight a war, you have to organise to do so.' He glared around at the delegates, most of whom hadn't uttered a single word since they had convened that morning. 'It's a time for democratic consent, but not for democracy. It's a time for decision-making – and time for a government with the organisational arms to implement those necessary decisions.' With empty-hand gestures, he flung Virtual words into the air to hang over the table. '*Army*: we need trained soldiers. *Navy*: we need ships to carry those soldiers to the Xeelee, to the war zone. *Organisation*: as well as a command structure over the armed forces, we'll need the industry to back all this up. *Ministries*, of supply, of production, a dedicated research and development force.

'*Security*. As the fear spreads we've already seen mass unrest, civil disobedience, even riots. This is only going to hamper our forthcoming efforts, from evacuations to armaments manufacture. The people have to be controlled, for their own good.'

Shamiso stood up, quiet, grave. 'And what of rights?'

'Rights? Rights will be respected, as far as is appropriate to the circumstances. But for now responsibility – duty if you will – trumps rights. If we get it wrong, when the emergency is over, Delegate Emry, you personally can lead the impeachment of myself and my team, or whoever is involved.' He glared at her until she sat down.

Then he began to pace again. 'And above all, we need *command*. In the age of the Roman Republic, as you may know, in times of emergency the senators would appoint a dictator, a *magistratus extraordinarius*, with absolute power to implement the decisions necessary to cope with that emergency. Absolute but temporary power.'

One woman dared object. 'You can't quote precedents from such a primitive age.'

But Harry was ready for that. 'The more recent past, then. The Bottleneck. The last great emergency to threaten the very future of mankind, when migrant flows threatened the stability of the nation-states that had been the foundation of governance for centuries. In that crisis the Stewardship emerged, a cross-national government agency with overall control of global resources, to manage the multiple issues of the time. Call this person – the *magistratus* – the Steward, if you like.'

Shamiso Emry looked more weary than angry – disappointed, Poole thought. Without bothering to stand, she asked, 'And who's to be this "Steward"?'

But Harry was ready for that. His finger jabbed at Shamiso. 'Do *you* want the job? Do you? Or you? . . .' He backed away. 'Let's take another break. I suggest an hour. Clear your heads, take some early lunch. When we reconvene, I move we vote on ratifying.' He glared at Gea, who nodded gently.

Poole saw that nobody, save Shamiso and Gea, was meeting Harry's eye.

Harry grinned at his son.

In the break, Harry quickly sought him out.

Poole was grudgingly impressed. Harry had always had huge energy, ambition, drive. It was just that before, those qualities had been directed entirely towards his own or the family's ambitions. Now, in this crisis, Harry had seen a bigger role he could fill – and, cynically motivated or not, he was stepping up to fill it.

'So, Harry. You finally got what you always secretly wanted. You're king of the world.'

Poole thought he had never seen his father look more alive. 'Maybe you have to be crazy even to dream of it. But now I have it – almost – listen, I feel like my head's on fire. Even while I was tweaking the tails of the rabbits in there – all watched by audiences across the Solar System, and you should *see* the instant-poll approval ratings – the whole time I was dreaming up a scheme. The next step in handling this Lethe-spawned Xeelee. Something to do with the talk of decoys, and my tame warriors' war-gaming on Mars, set me thinking.' He looked at his son. 'And I want you to be involved, Michael.'

Poole tried to follow this tangled chain of thought. 'How?'

'I said the Xeelee had been honest. It's begun the work of destroying us, and is making no secret of it. But *we* don't have to be honest.

'Let's lie to it.'

When the meeting broke up, Harry disappeared back into the elevated circles he now inhabited. Whatever new scheme he was cooking up, he didn't yet share it with his son.

Poole himself felt a need to do something more immediately practical.

A week after Kent, Poole retreated to the company facilities on the Moon. With the destruction of the nascent Serenitatis accelerator by the Xeelee Probe, the old Copernicus compound had become a still more essential location as the company's main surviving manufactory of GUTengines: a resource essential to any human future he could envisage. And so Poole went to work. In the months that followed, his contribution at Copernicus was satisfying and essential. And Poole took the opportunity to fit out a new GUTship for his own use, to replace *Hermit Crab*.

He tried to pay as little attention as possible to Harry's swift rise to power and his consolidation of his position.

But Poole did wonder what Harry had meant about lying to the Xeelee.

And then, after another six months, Harry summoned him to Mars.

45

At Phobos, Poole saw as soon as he arrived in the *Assimilator's Claw*, the Martian branch of humanity was building a navy.

For centuries already this little moon had been used as a shipyard, its own resources heavily mined. Now it was embedded in a huge zero-gravity nest of metal and carbon-fibre tethers, through which suited human figures crawled, and massive robot bodies edged cautiously. And from within this Tangle, as it was called, the carcasses of ships emerged. It was a striking spectacle, and all the more impressive for having been assembled in just a few months. And all this in unfiltered sunlight, the shadows clean stripes.

Of course, Poole knew, the very spectacle of this brilliant display of industry was part of the plan. It was meant to be seen, by all humanity: *look what we are already doing here, in orbit around this threatened planet, now that Harry Poole is in charge.* Poole just hoped that the ships and weapons that came out of here actually did some good against the Xeelee.

But as he settled the *Assimilator's Claw* into an orbit close to Phobos, Poole was distracted from all this frenetic industry by what he saw of Mars itself.

When he'd last visited the fourth planet it had seemed to him to be still lost in its own antique calm; ten million human beings hadn't made that much difference, not to Mars. The emptiness of the arid desert had been broken only by a few splashes of reflected sunlight in the Martian day, and artificial glows in the night: the big communities at Kahra and Cydonia, the bold green blister of the new Hellas arcology, a few ribbons of light marking out major surface transport routes, the scattered sparks that were the homesteads of individual families, trying to make a living out in the red expanse.

But now, he saw, there was light and motion everywhere.

All of Hellas sparkled with glassy reflections, like a window in the face of the planet, as if the tremendous arcology had been suddenly completed. To the north of Hellas, across the equator, blue-grey lines scraped through the desert from south to north, heading all the way up to the pole. And around grey knots that might be cities, fire sparked and flared: the unmistakable signs of war. Suddenly Mars was a crowded, highly developed, variegated, conflict-ridden planet.

Or anyhow it looked that way. And that, he began to guess, was entirely the point.

Without warning, Nicola Emry and Harry Poole materialised in the *Claw*'s cluttered lifedome.

Nicola, in an open skinsuit, head bare, scalp freshly shaved, looked around briskly, and grinned. 'Lethe, Poole, is that really you? This isn't just some fabulous dream?'

There was no perceptible time delay; they must both be projecting from within the Phobos complex, Poole realised. But that was no surprise. Six months after his coup, Harry spent a lot of his time here on the spot, to ensure that the resources needed by his massive new military build-up flowed in without impedance.

And Nicola, of course, was here to learn how to fly warships.

Harry wore a city suit, as Poole thought of it, a one-piece, black with silver piping – smart, not showy, practical, efficient. 'The crisis challenges us all. But we don't all have the luxury of tucking ourselves away in seclusion. Anyhow, thanks for coming.'

'We all have our work to do,' Poole said awkwardly. He felt thrown off balance by this intrusion into his personal space, Virtual or otherwise.

Nicola snorted. 'Like you had a choice. These days, when a Steward sends you a polite invitation—'

Harry scowled at her. 'Just remember who you're talking to.'

'How could I forget?' In zero gravity, she drifted around the life-dome, glancing over the control displays, the couches – even poking her Virtual head through the door of the bathroom. 'Nice ship. New?'

'Kind of,' Poole said. 'She was to be *Hermit Crab II*, under development on the Moon. After we smashed up *Crab I*, I accelerated her assembly.'

'And gave her a cuddly new name. *Assimilator's Claw*. Where did that come from, your kitten when you were a kid?'

Hesitantly, Poole confessed, 'My mother's archive. More bits of information fed to Michael Poole Bazalget by his girl from the future. One day the *Assimilator's Claw* will be remembered as a fighting ship that took part in the war for the centre of the Galaxy. That's twenty thousand years in the future, and the real *Claw* will probably be nothing like this, but—'

'Nice touch,' Nicola said. 'I can see she's tougher than the *Crab* used to be. Leaner. Faster, I'm guessing? And this lifedome is like a fortress.

'You must have seen the designs of the ships they're building in the Tangle.' She waved a hand at the vision beyond the dome. 'Warships, Michael. Centuries after the last time such craft were dreamed of. We have fast single-crew flitters meant to evade defences and launch close-in attacks, and big GUTship battle cruisers to deliver massive, sustained bombardments. But we're starting from scratch. We've lost the tradition of that kind of thinking – how to make spaceworthy craft nimble enough to fight, yet robust enough to survive an attack – *and* we're trying to adapt new technologies, stuff that our old warlike ancestors never imagined, to destructive purposes.'

'He knows all this,' Harry said, studying his son. 'He's a Poole, and most of it's our technology anyhow.'

Poole blurted, 'Why did you call me here, Harry? I need to be where I'm most useful. I *was* useful on the Moon. You know that. At Copernicus, trying to ramp up GUTengine production for your battleships. Look, I want to help fight this thing. But I'm an engineer. The best place for me is behind the lines.'

Harry shook his head. 'No. You are more than merely useful. You are unique, Michael. You know that the Xeelee's trajectory remains uncertain. But you also know we're trying to lure it to Mars. Right? And if it comes here, *this is where we will stop it*, before it goes anywhere near Earth. The strategy has been made known to every citizen who's participating in the Virtual-gaming programme going on down there. *They* know they will be in the front line, Michael, or anyhow that's the plan. And if *you* are down there, that's a sign of our commitment, to Mars, to their survival. Not only are you the hero who the whole human race saw ram that Lethe-spawned Cache Probe on its way to Earth, you're also my own son. A sign of my personal commitment, in fact.'

Poole glanced at Nicola, who pursed her lips, but for once she had nothing to say.

And Poole, thinking it over, knew he had no real choice in the matter – not for the first time when it came to his part in his father's schemes.

'Very well,' he said at last. 'We'll do it your way. Where do I start?'

'Jack Grantt wants to see you,' Harry said.
'Where?'
Nicola grinned. 'Barsoom.'

46

So, the next day, Poole descended to Cydonia. And Jack Grantt took him flying over Elysium Planitia.

Grantt's flitter was a robust two-man ship, adapted to Martian conditions and fitted out for long-duration fieldwork, with a compact life support system, a couple of bunks, a galley, and a small bench area set out with various scientific instruments, including a simple optical microscope. Lived-in, neat and mundane.

Elysium, meanwhile, north-east of Syrtis Major, was part of the vast, almost featureless system of lowlands and plains that dominated Mars's northern hemisphere. When Poole looked down through the big Virtual-transparent sections of lower hull, he saw dusty, rock-strewn desert, mostly unchanged for aeons. Familiar to Poole from many previous descents to Mars.

Familiar, except for the marching monsters beneath the flitter's prow.

Grantt, grinning at Poole's reaction, slowed the flitter and held it in a hover. 'Take your time. They can't see us; we're in administrator mode for this particular game-world . . .'

The procession was making its way across the plain, heading steadily south, moving no faster than the pace of the elephant-sized beasts that were doing most of the heavy dragging. Poole tried to estimate numbers: about fifty of those big draught beasts hauling what looked like chariots and travois, laden with furs and bits of broken statuary carved from crimson rock. In some of the chariots rode the evident masters of this march: big humanoids, each with what appeared to be an extra pair of limbs sprouting from the region of the hips, and a head with reptilian eyes that rolled back in their sockets. Green, leathery skin.

One of the chariots, a big one, bore what looked like huge, leathery eggs.

This parade was escorted by around five hundred smaller beasts, the size of horses maybe, with slate-black backs, and *ten legs* that gave their plodding motion an oddly crocodilian, low-slung look.

And behind this van came what looked more like regular people: men, women, children, their skin bright red, most of them more or less naked, blood-stained, many limping. Naked, on Mars: Poole felt his own deep-ingrained space traveller's instincts scream silently at the sight. And these were captives, bound at the wrists and ankles into one vast, shuffling chain gang. They were flanked by more of the big humanoids, armed but less adorned – warriors, presumably.

Poole had to remind himself that none of this was real – or rather, if anybody down there *was* real amid the crowd of Virtual projections, it was by choice, with their physical manifestation safely locked up in a booth somewhere.

'So are those prisoners people?'

Grantt's grin widened. 'Not quite. These "people" lay eggs too. Don't worry about it. This scenario isn't derived from a particularly modern scientific understanding . . .'

'This is the Discovery-era game zone, right?'

'Yes. When, through the best optical telescopes, all you could see of the surface of Mars was the waxing and waning of the polar caps with the seasons. And so people projected their dreams up here. This is a raiding party. Well, you can see that. They're heading back home after an assault on one of the more advanced cities, to the north. But the warriors live in a city of their own, a ruin, down at the ancient sea shore, south of here.'

'The sea shore. You mean the Discontinuity. The big geological dividing line between northern and southern hemispheres. That really *is* an ancient shore, isn't it?'

'Well, the old Discovery-era authors got some of their guesses right. *Their* Mars was a drying, dying world, just like the real thing – save that the north-hemisphere ocean actually vanished billions of years ago, not a mere million . . .' He turned the prow of the flitter sharply, and they swept away from the toiling caravan. 'The zone has got pretty extensive, with time. The work of many hands. And it stretches all the way to the north polar cap. It's the biggest of the planet's game zones, in fact.'

They came to a canal that cut across the landscape, grey and green and dead straight. Jack brought the flitter around so that it ran parallel to the great gully, heading almost directly north. In Mars's true air, which was closer to a vacuum than anything dreamed of in those Discovery-era fantasies, any open water would flash-freeze. But here, vegetation flourished along the canal banks – squat trees, what looked like cacti, even beds of moss – in some places spreading a few kilometres away from the canal itself, banding the waterway. And Poole spotted farms, neatly laid out fields irrigated by spurs from the canal.

In one place Grantt brought the flitter dipping low over a villa, surrounded by farmland. Graceful buildings, with pillars and arches of some glimmering crystal material, infeasibly tall. Before the main house stood a figure: a slim woman in a pale robe. She looked up as the flitter passed over. Poole saw that she wore a golden mask. Then she was lost, gone, the crystal pillars a fading glimmer.

'She looked like she could see us,' he remarked.

Grantt shrugged. 'Could be the protocols are slipping. Gamers like to challenge the rules, and the rule-makers. You know, gamers really are instinctive warriors – that's why they play. It's best they sublimate all that ingenious aggression into anachronous game worlds like this, rather than express it in the real world.

'And when Harry made his call for volunteers to help run this global game-world illusion – to get *all* the zones up and running together, to make the planet look as crowded as possible – the gamers responded with a will. A chance to fight for real, for once, if at one step removed. So here it is, the Mars of our dreams, fighting back against the invading nightmare. And you have to admit it looks convincing.'

'And Harry is gambling that it will all seem convincing to the Xeelee too.'

This was the logic, it turned out. Months after the Xeelee and the Cache had left the Sun, they continued to follow their patient spiralling trajectory out through the Solar System. And it still wasn't clear to the military analysts, drafted in from astronomy departments across the Solar System, whether the Xeelee was ultimately heading for Mars or Earth – or either. And so the Stewards, under Harry Poole, were trying to force the issue by giving it something to aim at . . .

'Well, that's the thinking. If the Xeelee is seeking to damage us on a large scale, maybe it will head for where it thinks it can do humanity the most harm, most quickly. It will try to decapitate us. So, Harry argues, we'll pull a bluff. Cover Mars with cities and canals, battles and disasters, make it look as if *it* is the dominant human world in the Solar System: not Earth, placid, peaceful, green, energy-conservative. And when we lure the Xeelee here, we'll hit it with all we've got – and above the surface of a sparsely inhabited planet instead of fragile old Earth.'

Poole marvelled at the deviousness. He knew he would never have come up with such a scheme.

'But will it work? It's all just spectacle; there's hardly any energy being expended down there. Hardly any *people* at all.'

'Maybe. But there are a lot of *minds* down there, simulated or projected. Look, Michael, I buy Harry's argument on this. I'm an exobiologist, remember. We're dealing with an alien species in the Xeelee – an alien, it seems, from out of time. Who knows what it perceives of us? It may understand little of our cool, carbon-chemistry biosphere. It may be of such a foreign nature that it can't even tell what's alive here, let alone sentient. It may think those hordes of simulated red-skinned warriors are as authentic a kind of human as you or I. Certainly we might confuse it, and if we achieve nothing else, that's something, isn't it?'

'I can see you've got heavily involved in running all this.'

'Thanks to your father. I was somebody on the spot he could use.'

'That's Harry.'

'For better or worse he knows how to reach people, Michael . . .'

Now a city lay sprawled across the desert below. Grantt lifted the flitter high in the air, for a better view.

Poole saw two mighty walled strongholds, each contained by a glittering circular rampart, set perhaps a hundred kilometres apart. Between the twin communities stretched a webbing of roads. Spires reached up from the heart of each city, kilometres tall, Poole judged. Even in the bright daylight, artificial light glimmered from rooftops, along narrow radial avenues, and from great structures like temples.

But all this was obscured by war. Armies clashed on the plain beyond the cities' walls: armies of foot soldiers, it seemed, their only vehicles carts drawn by more huge animals, with the spark and smoke of firearms everywhere. Poole could see that this particular conflict was a war of humanoid against humanoid – one band of the red-skinned people against another, without the involvement of the green-skinned giants he had seen earlier.

The war was being waged in the air too. Over the ant-like soldier hordes, huge, ponderous aerial vessels floated. They were like airships, Poole thought at first, long grey bodies strung from end to end with gaudy banners, and signal flags that fluttered in strings. But the ships moved too rapidly, too gracefully to be simple dirigibles, with turns and dips assisted by sails and propellers.

And they fought. The tactics were reminiscent of what Poole had read of ocean-navy clashes of the Discovery era. One ponderous craft would glide slowly alongside another, while cannon cracked between the parallel hulls, and crew threw nets and grappling hooks to try to board their opponents' craft. As Poole watched he saw one ship fall, its superstructure burning, drifting down slow as a paper lantern in the air.

'For cultures which have at least gunpowder, I can see an awful lot of swords being swung.'

Jack Grantt laughed. 'Oh, lighten up. It is supposed to be a game, Michael. Fun, you know? You won't be surprised that this is the most popular zone. Here, you get to swing a sword, *and* you can play with technology that's actually more advanced than our own. How do you think those airships fly? Not with some lighter-than-air gas mixture. They extract a kind of antigravity principle from the sunlight. Which, I would playfully suggest, isn't much more fantastic than the way you wormhole-builders claim to squeeze exotic matter from the vacuum. Come on. I'll take you to the Anthropocene zone. That's fun too, in a different kind of way.'

Glancing back one last time, Poole saw a new element enter the fight: more humanoids, short, squat, stocky, who could leap high in the air – high enough to reach the lower airships, and once aboard they laid about them with swords and clubs.

Grantt looked over his shoulder. 'People from Earth,' he said with a smile. 'On *this* Mars, they are super-strong. What a game!'

47

Heading for the other side of the planet, the flitter rose up out of the atmosphere for a brief suborbital hop. Grantt made the most of their few minutes of weightlessness to get out of his couch, stretch in the air, hand Poole a ration packet.

But once more Poole was distracted by the view: this time by something real, by rays laid down across the landscapes below, fresh and bright. Mars was a smaller, colder, *deader* world than Earth, and the great punch of the Xeelee Probe had done little global damage, compared to the Earth with its massive, easily perturbed oceans and atmosphere. But the rays of thrown-out debris from that new crater in Hellas had wrapped halfway around the planet. Thousands of kilometres from the impact, he was flying over its mark.

As the flitter began its descent, Grantt took back the controls and flew them down over an equatorial feature called Mangala Vallis, a place of chaotic gorges and huge, tumbled rocks. Here, waters trapped in aquifers within the ancient highlands of the south had long ago broken out and spilled into the desiccated bed of the northern ocean, smashing and tumbling the bedrock as they went. And here, in this intersection between two geographies – in some fictions – the first human landings on Mars had been made.

Poole could see the heart of it for himself now: a classic landing site, with a lone, fragile spacecraft, first-footstep trails in the crusty Martian dirt, a Stars and Stripes held up by wire in the thin air – the flag itself a symbol of a vanished polity that felt as remote in time to Poole as a Roman legion's eagle standard. But evidently the landing had been generations back, in the fiction; the remains of the cone-shaped lander were contained in what looked like a roughly roped-off, open-air museum, or shrine. Nearby was a township, primitive but thriving, a place of domes and bunkers of Mars-red brick, with cables snaking from a nuclear power facility, and fields of corn glimmering green under transparent plastic. Outside the domes people hopped around in clumsy pressure suits.

A consistency-violation alarm pinged.

Grantt checked a softscreen and laughed. 'Somebody shot at us. A rifle bullet. Only Virtual, but aimed with intent.'

'And we were hit,' Poole said, wondering. 'Good shot.'

'You probably don't survive if you're not a good shot out here.'

'You said this is the Anthropocene Zone.'

'Yes . . . A scientifically authentic Mars, more or less. And authentic spacecraft of the time, driven by chemical propellants or fission piles. In the reality of these games, the early age-of-heroes space ventures *weren't* abandoned as the Bottleneck closed in, as in our reality. And, with time, you got *this*. Pioneers and homesteaders in a new frontier. A Mars where Mangala City became the first capital, not Kahra. It never was like this, and maybe it never could have been. But it's another fine dream, isn't it? The big set-piece here is the revolutionary war. Kind of a rerun of 1776, with domed cities and Mars buggies.' He lifted the flitter higher in the air. 'Before we get shot at again, let's go see the later Bottleneck-era stuff. Smaller scale, but interesting in its own way . . .'

Again a loop out of the atmosphere. Poole watched patchwork fields, like scraps of ancient Kansas, recede beneath the ship. 'All these versions of Mars. And under it all, the real Mars. *Your* Mars, Jack.'

'The Mars of the Lattice, yes. And *that* can't be evacuated. I don't see how it's possible to save it, unless you save Mars itself. Of course, that's what I intend to do – to save the world. But if we fail I'm working on backup options . . .'

Once more they cut back into the atmosphere, and came swooping down on the equator, heading west. Poole recognised the crumpled gouge that was the Valles Marineris, where he and Nicola had trekked. But *this* version of the feature was littered with lights: communities, cities, but of an unearthly nature, with strange street plans and ungainly low-gravity buildings.

'So in these narratives we made it to Mars, and in the post-Anthropocene downturn the colonies were evacuated, contact with Mars broken. As in reality. But in the story, you see, a lost handful of colonists lived on, ragged, abandoned. And then . . . have you ever heard of the Mariner from Mars?'

Poole grinned. 'Heard of him? I *was* him when I was seven years old.'

'The franchise is so old we don't know who the original authors were. The Mariner was an alien – human in appearance, but alien. A million years back he was a refugee from a destroyed world. His spacecraft came sailing into the Solar System and collided with Mars. The first impact created the Hellas basin; the whole planet rang like a bell, and the Tharsis region with the big volcanoes, at the rough antipode of Hellas, was pushed up in response. Meanwhile the Mariner's ship, skipping like a stone on the water, came down again, and scraped across the ground for a thousand kilometres—'

'Digging out the Marineris gorges.'

'Hence the *true* origin of the name for that feature. You do know the story. Before finally smashing into Olympus Mons and being buried in lava, only to be chipped out much later by plucky human settlers. The immortal Mariner and his super-powered human-hybrid descendants lived on, built their thousand-kilometre-long city in the valley – and from time to time they returned to Earth, in secret. So, back on Earth, if you were lost in some Bottleneck disaster, just another migrant, desolate, plague-ridden, homeless . . . and if you were *really* lucky . . .'

'A Martian superhero would come down from the sky to save you. Nice dream. Although I always wanted to get hold of his interstellar-capable spacecraft and reverse-engineer it.'

'Spoken like a true Poole.'

The flitter soared up and away from the Valles and, skimming the atmosphere once more, made for the Tharsis region.

'Later I can take you to the fourth zone, the Recovery-era region, if you like. Covers much of Argyre. The whole basin brims with light. No rifle-toting homesteaders or egg-laying princesses there. Just peaceful aboriginal inhabitants, or visions of them. Mostly tall leathery humanoids. Wise old ones, who managed to save at least a portion of their planet from the great primordial drought, and have lived in peace with each other on their desert world ever since. For the more thoughtful gamers it's a kind of retreat, I think.'

'Sounds a little passive for me.'

Grantt grinned. 'Thought it might be.'

That was when Harry called.

The spotters had confirmed it at last: the Xeelee's trajectory had changed. It was bypassing Earth, and was making for Mars. Not only that, it was accelerating. The gaming, it seemed, had paid off.

The Xeelee would still take months to arrive, but it was here, then, at Mars, where the battle for the Solar System, for mankind, for the future, might be fought and won, or lost. But that put Grantt's precious adopted world, enigmatic Lattice and all, in the line of fire.

The biologist, at least, stayed calm. 'Let's get on with it, then. Lots to plan. One more sight I must show you first, though, up on Olympus . . .'

The butterscotch sky rapidly darkened as they rose on one more sub-orbital hop. The summit of Olympus, above Mars's air, was stripped, in this vision, of space-elevator infrastructure, and its true nature was revealed: a great caldera that could have cradled all the volcanic islands of the Hawaii chain.

And at its very centre, beings that looked like graceful low-gravity octopuses were assembling a cannon, pointing at the sky.

48

Poole headed back to Kahra.

He spent the next few months tucked into a suite in the Grand Martian, one of Kahra's better hotels. Poole knew the place well; it had supposedly been founded by a family, the York-Williams, who claimed to trace their origins back to the first Anthropocene-era pioneers, even though those first settler families had all been brought back to Earth during the Bottleneck. Be that as it may the Pooles had been using the hotel for generations, and indeed Poole Industries was a part owner. So Poole had the use of a suite, gratis.

And of course, Poole knew, the Martian was a place where Harry could keep tabs on him.

He had Jack Grantt for occasional company. The biologist had come in from his outpost in Acidalia to the capital, to witness this existential struggle for the planet he loved – and, he said, to work with the Martian regional authority on various contingency plans.

What Poole and Grantt witnessed going on in space, meanwhile, was an exercise in futility.

The Xeelee had picked up its pace, after it crossed the orbit of the Earth. It was expected to reach Mars in mere weeks. And from that point the continuing, plaintive attempts to contact it were finally abandoned. Instead, all the way in to its presumed target, the Xeelee was subject to constant attack.

Crewed ships maintained a moving cordon around the sycamore seed craft, with high-intensity lasers and the superheated exhaust of GUTdrives playing on that impassive black hull. The strategy, Poole knew, was simple. No single weapon made any difference to the Xeelee or its operations as far as anybody could tell, but by simply drenching the Xeelee with energy, some capacity for absorption might be overcome – that night-black armour might at last buckle.

Not yet it hadn't.

Then, as Mars neared, the assaults intensified, with missiles hastily adapted or improvised, tipped with everything from destabilised GUTengine pods to Anthropocene-era hydrogen-fusion bombs, cobbled together from ancient designs or even dug out of military museums. And, following the lead of Poole with his attack on the Cache Probe aimed at Earth, crude kinetic-energy weapons were thrown at the intruder too, massively built hulks fitted with little more than a GUTdrive pod, a guidance system and a payload of asteroid rock or ice, to be smashed brutally against the Xeelee. The strategy was, as Poole recalled, just as Harry's tame war-gamers had advocated it in Kent.

Many of these assaults were orders of magnitude more energetic than anything that had been tried against the Probes – and now, at last, were launched with unswerving determination.

Harry had observed this psychological shift. He'd said to Poole, 'We suddenly got serious. The Xeelee doesn't hold back, evidently. We have, so far. The warrior-nations of the Anthropocene would have responded to this situation better than we have, with less hesitation, more intent.'

'We are what we are, Harry.'

'Yes. A better breed, by most measures. But right now we need to fight with our hindbrains, as well as our intellect.' He had grinned at his son. 'And you, Michael, showed us the way. Makes me proud. People say we Pooles are too cerebral. Not when you smashed up the *Crab*, we weren't . . .'

But, just as Poole's own desperate resistance to the Earth Probe had proved futile, so the bombardment of the Xeelee itself en route to Mars made no difference at all to the alien's relentless approach.

Poole did find some comfort in the reports on Highsmith Marsden's ongoing studies. They were dry analyses laced with Marsden's habitually cryptic remarks, and occasional words of cold comfort: 'Remember, every failed attack is another data point. Every single time, we learn something.' Poole had even put Marsden, through Miriam Berg, in tentative touch with Harry's intelligence agencies – though Marsden had insisted firmly that his own location remain a secret. Despite the man's reclusiveness, Poole had faith that Marsden's researches and speculations, developed in the stealthed seclusion of Gallia Three, might eventually bear fruit.

But not yet.

For now, they had nothing to stop or even slow the Xeelee's approach.

And, early in the new year, the Xeelee came to Mars.

*

The sycamore seed ship, still accompanied by the Cache, sailed out of the Sun. While the Cache settled into a solar orbit about a million kilometres behind Mars itself, the Xeelee approached the planet.

And slowed to a halt with almost contemptuous ease over the south pole of Mars. Its altitude was about seven thousand kilometres, a little more than the diameter of the planet itself.

Meanwhile three smaller craft, featureless ellipsoids of hull plate that were immediately dubbed 'drones', were fired out of lesions in the Cache's flanks and sent to other stations, scattered over Mars's northern hemisphere.

On arrival, the Xeelee was immediately surrounded by the chasing fleet of ships, and more vessels thrown up from Mars itself – one of them piloted by Nicola Emry. Their relentless assault continued. The drones, too, were monitored, bombarded, with no effect.

But, for now, the Xeelee didn't respond. It just held its station, with its drones, silent and enigmatic.

Poole decided to go up to see the Xeelee for himself.

With a little help from local representatives of Poole Industries, he left his flesh-and-blood carcass lying under a light sleep-inducer field in a small sanatorium run by the Grand Martian. And he projected a Virtual presence up to ride alongside Nicola in her cramped, two-person, heavily armed flitter: a warship, at the fringe of a cordon of such ships surrounding the Xeelee. At this distance the lightspeed signal time delay from the ground was only a fraction of a second, a subtle disjunction that gave Poole no problems.

He and Nicola hadn't been in each other's presence, Virtual or not, for months. When he boarded her only greeting was a curt nod, before she returned to her inspection of the view through the windows and in her softscreens.

From up here – or *down* here, under the south pole, Poole reflected, if you thought in terms of a position in relation to a conventional north-at-the-top display globe – planet Mars was a shield of dull orange. The south polar cap was a swirl of dirty cream, right at the centre of that shield: water ice layers millions of years old, cut into an intricate spiral pattern by persistent winds. The few human settlements this far south were mere blemishes on that great planetary hide, splashes of glassed-over green. Most of them were the migrant communities living off the ice at the fringe of the polar cap. Poole wondered if the migrants had managed one last season's-end party at Hellas.

And, directly ahead of Poole as he looked with Virtual eyes out of the flitter's windows, there was the Xeelee. The alien itself was visible to him only with the ship's deep probes, with neutrino pulses and other subtle instruments, for the Xeelee was still surrounded by a dense cloud of human craft, a cloud that shifted endlessly as ships were moved into fresh positions, or pulled out of the line for relief, refuelling, or rearming. Warships, that even now bathed the Xeelee continually with ferocious energies.

Nicola fretted about the Xeelee's location. 'Why *here*, above a pole? And why this far out? It's not even in orbit; it's spending energy to station-keep every second it stays up here.'

Poole grunted. 'Somehow I don't think station-keeping energy budgets are a great concern for a Xeelee—'

A flash of light, cherry-red, in Poole's peripheral vision.

'Something's changed,' he said immediately.

'Yes.' They began to scan softscreens.

It became obvious.

From the heart of the rough sphere of human ships, beams of light now speared out, a gleaming, dazzling red – three of them coming from a common origin, arrowing dead straight through the cloud of ships. Beams scattering in three directions, separated by equal angles: beams that sheared off into the distance, to left, right, below from Poole's point of view, staying coherent, brilliant, as far as Poole could track them.

At first Poole assumed the beams must be aimed at the planet itself, but it soon became clear that their tracks passed over the surface of the planet before lancing on into space – but they terminated where the three beams each met one of the patient, waiting Xeelee drones.

It was no surprise when the source of the beams was revealed as the Xeelee itself.

The fleet of human ships kept its formation, but damage had been done as soon as the beams were fired up. Poole saw the hulk of a GUTship come drifting out of the crowd, spine sheared through, life-dome still pathetically bright. Poole had the intuition, though, that wrecking the ships of the escort fleet had nothing to do with the Xeelee's true purpose here.

Nicola was paging through softscreen displays, and Poole was aware of voices whispering in her ear. 'We're ordered to keep our positions, unless it's to evade mortal danger, or help survivors of the wrecks. Those beams have created a *lot* of wrecks.'

'What about the beams themselves?'

'Nobody knows. Energy densities off the scale. They've spread out at lightspeed; they span thousands of kilometres. Nobody even knows how come they are visible at all. It's not like a laser beam lighting up a cloud of dry ice. It seems they're more like some kind of wound in spacetime itself.' She looked up from her screens to peer through her window again, and Poole saw that terrible cherry-red light reflected in her face. 'Lethe. *Look* at it.'

Poole, trying to be analytical, was studying the geometry. 'The three lines, those precise angles. It's like looking down on some huge arte-fact. Like the Cache, when we visited it. Imagine hovering over one corner of *that*. You'd have the same impression, the convergent edges, thousand-kilometre lines meeting with the precision of a textbook diagram.'

'Maybe it is something like that. A vast artefact, I mean ... Look at this. There's something new.' Frowning, Nicola paged through a softscreen until she found a particular image, stroked the screen, Virtual-flung it into the air between them, where it rotated, three-dimensional. 'This whole-planet view is a synthesis, a composite from many sensors, many angles – even observations from Earth . . .'

The new image showed Mars, the whole of it, a globe the size of Poole's fist, floating in the air, quite detailed: the polar caps, the red deserts, one hemisphere in shadow. Even a blur that was a dust storm over Utopia Planitia.

But this was a Mars in a cage. A cage of light, connecting the Xeelee itself over the south pole to the three drones hanging over Mars's northern hemisphere. And now, Poole saw, more beams of that dread cherry-red glow had condensed, connecting these three nodes in turn, in great triangular linkings. Completing the cage. Closing it.

Nicola flicked the Virtual image with a fingertip; her gloved hand passed through the unreal projection, and it turned, slowly. That cage of light turned with it. 'And so Mars is contained. It must be visible from the ground. Quite a sight.'

Poole tried to focus on the cage itself. 'The three drones,' he said, studying detailed feeds. 'Spread evenly around the low-latitude northern hemisphere: over Tharsis, over Arabia Terra, over Elysium, roughly. And, that geometry—'

On impulse Nicola flipped the image over, so it was north pole down. Now Mars was like a marble sitting on the lower face of a tetrahedral box, a four-sided cage. The box couldn't have been any smaller and still able to contain the planet, Poole saw; the other faces, if solid, would have brushed the planet's surface. 'A geometer would call that an insphere. The largest sphere the tetrahedron could contain without its surface breaking through the facets.'

'A tetrahedron.' Nicola grinned, but it was a strange, mixed expression, Poole thought: bitter, awed – defiant. 'A tetrahedron the size of a planet. Seventeen thousand kilometres on a side. Earth's diameter is only thirteen thousand kilometres. Even you Pooles never thought of building *that* big . . . And it's precisely designed, too. I mean, to fit Mars, as closely as possible, just as you said. In fact, if those faces were solid, at their closest they really would come down to within a few kilometres of the planet's surface.'

'Why a tetrahedron?'

Now she laughed. 'Are you that dumb? *Because of you*, Poole. You and your tetrahedral wormhole mouths, and your tetrahedral amulet brought by some spooky alien babbling about the "Sigil of Free Humanity". With this Lethe-spawned tetrahedral cage around Mars, the Xeelee is mocking you. *Look what I can do.* And you can't stop it, can you?'

Poole, awed by this apparently effortless planet-scale display of power – and fearing, deep in his gut, that she was somehow right about the connection of all this to his own personal destiny – tried to stay defiant. To keep thinking. But it was as if his own mind was in a cage as confining as the Xeelee tetrahedron.

'Phobos,' Nicola said now, distracted again.

'What?'

'Phobos has suddenly become a priority.'

That threw Poole momentarily. 'Phobos? Oh – of course. Deimos should be OK; that little moon orbits around twenty thousand kilometres above Mars's surface. But Phobos is only six thousand kilometres up.'

'And those vertices,' Nicola said, 'are *seven* thousand kilometres above the surface. So they're evacuating Phobos, fast. If you've any stock in the Tangle shipyards, sell now—'

Poole grabbed the Virtual globe-in-tetrahedron out of the air with his Virtual hand; his consistency protocols assigned it solidity and weight. 'I'm going back down. Ask Grantt to meet me in the Grand Martian lobby. Good luck up here.'

She seemed to reach out to him, just as his view of the flitter cabin dissolved in a hail of pixels.

49

As soon as his consciousness returned to his body in the Grand Martian sanatorium, Poole was able to push back the cover of his couch and stand unaided, despite the close attention of a couple of med-equipped bots that seemed oddly disappointed at a lack of ill effects or disorientation. He grabbed a skinsuit, donned it. He made sure that he still had access to Nicola's Virtual, the Mars globe encased within its shell of cherry-red light; sure enough, it floated in the air at his shoulder.

Then, without a word, he walked out of the sanatorium.

The hotel lobby was a big, airy chamber, walled and roofed by glass, an elderly structure by Martian standards – and now almost like a scale model of the big arcologies that had been planned across the planet. And today it was crowded, with people sitting at tables or standing in clusters, looking out, talking in low tones. Some of them shimmered, blinked out of existence, reappeared; but most people seemed to be here in the flesh.

Including Jack Grantt, who stood by a windowed wall, softscreen in one hand. Like Poole himself he wore a skinsuit, open at the neck, ready to be closed in an instant – a basic precaution that few others had taken, Poole noticed.

As Poole approached, Grantt, evidently distracted, glanced at the Mars globe that hovered at Poole's shoulder. 'What in Lethe has been done to us?' He flicked a finger at the big enclosing tetrahedron, which trembled briefly. 'You want a drink? The bars are free of charge for the duration.' He grinned wryly. 'Always an upside, if you look for it.'

'No. Thanks.' Poole glanced around. 'But there are plenty of takers.'

Grantt shrugged. 'It's what people do, Michael. Ordinary people, not cerebral recluses like you and me. When a hard rain falls you want company, you listen to the news, you have a drink, you talk it over. That's my theory anyhow. Which is maybe why you came back down yourself.'

Poole shrugged. 'Or maybe it's just guilt.'

'Guilt? Get that out of your head. Whatever's to come, we need you thinking clearly.' He peered up at the sky, uneasy. 'You know, before the Hellas Probe hit, I sent my family to Phobos. Wife, kids and step-kids, grandchildren. Thought they'd be safe there, whatever happened down on Mars. Ha! Now I'm getting them off there fast.'

'I'll send a message to the Poole Industries people up there. If there's anything they can do—'

'I appreciate that.'

Poole murmured the message.

Then, moodily, he stepped to the window-wall.

This hotel was at the edge of the city itself. Looking west, he gazed out at a butterscotch sky, and a raw landscape sparsely cluttered with roads and masts and various support facilities: still, essentially, Mars. But when he turned north he looked across a human landscape: Kahra itself, its domes and towers. The heart of the city was an island, almost like a miniature Manhattan, crowded with skyscrapers of a delicacy and height that would not have been possible under Earth's heavier gravity. The most expensive single element, of course, was the deep, placid lake that surrounded that island: open water, the rarest of luxuries on Mars. This had to be pointed out to most visitors from Earth, where standing water was commonplace. This architecture, already centuries old, would have been dwarfed by the big dome at Cydonia, let alone the arcologies planned for Hellas and elsewhere, but still it was a monument to the ambition and style of a pioneering generation. Kahra had been a statement, a bit of Mars made like the Earth, a signal that humans were here to stay. But maybe that ambition meant nothing now.

Because, as Poole looked up into the pale orange-brown of an afternoon sky, he could see a cherry-red stripe. Dead straight, beyond the atmosphere itself, only slightly obscured and discoloured by the thin, dust-laden air. The Xeelee had come here, and in minutes it had overwhelmed everything humans had done on Mars in millennia.

'*Look* at that thing,' Grantt muttered at his side. 'There are some who are saying it actually casts a shadow, if you go outdoors. We're keeping up the Virtual camouflage, by the way. The armies of Barsoom and the Mariner from Mars. Maybe that ornery settler type in Amazonis is taking pot-shots at the Xeelee right now with his gunpowder rifle. Whether or not that worked in luring in the Xeelee, it can't make much difference now that—'

A flash in the sky, there and gone. More crimson, in the corner of Poole's eye.

He looked around, baffled. Grantt had shut up. Other guests flinched back from the walls, gathered in groups, muttered in hushed tones. Only the bots, circulating with trays through the crowd, seemed unperturbed. Something had changed, again. Poole seemed to sense it from the reaction of the people around him, as much as by the event itself. Superhuman energies were being wielded on a superhuman scale, and maybe it was just too big to see, for an individual to take in. And yet people together, the mass, sensed the change. Still that cherry-red gash across the sky was visible, strong, static – that tetrahedral frame must be turning with the planet, he realised. His sense of unease deepened. What, then? What was new?

Jack Grantt had pulled his skinsuit hood over his head; the suit was sealing itself up, a transparent visor dropping down before his face. 'Listen. Let's get out of here. Before they lock us up in our rooms with the other guests.'

Which, Poole knew, was the protocol. On Mars you didn't evacuate a hotel; the individual rooms were robust cells, virtually independent habitats in themselves, and people were safer there. A glance over his shoulder showed him that such a command was already being acted on; the drinks-serving bots had linked metallic arms in a kind of chain, and were herding guests back to their rooms.

'Agreed.' Poole pulled up his own hood and reached for his helmet. He and Grantt hurriedly walked out of the lobby, and to the airlock that led out of the city dome to the open terrain to the west.

Poole, oddly, felt safer out in the Martian air. At least he knew the variables out here; at least he could anticipate the danger. Or he thought he could. Over his head, he saw that tremendous beam in the sky, an edge of the Xeelee tetrahedron, like, he thought, celestial scaffolding.

Now Grantt pointed in the direction of the Tharsis volcanoes. *'There.'*

Poole turned and looked that way. Far to the west, towards Tharsis, something new: *another* beam, cherry-red like the rest, that seemed to drop straight down from the sky to the ground. Almost like a space-elevator cable, he thought, to match the one at Olympus Mons. That must be what he'd glimpsed before, subliminally.

All this in silence.

'Are you there, Michael?' Nicola's sharp voice.

Poole glanced at Grantt, and touched the biologist's faceplate with one finger. 'Copying Jack in.'

'Get outdoors.'

'Nicola, we're ahead of you, we're outside already. What's happening?'

'We're under attack, is what's happening,' she said grimly. 'About three minutes ago, each of the four vertices of the Xeelee tetrahedron let loose a beam – the Navy types up here are calling it a *planetbuster*. Same energy intensity as the beams that connected the tetrahedron in the first place. But now these four are blasting straight down at the ground, from each corner. You should be able to see the nearest, coming down on Tharsis, to your west . . .'

'We have it, Nicola.' Now, looking to the west, Poole saw a kind of glowing pillar following that line of cherry-red light back up towards the sky. And darkness spreading, very high.

'If you want the global picture take a look at your Virtual . . . downloading updates.'

The Virtual display Poole had brought down from orbit hovered patiently, an arm's length from his head. There was Mars, that fist-sized globe, one hemisphere still illuminated by an invisible sun, the other in shadow. There was that spiky tetrahedral cage of rich red light around the planet, looking oddly inverted, with its apex under the planet's south pole. But now new beams of light and energy, new cherry-red girders, had been added to the structure. They descended from each of the four vertices, apparently aimed straight towards the centre of the planet. Firing straight down at the surface, he saw, at the ground, and into it.

'As an abstraction,' Jack Grantt said, 'that looks almost beautiful. As if the Xeelee have made a pendant of Mars, put it in a setting like a precious stone . . .'

'So,' Nicola said, 'one target site is the south pole, under the Xeelee. The others are spread around the northern hemisphere, under the drones. One in Tharsis – about a thousand kilometres from Kahra, I think. One in Arabia Terra. One in Elysium.'

Poole saw that the central image of Mars was already changing. Even as he watched, where the four descending beams struck, a kind of dark blight was spreading across the planet's surface. And whole regions of Mars seemed to flicker and grow darker, plainer. The Virtual dioramas collapsing as the power failed, Poole supposed.

'Nicola, can I see a touchdown point?'

'Just magnify the image.'

Poole dug his hands into the turning planet, feeling nothing, expanding the image easily. He manipulated it until he had extracted a god's eye view of the Tharsis region, the great volcanoes like huge, shallow blisters.

The beam had grounded not far from the flank of Olympus itself, a cherry-red thread from the sky. Where it touched he saw a central bright spark, what looked like a walled crater around it, a wider area of smashed and broken ground. All this presumably caused in the first instants of the touchdown, an injection of energy, as if another huge mass, a greater Probe, had hit the planet.

But this wasn't a simple impact; the energy had continued to stream down from the sky. So there was a kind of continuing explosion going on in that central region, and more waves of smashed, semi-molten rock washed out, overwhelming mountainous crater walls themselves only a few minutes old. The ground around the strike was actually liquefying, Poole saw, staying molten, a lake of magma growing wide and deep and ever hotter.

Further out was a kind of ring, blurred, expanding rapidly: superheated air, he supposed, driving the ubiquitous Martian dust before it. And, behind that sweeping band, no sign of humanity was left, no settlements visible, no lights, no roads. Overwhelmed already.

'I think we may have trouble appreciating the scale of this,' Grantt said tightly, listening to feeds of his own. 'The apparent slowness is a clue. That central magma pool is already a hundred kilometres across. Much bigger than the crater in Hellas. A lot more energy being delivered. And that atmospheric shock wave, that looks like it's crawling, is spreading at the speed of sound. This is *big* . . .'

The ground shuddered and flexed under Poole's feet. He felt, as much as heard, a deep groan, as if the bedrock itself were being twisted and torn.

Jack Grantt reflexively grabbed his arm.

Poole, deliberately keeping calm, tried to figure the numbers. He was a thousand kilometres from the groundfall of that cherry-red beam; seismic waves propagated at a few kilometres per second . . . Only minutes since the strike, and the first effects were already here. And, in a few more minutes, they would be felt all across the planet.

Now came fear. A deep, phobic reaction. He had spent much of his life in space but he had been born and raised on planets, on Earth and Moon. Worlds weren't meant to buck and tremble like a ship with a badly tuned GUTengine. This was real, not just some light show, a distant, theoretical spectacle. The attack had reached out already and touched *him*.

There was a ferocious crack, loud in the thin air.

'The hotel,' Grantt said. 'Those glass walls—'

'Go.'

Out of instinct, Poole and Grantt ran, side by side, supporting each other, away from the building, Poole clumsy in the low Martian gravity, Grantt more efficient, faster once he hit his stride. The ground shook harder, making them stumble.

After maybe fifty metres Poole, still running, looked back. He saw that the big glass bubble of the lobby's wall had already cracked clean in two; shards were wheeling out in the Martian air. The roof of the lobby was sagging too. Poole saw bots rolling through the debris, patiently, as if preparing to begin the operation of sweeping up, despite the greater drama unfolding all around them.

Again the ground shook, still more violently. And again.

They ran on.

Poole gasped out, 'Tell me what's happening, Emry.'

'I've got softscreens full of numbers here. Projections. I'm trying to abstract what it all means.

'The Xeelee and its drones are just pouring energy down into Mars. From each of the vertices of the tetrahedron. Nobody knows *how* this is being done. Some of the police experts suggest it is something like a gravity-wave laser. Or even an antigravity laser, something that rips you apart from within.

'But what's important isn't the *how* but the *how much*. The numbers . . . Even the comparisons are extraordinary. It's as if Mars is suffering a dinosaur-killer comet strike, a Chicxulub, every hour. Or, a better comparison – those Probe strikes that did so much damage, on Mars and Earth and the Moon? Forty of those every *second*. And it just keeps hammering down. It's like an asteroid fall that won't stop.

'At the Tharsis site, an initial crater maybe a hundred kilometres across has already been obliterated, the rim walls dissolved, by a kind of spreading magma pool. From space it looks like a skin cancer, a blight. All that energy is blasting rock to liquid, even vapour – a hundred trillion tonnes of it at each groundfall so far, most of it being sucked up into the stratosphere along the lines of the beams. What else? Earthquakes. Seismic waves from the big shocks being inflicted on the bedrock, felt all over the planet already . . .'

Poole looked up. A shadow was crossing the sky, like a very high altitude cloud bank. Could that really be rock from Tharsis – the substance of ancient volcanoes pulverised and hurled out to the edge of space? He thought he could see the crackle of lightning.

'Why?' Grantt asked suddenly. *'Why?* Where is this going to end? What in Lethe does the Xeelee want? I'm an evolutionary biologist. I ought to be able to understand this. Maybe it is simply impossible for two tool-wielding, technological intelligences to coexist. One must inevitably displace the other . . .'

'Jack, come on, focus. Where's your rover?'

Grantt seemed to make a positive effort to think. He pointed, then led the way. 'Parked up at the city limit. Half a kilometre that way. We'll get organised,' he said grimly, as he walked, still distracted. 'We Martians, I mean. We're tough. They'll already be designating refuges, gathering points. Evacuation stations, even.'

Poole said, 'My father will see that your people get all the help there is. But it's one step at a time. Jack. Stay with me. The rover—'

'This way.'

When they got to the rover, they scrambled into its interior, slamming closed the airlock hatch.

It was a huge relief just to be in shelter. They opened their suits and gulped down water. Yet still Poole could feel the ground shake, through the vehicle's suspension.

There was fresh data, downloaded by Nicola.

She had found images of the damage being done at the south pole strike site. There, so much energy had been injected into the ancient landscape that the ice was *melting*, already, the whole kilometres-thick polar cap, a grand disaster spanning a thousand kilometres, those strange wind-scoured spiral valleys softening and slumping. Poole checked the time. It was less than an hour since the planetbuster beams had first touched Mars.

Nicola broke through their appalled silence. 'So, you two had enough of goofing off, and ready for some work?'

They looked at each other, and grinned. 'Patch us in, Nicola.'

Grantt quickly reported their own position and the rover's capabilities to the Kahra authorities, offering their service. In the last months, as the Xeelee had approached, preparations for an attack on the planet had been made as best they could be, including the establishment of an emergency command hierarchy with local controllers drawn from the

Federal Police, and from 'Steward' Harry Poole's new UN-peacekeeper army, stationed in each province. Already the Kahra commander was briskly ordering checks on outlying communities, settlements, even stranded travellers, the intention being to bring them into the more robust shelter of the city itself. It was a good start, although, Poole thought, the closeness of the planetbuster beam track to the Olympus space elevator was going to complicate the scheme.

Poole admired Grantt's focus now. With an immediate crisis to deal with, he didn't mention his family, or indeed the Lattice, once.

Within a few minutes the Kahra command centre gave them a destination, a young family that had got split up, half of them stuck in a low-tech habitat about twenty kilometres from the city. Emergency response required.

With Grantt navigating, they rolled that way and went to work.

Two hours after the planetbuster beams touched down, the dust storm hit.

The storm was a world-girdling wall that came from the direction of Tharsis, rushing from the planetbuster strike at the speed of sound in Martian air. The debris of a billion years, driven on supersonic winds. Such winds were being experienced across the planet now, driven by the unending storms at the four energy-injecting strike points.

It caught Poole and Grantt outside the rover, on their second call-out, as they were making for another small, isolated settlement. Dust, and bits of rock that pounded at their skinsuits like bullets. Suddenly Poole couldn't see, couldn't hear for the battering of the dust on his faceplate and hood; even his link to Nicola was cut off.

But Jack Grantt was still here, waving his hands in the murk. Poole grabbed his arms. Clinging together, moving by memory as much as by sight, they made their way towards the shadowed bulk of the settlement's domes.

They got the inhabitants back to the relative safety of Kahra. Then they responded to another call, and went out again. And then another. As long as the calls kept coming.

50

At the start of the second day Jack Grantt floated the idea of going to Cydonia, to do what they could to help co-ordinate the evacuation there. Though his own family had long been evacuated Grantt had grown increasingly anxious about the fate of friends, colleagues, students in the region.

So they travelled to Cydonia, by flitter, through a continuing global dust storm.

Cydonia, a glass dome over a forest of towers, was Mars's second largest community after Kahra, with two million residents before the Xeelee came. That number included a wide hinterland of smaller settlements, with a population who more or less depended on the central city for facilities such as medical care and manufacturing – and including Jack Grantt himself, who in normal times was to be found in his laboratory-base out in the wild country.

Poole and Grantt connected with the local relief efforts, and immediately got to work. But Poole, distracted, couldn't help but obsess about the numbers.

Two million people, then, in Cydonia. Ten million on Mars in total. Just a day after the planetbusters had come down – *the Cage*, as the commentators had started calling the Xeelee's lethal tetrahedral trap – it had become horribly clear to Poole that they would all have to be evacuated, taken off the planet: all the Martians, from Kahra, Hellas, Cydonia, everywhere. Because the Xeelee wasn't about to let up.

And Poole, consulting with Grantt and others, was getting a pretty clear idea of how much time they had left to achieve that evacuation. At the planetbuster touchdown points the surface bedrock and crust had already been melted all the way down to the molten mantle fifty kilometres below, so that, surrounding the vertical beams, lakes of magma, liquid rock, started spreading ever wider.

Given the energetics of the planetbusters, it was estimated it would take just thirty-one days after the Xeelee's arrival from orbit to have injected, in theory, enough energy to enlarge those lakes to a thousand kilometres wide. Ultimately, after a few years of this, the crust would be melted entirely. Of course it wouldn't be a smooth process; Poole imagined volcanism, earthquakes, islands of dissolving granite in a spreading magma ocean . . .

Whatever the detail, whatever the Xeelee's ultimate intention for Mars, the Stewardship analysts were saying now that they couldn't see how any part of the planet could remain habitable after a year, maybe less.

A year, then, to save the population of a world.

Already a heroic effort had begun. People, families, were lifted by flitters and commandeered cargo ships directly to orbit and then beyond. Or they were shipped by surface roads and monorails and even stately tourist airships to the foot of the Olympus space elevator, to be crammed into squalid compartments for dangerously hasty ascents to orbit.

But the elevator itself was a mere few hundred kilometres from the groundfall of a Xeelee planetbuster beam. The whole planet shook now with seismic waves, a response to the apocalyptic energies being poured into it at the groundfall locations. Passengers on the elevator said you could feel the cable sway, as you inched your way to space.

And all of this, the system working at its maximum capacity, seemed to represent only a trickle when measured against these crowds of people who needed to be saved. Poole was an engineer of interplanetary technology, and he was used to dealing with big numbers. Yet the sheer logistical, human, psychological complexity of shifting ten million baffled him. He worked, and worked. But his deeper mind churned too. How in Lethe could *everybody* be saved in time?

In another corner of his crowded mind, he kept obsessing over how his father's ploy, to lure the Xeelee to Mars, had worked out. He put in more calls, demanding that Harry meet him, in person or the nearest thing to it.

And during that second day, during his breaks, in an overtired mind fizzing with ideas, an evacuation scheme started to coalesce.

He and Grantt had more immediate assignments. But when he next got a break Poole took steps to put his plan, such as it was, in motion. He made calls to the Poole Industries shipyards at Jupiter, and ordered a trial GUTship called the *Carnot* to be flown in to Mars, with a few modifications made on the way . . .

On the third day a report came down from Nicola that a barrage of Xeelee Probes, launched from the Cache and having crossed space with virtually no human resistance, had destroyed the moon Phobos. Three human casualties, many artificial sentiences lost. Jack Grantt's family, though, were all long gone, to comparative safety. But the Tangle, the warship graving yard, was lost. It had just got that bit harder to fight back.

And Mars now had a ring, like Saturn.

Poole was barely distracted by this event, stupendous as it was in its own right, so immersed was he by now in the details of his own planning.

Then, on the fourth day after the arrival of the Xeelee at Mars, Poole got a personal distress call, from his own mother. She was on the scene of a collapse under Green Town Plaza, near Cydonia's Illinois Tower – somehow he wasn't surprised to discover Muriel had a presence here. And she'd found some trapped children. Nobody was going to die soon. But, she said, there was nobody around to help. Nobody physical.

So Poole got his gear together, and found Jack Grantt.

'I'll go myself. Nobody else to handle it.'

'I'll log it. Come back safe.'

51

In a battered rover, Poole soon found the location: a broken-open dome, already evacuated.

He released a swarm of rescue bots to find the survivors, put up a temporary airtight shelter, and do the heavy digging.

The bots found the trapped party within minutes. Poole closed up his suit, gathered his gear and walked to the site.

Soon Poole found himself looking down, through the dome's smashed, glass-strewn plaza, into a cracked-open bunker. He saw rooms dug out of the subsurface rock, separated by narrow partition walls, cluttered with rubble from a caved-in ceiling.

In the early days of both waves of Martian colonisation in the past, this kind of subterranean habitat had been a common building strategy. Mars's atmosphere was so thin it offered little effective protection from cosmic radiation or the Sun's ultraviolet radiation. So early pioneers, lacking the advanced materials that would later make soaring structures like the Cydonia dome possible, had erected pressurised domes that they'd covered with heaped up Martian dirt – or, as in this case, they'd just dug down into the ground itself, through layers of compacted, loosely cemented dust, maybe all the way down to impact-shattered bedrock. Thus, a protective cavern – and you found that you'd come all the way to Mars, to a new world, to live in a hole in the ground. But then, Mars never had been as welcoming as the dreamers of the Discovery era had hoped.

So he was looking into a bit of history here: a chamber that had once been a home, then maybe a storm shelter, then a storage cellar, until it was abandoned and probably forgotten entirely. But there was no time for archaeology now – and, perhaps, on Mars at least, there never would be again.

All that mattered for Poole now was the fact that, gathered there, maybe three, four metres down on the floor of the largest room, was a little huddle of children. And a single adult, an unreal figure, hovering over them. Angelic. It was, of course, Muriel, his mother.

She smiled up at him, radiating calm.

'Good to see you, Mother. But your projection is slipping.'

Subtle details: the shadows on her ageless face were wrong, as if she was illuminated by some invisible light source; her clothing, though a practical jumpsuit, was far too clean, unblemished. And, worst of all, she hovered maybe ten centimetres off the ground, and that was the detail at which the children kept staring.

'Not my fault,' Muriel said with a sigh. 'I keep sending back diagnostics, but the capacity for Virtual projection, like everything else on this wretched world, is being used to the maximum, even while the technological infrastructure to sustain it is collapsing . . .'

'You'll do. How many do we have here?'

'Just three. Two boys and a girl. Siblings. Family name of Thomas. They got separated from their parents, everything was in a rush.'

One of the children spoke up. 'There was an earthquake and the floor fell in and we fell in the cave and Robert hurt his leg.'

Muriel looked up. 'That's Timothy. He's the oldest. You're in charge, aren't you, Timothy?'

'Until Mom gets back.'

'Until then, yes. Doing a great job. And we have Alice down here, she's the youngest, and then we have Robert, the middle one. He has indeed hurt his leg.' She looked at Poole. 'Mars-born.'

He understood the implication: Martians were tall, lightly built, strong and wiry, but often with comparatively brittle bones. Probably a leg-break, then.

'Now, I don't think it's too bad and I showed Timothy how to improvise a rough splint, so it's stabilised. Alice helped a lot.'

Brave kids, Poole thought. Muriel would be full of advice but obviously she couldn't actually touch any of the children; Timothy and Alice must have had to set their brother's leg themselves.

'We know everybody's very busy, but—'

'But Robert needs to get to the doctor. OK. Just stay there.'

He had a good look around before he went any deeper.

The collapsed roof of the bunker had created a crumbled debris ramp – steep, but with plenty of ledges and protruding chunks. Not impossible for an adult to climb down, and back up again, Poole thought. And especially not for one with Earthborn muscles. Plus he had the right gear. Like everybody else involved in the rescue and evacuation operations going on across Mars, Poole had a basic kit in a pack attached to his skinsuit: medical stuff, a flashlight, a couple of knives, a length of fine rope. But he'd learned to take care.

He tied one end of the rope to a kind of podium, or lectern – he wondered if this level of the bunker had once been used as a chapel – and the other around his waist. Flashlight fixed to his shoulder, he inspected his route down into this hole in the ground one more time.

Then he turned, wary of his overpowered reflexes in the low gravity, squatted down, and dropped his legs into the breach in the bunker roof. Descending, he clung to the sloping wall, pulling the rope to ensure it didn't snag. His skinsuit boots were sturdy but the soles were fine enough for him to be able to feel for holds and ledges.

One last drop and he was on the floor.

He turned, put his flashlight on the floor so it didn't glare in anybody's eyes, fixed a smile on his face, and made straight for Robert. Cradled by his sister, Robert had a leg splinted by bits of plastic tied up with ripped-up cloth, and was evidently determined not to cry.

Poole fished an ampoule of anaesthetic out of his med pack and pressed it to Robert's flesh. 'There you go, it won't feel so sore now . . . Better?'

The kid managed a smile.

'Brave boy,' Muriel said. 'And, look, children, this is Michael Poole. *The* Michael Poole. He's my son, and he's an authentic hero, and he's come to save you.'

Alice stared. '*The* Michael Poole?'

He smiled. 'More to the point, I trained for situations like this during my Federal Service. I'll get you out of here.'

The younger boy stared too, but soon started crying again.

'You did well to find them, Mother.'

'Well, I can't administer medicine. I can't give frightened little children a hug. I never could, could I? . . . But I can go places others can't, or daren't, and I can find people and problems, and I can raise the alarm. And when I found these three – well, I had to call you. I knew he'd come, boys. He's like the Mariner from Mars, isn't he? *He* always came when you needed him.'

'*You* came,' Timothy said to her. 'Floating like an angel.'

Poole smiled at his mother. 'You said it, kid.'

'Now, Michael . . .'

'I found a spaceman.' Robert looked a little woozy from the anaesthetic. Wincing, he fished a lump of red stone out of a jacket pocket.

Poole took it. It was rust-red Mars bedrock, roughly carved into a tubby figure, with a faceplate, one arm raised in a vague salute, and what looked like a flag etched into his chest: stars and stripes. He handed it back. 'You keep that. It could be fifteen hundred years old.'

'It was on the floor, just there.' He tucked the figure away.

'So,' Poole said, thinking aloud, 'I'll get help, come back for you all. But I think I ought to take Robert straight out of here, to the doctor.'

Muriel said gravely, 'I'll stay with Timothy and Alice.'

Poole glanced at Timothy. 'Is that a good plan?'

The older boy thought it over, and nodded. 'Yes. Robbie first. We can wait. But how will you get him up that wall? It looks a difficult climb.'

Poole looked up. He wanted to get this over with quickly. 'I think I have a way. Timothy, Alice, help me lift Robert. Up on my back. This shouldn't hurt, kid, but you never know . . .'

Robert murmured only softly as Poole knelt in the dirt, and his brother and sister helped him wrap his arms around Poole's neck. Brave kids. Poole used a bit of his line, tied carefully around Robert's wrists, to ensure the boy couldn't fall.

Then he stood up. 'Now remember, all Earth people have super-strength on Mars. I learned *that* from Jack Grantt and his gaming buddies. Hold on now . . .'

On Earth, Poole could jump maybe half a metre from a standing start. Here, he could manage nearly three times as much, he reckoned. So, taking care to soften the spring so he didn't jar his fragile cargo, he bent his knees, jumped, and sailed up the wall face. He timed it almost right; he scrambled a little to get his feet firmly on the first ledge, then grabbed a support and steadied himself.

Timothy, down in the pit, actually applauded him.

'Now that,' said Poole's mother, 'is just showing off.'

Poole turned his head. 'You OK back there, little guy?'

'I found a spaceman.'

'I know you did.'

Another cautious spring, a jump, hands working at crevices on the wall, feet settling easily on the second step.

'It might have been made by one of the first people who came here. Somebody from Earth. Just like you.'

'Not like me. I'm a Martian,' mumbled Robert.

'Lethe, that's true,' Poole muttered. 'You always will be. And wherever you go, whatever you do, don't you ever forget it.'

'We won't,' Alice called up, her young voice containing an odd, emphatic finality that Poole found strangely disturbing.

He looked back at Muriel. 'By the way, I asked Harry to come see me. Stuff we have to discuss.'

She eyed him shrewdly. 'You have a plan, don't you?'

'Maybe,' he said with little confidence.

'A plan to save everybody. I know you. Make it happen.'

'I'll try. I'll see you, Mother.'

'You will.'

Holding the little boy's hands in his own, Poole prepared for his final leap out of the pit, and to safety.

52

When he had the time, while he waited for the *Carnot* to arrive, Poole followed the global picture.

By the sixth day it was estimated that the Xeelee, astonishingly, had injected enough energy into the Martian world system for all the planet's inventory of water ice to have melted. At the north pole, after a skim of dry-ice snow had quickly sublimated away, the kilometres-thick water-ice cap had all but vanished – taking with it, Jack Grantt pointed out, a record of Martian climate variations hundreds of millennia deep that could now never be retrieved.

And the Cage's heat energy was injected ever deeper into the crust, and spread along seams and fissures.

At last the waters of even the deepest aquifers were melted, and, heated to high-pressure steam, broke through the fragile lids of rock that contained them. All over the planet there were tremendous eruptions: fantastic, if briefly flowering geysers. It was a new hazard on the ground, a sudden, thick, superheated fog. Survival equipment meant to keep humans alive in a cold near-vacuum was stressed by heat and pressure; domes collapsed and blistered, and still more damage was done to the towers and arcologies as the sudden temperature changes caused cracking and collapse.

A hundred thousand people died that day alone.

But, briefly, liquid water flowed across the flat plains of the northern hemisphere. This whole tremendous basin had been created in the deep past by a single impact; once a world-spanning ocean had brimmed here. Now much of the released water refroze, or sublimated quickly, or simply sank back down into the aeons-dry, crusty dust. But across whole stretches of the ancient sea bed, for a while, ponds, lakes, even minor oceans glimmered. It was a moment of serenity, Poole thought, of spectacle, amid a new epoch of violence.

But soon the evaporation began. For much of the seventh day, most or all of Mars's water was suspended above ground, in fast-evaporating lakes, steam banks, clouds. The total mass of water Mars held was about the same as the mass of Earth's atmosphere. And so, for a few hours, Mars had an atmosphere as thick as Earth's, an air composed almost entirely of water vapour. From space Mars was a pearl of white cloud, as Venus had once been.

This phase too was brief. By the tenth day the superheated water was itself decomposing, its hydrogen leaking away to space, lost for ever, and the world clouds turned swiftly to rags. The temperature and air pressure plummeted back to something approaching Mars-normal. Humans emerged from their shelters to gaze at fast-sublimating banks of snow.

That was the day the space elevator came down. Now the migration off the planet was reduced to a trickle.

At noon of that day, Poole heard from Jack Grantt that his father was here. And that his experimental GUTship, the *Carnot*, was coming in to land.

53

Harry Poole, with Jack Grantt, stood waiting for his son near a rest station in the ruins of Cydonia. As Poole walked up he felt the ground shudder. The tremors were almost continuous now. It felt as if massive trains were crashing through tunnels dug deep in the Martian ground, day and night.

Harry was obviously a Virtual projection; Poole could tell by the lighting, just as with Muriel. But whereas Muriel had made the effort to clothe her projection in a coverall more or less suitable for engaging in a planet-wide catastrophe, Harry still wore what looked like capital-city elegance: jet black trousers, jacket inlaid with silver thread, polished boots. His blond hair, carefully coiffed, seemed to shine. He looked more like an angel than Muriel had, Poole thought.

Harry took a step forward. 'Michael. I saw the feed of you saving the little kids in the cellar—'

'What feed?'

'Come on. Surely you know. You're being watched, wherever you go – your various exploits. I don't have to tell you that there's a whole world in trouble here. Ten million people. But there's too Lethe-spawned *much* disaster. People like a story, Michael. Somebody they can follow: a single victim, saved by the hero. And the images of you giving it the full John Carter, leaping out of that pit in the ground with a sick little kid on your back? You got half a *billion* viewers. Half the population of Earth. And it's being rerun—'

'*Harry.*' Poole waved his fingers at Harry's face; Harry flinched. 'No time delay to speak of. So, if you're not some drone projection—'

'I'm the real thing, Michael. In spirit, at least. A real-time projection.'

'You're not on Mars itself, though, I'm guessing.'

Harry looked pained. 'How could I be? I'm offplanet, but close. Look, I can't put myself in personal danger. You know the situation. There are whole layers of our new cobbled-together interplanetary government that would rise in revolt, or collapse in incompetence, if I compromised my own safety. But you asked me to come, so I'm here.

You're still my son, Michael. Besides, it's good for me to be seen. To show the people of Mars that in this dire hour Earth is right behind them.'

Jack Grantt faced him now. 'Really, Harry? I heard rumours otherwise. That the people of Earth are less than enamoured of the idea of ten million ragged Martians dropping out of the sky on them. Resistant to the point where they are putting pressure on the government, on *you*, to slow down the rescue effort—'

Harry snapped his fingers.

Instantly the sound around Poole was deadened: the murmur of the exhausted relief workers nearby, even the groaning of the structure of the big dome, the towers and the roof.

Harry said, suddenly authoritative, 'If you're going to throw around accusations like that, you do it in private.'

Grantt said, 'Very well. But what's the truth? On Earth there used to be billions. Room for a few million more, surely.'

'Yes,' Harry said tightly. 'Yes, that's the rational point of view. But the first thing I learned in politics, and quickly, is that what drives people isn't rationality. It's primal emotions: it's fear, it's kinship. Priorities are placed on one's family and oneself. See? Right now on Earth we Stewards are having to negotiate our way through a cognitive minefield, because frankly, we're dealing with a population that is terrified. People fear that the Xeelee will come for Earth next, and laying down defences for the home planet has to be the priority, not harbouring migrants. We have to tread carefully. We have to appeal for empathy for the Martians, while not provoking resistance to helping them.'

Grantt glowered. 'And the result of all that is that you've set up this – this *funnel* of an escape route off the planet. Now that we've lost the elevator, the only way out is to line up for a ride to orbit on a flitter, then a limp across the Solar System on some GUTdrive scow, and *then* we are dumped in pens on the Moon. Pens. And don't give me any crap about high-gravity adjustments and quarantine stays. From a standing start to holding pens for migrants in ten days: pretty impressive, Harry.'

Harry replied, spreading his hands, 'I do understand, Jack. Seriously. But what more can we do? You speak of a "funnel". You know as well as I do that our interplanetary transport systems are simply not designed to transport millions of people between worlds in mere weeks or months—'

Harry was basically an engineer himself. So Poole knew his father was being honest enough. *But*—

'But,' Poole said, 'there are other ways to do it. We're Pooles, Harry. We find other ways. That's why I asked you here. One reason anyhow.'

Harry frowned, wary. 'What are you talking about?'

'Remember our *Cauchy*-class GUTships? Those concept discussions, before we got sidetracked by wormholes and aliens from another dimension? The test articles we completed?'

For years Poole had been tinkering with variants of his basic *Hermit Crab* design of GUTships, all adhering to the basic principles, of a spine with a lifedome at one end and a GUTengine with reaction mass at the other, but resized for more ambitious missions. The *Cauchy* class was a vessel that had been meant for pioneering interstellar journeys, with small crews, missions lasting many years – all built around a lifedome four hundred metres across, four times the width of the dome of the old *Crab*.

'The best-functioning test article in that class is called the *Nicolas Carnot*. Now, as soon as Mars was attacked and the consequences became clear, I called our colleagues at the Io shipyard to have them fit out the *Carnot* and bring her here. And make some modifications on the way . . .' He tapped his ear. '*Carnot*, you hearing this?'

The time delay was short. 'Loud and clear, Mr Poole. In high orbit – *very* high, what with that Cage and all. Been waiting for your call.'

'Modifications?' Harry asked uneasily.

'Simple but effective, I hope. Jack, can I use your softscreen?'

It took a few seconds for Poole to set up the display he wanted. He set it floating in the air before them: the *Carnot* foregrounded, a dazzling toy, the wounded planet behind her. That big lifedome was a glowing bowl of light, full of complexity.

'This is a recording. Here's the configuration she used to travel in from Io,' Poole said. 'And here's the manoeuvre she completed earlier.'

With a kind of flash at the top of the spine, the lifedome detached. Then the dome turned, evidently under its own propulsion system, and began to descend towards the planet.

'The dome emergency-detachment mode is what saved me when I rammed the Earth Probe with the *Hermit Crab*, of course. *Carnot* is a craft designed for deep space, not intended for landing on a planetary surface. But as you know we already designed our lifedomes to take the stress of extended periods of high thrust: years under multiple gravities, if necessary. So, putting those two design features

together . . . The lifedome isn't going to enter the atmosphere violently; it will come down under its own propulsion—'

'Wait. *Enter the atmosphere,*' Grantt repeated. 'Am I getting this right?
You're going to *land* a whole lifedome? What did you say it was – four
hundred metres wide?'

'That's the idea. And in this case it will come down right next to Cydonia. Jack, we may need a little help with the logistics. But I figure,
with a floor area of a hundred and twenty thousand square metres,
we might be able to cram in – what, fifty thousand people? – per ship.
Along with the air and food and other supplies they'll need.'

Grantt grinned. 'And then off into space. It's only a few days to Earth
in a GUTship. We're Martians. We can cope with a little crowding.'

'I've gone over the numbers with Miriam Berg, at Gallia Three.
Once this trial flight is out of the way – look, we have four more test
articles of this class of ship to adapt. But if we had to lift the whole
population of Mars off this way, you're talking two hundred flights,
each of maybe five days there and back – the operation will take us,
say, eight, nine months. Surely we can find ways to speed it up, but—'

'But that's within our deadline projection of a year to complete the
evacuation. Lethe, it's flaky. But for sure this is better than anything
we came up with before.' Grantt faced Poole. 'Thank you, Michael.
Maybe you are some kind of hero after all.'

'I just try to find solutions.'

But Poole saw anything but hero worship on his father's face. 'Ten
million immigrants to Earth,' Harry snapped. 'A million a month. And
where we put them all is my problem, is it?'

Poole stayed calm. 'What, are you going to turn them away?'

Harry glared at him, and at Grantt. Then he said, 'Sorry, Jack.' He
snapped his fingers.

Grantt looked bewildered. Then, when Grantt spoke again, Poole
realised he couldn't hear him. Even his mouth shapes were blurred, as
if pixelated. Grantt looked Harry up and down with a kind of disgust,
and walked away, back to the rescue workers.

Poole turned on his father. 'Why did you need to do that?'

'You should have told me about this *Carnot* scheme before you
blabbed it to the public. And believe me, Jack Grantt *is* the public.
Look, Michael, we're barely managing to hold everything together as
it is, and now you go throwing a bomb into the middle of all our plans.
What if the *Carnot* dome can't land after all? What if we can't ramp
up your evacuation scenario fast enough? What then? What should

we tell people? Did you think of that? If you're going to mix up public policy, company confidentiality and private matters like this, son—'

'*I know what you did*, Harry. Now it's just the two if us, I can say it. I know.'

Harry's eyes narrowed. 'What do you know?'

'It took me a while. I don't think the way you do. I don't think as fast as you. But I figured it out. It makes sense, in retrospect. You saw a chance, when that Xeelee came swimming out of the Sun. Surely its target was to be Earth or Mars. So you did all you could to lure it to Mars. That was the goal. You encouraged the Virtual-gamer camouflage. Fine.

'But *you made sure I was there too*, Harry. Down on Mars myself. And it was nothing to do with my being some symbol of resistance, was it? I was a big fat target. You knew the Xeelee was somehow drawn to me – that all this is somehow about *me*. And you used that. The camouflage, the gamers – all of that was a distraction. *I was the real lure*. All the Xeelee was likely to care about. You used me, without my consent or knowledge—'

'So what are you accusing me of – manipulating you to save the Earth?'

'You didn't tell me. You didn't give me a chance to do it voluntarily.'

'So is that a crime? Is that unethical? How do you think it made me feel? I did what I had to do.' Harry's expression hardened; his eyes narrowed. 'You always did lack ambition, Michael. But usually you show vision, at least – as with your scheme for the *Carnot*, here. Yes, that was the plan, the hope anyhow. Yes, I used you, if that's what's bothering you. And, frankly, I couldn't take the chance that you'd refuse.'

'So you never trusted me.'

'What does that matter? *It worked*. The Xeelee was drawn to Mars, and we've got that much more time to figure out how to stop it before it gets to Earth.

'And, listen, Michael – you can rail at me all you like, if you think I betrayed you. But if you're the genius everybody wants to think you are, *shouldn't you have thought of it yourself*? Huh? The lure scheme? You know, whatever everybody else thinks of you, you don't impress *me*. And every time you challenge me you remind me of that. You and your end-of-time Ghost and your Sigil of Free Humanity – that's nothing but tales for children, Michael. Like comic-book stories about the Mariner from Mars. And you, you are still a child—'

Abruptly the security bubble broke down. Some kind of override had been applied. Poole heard a babble of voices, that dreadful architectural groaning from the stressed building around him – and a message from his mother, clamouring in his ear.

Things had moved on.

The tetrahedral cage of planetbuster energy was still in place, still hammering at Mars. Still delivering a fresh Chicxulub every hour. But the Xeelee itself had broken away. Moved away from Mars, and had swum off into interplanetary space. Surely it had only one destination – Earth. And given the precedent of the Martian Cage, its intention there seemed clear.

Poole turned and ran, seeking a ride to a flitter to orbit. Gallia: that was his only thought. He had to get to Gallia Three, and Miriam, and Highsmith Marsden. That was surely where the only hope for resistance lay now.

Behind him he heard Harry call. 'You're nothing but a child to me, and always will be. I'm your father. Your father!'

SIX

With the Xeelee there has never been a possibility of negotiation, diplomacy, compromise. *None.* In fact there has been no contact at all – other than the brutal collision of conflict. The Xeelee ignore us until we do something that disturbs them – and then they stomp on us hard, striking with devastating force until we are subdued. To them we are vermin. Well, the vermin are fighting back.

Commissary Dolo, AD 23479

54

Not long after the Xeelee's arrival in the Solar System, under Highsmith Marsden's orders the Gallia Three habitat had abandoned its ancient cycler orbit. No longer did it patiently cruise between inner and outer planets; now Gallia was suspended forever in Jupiter's orbit, at the fifth Lagrangian point, hidden in a diffuse cloud of asteroids at this place of stable gravitational equilibrium.

Hidden here too was a cluster of GUTships of various classes: all of them Poole Industries vessels, though many were owned by other parties. They were all that Poole, with some covert help from Harry, had been able to commandeer in the eight months since the Xeelee had caged Mars. A rough and ready war fleet.

And here at Gallia, with only weeks left before the Xeelee was expected to arrive at Earth, Highsmith Marsden had his weapon, at last.

In great secrecy, Poole learned, prototypes had been manufactured using the huge energy flows of the Io flux tube, shipped cautiously to Gallia in armoured GUTships, and were now stored in a detached laboratory outside the Gallia habitat itself. This lab unit was a cylinder crammed with instruments, and fed with energy by two interplanetary-capable GUTengines. Nobody built of flesh and blood was allowed inside. Only Virtual projections.

So now Poole, with Highsmith Marsden, Miriam Berg, Poole's mother Muriel and Nicola Emry, drifted inside a space dimly lit, full of shadows, and so crowded that Poole was distracted by sharp flashes of pain as he bumped up against surfaces, and consistency-violation pixel showers were constant glimmers in the corner of his eye.

Nicola Emry grinned. 'Just as well we're all such good friends.'

Miriam said bluntly, 'You want to try working in these conditions.'

'Play nicely, children,' Muriel said softly. 'Just remember it's like this for me all the time—'

'Then you should have stayed away,' Poole said bluntly.

Miriam glared at him, evidently disapproving.

Muriel herself looked saddened, Poole thought with a stab of regret. But she understood, he thought. She tended only to show up in his life when she had some new bit of spooky, disturbing information about his clinging past to force on him. He ought to resent that, the lost generations of Pooles, rather than her, he thought now.

He tried to focus on the here and now.

Evidently Highsmith Marsden felt the same. 'All of you shut up,' he said. 'And pay attention to a miracle.'

Nicola laughed out loud.

Then, in respectful silence, they took turns at the eyepiece of a small optical microscope. Poole thought that the simplicity of the equipment, in this setting, actually enhanced the significance of the achievement.

When it was his turn, Poole saw only a speck of light, glowing brilliantly.

Marsden seemed irritated at their subdued reaction. 'Are you impressed? No? You should be. That, my unsatisfactory audience, is a magnetic monopole. Manufactured using the Io flux tube energies, and held in place with a strong magnetic cage.'

Miriam was nodding. 'And with this we have at last a fighting chance against the Xeelee.'

Her mood was not like Marsden's, Poole saw. Marsden was the mannered, academic eccentric. Whereas Miriam was – *eager*. Poole had known Miriam a long time. She'd changed, her attitude harder. Bleaker. She looked older than her age, AS treatments notwithstanding – older than Poole, though he had been born a few years earlier. And, ever since the lethal incident on Io, this had been a personal fight, for her. They were all different people, he supposed. Not who they might have become if not for the Xeelee.

'As to the design of weapons—' Marsden moved back, clapped his hands, and now the awkward space was further crowded by a Virtual display that hung in the air between them: the Xeelee, the now infamous sycamore seed craft. 'Naturally we've been studying the Xeelee closely since it first burst out of the wormhole into the Solar System, and especially since its hostile intent became evident. And through that deeper scrutiny we have learned much. Particularly concerning the way it *moves*.'

The image of the Xeelee shimmered and flickered, and Poole realised he was seeing a composite of many records, crudely spliced together. But he could see how, out of those swept-back, lobe-like wing stubs, further extensions emerged, or unrolled perhaps, flickering into existence, morphing: elusive geometries.

'The imaging is uncertain,' Marsden said now. 'Of course we haven't always known *what* we are observing, so that is always a challenge as to *how* to observe. The best clues came from gravity-wave measurements, in fact, which are a particularly strong signal from the Xeelee.

'But the wing extensions you see here – and we don't believe we've seen the full extent, we think the Xeelee's motions have been relatively cautious – are clearly the secret of its propulsion method. They are not material, not mass or energy. They are discontinuities in spacetime . . .' He paused, looking around at them, showing comparatively mild irritation – mild for him – at the blankness of their faces. 'Well?'

Nicola whispered to Poole, 'He's like a tutor I had in the remand centre at Aristarchus.'

He glanced at her. 'You never told me about *that*.'

'One of my mother's ideas to improve my character.'

'That worked well.'

'You just have to let him run down, until he tells you what you need to hear.'

Miriam was glaring at them; Poole shut up.

'The vacuum can take many energy states,' Marsden said at last. 'It is just as water can be found as a solid – ice – or a liquid, or a vapour – as steam – or a plasma. And just as water releases energy, latent heat, when it collapses between states – from steam to liquid water, or liquid to ice – so the vacuum releases energy as it collapses from one state to another. These pulses of phase-change energy had a key role in the shaping of the universe, in the very early moments after the singularity itself.

'*But* – when water freezes, ice rarely forms uniformly and regularly. Which is why, in a cube of ice you would drop in your drink, you will often find defects: bubbles and lines and planes of fracture. And so, as it congealed, spacetime too has been left full of flaws. Now, since spacetime has extensions in three space dimensions, then just like an ice cube it contains flaws in lower dimensions: two, one, zero.'

Miriam said, 'The defects most commonly experienced in nature are one-dimensional. Enormous threads—'

'Cosmic strings,' Poole said. 'My astrophysics is coming back to me.'

'Right. Stretched out across the cosmos, endlessly on the move, propagating at near lightspeed. And essentially tubes of high energy – a relic of the state of the early universe – just as a linear crack in an ice cube will be full of liquid water. A remnant of the previous state, you see. Cosmic strings are massive enough to distort spacetime itself. To bend space around them.'

Muriel said with a trace of impatience, 'So that's one-dimensional flaws. And in two dimensions – some kind of sheet?'

'Indeed,' Marsden said. 'An extensive, planar crack in spacetime. Domain walls, these ruptures are called. Again their tendency, once formed, would be to propagate away at lightspeed.'

'Ah,' Nicola said. 'I get it.' With a delicate Virtual finger – delicate for her anyhow, Poole thought – she poked at the profile of the flickering extension of the Xeelee wing. 'We know the main hull and these lobes are made, like the Cache, of what we've called hull plate. Right? Which is a marvel in itself. But this wing, I'm guessing, is your planar spacetime defect.'

Miriam said, 'As Highsmith pointed out such a defect will propagate in space. Imagine a shock wave in spacetime itself – like an ocean wave on the point of breaking. A nonlinearity. And if you could harness that motion . . . A *discontinuity drive*, we are calling it. It's a little like our wormhole design strategy, Michael. The Xeelee essentially rides instabilities.'

Watching the simulation, entranced, Poole saw how the spacetime-defect wings were not static structures; they folded, twisted, changed.

Miriam described this as a 'geometric phase' motion. 'The Xeelee swims by changing the shape of these defects and pushing at spacetime itself. It's rather like the way some bacteria swim through water . . . To a Xeelee sycamore seed ship, spacetime is as dense as water is to a bacterium. Thick as treacle.'

Marsden said, 'All this, if I may speculate, may be another relic of the very early universe. In an age even before the time of the quagma phantoms – even before the GUT era, when gravity was still combined into the single superforce – spacetime itself was a young, frangible thing, twisted and torn by the relic energies of the singularity. And it was full of defects. Perhaps, if life in that chaos was somehow possible, it might have survived in subsequent epochs, even achieved symbioses with other kinds of life. Just as we appear to see here.'

Poole said, 'Tactically, though. This discontinuity drive of yours would make a ship highly manoeuvrable. We've studied military technology of the past: fighter planes of the Anthropocene wars, for instance. As soon as they could, they made their planes smart, and deliberately unstable. Because if you can control that instability, with fast enough reflexes, you can slip quickly from one mode to another – faster than between stable states. Manoeuvrability was the key to winning a dogfight.'

Marsden glared at him. '"Dogfight." Miraculous science expressed in language little more sophisticated than a chimpanzee's pant-hoot.'

Nicola stared at Marsden. 'Did he say "pant-hoot"? I love this guy. I want to have his babies.'

Miriam suppressed a laugh, coughing. 'But,' she said, 'that is a valid perception in the circumstances, Highsmith. A pilot's perception, and that's the point of all this. Yes, a warship driven by spacetime discontinuities would be highly manoeuvrable.'

Muriel said thoughtfully, 'But you say this drive, miraculous as it is, is restricted to lightspeed, or less.'

'That's correct,' Miriam said. 'The Xeelee must surely have a more capable interstellar drive. Some kind of hyperdrive, we think. I mean, a drive capable of transcending the normal dimensions of space and time altogether. But if it does, we haven't seen it in action. The Xeelee, after all, arrived in this System through the Poole wormhole.'

Muriel said now, 'Our descendants will have hyperdrive capability. At least, so the family archives hint. We will fight a faster-than-light war with the Xeelee at the centre of the Galaxy.'

Marsden eyed her. 'Really? Now *that* would be interesting. Because FTL ships are also time machines, potentially. A war of time paradoxes . . .'

Muriel, rather awkwardly, turned to Poole. 'Actually, that's something we need to talk about. Time travel. History-tinkering. Paradoxes.'

Poole's face felt hot. He stared down once more at the shining dot in the microscope's field of view. 'Getting back to the point – defects in spacetime – *this*, I'm guessing, is a zero-dimensional defect. A point.'

'A magnetic monopole,' Marsden said, with allowable pride, Poole thought. 'Produced naturally in the early universe when phase-change GUT energy powered a surge of expansion – we call it inflation. Space swarmed with monopoles, like bubbles of water locked in ice, all merrily decaying away. Now we are using GUT energy again, as harnessed by Poole Industries engine pods, to create this new batch.'

'And weaponised,' Miriam said with that grim tone. 'Built to a uniform size and mass. A monopole is a few hundred nanometres long, so it's visible through this scope, but it has the mass of a trillion protons – about the mass of a DNA molecule. I like that, don't you? A good mass for a human-made bullet. And soon we'll be churning these things out like an Anthropocene war-industry armaments factory.'

Nicola glared down at the microscope, as if she could make out the captive monopole through sheer will power. 'Ah, I get it. Bullets. Because the way you puncture one spacetime defect—'

'Is by firing another spacetime defect at it,' Highsmith Marsden said.

The meeting broke up with a kind of grim satisfaction. Nicola in particular fizzed with energy, and immediately started work on preparing the new technology for tactical use. Poole made sure she had the support she needed.

But, he knew already from earlier briefings, though the monopole weapon was indeed a miracle, it wasn't likely to be enough. While Marsden had developed useful hypotheses about the structure and function of the Xeelee's sycamore seed vessel, the planetbuster technology behind the Cages, though heavily studied at Mars, remained a mystery. Unfathomable and, for now, unbreakable. So Poole believed that, when the Xeelee came to Earth, to win a battle they dare not lose, they needed more. A Plan B.

Right now he had no Plan B. Only vague notions of more or less outrageous implausibility, impracticality and unacceptability.

As he worked on these schemes, he was summoned by the Virtual ghost of his mother.

55

When he went to see her, in the small bamboo hut she'd been assigned inside Gallia as a polite nod to her Virtual privacy, Muriel sweetened the pill with new reports from Earth and the inner System.

She had always had privileged information. Poole suspected, in fact, that behind her lay a kind of shadow Virtual society, a network of artificial sentiences and simulated humans like herself – subtly disconnected from corporeal humanity, lacking true sensation, true joy, true pain, and yet deeply tied to their flesh-and-blood progenitors by the simple fact that if human civilisation collapsed, so would the power systems and information stores that such minds inhabited in the first place.

Anyhow, now Muriel was able to show Poole a stream of reports from Mars, pinned within its deadly Cage.

Eight months on, much of the atmosphere had been stripped off, all the water was broken up and gone, and most life was extinct – Jack Grantt and his colleagues had done their best to salvage something at least of the world-spanning Lattice – so that there was nothing left but geology, and even that was dissolving as swathes of the crust melted, exposing the liquid mantle beneath the skin. The great Tharsis volcanoes, destabilised, were all erupting now, blanketing the planet with a layer of dust and ash that obscured the surface, which itself was fracturing along billion-year-old fault lines. The Marineris valley system brimmed with magma, a shining river a thousand kilometres long. The northern hemisphere, that ancient sea bed, seemed to be shattering into islands of rock isolated by a new rising sea of lava. Poole almost felt the planet's chthonic agony, as if in sympathy.

But still, Poole knew, the great GUTship evacuation of the planet continued, with hundreds of thousands of people being lifted off the doomed planet every week. Already less than a million, one-tenth of the original population, remained – though some volunteer monitors, like Jack Grantt, were staying in orbit, determined to witness as much of the final reckoning as they could. Hence the reports Poole was tapping now.

Mars, though, was old news.

Long before the Xeelee itself reached Earth, more damage was being done elsewhere in the Solar System. Muriel was able to show Poole records made from an Eyrie, one of a number of small science stations that followed orbits which took them high above the plane of the ecliptic, the plane of the Solar System itself. From that celestial elevation the observers could see the whole orbital tracks of the planets, a set of neat circles around the central fire of the Sun – as well as such novelties as the polar regions of the Sun itself.

And, seen from that vantage, it was being observed that, in the dark gap between the circles of Mars and Jupiter, sparks flared and died.

'The asteroids,' Poole said grimly.

'They're targeting the main belt now. Probes sent from the Cache. You know that when the Xeelee left Mars and sailed inward towards Earth, the Cache went the other way, towards the outer System. Right now it is lodged in orbit around Ceres. Most of the bodies hit are just smashed to dust. But there's a subtler process going on, we think. Larger chunks of debris, and some of the remnant dust clouds, are being swept up to make *more* Probes. Some kind of self-nucleating, self-replicating mechanism is at work in there – so Marsden and his team speculate. Something else we know nothing about. Anyhow you can see the logic.'

Poole nodded. 'An exponential spread. Like a virus, hijacking the resources of a host body to make more copies of itself, and more again, in a cascade . . .'

'It's hard to see what can stop this process, now it's started. Eventually, it's believed, the whole of the asteroid main belt could be reduced by this process. I mean, reduced to dust. Presumably the next target will be other clusters of objects, less accessible than the main belt: the Earth-crossing asteroids, the Trojans that trail Jupiter . . . Wherever people have gone, so the speculation goes, the Xeelee will follow.'

'The Trojans? Finally they'll come here, then. We'll need to move Gallia.'

'Yes. As for Earth – well, we aren't responding too well, so far. Your father is doing as much as anybody could in his position.' She smiled. 'Even if he stole the job. But the world is in turmoil. Of course there's a clamour to fight back: well, the authorities are trying. There are rumours of the super-rich digging super-bunkers – the government too – but the example of Mars shows how futile that will be, when the Xeelee comes. Above all, people are looking for somebody to blame. Or just to hate. Very primitive reactions. There are noisy complaints about the flood of Martian migrants, poor wretches who must feel they're running from one blazing building into another.

'The consensus behind the world government is cracking, I think. There have been riots outside UN buildings, assassination attempts – including against Harry, though he doesn't talk about it to me. The commentators are even predicting war, between regions. It's all a distraction from planning for how to cope with the Xeelee attack, if it comes, when it comes. As to *why* the Xeelee is doing all this—'

'It seems clear enough,' Poole said. 'To leave us with nowhere to live. Nowhere we can even hide. And then what? That expansive future you dug up from the archives, Mother. The future that the lost girl told Michael Poole Bazalget all about. Doesn't look like it's going to come to pass, does it?'

She smiled, an oddly weary expression. 'As we've suspected from the beginning. Maybe we've been a little slow, we Pooles. As I understand it, any FTL ship is potentially a time machine. Because when you travel faster than light, effect can precede cause.'

'You have to get the relative velocities right . . . That's essentially correct.'

'Marsden, faced with the likelihood of the Xeelee having FTL technology, immediately grasped its implications for time travel.'

'He is an authentic genius, Mother.'

'There is that. Anyhow these studies have shed new light on our archive material. We already knew of previous reverse-time interventions: the Transcendents, the Wormhole Ghost. And now we know that someday, we will – *we were going to* – fight a faster-than-light war at the centre of the Galaxy, against the Xeelee. And, just as Highsmith realised, with FTL warships flying around on both sides, this kind of future-past entanglement will happen all the time. The archives talk of a Library of Futures, where survivors of battles *yet to be fought* will lodge accounts of those battles, and the commanders and strategists can use that information systematically, to plan their war.'

Poole frowned. 'Quite a resource. But it ought to lead to endless stalemate, as each side sought to avoid defeat.'

'Maybe it did. It *was* a millennia-long war . . . But, Michael, a FTL warship isn't the only way to travel into the past.'

'You mean, wormholes.'

'You build the things. I barely understand how, let alone their consequences . . . A wormhole isn't some simple tunnel. After all, you break lightspeed by travelling through it.'

'We've studied this, Mother. Theoretically. You could build a wormhole, use a GUTship to drag one portal off on a long interstellar jaunt, travelling close to lightspeed so it ages slowly through time dilation . . . A wormhole time machine.' He sighed. 'I used to dream of putting that to the test some day. Perhaps they occur in nature. I see where this is going. The Xeelee may have used my wormhole, or some hyperdimensional extension of it, to come here, to its past, from the future.'

'And if so, its purpose is clear now, isn't it? To cut down the tree of humanity at the root. Thus winning the Exultant war before it starts. And to divert you from your own destiny. You should be "remembered" – the events of your life celebrated, reworked, reinterpreted.' Her eyes were bright. 'Even your death, like Christ's, but not as a dark moment. Why, even alien creatures will see you as a symbol of hope. We know that; the Wormhole Ghost came back to tell you so. And the amulet it left you, by the way. We're still studying that. There seem to be images, trapped in there, folded up in spacetime . . . We think we're close to some results, which may tell us more. If you want to see them.'

He looked at her; that was an acute remark. No, he didn't want to find out about the amulet's secrets. Poole was already profoundly uncomfortable with all this. 'It's all a dream, Mother. A lost future. That won't be *me*. As you said, it all seems to have changed now. What am I actually supposed to do?'

'Just follow your heart. You will reflect on this background. On the destiny that might have been. The Michael Poole you might have become. *The Poole the Xeelee came here to destroy.* But you'll know what's right.'

And somehow, suddenly, as he thought through this mystical muddle, he felt as if his own thinking had been clarified, his own future course suddenly clear.

He knew what he had to do.

He stood. 'I have briefings to give.'

She frowned, looking into his face, searching. 'Briefings? About what? Highsmith's monopoles . . .? No. Something else. I know you. A Plan B? In case the monopoles fail . . . *That's* a Poole family tradition. Always have a Plan B. What are you going to do, Michael?'

He smiled, and put a finger to his lips. 'Shh.'

56

He decided to try it out on Nicola first.

They met in a tiny conference room – just another hut, really, in the green heart of Gallia Three. They sat at an elderly bamboo table, drink flasks set on its top.

Nicola didn't waste time.

'I know you, Poole,' she said. 'You're up to something. And it's a secret, right? Like the time you decided to ram our GUTship against a Xeelee Probe, without telling me first.'

Poole shrugged. 'Yes, I've got something. In case the monopoles fail. I didn't have this two days ago; I have it now. What do you want from me? Here I am telling you about it.'

'Just me?'

'Just you for now. Miriam next. Look – the Xeelee is heading to Earth. And it must be a safe assumption that it's going there to inflict the same kind of pain on the home planet as it did to Mars. A planet-buster Cage.'

'Earth will defend itself,' Nicola said bluntly. 'And we must help. You've got a small armada of ships here, and Marsden's monopole weapon.'

'Indeed. That's probably the best chance we have of harming the Xeelee directly. So, before the Xeelee closes on Earth, I intend to pack it all up and send it to the inner Solar System – to Earth. Along with technicians trained in its use. And you, Nicola. I know you're already working on its tactical deployment. If anyone can make this work, in my circle of acquaintances anyhow, it's you.'

She laughed. 'Praise indeed. So while I'm holding the monopole line, you're doing what, Michael?'

'Preparing a fallback. The details are still sketchy . . .'

Nicola shrugged. 'Tell me.'

He waved in the air.

A Virtual appeared over the tabletop: a cut-down Solar System, just the Sun, Mercury, Earth, Jupiter. Now wormholes appeared in electric blue, a pair of them, threads through space the same colour as their exotic-matter portals. One connected Mercury to the Sun, the other Earth to Jupiter.

'Here are our two existing prototype wormholes. Both still intact – despite the Xeelee's own disruptive entrance through the Jupiter portal. Sun to Mercury, Earth to Jupiter. And this is what we're going to do.' Using two hands, he manipulated the wormholes, drawing one end of the solar wormhole from Mercury towards Earth, the Jovian end of the other out beyond Jupiter itself. Connecting Sun to Earth, and Earth to the edge of the Solar System. 'And then—'

She covered his hand. 'Wait. Before you tell me more. This plan of yours. I imagine it's megalomaniac.'

He shrugged, tense. 'I'm a Poole. Of course it's megalomaniac.'

'Have you told your father?'

'No.'

'Why not? Because he'd stop you?'

'Right.'

She looked at him. 'You know I'm no fan of Harry Poole. But he is the government. If he would think it's a bad idea, if the government would think so, what makes you think you're right, and they're all wrong?'

He shrugged. 'The Wormhole Ghost came for me, remember. Somehow this is all about me, like it or not. Anyhow—'

'Have you ever heard of the Norns, Michael?'

He frowned. 'Were they in the one where the Mariner was fighting the Mole Men?'

'I'll ignore that. The Norns, Michael. The spinners of fate. Three sisters. The Norse believed they water the roots of the world tree. And their spinning controls the lives of all of us, all us mortals.

'You have your own Norns, Michael Poole. Spinning your fate. That girl from the future who haunted Michael Poole Bazalget. Second, the Xeelee, of course. And third, your own future self. The messiah of the Galaxy-core soldiers. The hero at Timelike Infinity. He looms over everything you do. You're trying to live up to him, aren't you? Even though you know he will never exist.'

He found he was trembling.

She sat back. 'Maybe the spinners put this latest idea into your head. But it's your decision whether to go ahead with it. Your life to control. But whatever you decide—'

'Yes?'

'I'm with you. So tell me about your plan.' She began to tease the ends of the two Virtual wormholes together, and looked at him frankly. 'Lead us, Michael Poole.'

57

With Nicola's help, he quickly worked up his proposal into a compact briefing.

Then he and Nicola brought Miriam Berg up to speed. It was a tense session.

Poole knew they had never got on. Miriam, a friend since schooldays, his partner in so many projects since then – Miriam, with whom, before the Xeelee, he'd expected to be working for ever, effectively, on one expansive project after another. Following his father's advice, he'd always postponed any deeper entanglement. Time enough for love. Yet whenever he'd imagined any kind of personal future, Miriam had always filled a certain hypothetical role in his head. And after all she deserved to become a Poole, if anybody did – though he knew that if he ever raised that idea she'd point out that it would be an honour for him to become a Berg. But maybe that future, like so many others, had been obliterated. One more grudge to bear, he thought bleakly.

And Nicola. Nicola, who he probably never would have met at all if the Xeelee crisis had not so disrupted his, and everybody else's, life. After all, she and her mother had only come out to the Jovian construction site in the first place because of queries about those initial anomalies with the Jupiter–Earth test wormhole. But since then, through her goading and sheer randomness, she seemed to have dug out of him qualities he'd never known he possessed.

Miriam was his past. Nicola the future. And a future of which the family archives and the Wormhole Ghost's words and all those other enigmatic bits of prophecy had nothing to say.

They got through the briefing. It was characteristic of Miriam, he thought, not to react to the sheer monstrous audacity of the scheme, but instead to interrogate him on details.

Then they worked out a strategy. A plan, that unfolded in the next few days and weeks.

Meanwhile Nicola took her squadron of 'Monopole Bandits' off to the inner System.

When Poole himself hurried back to the inner System, it was already September. Two months out from the expected encounter of the Xcelee with Earth. Frantic preparations for the defence of the planet were under way. Poole wanted to contribute to these preparations as much as he could.

Because if they worked, there would be no need for Plan B, and the worst choice he'd ever have to make.

As the deadlines approached, Harry summoned Poole to Earth's L5 point, in the planet's orbit, sixty degrees away.

As it happened, as the sycamore seed craft spiralled in from Martian orbit, moving with roughly Earth's own orbital speed, it was already clear that the Xeelee would pass close to L5. And, Poole learned, the military analysts saw this as an opportunity.

A gravitational well like Mars's L5 and Jupiter's Trojan points, L5 itself was a loose Sargasso, Poole saw as he flew in aboard the *Assimilator's Claw*: a pit in the sky cluttered with a ragtag bunch of battered minor asteroids, and a glittering swarm of spacecraft, some of them monitors and science stations intentionally deposited here, mostly wrecks, relics and fragments.

'A self-organising museum of space, I like to think of it,' Harry had said, when he had proposed meeting Poole here. 'Someday, if we ever get the chance, we might come out with a team of archaeologists and sort it all out. But for now we have the Xeelee coming to visit. And so, deep inside this cloud of junk, we built a fortress . . .'

The crew wouldn't let Poole bring the *Claw* closer than half a million kilometres; he had to make his final approach in a small, low-powered flitter.

Harry's fortress looked like just another lump of comet ice to Poole, with not a stray photon of heat radiation to reveal the fact that humans and their machines were hiding in there, eating, breathing, living. Waiting for the Xeelee, heavily stealthed. Poole wasn't given the station name, even. He had a feeling the Solar System was filling up with such refuges, as humanity learned to hide. Highsmith Marsden had had it right from the beginning, he reflected now. From the very first day.

Harry met Poole when he docked at the axis of the spinning mass. 'So I'm here in the flesh, just for you. Impressed?'

To validate the claim, Poole poked at his father's arm. He was real enough. The sleeve of his smart jet-black-and-silver uniform had a peculiar texture. 'This feels like a carbon-fibre composite. Some kind of armour?'

Harry grunted. 'Follow me.'

He led Poole through cramped, empty corridors, cut into glassed-over ice. The base, dug into this comet-ice fragment, appeared brand new, but was small, poky – no doubt a consequence of the stealthing. There was gravity here, thanks to the spin-up.

'Do you blame me for wearing protection? This armoured suit won't save me from a Xeelee planetbuster beam, but maybe from an assassin's laser. A human assassin, I mean. Here we are.'

They had come to a kind of observation lounge, Poole saw, the walls plastered with high-specification softscreens – he would not have expected a window, leaking light and heat, in an installation like this. There was nobody here, not much equipment beyond the softscreens, chairs and a table and a dispenser of drinks and food. It struck him now that he'd seen no other human being at all, save his father, in his time in the station.

'You want something? There's only a handful of crew here and they lead a monastic life, but the food synthesis machines are top of the range.'

'Just water.' Poole walked to the largest screen, which showed an expanse of starry sky. He picked out the constellations, figuring his orientation. 'Sun to the left, Earth–Moon to the right. And the Xeelee, right now, is about – *there*.' He pointed at a patch of empty space – but not far from the Xeelee's position was a light, sliding through the dark. 'What's that? Looks too big for a ship, and too slow . . . What are you up to here, Harry? And why did you want to see me?'

Harry brought two cups of water, set them on the room's only table, and sat down. 'Well, I think we need a little honesty between us, you and I. I brought you here to discuss strategy. That is, our defence strategy. The Stewards'.' He glanced at his watch. 'In fact, to show you it in action. And I do it in the hope that you in turn will be open with me. I know you're up to something, son; our spies are good enough to tell me that. But not *what*. We both want the same thing here, surely. The security of Earth. And surely we have a better chance of achieving that if we work together.'

'Maybe. You start.'

Harry sighed. 'Wise-ass kid. Well, in the last few months we all studied military strategy pretty hard, from the history books. And we've been tutored by a few entities like Gea, some of whom are old enough to have *witnessed* some of the Anthropocene and Bottleneck wars.

'We think we have the Xeelee's trajectory pretty much mapped out now. It's been a long haul in from Mars – it doesn't seem to do anything quickly, does it? – but now it's clearly closing in on Earth. So we have set up three stop lines, as we've called them. Three locations we're going to try to hold the Xeelee. The first is here, close to L5. With the Xeelee two months out from Earth.'

'You're going to try to hit the Xeelee here? What with?'

'You'll see soon enough. Don't spoil my surprise. The next stop line is ten light-seconds from Earth, roughly. Three million kilometres; a day's transit to Earth for the Xeelee. If it gets that close we're going to hit it with all we've got left, from kinetic-energy weapons to fission and fusion bombs to GUTengine missiles—'

'We tried that stuff at Mars. Did no good there. What makes you think it will work now?'

'This will be an assault on a much larger scale. Mars was remote, Michael; it was impossible, politically as well as logistically, to move all our assets over there. And besides, we still didn't understand the Xeelee's capabilities at that point; for all we knew it might have worked. Now we can throw in *everything*. We may yet exhaust the Xeelee's capacity for punishment; we may just burn the thing down. We certainly have to try – but if the Xeelee does break through that second stop line, it will be just a day out from Earth.'

'You said there's a third stop line.'

'It's kind of arbitrary. We defined it as one light-second from Earth. That's about the Moon's distance. A psychological barrier, you see. But only a few hours out, for the Xeelee.'

'And you'll be defending that line with—'

'You.' He eyed Michael. 'Your weapons from Gallia Three. Whatever you've got. And however we can back you up. Look, we have our eyes and our ears. We know you have some pretty impressive work going on out there at Gallia, though we haven't been able to get hold of the results in detail.' He held up a hand. 'Don't tell me. But if you think this system might work against the Xeelee—'

'Highsmith Marsden thinks it might.'

Harry smiled ruefully. 'That screwball loner? Well, there you go, humanity is saved.'

'This was why we kept it discreet, Harry,' Poole said, annoyed. 'So there'd be no scepticism, no second-guessing. We knew this was the best we could do – the best anybody had. We couldn't afford a loss of focus. And that's why we insist on the final say in the system's deployment.'

Harry held up his hands. 'Look, Michael, if you have faith in your system, I trust your judgement. Well, I've no choice. But – work with us. Put your ships on the lunar-orbit stop line. We'll stand with you, with whatever we have left, whatever we can do. Even if it's only to distract the Xeelee for a few seconds.'

Michael considered that. 'Seems reasonable.'

Harry nodded, looking more grim than relieved. 'OK. We'll get our staffs together to talk and work it out.'

'I don't have any staff. Talk to Nicola Emry. She flew in with the Gallia crews.'

'That mouthy kid?'

'Harry—'

'OK, OK. Whatever you say. Now, look, Michael, I've one more question for you. I am your father – I am the Steward of Stewards – and I want you to do me the courtesy of answering. However briefly. Will you do that?'

'Ask.'

'Suppose we fail. Suppose the Gallia stuff fails. *Do you have anything else?*'

Poole considered. Was it more productive to lie at this point, or to tell the truth? That was the kind of calculation Harry would make, he realised. Maybe he had more of his father in him than he sometimes liked to believe.

'Michael?'

'Sorry. Yes. I have something else.'

Harry held up his hands. 'A supplementary, OK? You don't want to tell me what this is?'

'No.'

Harry considered that. 'Fair enough. I guess that if we get to that point, it won't make much difference if the Xeelee wrecks the Earth or you do.'

Poole sat silently. That was unfortunately evocative of his own fears.

'I'm trying to tell you,' Harry said heavily, 'that I trust you, son. I know you'll do your best. I'll keep your secret. Because at least I'll know that if all else fails—'

Light flared, at the centre of the big viewscreen.

*

Poole stood and stared at the image, at light that was already quickly fading. Fragments dispersing as if from some immense explosion.

Data started to chatter in, scrolling across the secondary softscreens. 'What in Lethe—'

'The Xeelee,' Harry said. 'Well, it crossed the stop line. And we hit it, right on cue. I got too interested in our conversation; I lost track of time.'

Poole remembered the speck of light he'd seen drifting close to the Xeelee. 'Hit it with *what*?'

'Cruithne,' Harry said grimly. 'You heard of that? Earth-crossing asteroid, co-orbiting with Earth. Our second moon, some called it. Stealthed as best we could, arrays of GUTdrives fixed to its surface. We've had it sailing out this way for months; it should have *looked* like it was going to miss the Xeelee by a comfortable margin. But at the last minute, a big deflection from the GUTdrives – *wham*. We hit that bandit with sixty billion tonnes of rock and ice, moving at interplanetary speeds, out of the blue.'

Poole was astonished. 'Lethe, Harry – well, it was worth a try . . .'

But when the images cleared, and more data was captured, it soon became clear that the Xeelee had sailed out of the impact site with no evidence whatsoever of physical damage, no evidence that the assault had deflected its course by so much as a fraction of a degree. The sacrifice of a moon had done the Xeelee no more harm than had Poole when he had similarly sacrificed the *Hermit Crab*, and, nearly, his own life.

Father and son sat together for a while, considering the aftermath. Michael Poole, for one, wondered if he'd ever see his father in person again.

Then he went to Earth.

Poole stayed with his mother. Physically he was resident with her at the Poole family complex at Princess Elizabeth Land in Antarctica. He spent the next two months working on his own secretive project. The study itself was absorbing. Poole had always been able to lose himself in work. At times he lost track of the time, even the date.

Then the Xeelee came.

58

It was November, in this year AD 3650. And there was fire in the sky of Earth.

You saw it at night, flickering and sparking. Some of the great detonations could even be glimpsed in the daylight. In the thirty-seventh century, Poole supposed, there were few who feared visions in the sky. Evidence of artifice in heaven was commonplace: sunlight glinting from the solar panels of an orbital factory, or the contrail of a great profac ship mining nitrogen from the air. Sights of a kind that had been seen for a millennium and a half.

But now the lights in the sky were a signal of something that was anything but routine, or benign. Up there, the resources of Earth, a world that was the centre of an interplanetary civilisation, were being hurled at an intruder with nothing but lethal intent. Resources and lives, Poole knew: human lives that might have spanned millennia, spent like coins.

And through it all – drenched in a bath of energy from its assailants' weapons, powered by wings of fractured spacetime – the Xeelee sailed on. Relentless. Unwavering.

Now it approached Harry's second stop line, a day out from Earth. If it broke through that crowd of ships and weaponry, nothing stood in its way, save for Marsden's experimental weapons at the third and final stop line.

That, and Poole's own, desperate last resort.

In the final days, in his time off, though he stayed physically in the Princess Elizabeth Land compound, Poole travelled the world with his mother in spirit. It seemed appropriate. Last chance to see, perhaps.

And now, on the very last day before the Xeelee was due to arrive at Earth, Poole stood with Muriel on a high balcony of the Waukegan Tower, in Illinois, United Americas. Virtual angels together, they were a kilometre and a half high atop a sculpted pillar of glass, steel and carbon composites, and the unreal air in their Virtual lungs was authentically thin, even chill.

To the east stretched the placid waters of Lake Michigan, to the west a green, flat country with scattered lakes. But, unlike much of the continent, this land had not been given back to the wild. At the Tower's foot the remains of old Waukegan had been largely preserved, ancient buildings of concrete and stone. Further out were the rectangular layouts of farms: an open-air museum, Poole knew, a monument to the days when humans had had to coax all their food from the stubborn ground of Earth.

The sky was bright, sunlit, though marred by silent detonations overhead.

They were alone up here. In fact, Poole knew, the Tower was mostly abandoned. People were seeking refuge wherever they could, wherever seemed safe. Many had gone underground, to basements, ancient cellars, even a few Anthropocene-era museum-piece nuclear war bunkers. Some had taken in weapons, to keep out anybody who tried to follow them into whatever refuge they had found. Others had congregated around government centres, pleading or protesting, stretching the resources of the Federal Police.

The mostly empty Tower, though, seemed peaceful.

'I'm still not sure why you brought me here, Mother. Today of all days.'

'I've been thinking of witnessing,' she said thoughtfully. 'You know that some groups have been formalising this, ever since the Xeelee threat to Earth became apparent. Jack Grantt's doing the same thing at Mars, of course. Whether or not we can stop this blight on the Earth, at least we can watch, remember.'

Poole grunted. 'What for? So we can hold the Xeelee to account some day?'

She smiled. 'Well, it's not impossible. We discussed this, Michael. Whatever we Pooles believed we knew of the future, surely all that is gone now. Lost. The future is as open as most people always thought it was. Who knows what's to come, what we'll achieve?

'And so, here I am. Taking a last chance to see the world the way it should be.

'In the end we did a good job, didn't we? Of saving this world which we accidentally inherited – saving it from ourselves. And then we built it all up again, the way it was before us. So, in North America alone, you have Yellowstone, a rich biosphere lodged in the throat of a supervolcano, and further north the redwood forests and the taiga and the subpolar scrublands . . .

'But I think it's the very old places I like the most – old in human terms, I mean. Deep in central Asia you'll find the Altai mountains, one of the last refuges for Ice Age fauna: moose, reindeer, musk ox, lynx, wolverines. I must show you if there's time. Go there, Michael, and you have a deep sense of *belonging*. Because these were the environments in which we evolved. And which our more recent ancestors restored and preserved, as one would shelter an ageing parent.'

'Yet you come *here*, on the last day. To this museum of farmland?'

'But this is an ecology too, Michael. If an artificial, heavily engineered one. Engineered by us. And perhaps there's a lesson in that. There are some ethicists, you know, who question whether this is a crime at all. The Xeelee's crusade against us.'

Poole grunted. 'I don't follow. How can it not be?'

'Here we are on top of a Tower. Look at it from an elevated point of view, Michael. We ourselves have managed ecologies for millennia – like this one – and we know that death is as essential a process in keeping an ecology healthy as is life. Even the primitive conservationists of the Anthropocene understood the importance of predators, especially top predators. In the Yellowstone forests, wolves prey on elk populations, which would otherwise breed out of control, eat all the tree saplings, and produce a wilderness. In the waters too—'

Poole scowled. 'Are you suggesting the whole Galaxy is some kind of ecology, Mother? And that the Xeelee is nothing but a pike in a pond full of little fish?'

She glanced out at the expansive fields of swaying grasses. 'Sometimes I find it comforting to think that way. That for all our intelligence, all our technological ingenuity, we're really nothing more than components in a great natural cycle. Even the Xeelee.'

'But you don't believe it.'

She grinned, fiercely. 'Not for a second. And even if it were true, maybe today is the day of the herbivores.'

He felt a subtle vibration at his wrist: a monitor, bearing news. He glanced at it. 'Ah. The Xeelee broke through the three-million-kilometres stop line. The defenders fought hard . . .'

She absorbed that bit of information. 'We always thought it would come through. So, one more day and it will be at lunar orbit. And after that . . . Michael, I've got every faith in you. And so has your father.'

'Harry?'

'Believe it.' She smiled. 'Anyhow, at this point he doesn't have much choice.' She stepped back. 'Go to work. Come what may I'll wait for you at Princess Elizabeth Land.' And she winked out of existence.

59

Well before that final day, as the Xeelee had sailed towards the last stop line at lunar orbit, Nicola Emry and her Monopole Bandits had gathered on the Moon itself, training incessantly, preparing the technology of war.

And in these last hours, in his own flitter, Poole impulsively made a hurried flight to meet her there, in person, at the Copernicus Dome. He'd tried a Virtual projection, but the exclusion protocols were even tougher than for a physical visit.

Even so it wasn't an easy journey. Cislunar space was crowded. As the Xeelee loomed, and people instinctively sought refuge, there were massive migrant flows travelling from Earth to Moon – and even, remarkably, some coming back the other way.

But as Poole came in for a final landing close to the venerable Copernicus Dome, on a landing apron scarred by centuries of rocket blasts, he saw a small, brave fleet gathered: modified flitters, small, fast, highly manoeuvrable craft. These were the ships dedicated to Nicola's special mission, equipped with Marsden's monopole weapons. Just six of them, six ships. From Poole's vantage as he approached, they were fragile specks against the grey face of the Moon.

But each bore, incised on its flank, the Poole Industries corporate logo, and a green tetrahedral frame.

He found Nicola in a mess room, with a handful of her colleagues from Gallia.

The Copernicus Dome was an old facility, built into the shell of a big, long-abandoned Anthropocene-era Moon base. The lighting seemed poor, the fittings shabby, and even in this mess room there was always a smell of burning, as if the dome still leaked Moon dust which oxidised enthusiastically in the air.

The fliers stared at Poole as he approached, and fell silent.

They all had tattoos right at the centre of their foreheads, angular and green. So did Nicola, in fact, a new acquisition. Ugly, crude markings, disconcerting in their very placement. Casual in their mess suits, showing no signs of nerves, the crew looked like they fitted in here. In fact Poole suspected they all were genuinely young, like Nicola not AS-preserved but with the fast reflexes and reckless courage of true youth. Poole was twenty-nine years old now. They made him feel antique.

Nicola introduced him briskly, parroted names that he knew he would never remember, and then led him over to a table in a corner of the hall. She snapped out commands for water and bread to hovering bots. 'Had to get you away from my Bandits. Didn't want hero worship closing down their thinking, not now.'

'Hero worship?'

'Come on, Poole. You must be aware of the propaganda the Stewards have been putting out about you and your daring feats. Especially your dad, who is not averse to glory by association. To them, you're Michael Poole the hero pilot—'

'Poole the idiot.'

'Who rammed a Xeelee Probe, trying to save the Earth. What's not to worship?'

He reached out, tentatively, and pushed back her short hair so he could see her forehead better. The tattooed tetrahedron was green, just like on the hide of the Wormhole Ghost. Just like the amulet which his mother still studied.

'That's your fault too,' Nicola said.

'The Sigil of Free Humanity?'

'It's become a kind of fashion. Look, I don't care what they believe about you, as long as it motivates them to fly their ships that little better.'

'And what motivates you, Nicola?'

'You know what. I need to fight, for once in my sorry life. As opposed to rebelling against my mother, which is what I've mostly been doing up to now. Fight this thing that's threatening my home planet . . . Pretty good reason for getting out of bed, right? How's Plan B coming along, by the way?'

'Never to be used, I hope.'

She shrugged. 'Well, it's evidently kept you busy. I suppose I appreciate you coming out to – what? To say goodbye, before I get my head shot off?'

That was exactly why he had come, of course. But, sitting here, he suddenly felt that wasn't enough. On impulse he asked, 'Will you take a passenger?'

Her eyes widened, but she quickly snapped back to her usual cynicism. 'I don't need ballast.'

'Not physically. I'll send my carcass back on my flitter to Earth—'

'Ah. You want to project a Virtual into my ship? Just like Mommy Poole.'

'Why not? The stop line is only a light-second from Earth. Come on. We've been through a lot, Nicola. Just like old times. And you never know, I might be some use.'

She stood up. 'No, you won't. And if you get in my way you're turned off.'

'Noted.'

'*And* I want a mute button. Oh, one more thing. If you're going to fly in my squadron—' She produced a kind of stylus. 'It's almost painless. Come on, on your feet.'

The tattooing felt like a Xeelee planetbuster beam working on his forehead.

After that, everything came in a rush.

60

'Strap in,' said Nicola.

Suddenly he was in a flitter's co-pilot's couch, with Nicola at the controls to his left-hand side. He'd barely got his own ship Earth-bound once more when the Virtual projection had abruptly cut in, and he was cast into Nicola's craft. He gasped; it felt like he'd been dropped from a height.

Evidently they were already under way. Nicola was busily sliding icons across softscreens around her, and manipulating floating Virtual controls with big, physical gestures. Poole had always remembered that of her, the physicality of her flying.

And when he looked out, he saw they were peeling up and away from the Moon. The surface receded, the big, ancient Copernicus Dome a blister as dust-grey as the rest of the lunar ground. He glimpsed other craft rising up around them, like sparks from an invisible fire, in a loose formation maybe a half-kilometre across.

'I said, strap in – oh, into Lethe with it.' Nicola tapped a softscreen, and a Virtual harness appeared in place around his Virtual body. Another brisk manipulation and the flitter surged forward, with an acceleration like a punch in the stomach. 'Hope a desk pilot like you hasn't got too soft to take a few gravities.' She glanced at him. 'Assuming you can feel it at all.'

'Oh, I felt it all right.'

'Good.'

He glanced around, at that constellation of risen sparks in the sky – a sky black and empty otherwise, thanks to his Sun-dazzled vision. 'You keep a tight formation.'

'No accident. We rehearsed, over and over. For *that*.' She pointed to a corner of the cabin's big window, where light flared.

'The stop line.'

'Yes. Where the fighting has started already.'

'We're going in pretty fast.'

'Well, this is the battle plan. We knew the Xeelee happened to be coming in pretty close to the Moon. Another lucky break, like the approach to L5. Why not use that? So we climb out of the Moon, go in fast, get the job done, and come out just as fast – hopefully. There's no value in a long, slow approach; all you do is give the Xeelee a chance of taking a shot at you – not that it's shot at anything smaller than an asteroid so far; the wrecks we've had have mostly been sideswipes from the planetbusters. Coming up on our attack vector.'

'So soon?'

'Now!'

They fell through a veil of fire.

This was the barrage kept up by the conventional weapons of a first wave of defenders. Poole glimpsed the flare of GUTdrive exhausts, the dark silhouettes of ships, sharp pinpricks that must be the detonation of fission or fusion bombs.

Then, just as swiftly, they were through. Poole saw a black sky.

And, dark against dark, that strange yet familiar shape: the central pod, the swept-back wings – the Xeelee, right in front of him.

'Hello again,' Nicola said. 'Remember us?'

Suddenly it was very close.

Then passing *under* the flitter.

'We're beyond it!' Nicola hauled icons through the air.

The ship turned with a savage jolt that pushed Poole back in his seat, hard. 'Lethe! Can a Virtual get broken ribs?'

'I *will* mute you if you don't shut up. All right, kids, here we go. Lethe knows we rehearsed it so often you're already bored, right? Bandit One, you're up – go, go! Bandit Two, line up to follow her in. Then you, Three . . .'

As Nicola's flitter banked and settled on its own approach path, Poole's view opened out. Now they had swivelled in space so they faced the Earth, a blue pendant in the dark, gibbous and beautiful. Before it hung the wings and body of the Xeelee, black as night. And there, above the Xeelee, the first of Nicola's flight of ships was already diving down on that wide black carcass. The assault craft looked like some raptor bird, hunting in the night. The Xeelee made no attempt to evade or destroy it.

And at the moment of closest approach, Poole saw the flitter's improvised cannon fire from its underbelly – saw the sparks of the shells it emitted sail down at the bland back of the Xeelee craft – and saw those monopole bombs flaring as they came into contact with the Xeelee.

Cutting visible holes in that slim central hull. Creating wounds that punched right through the graceful wings.

'It worked,' he breathed. 'Highsmith's Lethe-spawned monopoles worked!'

Nicola whooped. 'You're on the line, Michael. Do you hear that, kids? Confirmation from the man himself. We *hurt* that lousy thing, the first to do so since it came sailing in from Jupiter. We hurt it! But it's still heading for Earth, we haven't earned any medals yet. Why, I don't think we even got its attention. Bandit Two, you're up, make sure that thing knows we're here . . .'

Poole watched the next ship line up for its run, and the next. 'Six ships,' he said, remembering what he'd seen on the Moon. 'And we are?'

'Number six. If anybody has to take the final flak it's going to be us.'

Poole nodded, feeling a sharp stab of fear, even though he knew his own physical manifestation was safe, comparatively, in its flitter en route back to Earth. An Earth that seemed to loom terribly close: close and undefended, save for this last handful of warriors.

That and his own insane final-fallback scheme.

Nicola was studying her sensor screens. 'Bandit Two inflicted more damage. And Three. Lethe, it's slowing down. Hasn't adjusted its course, but it's slowing down!'

'You hurt it, and now you made it respond,' Poole said. 'For the first time. Well, that's something. Is being ignored worse than being killed? I—'

Cherry-red light flared across the window, dazzling, blinding. Alarms shrieked. The flitter's automatics cut in, and the ship was wrenched sideways.

Poole saw a thick rope of energy, cherry red, surge past the window.

'Planetbuster! Used as a combat weapon. We haven't seen it do *that* before.'

Nicola ignored him and worked her controls. The flitter ducked and swerved, and Poole glimpsed the Xeelee again, with brilliant planet-buster beams flashing out in all directions from what looked like an emplacement on the top of its central body.

'We lost Bandit Three,' Nicola said. 'Oh – and Five. Into Lethe with it. The rest of you, abandon formation. If you're dry, go home. If you have shells left follow me in, any way you can. Let's not waste these gifts we came so far to deliver . . . Poole, hang on.'

She threw the flitter across space and *down*, down at the Xeelee, the nimble craft dodging around the flicker of planetbuster beams as it went. Poole remembered how once she had piloted her way through a tangle of flux ropes, deep in the heart of the Sun. She really was some pilot.

And the fight went on. Out of the corner of his vision Poole glimpsed other craft, one plummeting down ahead of them at the Xeelee, another flaring into sudden light as the Xeelee weapon caught it.

Then they were on the Xeelee, again.

It was only a hundred metres below them, less. Poole saw it close to – closer even than during that extraordinary encounter inside the Sun. That central body was a pod, a spindle-shape, small, with not much more room than would take a human pilot. The lobed wings that had given the ship its sycamore seed label swept back, planes under him, very smooth – and very fine, he saw; towards the edges the cherry-red glow of the Xeelee's own weapon was shining *through* the fabric of the wings. And at their edge a subtler darkness, elusive, that might be the discontinuity drive itself, or its wake: the fractures in spacetime which the Xeelee rode across the Solar System.

Now this elegant form was damaged, Poole saw with a surge of exultation: ragged holes had been punched in those domain-wall wings, wounds that were edged by flaring white light. There were even craters in the hull of the central pod.

The flitter shuddered and shook as it fired, and again Poole saw more shells rain down at the Xeelee, each slug a metallic crust around a bitter monopole core, a knot of broken spacetime. One, two, smashed into the Xeelee, ripping more holes in those delicate wings. Again Nicola whooped.

But more alarms flared, the flitter twisted and tumbled, and planet-buster light glared through the window.

'Hit!' Nicola yelled, angry, frustrated. 'But we got the weapons away.'

'Nicola—'

'We're done for.' But now, as the flitter tumbled, the face of Earth was large before the window. 'Or maybe not! If I can get us down to some kind of controlled landing – us? What am I saying?'

'Nicola, let me help you—'

'Give my regards to your mother.' She slapped a control.

Darkness.

*

Another fall through emptiness.

Slam. Suddenly he was lying on a floor, sunlit. His mother standing over him. He gasped; he felt like he'd been punched.

He knew this light, flat and low. He was back in Princess Elizabeth Land. The Poole complex. Low Antarctic-summer sunlight. He tried to sit up; he felt winded, disoriented.

His mother knelt, put her arm around his shoulders, and helped him. For once she was able to touch him; the simple contact seemed to surprise them both. 'Don't try to talk. You've had a shock, I can see that.'

Poole rubbed his hand on the floor, deliberately. His palm broke up into pixels with sharp fragments of pain. 'Still a Virtual, then.'

'Evidently. What have you done to your forehead? It looks infected.'

'Ask Nicola Emry. Where am I? I mean, my physical body?'

'The last I heard, you're still in a flitter coming down from the Moon. Should be here in—'

'Never mind. No time. This will do.'

With Muriel's help he got to his feet, struggled to the window. The light was soft here, crimson to the east, a deep blue above. Very early summer morning in Antarctica.

'Miriam Berg? Can you hear me?'

The signal delay was only a fraction of a second. 'Loud and clear, Michael. The monopoles?'

'They cut that Xeelee up. We slowed it. But we didn't stop it.'

'Well, then,' Muriel said softly.

Michael Poole held his mother's unreal hand, and looked up; there were still stars to be seen at the zenith, in the Antarctic sky. And he looked east, into the dawn sky. Where Miriam Berg and her hand-picked crew were manipulating Solar System-spanning wormholes. 'From here we will probably see it.'

'See what?'

'Plan B.'

61

Poole's scheme was conceptually simple. And, he believed, despite a lack of prototyping or testing, physically plausible, given that it made use of two experimental wormhole systems that had already been opened up, stabilised, traversed. It was the scale of it that staggered most people who had worked on it.

Even Miriam Berg, who had shadowed Poole in everything he had done since he was nineteen.

Even, in the end, Michael Poole himself.

Take two wormholes: one that connects the Sun's interior to Mercury, and a second that connects Earth orbit to Jovian space . . .

In the months before the Xeelee's final, relentless approach to Earth, Miriam and her crews, in *Hermit Crab*-class GUTships, had used magnetic grapples to haul the Mercury terminus of the solar wormhole to Earth. And they had plunged the wormhole's other portal deep inside the body of the Sun itself: down through the layers Poole himself had explored, down through the great convective plumes, through the slow-churning radiative zone – deep down, in the end, into the fusing core itself (where enigmatic dark matter creatures swam, which would, it was hoped, leave this fragile human construct alone for a while). For now the wormhole's throat had been kept closed, so that the surging energy of the solar heart could not yet escape – could not pour into near-Earth space. Not yet.

The Jovian terminus of the other wormhole, meanwhile, was dragged by another cluster of ships, out away from Jupiter, into deep space, beyond Neptune, most distant of the giants, beyond the scattered Kuiper Belt – out into the mighty Oort Cloud, far beyond Pluto's orbit, a spherical domain of cold and deep-frozen worldlets circling in attenuated sunlight. That itself was a monumental effort, with the GUTship convoy thundering at thrusts of multiple gravities to meet the deadline.

All this had been hidden in the open. Proxies had informed Harry's government that the solar wormhole was being towed out to serve as an emergency energy source for Earth, and the government had swallowed that – although Poole would always wonder if Harry had turned a blind eye. As far as he knew the authorities hadn't even noticed the displacement of the Jovian-orbit portal.

So now there were two wormhole mouths, both close to Earth: one connected to the core of the Sun, the other to the edge of interstellar space. Hastily dragged to a halt, relative to the Sun – and set directly before the Earth, in its own path around the Sun.

Two portals brought so close together they almost touched. Waiting.

Until, from Antarctica, Poole gave his final command.

'Miriam?'

'Ready. Michael, are you sure?'

Poole felt exhausted. As if he could barely stand.

A last heartbeat. A last agonising doubt.

'Let's do this.'

The solar wormhole's throat yawned open.

Fusing solar-core hydrogen, at a temperature of nearly fifteen million degrees, spewed out of the portal.

Pulsed out into near-Earth space.

Hosed straight into the structure of the portal of the second wormhole, the route to the Oort Cloud.

And, as Poole had intended, from an object just big enough to pass a *Crab*-class GUTship lifedome, that portal began to grow dramatically. Solar energy, wormhole-mined and intelligently applied, was rapidly transmuted into more of the exotic matter that constituted the threadlike struts that framed the portal. This was how you force-grew a wormhole, as Poole had once tried to explain to Nicola and her mother. But it had never before been attempted on such a scale. He wondered if it ever would be again.

The portal seemed to blossom, some observers said later.

Poole and his mother, Virtuals both, wrapped in illusory, protocol-complying cold-weather gear, walked out of the Princess Elizabeth Land residence and looked to the east, to the Antarctic dawn.

And they *saw* the wormhole portal grow, high in the sky, fed by a spark of fire far brighter than the surface of the Sun itself. Grow into a frame that was soon easily visible to the naked eye, an electric-blue diagram across which stretched evanescent sheets, like gold leaf.

Muriel stared. 'It's like an immense building. A structure *beyond the sky*. Like an aurora perhaps, those curtains of light you see . . . I can't think of another point of comparison.'

Poole had no words at all. There was only the spectacle, which seemed to overwhelm him – even as he followed its progress analytically, even as he watched the unfolding geometry, estimating growth rates – a spectacle that seemed to implant dread deep in some animal core of his mind. *There aren't supposed to be things like this, up in the sky.* Even if Poole himself had put them there.

The frame grew fast in his vision, as it continued to expand, and as the Earth plummeted closer to it with its own orbital velocity of over thirty kilometres every second. Soon Poole had to crane back his head to see it all, that single immense triangular face that now dominated the sky. One vertex loomed up towards the zenith, a meeting of dead-straight struts, dazzling blue beyond the air, while the other two vertices of the face dropped below the horizon.

In the end the portal would grow to become a tetrahedron with sides some thirty thousand kilometres long – every bit as large, probably, as the tetrahedral Cage of planetbuster beams the Xeelee would have built around the Earth, just as it had at Mars, if it had had the chance. Already so large that the frame itself, as seen from Earth, was sweeping out of sight.

Poole imagined eyes lifted like his own and his mother's, all over Earth, watching this astounding spectacle. Imagined Nicola Emry in her fragile, broken flitter, tumbling out of the sky even as an immense shadow fell across the world. Imagined his own physical body in yet another descending craft, fleeing a sky growing very strange indeed.

Now Poole could no longer see the frame at all. Only that one tremendous face, directly ahead of Earth, a sheet of elusive gold, with hints of a starlit darkness glimpsed beyond the pale morning sky. A face large enough to swallow the whole Earth.

There was a final flicker of gold, all across the sky. Like a dazzle from the surface of a tremendous sea.

Then the dawn was snuffed out, a hideously unnatural collapse of the light.

Darkness fell.

'I did this,' he whispered.

His unreal mother squeezed his hand.

*

Later, Poole was able to access records from witnesses left behind in the inner Solar System.

The timing had been exquisite, the solar heat wormhole mouth closing down just as the planet made its own rendezvous.

Then the whole Earth took seven minutes to pass into the wormhole. As observed by probes outside the portal, it looked as if the planet itself was being burned out of existence, metre by metre, by the shining plane into which it crossed.

After that, it took more minutes for the planet to traverse through the wormhole's huge throat. It was not like a passage through a tunnel, more as if that tetrahedral cage closed in on the planet, then opened out again. A wormhole was a paradoxical nesting in a higher dimension – and a nesting associated with extreme spacetime distortions. In those long minutes the Earth suffered a severe tidal flexing, that triggered landslides and earthquakes, and sent immense ripples marching across the oceans – events whose after-effects would be, Poole knew, hideously familiar to anyone living on an Atlantic shore so recently battered by the Probe tsunami.

Once the planet was through, the wormholes were immediately collapsed, with electric-blue negative energy surging out of the fading portals.

In the inner System, in the space vacated by the Earth, a constellation of satellites and orbital habitats, suddenly bereft of their anchoring world, drifted slowly apart. The Moon too, shorn of its gravitationally dominant partner, began to settle into a new, solitary orbit of its own.

And a single Xeelee craft, damaged itself, brooded in the sudden emptiness.

While on Cold Earth, far away, under a sky suddenly black and star-littered, it began to snow.

Harry Poole made a quick call to his son. 'OK. Now I'm impressed.'

62

Earth came through the wormhole with its ocean, atmosphere, cargo of life more or less intact, dragged through by gravity. And through too came craft in the air and near-Earth space at the time, a handful of low-orbit satellites and habitats. At first all was confusion, as these craft – and their controllers on the ground, in the air and in space – tried to figure out where they were.

It took a full hour after the event the commentators were already calling the Displacement before Poole's flitter landed at last, bringing him physically to the Earth, at the family complex in Antarctica.

One hour after that, Poole walked out of the villa, alone. He felt he had to experience this new world directly. The Antarctic compound was full of specialised cold-weather gear, but Poole wore his own skinsuit, taken from the flitter. Adapted for space, it was more than capable of protecting him from the climate outside: even this new night, colder than any this chill southern continent had ever known.

A night that would never end.

Outside, the air was still and calm, the sky clear, the steady stars like shards of bone. This was the sky of the Oort Cloud. In minutes, Earth had been hurled more than a thousand times as far from the Sun as the orbit of its birth. Of course the constellations looked no different, even across the distance traversed by the planet during the Displacement; immense it might be in human terms, but that great dislocation was dwarfed by the gap even to the nearest star. At least he had not challenged the stars, Poole reflected. It was no comfort.

But, as he gazed up, he thought he saw some of those stars flickering now. High clouds forming, already. Even over Antarctica.

I did this.

His mother joined him, her footsteps soft in the huge night. She was bundled up in her consistency-protocol-compliant coat, quilted, ground-length, though she wore no hood. And she carried a kind of manikin, maybe ten centimetres tall. It was a doll-sized version of Harry, Poole saw with some bemusement, his father smart in his customary black and silver suit.

Poole didn't know what to say. So, as was his custom, he didn't say anything at all.

Muriel lifted her face to the sky. 'I once saw a solar eclipse. I mean, when I was young, still flesh and blood. Did I ever tell you? We were on a ship, a cruise to view the event. The totality crossed the Pacific. We stood there, on deck, under the sky, as the shadow of the Moon swept over us. I had anticipated the central event, the black disc of the Moon over the face of the Sun, the corona – the usual special effects, like in the Virtuals. I *hadn't* anticipated the scale of it all. The way the light dipped across the sky, all the way down to the horizon. As if the whole world was changing around me, above my level of existence. I felt a kind of primitive awe. I think today will have been the same for many people. A profound, visceral shock. Some will never recover, perhaps.'

Guilt twisted at Poole, and he knew that was a feeling that wouldn't go away any time soon. 'I'm sorry.'

'You don't have to say that.'

'It wasn't possible to give any warning. Even if we had, it would only have caused panic.'

She shrugged. 'And you would have been stopped. By the Stewards, the other government agencies. By Harry – he'd have had to. Stopped from saving the world. What's done is done. I'll tell you what strikes me as the single most impressive imagery I've seen so far today. After the loss of the Sun itself, of course . . . The space elevators. The orbital stations were detached, in the last moments before we hit the wormhole. There are recordings of that, brought with us through the wormhole.'

Again Poole felt pangs of regret. 'We couldn't warn the crews. I guess they figured it out. Smart guys.'

'Those Node stations must still be drifting in space, back at Earth's old position, in its orbit. But their cables were left dangling, engineered carbon threads thousands of kilometres long, and they came through with Earth. There are already flitters up there cutting it up; you don't want that stuff wrapping around the planet. So in some ways the government arms are already reacting.'

Poole thought he felt a drop of cold water on his bare cheek. He glanced up, and saw that the stars were almost obliterated now by an empty darkness, creeping down from the north.

'I felt that too,' Muriel said. 'The consistency protocols. The rain, sleeting through me, is like an itch. Rain, in Antarctica.'

'We did some modelling,' Poole said. 'The team at Gallia Three. Of the consequences of this, the Displacement. Under the Sun, Earth's energy budget was pretty much at a balance. The planet continually radiated away as much heat as it received from the Sun, more or less.'

'But now that the Sun has gone—'

'Earth is still radiating. For now it's like a bathtub with an open drain, and the taps suddenly turned off. Shining in the dark, in infra-red anyhow. But once the warmth is lost, it's lost. The oceans will keep their heat a little longer, but the air over the land will cool quickly. And the first thing the cool air will do is dump its water vapour.'

'Rain. Snow?'

'By this time tomorrow, yes. From pole to pole. Snow on Amazonia, in the Congo. Mother – what's with the scale model of Harry?'

She glanced at it, as if she'd forgotten she was holding it. 'This? He's been addressing the world. Began an hour after the Displacement, and has been on a loop with a few updates since. I thought you'd like to see.'

She threw the manikin into the air before her; it grew to life-size, the resolution only slightly imperfect.

And Harry Poole, still clad in an entirely inappropriate city suit of black and silver, began to speak, solemnly but calmly.

'. . . obvious to every citizen of Earth by now that the planet has indeed been displaced, by a passage through a wormhole. Whereas we were orbiting the Sun at a distance of some one hundred and fifty million kilometres – one astronomical unit – we are now more than a thousand times further out. A thousand AU.

'We are now in a part of the Solar System called the Oort Cloud. We are not alone out here; this is a region in which can be found many massive objects, even planets, dwarf worlds the size of Pluto or larger, even a couple of ice giants. There are humans too, exploration ships, even ancient colonies living off ice and gathered sunlight. In time we will be in touch with these pioneers.

'The Displacement has been a profound shock to the planet itself. A jolt. In the immediate term there have been reports of earthquakes, landslides, slippages – on the oceans, exceptional waves. We already have emergency agencies working in problem areas. In the longer term we will have to manage the loss of the tides, incidentally; we

have lost both Sun and Moon . . . That's the short term. As to further
out—

'Well, we are still within the Solar System. The nearest star is more
than two hundred times further yet than we've travelled. But sunlight
is sparse here. At a thousand times further from the Sun, the Sun's
energy as it reaches us is diminished by a factor of a *million*. And that
simple fact will shape all our lives from now on. Without sunlight,
this is a night that will never end, for Earth. Soon it is going to grow
cold. Very cold.

'Your government, however, the other Stewards and I, are responding to the emergency. And we have a period of grace, the
meteorologists tell me. Seven days, perhaps. Seven days before the
surface of the Earth becomes uninhabitable for human life, without
protection, without specialised vehicles or space-capable clothing like
skinsuits—'

Muriel said, 'This is an emergency that I suppose he never dreamed
he would have to deal with, only a few hours ago. Yet here he is. Calm,
in control.'

'Mother, nobody is in control.'

'Maybe not. But, right now, *sounding* as if he's in control of events
is absolutely the best thing Harry could be doing. Maybe this will be
his hour.'

'I hope so,' Poole said fervently. 'Because he's all we've got.'

'. . . What we have to do is to use this week, this time of grace, to
get everybody into the warm. And by that I mean the great Towers.
These are enclosed environments, capable of being sealed off, with
controlled inner climates; there you will find water, warmth. We are
a billion, on this Earth. Estimates indicate that the entire population
could be housed in the Towers. The government has already taken
steps to take the Towers into common ownership; you will be made
welcome.

'Beyond that – well, it won't be easy, especially at first. But one
thing we do have is power. For centuries humanity has been living
off the natural flow of energy from the Sun, from the planet's own
deep heat. That has been our conscious choice. But we do have available tremendously powerful artificial energy sources. The engine of a
single Poole Industries GUTship . . .'

Poole had to grin. 'Not really the moment for a product placement,
Harry.'

'. . . generates power of orders of magnitude more than the whole of human civilisation at the peak of the energy-hungry Anthropocene. The planet brought with it a number of such craft, on the ground or in orbit. Those craft will be landing soon. Bringing down heat and light.

'We have many more such craft in the planetory system, of course– meaning within the orbit of Nepture. But I have to tell you that the distance from home is very great – greater, perhaps, than our own imaginations have yet been able to absorb.

'Earth was once eight light-minutes from the Sun; now we are six light-*days* out. So far that we have not yet been able even to make contact with our remaining ships, or indeed Mars or the other colonies. Our first messages are crawling at lightspeed back to the planetary System right now – messages to stranded friends who must be even more bewildered than we are. Even when we do make contact, a GUTship driving at a full gravity's thrust would take no less than ninety days to get here.

'They will come. For now we are on our own.

'We have a week, then. You must do all you can to get yourselves and your families to shelter – and please help others. Let nobody be left behind. Meanwhile we're going to need volunteers to help with rescuing the rest of our world. I mean the flora and the fauna . . . Efforts are already beginning in the great reserves. Whole biomes are being preserved, under heated domes. And beyond that we must prepare for a new future – a different future.

'Most people already know, I think, that my son is responsible for this huge, bold act. It was indeed Michael Poole's scheme, his design – his wormhole – that brought us out here.' A faint smile. 'Judging from the contacts I have had so far, half of us want to give him a triumph to match any Caesar's. The other half want to lynch him.

'But, listen to me now. If Michael had asked for consent, he would not have got it. Not even from me, his father. And if he had not acted, by now Earth would be pinioned, as Mars already is, pinioned inside a Xeelee Cage, and doomed. Along with all of *us*.

'This is not a perfect solution. Millions of us will die.'

Muriel tried to touch Poole, to rest a hand on his shoulder; pixels glittered, but he felt nothing.

'But because of what my son has done today, most of a billion have survived – *will* survive. And Michael will be remembered as a hero, for ever . . .'

Muriel murmured, 'That was true already.'

'Mother, I need to go and help.'

'You should stay here, Michael. Earlier generations of paranoid Pooles made this place not so much a mansion as a bunker. And of course it's built to withstand the Antarctic winter. You'll be safe here.'

'Safe?' He shook his head. 'Nobody is safe. I have a flitter. I'm a pilot. I need to go help the evacuation effort. If somebody takes a shot at me, so be it. And I need to find Nicola. In the final battle, she took a hit. Hopefully came down somewhere. On Earth, I mean.' He hesitated for one more heartbeat, looking up at the sky, now almost a solid bank of clouds. 'And besides, it's all my Lethe-spawned fault.'

With a last regretful glance at his mother, he pulled closed his skinsuit and made for his flitter.

63

So Poole searched for Nicola.

Planet Earth remained interconnected. Even though when it crossed into the wormhole the planet's orbital family of artificial satellites, habitats, power stations and factories had mostly been lost or disrupted, Earth's own deep-embedded connectivity of fibres and cables, much of it very ancient, had survived almost intact. Poole made sure his flitter's systems were locked into this robust net of information and messages. He knew that if she lived, Nicola would be posting messages somewhere, somehow – and if so, he would pick them up.

But for now, almost at random – looking for migration efforts to support – he flew north, out of Antarctica, and headed for Australia.

He descended on Melbourne, a city he'd visited many times before; Poole Industries had offices and facilities here.

Now, at first glance as he descended from the dark sky, as seen by its own artificial light, the place looked much as he remembered it, still huddled behind walls that had protected riverine landscapes during the age of sea level rise. The core of the old town was easily visible, a grid of stately boulevards, and along the banks of the Yarra river was a later development of taller, more airy buildings. Australia as a whole had suffered savagely in the post-Anthropocene climate collapse. With the coming of the Recovery it had found a new balance, with a skim of population living in equilibrium with a restored flora and fauna: gum trees and giant kangaroos. But the old cities, like Melbourne, had survived as nodes of population and relics of the past.

There was no shelter now in Melbourne, however; the nearest modern Towers were in Canberra, about six hundred kilometres away. And that was where the population of Melbourne was going to have to find refuge, along with the inhabitants of all the coastal communities as far north as Sydney. The more scattered populations of the interior, too, were being gathered at hastily designated evacuation centres. Even in the oceans there were underwater communities, whose elaborate, beautiful habitats were being cut loose of their moorings, floated to the ice-littered surface of the raging seas, and emptied.

So Poole descended, through thick falls of snow, towards the dying city.

This was the third day since the Displacement. The heat dumped into the air by water vapour, as the falling snow crystallised out, had kept the air temperature at no lower than freezing point, for now. But whole swathes of Melbourne had already fallen dark. The snow was lying thick on the rooftops, and along those late-second-millennium avenues – any surviving trees must have been cut for firewood.

And he saw people moving everywhere, in crawling vehicles, even on foot, struggling towards the evacuation centres. From the air they were black dots, lumps of misery against the white snow. Poole had a sudden, sharp memory of the evacuation of Io, right at the start of all this, after the Xeelee incursion at Jupiter. It must be like this all over the world, he realised, communities draining, social structures collapsing, humanity reduced to a rabble with no goal but to find shelter. Each of those dots a human being, living, breathing, feeling. Nobody right now was even able to estimate the number of lives being lost.

I did this.

Poole reported his readiness to pick up evacuees to the Melbourne city authorities. Then, following instructions, he allowed automatic systems to lock on to the flitter and bring him down over Federation Square, an open space where bots fitted with huge improvised shovels laboured to keep the snow clear from a central apron. As soon as he was down Poole flung open the doors of his passenger cabin and cargo bay. Before he left Antarctica, both chambers had been fitted out with racks of couches.

Soon ground crew, sweating in thick snowproof gear, began to supervise the loading of people into the flitter.

Poole himself didn't climb down to the ground. Stuck in his cabin, he hastily organised the small party that came crushing through the port into the cabin itself. Three adults, three children – no, four, he saw, one small child, which made it one above the regulation number for the space. He wasn't about to complain.

One of the adults, an exhausted-looking woman, settled into the vacant co-pilot seat beside Poole. She picked up that spare child and held her close on her lap, and glanced at Poole. 'Thank you. We're the Bartons. From out in the suburbs. We're an awkward number, but it's not a time you want to get separated.' She hugged the little girl close.

But, in the sudden heat of the cabin, the child began wriggling out of her heavy coat.

'Hey,' Poole said gently. 'You need to keep wearing that. Just in case we have to come down quick.'

'Is she OK on my lap like this? I know she doesn't have a harness.'

'I'm not planning any stunt flying. You're her mother?'

She grinned, tired, and pushed a hank of wet hair back from her head. 'Her great-grandmother.'

The little girl was staring at Poole, with one small finger stuck up a nostril; a glove dangled on a thread from her sleeve. Something in that big-eyed glare made Poole uncomfortable.

He asked, 'Do you know who I am?'

'Yes.'

'Who, then?'

'You're the man who's driving the airplane. Granny, are we there yet?'

'Not quite, sweet pea.'

At last they got clearance from the ground.

As the flitter lifted smoothly into the air, Poole felt an odd pang of nostalgia for his long, solitary missions in deep space, of which he had grown increasingly fond. Sabbaticals, his mother had called such jaunts, and she had tried to break him of the habit. Well, now he was at the other extreme. He had made it to the Oort Cloud, he supposed, but here he was crammed with strangers inside a tiny ship, his mission a mere six-hundred-kilometre hop.

And it wasn't even under his control. As soon as he lifted from Melbourne, the flitter was taken over by a hastily improvised traffic control system and driven north-east, skirting the great up-draughts around the Australian Alps. The control was necessary; the airspace was so crowded that he could see the lights of other craft streaming through the snow all around him, and, close by, a lane of empty vehicles coming back the other way. He was kept low enough, too, to make out ground traffic: vehicles on the roads, and the glittering lights of monorail trains.

He was ordered to make a detour around a particularly savage storm system over Bombala. The traffic got still more jammed up, slowing them all down even further. Poole was getting used to this. The vast climate adjustments were not proceeding in an orderly or uniform fashion: all that lost heat energy seemed to rage as it leaked into space. So, vast hurricanes stalked the oceans and battered at the coasts, and the snow came in blizzards driven by ferocious winds.

His passengers didn't utter a word of protest or complaint. They had water and food bars and basic medical supplies, from packs handed to them by the ground crews. And after the first hour they seemed to be falling asleep, including that child on the lap of her great-grandmother next to him.

An alarm chimed softly: a privacy notice. He hit a tab that would cast a Virtual translucent curtain around his pilot's position, making him inaudible and all but invisible to his passengers.

Harry's head materialised in the air in front of him.

Harry looked exhausted, unshaven, his eyes rimmed red. But he smiled at Poole. 'Your passengers are asleep, I see. Sweet, isn't it? It's good to put yourself in somebody else's care for a while. A vacation from responsibility.'

'I wouldn't know. What do you want, Harry?'

'Just to talk. A few minutes. When I saw you were in the air, I took the chance. In the air and away from your mother, of course.'

'You've been watching me.'

'Of course I've been watching you. There's still a massive but discreet security operation revolving around you, Michael. I'd have thought you'd guessed that. Right now you're the most famous human being on the planet. Or the most notorious. What did you expect? To most people on Earth the Xeelee was an abstraction. Even what it did to Mars was just pictures from the sky. You, though, have thrown us all into an Ice Age. In itself, this was a hugely destructive act. You're being called a mass murderer, Michael. Or, the most notorious fascist since the worst of the Anthropocene. After all, you didn't consult anybody before making a decision on behalf of all mankind. We Pooles have probably been getting it in the neck since the time of Michael Poole Bazalget, but you've taken the crown.'

'I had no choice—'

'I know that! But for now, if you insist on being out in the world, if you won't just stay back in Princess Elizabeth Land as your mother suggested, stay anonymous, OK?'

'I'm surprised you've got the time to talk.'

'Even Stewards get time off, you know.'

Poole said grudgingly, 'I saw your broadcast. The first day. You did well. It must have been a Lethe-spawned shock for all of you in the government.'

'We did have help,' Harry admitted. 'From the artificial sentiences in particular – Gea, for instance. When you pushed the world through that big electric-blue hoop, Michael, they were quick to begin figuring out the implications. So we got off to a good start. But we're already thinking through the wider consequences, the longer term.'

'The longer term?'

'Well, we didn't defeat the Xeelee, we just ran away. It might take a while for the Xeelee and its drones to come out here, but we don't imagine we can hide away a planet like Earth for ever, not even a thousand AU out. Although we need to think about ways to try. But you've bought us time, Michael. And most of the people alive on Earth before the Xeelee came are still alive, because of what you did. You have to hang on to that.'

Some of Poole's reflexive cynicism cut back in. 'What's with the comforting words, Harry? Are you angling for something?'

Harry shook his head. 'Not this time. Just this once . . . I do have two things to tell you. One is you have clearance for your final approach to Canberra. I'll get off the line. And the second—'

'Yes?'

'We found Emry for you. Downloading now. Stay safe, son.' And he winked out of existence.

Nicola's damaged flitter had tumbled with Earth through the wormhole, and had come down on the other side of the Pacific: in the Andes, close to an isolated community of Quechua speakers. Thinking about it, Poole realised she had been lucky to come down on dry land at all. Reeling out of the fight with the Xeelee, descending almost at random, she'd had a seventy per cent chance of coming down in the ocean, or on the ice – and if she had, in the aftermath of the Displacement, her chances would have been poor.

As it was, local people had been able to save her. They extracted her, broken leg and all, from the wreck of her flitter. And then, a day later, when the snow started to fall, she in turn had needed to save them, by helping them rig up cover over their small town hall, and using the flitter's GUTengine to pipe in heat and light.

Thus she survived.

Poole was able to home in on a small transmitter embedded in that Poole Industries GUTengine, a routine relay of maintenance data back to the manufacturer. But it took days for him to get clearance for such a flight, such was the chaos in the air of Cold Earth.

At last, on the tenth day after the Displacement, he flew around a freezing planet. Over ice-coated oceans.

The snow was over now. In the end there had been enough water vapour in the air to deposit a global layer of snow ten or twenty metres thick. The oceans, meanwhile, were steadily cooling too. On the surface waters, in fact, even at the equator, the ice floes had started to form from the very first day.

But by the seventh or eighth day the first great pulse of heat loss was over. The snow stopped falling, the clouds had dissipated – the skies had cleared for the last time. The oceans were already covered by a uniform skim of ice, steadily thickening. Earth lay still, under stars like bone. Even the rivers had frozen solid, an eerie sight.

And, with the skies permanently clear, there was nothing now to trap the remnant heat. Nothing to stop the temperature from falling, and falling.

Poole landed his flitter over the position of the GUTdrive beacon, buried somewhere under the snow. Then he staggered through the clear, deep cold air, broke through the snow layers with the help of shovel-wielding bots, and forced his way into the buried town hall.

When he cracked the roof, hot, moist air billowed into his eyes. He saw circles of faces, wide-eyed, shocked, scared, relieved. There were even a few llamas, off by one wall, grubby, treading in their own dung. And in one corner, her legs hidden under heaps of colourful blankets – skinsuit torn open at the neck – holding a set of pan pipes, evidently hand-made—

'You took your time,' Nicola said. And she went back to picking out a tune on the pipes.

'I—'

She looked at him now. 'What?'

'I haven't slept. Not since—'

'Hush.' She got up now, limped over, and wrapped her own blanket around his shoulders.

SEVEN

We are just a handful of people in this desolate, remote place. And yet here a new epoch is born. They are listening to us, you know – listening in the halls of history. And *we* will be remembered forever.

Admiral Kard, AD 12659

64

Ten years after the Displacement of Earth, Michael Poole, thirty-nine years old, wrapped in a non-reflective skinsuit, stood on the surface of Chiron.

Chiron was one of a wandering class of natural bodies called, in ancient jargon, 'centaurs'. It followed a leisurely, eccentric, fifty-year orbit through the Solar System, between the circles of Saturn and Uranus. Its ground was stained dark with organics, purple and crimson, exotic chemistry created by the pallid energy of the distant Sun. Only the fact that the rock percentage outweighed the ice made this worldlet an icy rock rather than a dirty snowball.

Poole, cautiously, tested the gravity; he flexed his feet, and drifted slowly up off the ground. He knew the gravity was only around one per cent of Earth's – barely there at all. Rather like himself, he thought. After all, this Virtual copy, though full of memory and self-aware, wasn't Michael Poole. Barely there at all.

But Chiron, as an inhabited refuge, was meant to be elusive. Its surface, heavily but subtly modified, bristled with spindly cones of ice-rock, some waist-high, some towering over Poole's head. These were coated with smart material that made them work as solar energy collectors in the sunlight, waste heat radiators in the shadow. From a distance it would appear that the energy of the Sun washed through an inert mass, without modification, without evidence of occupancy. In fact that flow of radiation was trapped, used, the waste heat scrambled and released, by the new inhabitants of Chiron.

In the ten years since Earth had been thrown out of the inner System, humanity had learned to hide.

The Xeelee and its collaborators, or symbiotes, had been observed operating actively as far out as Saturn, so far. Yet mankind survived, in caches like this even within that orbit, and in greater numbers further out – notably, of course, on Earth itself. So the Stewards' mandate was that there should be minimal evidence of human activity, anywhere. Certainly no GUTships flew, big, bright energetic objects.

And that meant, if Poole wished to visit the planetary System, it could only be by the projection of Virtual copies on elusive, tight-beam neutrino links.

This little world had its own natural wonders, however. Remarkably, Chiron had rings, like Saturn's, thin bands of water-ice particles orbiting a hundred kilometres or so above the surface. Poole was close to the equator here, so the rings were edge-on. He leaned back, lifting his head, trying to convince himself he could make out the rings' elusive glitter.

A few paces away, a hatch opened in the rough ground, a lid of rock and ice. It had been well concealed, camouflaged like the rest of the surface. From a dark interior a figure in a skinsuit jumped up with accustomed ease, to stand by Poole. Vapour plumed around his feet, volatiles stirred by leakage from the suit – Poole's unreal footsteps made no such marks, a failure of the simulation.

Behind a faceplate, in the low, distant sunlight, Poole made out the features of a grinning Jack Grantt.

'Michael! Welcome to Chiron. Or, as we sometimes call it, Little Mars.'

Uncle Jack. Poole had to grin back as they stumbled through the low gravity towards each other.

From what Poole could see of him, Grantt was scarcely changed from the days when he had been busily prospecting for advanced native life on Mars. If anything he was a little younger looking, and that wouldn't be a surprise. Mankind had responded to the great shock of the Displacement in unexpected ways. After the initial pulse of casualties, the birth rate had surged, and there had been a clamour for already stretched medical services to provide more AntiSenescence treatments. People wanted to live, they wanted children, and wanted them to live too. And a younger-looking Jack Grantt was an exemplar of that.

Now Grantt held out a hand to shake. Poole's gloved hand disintegrated to pixels as it passed through Grantt's.

'Ouch,' Grantt said. 'Sorry. Those consistency routines. We're not used to it, not any more. We don't have the spare capacity for Virtuals here.' He was gazing at Poole, oddly fascinated. 'In fact I've never spent much time around Virtual people. Aside from a few Barsoomian gamers. You *aren't* Michael Poole, are you? Because Poole himself is light-days away, on Earth. Probably awake, doing stuff, leading his own life. When this visit is done we'll transmit your memory store back home, where you will be synced back to the original, and nothing else will be left of *you*, the entity standing in front of me now . . . That doesn't trouble you?'

Poole shrugged. 'Best not to think about it.'

Grantt looked directly at Poole. 'Of course if I was a psychologist instead of a biologist, I might think you're putting yourself through this, these mini-deaths, as a kind of punishment.'

Poole said nothing to that.

'Well, Michael, deep down, I don't know what you are. And frankly I can't imagine how it must be for you to have to live with what you did. But for sure I'm glad you did it. And my people here will be glad to see you.' He raised a welcoming arm. 'Come inside.'

65

Inside Chiron, exiled Martians had carved out a hollow world.

Buried a couple of kilometres deep within the carcass of the world-let, the main chamber was roughly egg-shaped, and full of light. Walls of ice, smoothed over, sealed behind plastic, glistened purple-red in the light of sunlight strips. The gravity was much as it had been on the surface, one per cent of Earth's – or about three per cent of Mars's, Poole reminded himself – so little it hardly made any difference, and he saw people leaping high and confident, swarming over nets and cables flung across the open inner volumes.

Of course breathable air, clean water, food were essentials, and hidden out of sight there were no doubt hydroponic banks and recycling suites to ensure those provisions. Poole imagined there would be food machines too, used only as a backup, power-hungry as they were, and with visible signatures.

But here, out in the open where people lived, old-fashioned farms sprawled across the inner walls, a relic of the long-vanished age of agriculture on Earth. Cabbages grew huge. Meanwhile people lived in houses on stalks of insulation-clad ice that rose from the floor, or stuck out of the walls. Grantt told Poole the stalks had been deliberately left in place when the hollow had been carved out.

The place was busy, in a low-key, domestic way. People were working in the fields, or fixing up the houses, or they just gathered in little knots in the air, talking. In one corner was what looked like a school group: young kids and a couple of adults clustered around a chicken coop. In another, a party was working its way down one of the sunlight strips, cleaning, polishing, mending. They cast huge shadows across the habitat.

This bubble of light was a place where people were getting on with their lives, so much so that few of them even glanced over at Poole, the stranger, the famous – or notorious – world-mover. He felt all the better for it. Comforted, almost.

'I was always confident we would survive here, once we gathered a decent population,' Grantt said, guiding Poole through the space. 'I mean, we already had the necessary skills, we Martians. The whole of Chiron is only a couple of hundred kilometres across; we were building arcologies bigger than that on Mars. And Chiron is generous. It is twenty-five per cent water ice by volume, and full of organic chemistry. At first we considered spinning her up to give us normal gravity – I mean Mars-normal.'

'But that would have made you too obvious.'

'To the Xeelee, yes. We instinctively stealthed everything we did, from the beginning. We came here to hide, after all. And to keep an eye on the Xeelee.

'We broke up most of the ships that brought us here, and took the salvage down into the ice. All our internal communication is by cable – closed systems. We have a number of GUTengines, taken from the ships, which we could dig out of store if we really needed a lot of power in a hurry. Otherwise we're living, ninety-nine per cent, off the flow of energy from the sunlight that hits Chiron's surface naturally.

'We live modestly, and quietly, and so far it's worked. And,' he said testily, 'when you go back you might tell that father of yours and his colleagues in the Stewardship that we don't need directives and reprimands and lectures on how to stay stealthed. We *know*. We've already survived a decade a few astronomical units from a rampaging Xeelee. In fact Stewardship messages are themselves among the worst compromises to our security . . .'

Poole grinned. His father knew all about Martians. Most of the ten million former inhabitants of the planet, after all, had finished up as refugees on Earth itself, and most of them were still there, on Cold Earth, out in the Oort Cloud. In fact, in the early days after the Displacement, the Martians had made invaluable contributions to Earth's survival: unlike most Earthborn they had personal experience of life on a cold, all but airless world.

But Martians, said Harry, were a self-reliant, ornery, argumentative bunch who were the bane of his life. So one more complaint from Jack Grantt, Poole thought, wouldn't really make much difference.

'. . . It *is* him. I told you. The tattoo on his forehead gives it away.'

'It doesn't look right, though. The tattoo.'

'That's because his was one of the first, dummy. Must have been if you think about it. They hadn't got it stylised yet . . .'

Two young people came drifting down towards them, from a sky full of houses.

*

A male and a female, they looked alike, with tousled blond hair grown long and tied back. Clear blue eyes. They might have been seventeen, eighteen. Wearing loose, practical coveralls, with knees and lower sleeves dirty, they looked as if they'd come straight from farmyard chores. And they both had stylised tetrahedral sigils, picked out in lime green, on their foreheads.

Grantt clucked. 'Stop staring, you two; you've no manners. Yes, it's *him*. Michael Poole, meet Flammarion; her brother is Weinbaum. My stepchildren.'

Poole made a double-take. 'Stepchildren?'

The girl snorted. 'That's typical of you, Jack. The most important person in the Solar System comes visiting, and you didn't tell us about him. You didn't even tell *him* about *us*.'

Grantt looked weary rather than embarrassed. 'If I owe anybody an apology, fine.'

Poole said, 'I met step-children before, years back. You married again, Jack?'

He nodded. 'I'll introduce you to Tania. These kids lost their father during the evacuation. Lots of broken families, here in Chiron. Lots of new families being put together. Like a living jigsaw.'

'Well, I'm happy for you.' Poole studied the boy. 'Weinbaum, though. An Anthropocene-era fiction writer, yes? I heard of him.'

The boy looked puzzled. 'No, it's a crater on Mars. Or was.'

Grantt said, 'Another fashion. People have started naming their kids after features on Mars – so we don't forget, you see – and some of the youngsters, like these two, have adopted names of their own. They were six and seven years old when the Cage came down. But of course those features were named in the first place after mythological entities and famous figures and whatnot from Earth. I know Flammarion was an astronomer.'

The girl eyed Poole critically. 'You're not as tall as you look in the Virtual dramas.'

He grinned. 'I've heard that before. They use actors. Even in the documentary features, they clean up the imagery.'

'You should have had that tattoo fixed,' Weinbaum said, glancing at Poole's forehead. 'Although it has got a kind of primitive authenticity.'

'Thanks.'

'Ours were properly designed.'

'Some people are programming it into their genes,' Weinbaum said.

'So your baby is *born* with the tattoo. The Sigil of Free Humanity. But we think that's wrong. It makes more sense if the child has to choose to wear it, or not, when it grows up. Some people are having a kind of ceremony when the tattoo is made.'

'Like a baptism,' Jack Grantt said, with a warning look at Poole.

Poole longed to turn away from the intense gaze of these two bright, hardworking teenagers, with their vivid tattoos. He wasn't sure if it was worse to be worshipped or reviled. Either way, he suspected he spent too much of his time these days hiding away from it all. 'I'm no messiah,' he mumbled.

'Maybe not. But you're all we've got.' Grantt tried and failed to put an arm around Poole's Virtual shoulders, an instinctive category error that reminded Poole of his mother. 'Come on. Look, I arranged for you to give a talk at our school later. I'm sure you won't mind that. But for now, come see what we've been doing out here. We don't just play at farmer in the sky . . .'

Grantt led Poole up an ice stalk to one of the more complex structures. It turned out to be a cluster of workrooms. There were people apparently on duty in here, and the space was heavy with information technology, with softscreens on the walls, and Virtual figures, abstract and figurative, that floated in the air.

'This,' Grantt said cryptically, 'is where we keep our own eye on the Xeelee. And where we entertain guests.'

'Guests?'

They turned a corner, and Poole found himself facing Highsmith Marsden and Miriam Berg, both shimmering with the faint, glistening unreality of Virtual projections.

66

Poole and Miriam stood in the gentle gravity, facing each other. One projected from Jovian orbit, the other from the Oort Cloud.

At length Poole said, 'Not like you to be lost for words, Miriam.'

'On the other hand,' she snapped back, 'it is entirely like you. Do you even remember when we last met in person?'

'I—'

'I'll tell you. Eight years ago. Not long after the Displacement, when Highsmith and I came out to Cold Earth in person for one of Harry's super-secret summits. Creeping across the outer System for two hundred days in a low-thrust, low-emission GUTship . . . And it's not actually face to face now, is it?'

Highsmith Marsden was grinning, his grey-white hair a drifting halo in the low gravity. 'Oh, must you behave so, you two? All this fencing. Sometimes you seem so immature I find myself looking for gills. Miriam, give him a hug.'

Their collision, two Virtual spin-offs embracing, was uncomfortable. Then Poole stopped thinking and gave in to the moment.

Holding him tight, she whispered sternly, 'You haven't changed, Michael. I don't believe the hype about you, for good or ill, any more than you do yourself. But we've got work to do. So pull yourself together.'

Grantt smiled. 'And come see what the Xeelee is doing to our Solar System.'

He led them through the rest of the rooms, where technicians adjusted displays, and earnest-looking observers made notes on softscreens. Virtual models of planets and moons hung in the air.

Highsmith Marsden looked on with apparent approval. 'A museum of orreries. We have a very similar set-up back on Gallia Three.'

Grantt said, 'Of course we share all our data and interpretations with Earth, Gallia and other refuges. But here's our intelligence-gathering operation in action. Not that things change much day to day. The Xeelee is nothing if not deliberate.'

In one room the Caged Worlds were shown. These were the major bodies once inhabited by large numbers of humans, and now on notice of destruction by the cherry-red frames which trapped them. By this point they included Earth's detached Moon, and Venus, where lava gushed through a thick layer of an atmosphere long since frozen out by mankind's sunshield. Even Mercury. And Mars, of course. The first victim. Mars was almost featureless now, Poole saw. Even the great Tharsis volcanoes had slumped. Islands of a kind of dark slag floated on a global ocean of sullenly glowing magma. After ten years enough energy had been injected into that world to melt the planet's fifty-kilometres-thick crust almost entirely. But still that Cage kept the planet pinned.

'We think,' Marsden said, 'that with time, the Xeelee, or its devices, will dismantle Mars entirely. And ultimately, presumably, all the Solar System's planets and moons – first, those which have, or had, trace human populations, but we see no reason why it should stop there. This will take some time. It's estimated that it will take fourteen centuries to pour in enough energy to take Mars apart, for example. We know the giants – Jupiter, Saturn, Uranus, Neptune – are receiving attention too. We had to evacuate our stations in the high clouds. Some different kind of gravity weapon, it seems, missiles sent down into their interiors. A long-term destabilisation seems to be under way. Perhaps, ultimately, implosions will—'

'And the smaller worlds? The lesser moons, the asteroids?'

'The Dust Plague,' Grantt said grimly. 'Come take a look.'

He led them to another room, which hosted a big schematic display of clusters of the minor worlds and asteroids of the Solar System. These images were returned by the high-inclination Eyrie stations, which were still crewed, and ran as silent as the rest. The asteroid belt, a ring around the Sun, sparkled with light, the markers of attacks, as it had in such representations for a decade.

'This all began with the Cache,' Grantt said. 'And the Paragons who inhabit it. They're still producing Probes – and you know that one of those babies can entirely dismantle a body seventy kilometres across in a single blow.'

'Beyond that, however,' Marsden said, and Poole thought his tone sounded very pedantic-scholar for such a narrative of destruction, 'as we have been monitoring, what we call the Dust Plague continues.

327

Quasi-biological technology, using the mass-energy of our asteroids against them: converting debris to weapons to take out yet more asteroids.

'*Quasi-biological:* we have been observing this self-replicating strategy for some time, but now we think in fact that to achieve this the Xeelee may have unleashed yet another kind of life in the Solar System. Another of their client species? Another relic from the early days of the universe? These seem to be nasty little knots of animated spacetime – quite unlike anything we've seen before. Feeding on the gravitational binding energy of the very objects they destroy. Eating them from the inside out, bursting them open, to make more copies of themselves. And so it spreads, until nothing is left. Ultimately even the smallest bodies, even pebbles in the sky, will be reduced to dust.'

Miriam regarded the images. 'With the benefit of hindsight we think we can discern distinct phases in the Xeelee's attack. After the initial emergence from the wormhole, and its gathering of equipment and energy from Mercury and the Sun, it unleashed its initial Probes to test us, to explore. Then followed its programme of targeted destruction of inhabited worlds and bodies: from Mars, Earth and Moon to the smallest deep-space habitat. Now it is proceeding to assail bodies where we have yet to establish a significant presence, resources we have yet to tap: the giant planets, the uninhabited rocky worlds and moons, the asteroids and comets. All of it. And surely the wave of destruction will expand beyond the planetary system, to the Kuiper Belt, ultimately the Oort Cloud. So that we can never recover, I suppose: not here, in the Solar System, at any rate. But as Jack says, this programme will take some time to complete.'

Grantt said, 'And that gives us a fighting chance. For now there's a healthy number of humans surviving in the Solar System. In fact because Earth itself survived, most of humanity, in terms of the pre-Xeelee population, is still alive.'

Most. Poole turned away at that word. He felt Miriam's Virtual hand slip into his.

Highsmith Marsden proclaimed, 'It can't be doubted that the Xeelee strategy has been flawed – well, that's clear, if even a fraction of humanity still has a decent chance to survive. We know that the Xeelee had to wait until the human creation of a wormhole before it could complete its journey here from the future; by definition we already had an off-planet presence by then. We were *already* scattered, and couldn't be caught by a single strike on Earth, for instance.

'Since it arrived it has moved on us slowly, deliberately, remorse-lessly – but without covering our avenues of retreat, such as out to the Kuipers and the Oort Cloud. It seems to have created no global observation post such as our own Eyries. Perhaps its previous experiences have shaped it. Perhaps it did not *expect* us to be so resourceful, so elusive.'

Poole thought that over. 'And maybe that's how we managed to beat them in the Exultant War. Or would have.'

Marsden eyed him. 'And if that means that *you* are one of the most highly developed intelligences in the Galaxy, then I despair, Michael Poole, I despair.'

Grantt went on, 'So we have this interval, this respite, and we have to use it wisely. We of Chiron have figured out a plan of our own . . .'

Another room, another display.

Chiron was actually a relative newcomer to the planetary Solar System, Poole learned now. It had probably begun its existence as a bit of orbiting debris in the Kuiper Belt, beyond Pluto, left over from the formation of the planets. Chance encounters with other bodies, collisions or gravitational slingshots, had brought it drifting into the inner System, and had jostled it into this present orbit, looping be tween Saturn and Uranus.

'But it's probably only been here for ten million years or less,' Grantt said. 'And, left alone, in ten more million years close encounters with Saturn or Uranus would probably have thrown it out of its current orbit. After that, maybe it would sail close to the Sun and become a short-period comet; maybe it would collide with Saturn or Jupiter. *Or* – it might be flung out of the System altogether.'

Miriam smiled. 'Ah. And maybe if you give it the subtlest nudge, next time you sail close to Saturn—'

'That's the idea. Chiron's escape from the Solar System can be made to look natural. No cause for alarm, for the Xeelee. And then we'll ride a slow boat to the stars. Even if we aim right, it will be millennia before any kind of landfall, but Chiron has all we need to survive. After that – well, if the Xeelee doesn't hunt us down, we'll see what the future brings.'

Poole turned to Miriam. 'And you? Gallia Three is hiding in the Trojans right now – in Jupiter's orbit, that much closer in than Chiron.'

'And at a stable location, gravitationally,' she said. 'If we wander out of there it won't be nearly as convincing in terms of fooling the Xeelee. Which is one reason we aren't going anywhere soon. But the Xeelee's programme of asteroid-busting will reach the Trojans eventually.'

Marsden nodded. 'I am determined that even if we must move the habitat, *we will not flee*. We were the first human sanctuary to go stealthed – as you will remember, Michael Poole, at my recommendation, right at the beginning of all this, despite a squawk of objections. And we have achieved a great deal. I believe that we have a duty to leave at least one human community *inside the System* that birthed us, even as the rest scatter.'

Grantt nodded. 'I don't envy you. But I can see that's the right thing to do.' He turned to Poole. 'But that leaves the biggest issue, of course. The largest human refuge of all.'

'Earth,' Miriam said. 'A billion people. Stuck on a world slowly turning into a huge cryogenic lab. What next for them?'

'We're working on it,' Poole said bluntly.

Marsden looked at the Virtual images, hanging in the air around them. 'There is a kind of abstract, silent beauty in all this. Mars has rings, now, like Saturn.

'But this phase won't last long. The Xeelee may take a hundred thousand years to finish the job. But in geological terms, or astrophysical, that's a blink of an eye. And after that blink the Solar System will be rubble,' he said brutally. 'Less than rubble. Dust. All of it. It will be as if the Solar System has been taken back to its birth, when there was nothing but the young Sun and a disc of rubble, yet to form into the planets. Nothing here save the Sun, and the dust, and the Xeelee.'

Marsden gazed into the Virtual sunlight. 'I was born on Earth, you know. I grew up in Achinet, in fact. We were not rich, not well-connected. But I was privileged. For no human child will ever again be raised as I was, under the open sky.' He faced Poole, and gripped his arm hard, Virtual flesh against Virtual flesh. 'Make it pay, Michael Poole. I will do all I can to give you the tools you need. Make the Xeelee pay.'

Poole stayed a week on Chiron.

He spent time with Flammarion and Weinbaum and their friends, all of them sporting tetrahedron tattoos. Most of these youngsters were already forgetting there had ever been any other world than this, the heart of a centaur, to grow up in, and they had no need to forgive Poole for what he had done to Earth. Poole hoped some of the sense of renewal that he got from these kids would transmit back to his original, on Cold Earth.

Miriam and Marsden uploaded back to Gallia on the sixth day. Poole suspected he would never see Miriam again; not for the first time, he had plans, not yet revealed. He sensed she had the same intuition. Their farewell wasn't cold, but it seemed perfunctory. A brief embrace. A lost future. They parted with secrets.

On the seventh and last day Grantt threw a party. Poole morbidly called it a wake, for his short-lived Virtual.

Then, that evening, there came at last the time for the transmission back to Earth, the uploading back to his original. Because of the need for stealth, the timing was quite precise, a question of obscure algorithms; transmission directions and timings had to be optimised for minimal detectability, given the relative positions of the Xeelee and its known agents in the Solar System.

And it was because of this last-minute analysis of the Xeelee's movements that this copy of Poole became aware of a striking new development, just as he prepared for his own Virtual death.

Across the Solar System the Xeelee's great projects continued unhindered. The Cache remained, a source of Probes, a refuge for Paragons and Dust Plague fabricators and other entities.

But the Xeelee had gone.

67

On the fifteenth anniversary of the Displacement, Poole and Nicola called a meeting in the family compound on Princess Elizabeth Land – a location that was no longer among the coldest on the planet, as Poole reflected with bleak humour every time he came here.

Of course no Poole family gathering was without an agenda. This time it was Poole and Nicola who had an announcement to make. So they gathered in the lounge: Michael, Harry, Muriel – Gea too – were all here, and Shamiso Emry. They sat with drinks. Poole was handed a single malt by Harry, serving bots being rare nowadays – though not so rare as the malt whisky itself. At first the talk was quiet. Poole sat still for only a little of it.

Feeling detached, he walked to the lounge's huge picture windows.

And, standing there, with a soft, almost subvocal command, he threw a Virtual projection into the sky.

Michael Poole rose like a stone thrown from a bowl of ice. And he looked down on Cold Earth .

From up here, Earth looked spectral in the starlike glint of its distant Sun, pure white, an abstraction of its former self. But it was still possible to discern its geography, the familiar shapes of the continents like plaster sculptures, textured with frozen lakes and mountain chains, and the smoother plains that coated the oceans.

And those pale landscapes were broken by specks of green. Dots of light in the dark. These were the surviving Towers and other human shelters – heavily reinforced and supported by independent power supplies – and the ecohabs, as they had come to be called, scraps of wilderness preserved by the descendants of the Recovery-era generations who had first restored those ancient landscapes centuries before. In North America, in such shelters, bison and short-faced bears and dire wolves wandered, baffled; in the relics of the north European forests, steppe mammoths and woolly rhinos; in Australia huge wombats and marsupial lions. There were habs even under the oceans, domes of water inside the thickening ice kept liquid by the energies of GUTengines.

And if Poole watched closely, he could see the slow movement of vehicles across the ice. Lights, crawling bravely through the dark. Even now, fifteen years on from the Displacement, it was still possible to find scattered groups of survivors, living in more or less improvised nests of air and warmth, scraping up frozen oxygen to stay alive. When such caches of people were found and rescued, Poole was always reminded of another fragment of his reading of Anthropocene-era fiction. Pails of air.

Poole's initial dramatic gesture, throwing open a wormhole to move the whole Earth and its population of a billion people, had only been the beginning of a struggle for survival that, everyone now suspected, could probably never be regarded as over. By the end of the first week, after the great blizzards had finished, and the skies of Earth cleared, the temperature had started dropping fast – the global average plummeting by three degrees or more per *day*, after the first month easily breaking pre-Displacement records set here in Antarctica. Meanwhile, out of sight, the freezing-over of the oceans had inflicted an immediate catastrophe on the great, lovingly restored whales and other ocean fauna, which suddenly had no access to air. And with time, as the plankton of the upper waters died off without sunlight, wider food chains collapsed. After a few months or years, the extinctions would have cut to the deepest waters

People fought to survive. The immediate chill-down was like a slow-burning global war, as swarms of refugees battled over shelter and provisions. In some cases the wars were literal, such as the aggressive conquest of Iceland, rich in geothermal energy, by a band from northern Europe. After five or six weeks the cold had locked down everybody left alive, in whatever scattered shelters they had been able to find. Work parties began the job of retrieving the corpses of the rest.

Then, almost unbelievably, just two months after the Displacement, the air itself started to rain out. Seas of liquid oxygen pooled over a crust of water ice, itself by now hard as rock. These seas, metres deep in places, froze in their turn.

And the nitrogen rain began . . .

On impulse, Poole the Virtual angel threw himself down at the planet – to New York, to Central Park, where, he always remembered, Harry had once gone to witness the effects of the Xeelee's Atlantic Probe on the American east coast. Now, the surface of the Park itself, swathes of dead grass, was lost under metres of water-ice snow, frozen as hard as basalt. The taller buildings still protruded from the ice, smashed, broken, mostly abandoned – the big old Paradoxa carbon-sequestration dome still stood – and drifts of nitrogen snow metres thick were heaped up against the walls of the dark towers. Exiled Martians laughed that nitrogen and oxygen, this stuff that Earth had been so reluctant to ship to Mars, now lay around for the taking, ready frozen for convenience of mining.

But the city looked oddly beautiful, as if asleep under an ethereal snowfall. And it was not dead. Walkways had been cast over the banks of frozen air. Even now people moved through the city.

Through these evolving horrors, blame was heaped on Michael Poole. The inquests were endless. There were demands for trials, and when the authorities refused mock hearings were held anyhow. Effigies were burned or hanged. Harry would give Poole bleak, occasional summaries of how many assassination attempts had been averted lately, along with pleas for Poole to stay out of sight. Sometimes Poole thought it was as if people had forgotten the Xeelee which had impelled him to take this action in the first place.

None, however, was so critical of Poole as Poole himself. Was there after all something he had missed? Some way of saving the world other than plunging it into this deep-freeze? He felt as if he had grown old. Old and alone, no matter who was with him. He was forty-four years old.

Meanwhile, fifteen years on, still the temperature fell. The thicker the sea ice, the slower the heat loss, and the more gradual the planet's overall temperature decline. But the heat leak would not stop until the Earth neared the temperature of interstellar space, a mere few degrees above absolute zero: a temperature set by the faint afterglow of the Big Bang itself.

Nothing in the universe was colder. Mankind huddled for warmth.

Poole rose up once more. Suspended in space, he turned away from the planet, and gazed out at the sky of the Oort Cloud. At stars – hard and brilliant and uncomfortable stars, here at the edge of interstellar space.

He was distracted by a glimmer of light, a flash against the patient, unblinking stars.

That was probably one of the sun-catcher colonies, strange, remote communities who had moved out here long before the Xeelee had come to the Solar System – isolated, introverted folk living off the resources of comet cores, gathering sunlight so faint you needed a mirrored sail a kilometre wide to reflect enough heat to warm the palm of your hand. Shy they might be, but after the Displacement, cautiously, they had come flocking to a suddenly stranded Earth. Like the Martian refugees already present on Earth, they had known the cold, and how to survive it. All of this fifteen years ago.

Fifteen years. Any anniversary on Earth was somewhat abstract now, Poole knew. Earth still had its day; it had kept its rotation on its own axis. But the Sun was gone, and a year was a mere abstract interval. Still, people almost obsessively counted the days, and accumulated them into years, and they marked anniversaries, like this one, the fifteenth of the Displacement.

And on such anniversaries Poole himself took time to reflect. To come out and see, like this.

He found Sagittarius. That was where the centre of the Galaxy lay, itself hidden by clouds of dust and gas. Poole stared hard, wishing he could see through the galactic murk to that crowded Core. Because, it was believed, according to the best observations, that was the direction the Xeelee had gone.

With a kind of phobic reluctance, he descended, angelic, to the estate at Antarctica.

68

His family acted as if they hadn't noticed his absence. But he was sure that was just an act. His habit of disappearing was tolerated, barely.

When Poole had taken his seat, Harry handed him another glass of single malt. 'Lethe knows we've got enough ice these days, though the whisky is an endangered species.'

'No. Thanks.'

Harry raised a glass to the window. 'You noticed the sun-catchers out there? Those guys have done what they can for us. But we've got to learn a lesson from them. After generations in the dark, most of them have grown up without even a thought of returning to the inner System, where their ancestors came from.'

Shamiso Emry nodded, her daughter sitting beside her. 'That's true. They were already looking outward, long before the Xeelee invaded. That's a model we can emulate . . .'

Poole murmured to Nicola, 'Not like our families to be so upbeat.'

'Shut up and listen,' she snapped back. 'They deserve that, just this once.'

'. . . And there is plenty of room out there.' Gea, in her ancient avatar as the comical toy robot that had once comforted an elderly and bitterly nostalgic George Poole, rolled silently to and fro on the carpet. 'This Oort Cloud stretches far out into interstellar space, and is full of places to go. We've recently identified a new planet, about twenty-five thousand astronomical units out – a super-Earth, really – which has retained, in the cold, such a thick primordial atmosphere of hydrogen that its surface is actually temperate. Warm enough for liquid water to gather. At least in theory.'

Harry grunted. 'We've already targeted a few of our scatterships at it. They're calling it *Thule*.'

Shamiso shook her head, as if in wonder. 'A "few ships"? No less than a couple of hundred thousand people, then. What times we live in!'

Harry grinned, and poured himself another glass. '*That* is what everybody's watching,' he said. 'I hope. The Scattering. And counting the numbers of successfully despatched evacuees as they stack up.' Despite his bragging Poole thought he could see strain etched into Harry's face, despite continued AS treatment; the smoothing of artificial youth, the strain of fifteen years of leadership.

Poole knew the logic behind the Scattering was elemental. Cold Earth had to be hidden. So, what would make a planet like Earth stand out among a trillion Oort Cloud objects? There were plenty of bodies with a similar mass. Earth had come through the wormhole with a relatively high velocity – a relic of its rapid close-in orbit around the Sun, the planet's momentum carried through – but even that wasn't such an anomaly out here.

Earth's still-high temperature was, however. Humanity could not afford for the planet to emit more heat energy than naturally leaked from its interior; any more would be an unmistakable sign of a technological civilisation – of people. And that inner energy flow was only one five thousandth part of the energy that had once poured down on it from the Sun.

So, even a crude estimate suggested, Earth could not safely support a human population of more than one five-thousandth part of the billion who had been living here, in the warmth of the inner System, before the Xeelee came. A mere few hundred thousand people, who would have to survive on a drizzle of sunlight and the Earth's own leaked inner heat.

But to reduce the population to such a thin scraping meant that there needed to be the best part of a billion people *less* on the planet, within a period of a century or less – such was Harry's government's nominal target for the completion of the camouflage of Earth. Some of this could be achieved by a drastically reduced birth rate – but the death rate, on the other hand, was minimal. Most of the billion alive were already supported by AS technology; they were a billion potential immortals.

So from the beginning Harry and his government had pledged a programme of evacuation. A billion in a century. Ten million a year.

It was a fantastic challenge. And Michael Poole had got to work. He and his father had kick-started the construction of a whole fleet of mighty new GUTships.

Cautious raids on Io had extracted dockyard technology from that lost moon. For resources to build the ships, they had quarried a chunk of rock and ice: a nameless inhabitant of the Oort Cloud as old as

337

the Solar System, tethered and cautiously brought into orbit as a new moon for an exiled Earth. The energy for the ships' GUTdrives was extracted from the collapse of the exotic-matter portal of the wormhole which had brought the Earth here. All to build ships to Poole's design.

The ships were all of the class he had tentatively labelled *Great Northern*, each with a lifedome at least a couple of kilometres wide and fifteen or more decks deep. Once Poole had envisaged these as generation starships, capable of supporting populations of a few thousand people on one-way interstellar migrations lasting millennia, or even longer. Now this design had been upgraded. Each ship would carry, not five thousand active colonists, but an awake crew of fifty or so, and a *hundred* thousand passengers in deep cryo storage, stacked in banks of cells within the lifedomes. Each lifedome would also shelter a sample of Earth's ecologies, carefully tended by the active crew. (And, as devised under Jack Grantt's supervision, two precious ships, full of thin carbon-dioxide air, had already carried away samples of the Lattice which had once embraced Mars: a lengthy working-out of Grantt's own Plan B to save his Martian mind.)

A hundred ships a year. Two or three launches a week. On Earth, people actually lived in the lifedomes that were being built to take them to the stars. Even finding the technical crew was a challenge; Poole had set up a kind of cascade system, so that those trained up in Year Two helped bring the Year Three batch up to speed, and so on.

This was the Scattering: the dispersal of mankind. So far, the job was getting done. Of course there were problems – mostly with the people. Harry's Operations Division had tried to put together more or less compatible crews. The Division swiftly became the single most hated government department. Some of the ships were more like prison hulks, it was murmured.

Yet the scatterships were beautiful, as they launched in their mutual-support convoys, their GUTdrive flames bright as stars. In the telescopes they were droplets of Earth green and gleaming light: cities in flight. Dispersing, each was soon locked in a time-dilated deep-freeze, as more were launched, and more, spreading into the sky, heading for new Earths and red dwarf planets and starbirth clouds.

Publicly, Harry had stayed upbeat throughout. Now he grinned as his display showed the latest members of that fast-growing fleet. He read out their names: '*Magellan. Mayflower II. Valley Forge.* A third of a million people in this flotilla alone.'

Muriel reached out to him and made one of her odd, tentative reality-defying gestures; perhaps she meant to hold Harry's hand. She never had got used to being a Virtual, Poole thought.

She said, 'In the end the Xeelee underestimated us. It underestimated *you*, Harry. Flawed you have always been—'

'Well, you married me.'

'But nobody can deny you rose to the occasion.'

Shamiso smiled. 'As for me, I choose to stay on Earth. One of Harry's caretakers. Because of the even longer term.' She regarded Poole. 'Michael, it may be that a titanic effort still remains, to save mankind in your mighty scatterships. But *you have already saved the Earth*. Even without the Sun – even without human intervention – Earth life will survive. Ultimately the oceans will freeze to their beds, but even then there should be islands of life around the black smokers, vents in the ocean-floor crust whose heat will hold the ice back. And the deeper biosphere too: the very rocks of the crust are a vast reservoir of bacteria, leaching minerals, reproducing slowly, slowly . . . Those bugs will barely stir from their aeons-long slumber, whether we live or die. And they preserve in them the DNA mechanisms that are the result of billions of years of evolution and selection. The central hardware of life. This isn't a trivial legacy, Michael. Even if humanity were to die out completely, the planet lives.'

Now Gea rolled forward. 'One day, in fact, the Earth may grow warm again . . . It's pure chance, Michael, but when you created the Displacement it was early winter, in the northern hemisphere at least. And at that point in its orbit, Earth happened to be heading for the stars in the constellation Leo. Well, now, released from the Sun's gravity, Earth still *is* heading for Leo, and always will be. And now we think that in about eighty thousand years' time, we will be nearing the star Wolf 359. Perhaps our descendants will choose to deflect their course a little, and slow down – how, we don't know yet. Of course 359 is a variable star, so that will present fresh challenges . . .'

Poole absorbed all this in silence.

Harry was studying Poole. 'Look, son, we're trying to help you, in our clumsy way. So if we're all praising your efforts, if humanity is coming out of this long cold tunnel you had to push us into – why the long face?'

Poole said abruptly, 'Because this could be the last time we meet like this.'

Harry and Muriel shared a sharp glance. Poole recognised that look from his boyhood: *wary parents*.

Harry snapped, 'Is there something you two aren't telling us?'

Poole glanced at Nicola. She shrugged. 'Get it over.'

'We're leaving,' he said.

Muriel frowned. 'Leaving?'

'Nicola and me. That's why we asked you here, to get you together. To tell you—'

'Are you joining one of the scatterships?'

'Not that. Mother, we've been fitting out the *Cauchy*. You know she's the prototype of a class of small-crew ships meant for exploration. Interstellar or even extragalactic. That was back in the day when we still thought in terms of such goals as exploration. Well, now we have a different destination. We'll need some reaction mass. A kilometre-wide block of rock and ice should do it.'

'Do the sums for me, Michael,' Muriel said gently. 'How far will that take you?'

'To the centre of the Galaxy,' he said bluntly.

Even Gea seemed shocked. 'That would take a few decades of your lives. But twenty-five *thousand* years in the external universe. Another twenty-five millennia to come home . . .'

'Coming home isn't the point.'

'Then what is?' Muriel asked.

'The Xeelee,' Harry said. 'That's the point. Isn't it, Michael? That's where the Xeelee went. It limped away wounded maybe, after we shot it up with monopoles, and left its clients and machines to finish us off. And so you're going after it. For you it's not enough to wait until mankind can recover from this low point, grow strong enough to take on the Xeelee. For you it's personal.'

'Wouldn't you feel the same?'

Muriel protested, 'But even if the Xeelee started out towards Sagittarius – we believe it has a hyperdrive. It could go anywhere. Even that image we just got from the amulet is ambiguous . . .'

Nicola glared at Poole. 'What image?'

Poole ignored her, for now. 'Oh, I think it's heading for the centre. One day there will be – should have been – a kilometres-high statue, to *me*, there in the core light. There's something there that the Xeelee care about, something we took from them. So that's where it will be going. And so am I.'

Shamiso regarded her daughter. 'And you're following him?'

Nicola grinned, the green tattoo on her forehead vivid. 'Sure I am. Because it's fun.'

Shamiso sighed. 'No. You're going because, as has been obvious since the moment you first met, you belong at his side, Nicola. And he at yours.'

Still the family arguments continued.

Poole, restless, walked away from the group once again.

He went back to the window. He could see a handful of bright, drifting stars: the latest ships of the Scattering, still visible across distances comparable to the width of the inner Solar System.

He always carried the amulet, these days, the green tetrahedron delivered from another universe by a dead alien. He kept it in a fold of soft cloth, tucked into his belt. On impulse, he took it out now, and unfolded the cloth, and looked at the amulet sitting there, green on black.

He grasped the amulet in his bare fist. Its vertices were sharp, digging into his flesh. Drawing blood.

Nicola joined him. 'Careful with that.'

'Got it back from my mother. Taking it with me.'

'She mentioned some kind of image, retrieved from the interior.'

'We only just got it out. Very advanced data compression. Took years to extract it.'

'You didn't tell me.'

He shrugged. 'I didn't want to have to discuss it in front of *them*. The family. Let Muriel tell them.'

'Show me.'

He glanced at her. Then he waved a hand in the air.

A Virtual image coalesced. A jewel-like object, like a black ball, wrapped in an asymmetrical gold blanket, lay on a carpet of stars. And, some distance away, a fine blue band surrounded it.

Poole said, 'Tell me what you see.'

'That looks like gravitational lensing. The gold, the way it's distorted. Light paths distorted by an extreme gravity field . . . A black hole. Like the one at the centre of the Galaxy?'

'Tell me what you see.'

'It looks like a black hole with a ring around it. What is it?'

'A black hole with a ring around it.'

She stared, and grinned. 'And that's where we're going?'

He glared out once more at Sagittarius. Overlaid on the constellation's stars he saw a reflection of his own face, dimly outlined. The dark complexion, dark hair: the face of a Poole. And that tetrahedral scar on his forehead was livid.

He whispered, 'Are you out there, somewhere? Can you hear me?

'My name is Michael Poole.

'Xeelee, I am coming to get you.'

In the pale rocket light the face of Michael Poole Bazalget was like an upturned coin, but his mouth was set with a kind of determination, his eyes shadowed. I felt unaccountably disturbed. I wondered what this child, and his own children after him, would do with the world.

George Poole, AD 2005

Afterword

This novel and its sequel, *Redemption*, are a pendant to my 'Xeelee Sequence' of stories and novels. The epigraphs to the sections are taken from earlier works in the Sequence.

A recent and accessible account of the theory of wormholes and relativistic time travel is *Time Travel and Warp Drives* by Allen Everett and Thomas Roman (University of Chicago Press, 2012). A wormhole mouth contained by a frame of exotic matter was suggested first by physicist Matt Visser in 1989 (*Phys. Rev.* D 39, pp. 3182ff, 1989). The theory of defects in spacetime was worked out by A. Valenkin *et al.* (see *Cosmic Strings and Other Topological Defects* by A. Valenkin and E. Shellard, Cambridge University Press, 1994).

New models of the surface of Mercury, as depicted here, have been described by Peplowski *et al.* (*Nature Geoscience*, vol. 9, pp. 273ff, 2016). One of the best reviews of concepts for terraforming Mars, Venus and other worlds remains Martyn Fogg's *Terraforming* (Society of Automotive Engineers, 1995). Paul Birch set out a design to freeze out Venus's blanket of air quickly (*Journal of the British Interplanetary Society*, vol. 44, pp. 157–67, 1991), while Stephen L. Gillett, PhD., suggested fixing the planet's atmospheric carbon dioxide in a chemically exotic solid form (in *Analog*, November 1999, pp. 38–46).

The 'paraterraforming' of Mars, the covering of vast expanses of the surface with glass roofs, was suggested by Richard Taylor in 1992 (*Journal of the British Interplanetary Society*, vol. 45, pp. 341ff). A migrating settlement to avoid the Martian winter was proposed by Charles Cockell (*Journal of the British Interplanetary Society*, vol. 57, pp. 40ff, 2004). My friend Javier Martin-Torres of the Instituto Andaluz de Ciencias de la Tierra, Spain, led a study on a possible, very slight, water cycle on present-day Mars (*Nature Geoscience*, vol. 8, pp. 357ff, 2015). The 'Lattice' life form described here is my own speculation.

A recent survey of the outer planets is Michael Carroll's *Living Among Giants* (Springer, 2015). The Jupiter-cycler habitat Gallia Three was partly inspired by the Mars–Earth 'Aldrin cycler' proposal (see D. Landau *et al.*,

Journal of the British Interplanetary Society, vol. 60, pp. 122ff, April 2007).

Speculation that there may be many planets between the stars was given by L. Strigari *et al.* ('Nomads of the Galaxy', *Monthly Notices of the Royal Astronomical Society*, vol. 423, pp. 1856ff, 2012). Suggestions on how to colonise such remote realms have been given by Roy *et al.* (*Journal of the British Interplanetary Society*, vol. 66, pp. 318ff, 2013). The idea that an Earthlike world far from its parent star might retain a thick hydrogen atmosphere was originated by D. Stevenson (*Nature*, vol. 400, pp. 32ff, 1999).

The suggestion that the Sun may contain a knot of dark matter in its core has recently been revisited to explain anomalies in the Sun's energy flow; see for instance Aaron Vincent *et al.* (*Physics Review Letters*, vol. 114, 081302, 2015). Abraham Loeb (*International Journal of Astrobiology*, vol. 13, pp. 337ff, 2014) made the suggestion that life could have evolved in the afterglow of the Big Bang. Natalie Mashian and Abraham Loeb (*Monthly Notices of the Royal Astronomical Society*, vol. 460, pp. 2482–91, 2016) discussed the formation of carbon-rich planets in the early universe.

The space elevator terminology used here is the standard established by the International Space Elevator Consortium (ISEC) (www.isec. org); I'm grateful to Dr John Knapman, Director of the ISEC Research Committee. Martian space elevators are discussed in *Leaving the Planet by Space Elevator* by C. C. Edwards and P. Ragan (Lulu.com, 2006). The notion of borrowing design ideas from termite mounds for human architecture has been explored by, among others, a collaborative project funded by the Human Frontiers Science Programme and led by Professor J. Scott Turner of the State University of New York. Freezing out sea-level-rise water on the Antarctic ice cap has been suggested by K. Frieler *et al.* (*Earth Systems Dynamics*, vol. 7, pp. 203ff, 2016). And the idea of freezing out carbon dioxide there has been suggested by Ernest Agee *et al.* of Purdue University (*Journal of Allied Meteorology and Climatology*, vol. 52, pp. 289ff, 2013).

The fate of an Earth deprived of its Sun has been considered for example by Gregory Laughlin and Fred C. Adams (*Icarus*, vol. 145, pp. 614ff, 2000). Of course, as Michael Poole knows, Fritz Leiber got there first ('A Pail of Air', *Galaxy Science Fiction*, December 1951).

All errors and misapprehensions are of course my sole responsibility.

Stephen Baxter
Northumberland
October 2016